MW00812676

THE DARK ATONEMENT

THE COLD WAR LEGACY SERIES
BOOK TWO

SARAH HAMAKER

Katherine -
Happy reading -
Sarah

Seshra
Press

Copyright © 2022, Seshva Press. All rights reserved. Without limiting the rights under copyright reserved above, no part of this publication may be reproduced, stored in or introduced into a retrieval system, or transmitted, in any form, or by any means (electronic, mechanical, photocopying, recording, or otherwise) without the prior written permission of both the copyright owner and Seshva Press. The only exception is brief quotations in printed or broadcasted articles and reviews. Contact Sarah Hamaker via her website, sarahhamakerfiction.com, for permission.

This book is licensed for your personal enjoyment only. This book may not be resold or given away to other people. Thank you for respecting the hard work of this author.

Names, characters, places, and incidents are either the product of the author's imagination or intended to be used fictitiously. Any resemblance to actual events, organizations, places, or persons living or dead is purely coincidental and beyond the intention of either the author or the publisher.

ISBN ebook: 978-1-958375-01-3

ISBN print: 978-1-958375-02-0

Cover design by 100 Covers.

Created with Vellum

When I look at your heavens, the work of your fingers, the moon and the stars, which you have set in place, what is man that you are mindful of him, and the son of man that you care for him?

Psalm 8:3-4 (ESV)

ONE

The trains were running late tonight, and the press of bodies on the platform of the Farragut West Metro stop pushed against Lena Hoffman. Nothing unusual during rush hour in the nation's capital. She tightened her grip on her messenger bag strap. The beginnings of a headache pulsated along the base of her neck.

"Sorry," someone mumbled as the crowd shifted and bumped her closer to the edge of the platform.

Her cell phone buzzed, and she inched it out of her coat pocket to glance at a text.

Where R U?

Lena glanced down the tracks. The electronic signs indicated the next Orange Line train would be arriving in two minutes—the same message it had been proclaiming for the past fifteen minutes. Conversing with Belinda Travers would help to make the time pass more quickly.

@ Farragut West. She managed to text back coherently in the cramped space.

Did U work L8?

1

No. Trains L8.

The unreliability of DC subway system often caused Lena to rethink her dependence on public transportation, but the convenience of not having to drive and park in Washington, DC, made it worth putting up with evenings like this.

Guess you'll miss seeing your hunky neighbor tonight.

Lena smiled at Belinda's text. Her best friend frequently teased about timing her return home to coincide with a new neighbor. In the six months since he'd moved into the condo across the hall, Lena hadn't exchanged more than a handful of words with him. She also had yet to see the tall man with the dark brown hair and brown eyes with a female.

Warmth dotted Lena's cheeks as she recalled Belinda's suggestion to ask him over for dinner, but she could hardly get the man to look her in the eye much less linger in the common hallway long enough to ask that question.

U know I'm not sure about dating again after being dumped.

Lena shuddered at the memory of Capitol Hill staffer Stan Monahan. To think she'd wasted the better part of a year going out with him. Stan's handsome face had taken her eyes off his political ambitions, so his parting statement had stung. He'd said as casually as if he'd asked for cream in his coffee that he could no longer date a woman who brought nothing to the table in the way of connections.

Flashing lights and a collective sigh of relief from the crowd on the platform signaled the arrival of a train. Lena texted the good news to Belinda and wedged the phone into her coat pocket. Only a few people exited the car, but Lena pushed her way into the crowded compartment, finding a small space to occupy for the three stops until she could exit. At Rosslyn, she moved off the train and up the escalator to North Moore Street, glad for the fresh air after the long wait on the platform.

The afternoon's warmer temperature had plummeted with the descent of the sun, and a breeze brought a decidedly chilly wind. As she turned right onto Wilson Boulevard, she pulled out her phone to check the time. Six-forty-five. Definitely too late to cross paths with her neighbor. She hadn't told Belinda she'd seen his name—Dr. Devlin Mills—on a piece of mail he'd dropped last week. If her friend knew that juicy tidbit, her admonishments to ask out the hunky doctor would be constant.

A few blocks later, she waited at a light to cross North Quinn Street. The crossing light flicked to the walking man, and she stepped off the curb, her focus drifting to the Mexican restaurant a little way down the block. Maybe she'd treat herself to takeout from Guajillo. Her mouth watered at the thought of biting into a hot, crispy pork chimichanga.

Halfway into the intersection, Lena curved slightly to the right to enter the parking lot of the small strip mall. An engine revved. Then a black SUV roared out of nowhere like a bull charging a matador's cape. Lena froze, not sure which direction the car would go. From behind, someone yanked on her messenger bag. She reflexively clutched at it but the movement propelled her directly into the path of the oncoming car.

DR. DEVLIN MILLS ROTATED HIS SHOULDERS AS HE WAITED WITH ABOUT twenty others for the light to change at the intersection of North Quinn Street and Wilson Boulevard. He had stopped by Heavy Seas Alehouse in Arlington after driving home from work for an impromptu thirtieth birthday celebration of one of his co-workers. Devlin wasn't into the bar scene, and he skipped many happy hour gatherings. However, he liked working with Dr. Nancy Orleans and so had stayed long enough to down a seltzer water with a twist of lime and wish her a happy birthday before departing for his quiet condo. He didn't blame her for wanting to celebrate off the National Institutes of Health campus, given their immediate supervisor, Dr. Walter Shan, frowned upon socializing in the office.

The streetlights cast brightness into the cold, January evening.

Once again, he'd miss seeing his lovely next-door neighbor. Granted, he'd yet to gather his courage to actually introduce himself. His co-workers lightheartedly teased him about being the embodiment of the stereotypical reserved scientist, especially around women he found as attractive as his neighbor. Her long blond hair and blue eyes sent his blood racing and tied his tongue in knots.

The light changed, and the group moved off the sidewalk and into the crosswalk. One figure broke off to veer toward the entrance to the shopping center's parking lot, and he caught a glimpse of a familiar face. He quickened his pace to catch up to his neighbor. Then a black SUV gunned its engine and headed right toward her.

The woman turned at the sound and froze, her eyes wide and mouth open as the vehicle raced closer. Devlin dashed forward, but the SUV came between him and his neighbor, scattering the group crossing the street and eliciting curses and shouts as the driver negotiated a tight right turn and sped away up Wilson Boulevard.

His heart pounding, Devlin ran the last few feet to reach the woman, who lay on her side on the curb of the parking lot apron. Kneeling, he gently touched her shoulder. "Are you okay?"

"I think so." She slowly pushed herself upright, her hair falling across her cheek.

He brushed it back, his fingertips lightly grazing the soft skin. "That was close."

"I've got 911 on the line. Does she need an ambulance?" said a woman's over Devlin's shoulder.

His neighbor shook her head. "No, I wasn't hit. I moved out of the way just in time."

Devlin turned to the bystander, phone to her ear. "Thank you, ma'am. I'm a doctor. I'll make sure she goes to the hospital if she needs to."

The Good Samaritan nodded and spoke something into the phone Devlin couldn't hear. His attention returned to assessing his neighbor's injuries. "Are you sure the SUV didn't clip you?"

The woman nodded slowly. "Someone grabbed for my bag, and

that turned me away from the car just in time."

Devlin frowned. He'd seen the SUV gun its engine as it approached the intersection, but from his view, the car had swerved toward the parking lot entrance. The driver must have realized someone was walking there at the last minute and missed her. "It looked like he didn't realize you were about to cross the parking lot entrance and overcompensated."

"I could have sworn the car headed right toward me, but it happened so fast, maybe you're right." She gathered her bag and started to rise.

Devlin offered his assistance. "Let me help you. You're probably still shaky from the close call."

"Thank you." She straightened and winced, her hand going to her hip. "Oh, that's going to leave a bruise."

The woman leaned into him, and Devlin inhaled the scent of spring as a lock of her hair brushed his shoulder. Then she met his gaze. "Wait a minute. Don't you live across from me?"

"Yes. Devlin Mills, at your service." Devlin placed his arm more firmly around her waist, liking how she fit snugly against his body, her head rising above his shoulder. He liked tall women. This woman was easily five-foot-nine, a nice height that complimented his own six-foot-one.

"Did you say you're a doctor?" Her gaze captured his.

Now looking into her sky-blue eyes, words deserted him once again. Then she blinked, and he found his voice. "Yes. I work as a researcher at the National Institutes of Health."

"I'm Lena Hoffman, translator at the State Department." She shifted under his arm. "It's nice to finally meet you."

Devlin had been so concerned for her well-being, he'd forgotten to be nervous. Even though the immediate crisis was over, the nerves he'd previously experienced around her hadn't returned. "I'll walk you home. I have some gel ice packs for those bruises." He guided her onto the sidewalk.

"Thank you." She gestured toward the Mexican restaurant as

they passed it. "I was going to get a chimichanga for dinner tonight, but my appetite has gone."

"A stressful situation can take away a desire for food." He adjusted his pace to match her slower one. "Thank goodness you weren't seriously hurt."

Lena paused at the sidewalk junction leading to their gated condo community. "I am grateful, but I can't shake the sensation it wasn't an accident."

"It didn't look deliberate from my perspective." Devlin released his hold on her and walked a couple of steps ahead to punch in the security code to unlock the gate. He swung it open for her to pass. Funny how much he missed having her tucked into his side.

"Maybe not." She shrugged. "I can't think of any reason someone would want to run me down, so it's probably just my imagination." Lena went through the gate, the earlier tremors from the near-miss not evident in her stride.

"You seem steadier on your feet now." He pulled the gate shut and returned to her side.

"I'm still a bit shook up, but I can walk unassisted." She demonstrated by continuing down the sidewalk. "I have ice in my freezer, so you don't have to bother with gel packs."

"It's no bother. The gel cold packs will be more effective and are less messy." He held open the outside door to their condo building.

At the mailboxes in the common hallway, she stopped and inserted a key into hers. "Okay, you've convinced me." She tucked the envelopes into her messenger bag.

He pulled his own mail out and shoved it under his arm. "I'll come by in about fifteen minutes with the cold packs."

"That sounds good. Thank you." With a little wave over her shoulder, she disappeared into her condo.

Devlin entered his own apartment and headed straight for his freezer to check on his stash of cold packs. Guilt claimed his thoughts as he acknowledged a fleeting desire to thank the distracted driver who had finally brought them together.

CHAPTER

TWO

It wouldn't do to reveal too much of his identity within this first missive. Dr. Wolfgang Hoffman had no idea what she knew about him or his work. She might not even know his name, and even if she did, she would have been told he was dead.

He turned over the innocuous postcard promising a delightful time in Bryce Canyon, Utah. Slowly, he uncapped the writing instrument with his cotton gloved hands, necessary to avoid leaving fingerprints but difficult to hold onto the glossy piece of cardboard. He poised the tip above the address block and wrote *Lena Hoffman*. He added her address in Arlington, Virginia.

The sojourn to his adopted country had not been without regrets. His eyes had been on the prize rather than on the cost. Now in his twilight years, he had come face to face with the reality of what his arrogance and conceit had brought about, and he'd not liked the picture it formed.

The blank space of the postcard's message yawned up at him. He must choose his words carefully, just enough to entice Lena to further investigation but not enough to lead her too far down the path into danger. If he played his cards right, he would be reunited with his granddaughter and start the third chapter of his life without the secrets and lies his first seven decades had wrought.

With a decisive nod, he continued writing in the same style as the address. Finally he capped the pen, pleased with the resulting message.

The sun streamed through the kitchen window and warmed his back as he sat at the small table, rereading what he had written. He peeled off a Forever stamp and affixed it to the card.

Pushing to his feet, he put on a light jacket before tucking the postcard into its pocket, stripping off the gloves and putting them in the pocket as well. Then he walked out of his condo and down the street, pausing to greet neighbors along the way. Making his way to the corner store a few blocks from the apartment complex, he used one of the gloves to drop the postcard into the blue mailbox with a twinge of fear. What he had set in motion could not be stopped. He only hoped his calculations proved correct. If he made a mistake, he might have just signed Lena Hoffman's death warrant.

Back at his condo, he went directly into the master bedroom. The large walk-in closet had been converted to a secret enclave with a pulsating keypad and fingerprint recognition software beside the door, embedded into the wall and hidden by a small piece of artwork. The soundproof closet had a desk, a comfortable chair, a laptop, and a filing cabinet.

He keyed in the seventeen-digit code, then pressed his forefinger onto the smooth surface of the keypad. A soft click gained him access to his fortified office.

Closing the door, he took a seat at his desk, then opened a drawer and selected a new burner cell phone from his stash. Untraceable cell phones would have been a godsend when he lived in East Berlin. But the Stasi probably would have come up with a way to jam tower signals and keep the German Democratic Republic citizens under their thumb like they had anyway. He'd always been an early adapter to new technology and had been using the disposable phones for years. Dialing a number he had long since memorized, he didn't have to wait long for the other person to pick up.

"Yes?" A crisp voice answered.

Hoffman leaned against the high back of the chair. "General, we had an understanding my work was finished."

"Then why are you calling me?"

The thread of concern in the other man's voice triggered a smile. "I might be out of the game, but I still have ears. Someone is trying to contact me."

General Marvin Pettigrew barked a short laugh. "Believe me, I've got better things to do than track down an old dog like you. Enjoy your retirement."

Hoffman pushed the end button. Selecting another phone, he punched a number he had used only once before, when he had seen the writing on the wall that his days as a scientist in East Germany were numbered.

The call was answered on the second ring. "Yeah, good morning." The impatience in the man's voice was an act Hoffman wasn't buying.

"An east wind is blowing across the Danube." The code phrase tripped off Hoffman's tongue as easily as if he had memorized it yesterday instead of nearly four decades ago. He only hoped he hadn't been foolish to call in the favor.

A short pause. "You realize we cannot guarantee the arrangements."

Hoffman gripped the phone, adrenaline pulsating through his veins much like it had when he set into motion his escape from East Berlin. "I think by now I know the risks as well as any man."

"I suppose that's true. Call again tomorrow for instructions." He disconnected the call.

Hoffman turned the phone over and popped out the SIM card. Placing it on a stone slab resting on the floor, he took up the hammer beside his desk and crushed the card into bits. One couldn't be too careful when awakening sleeping giants.

~

Lena opened the door of her apartment to a loud *meow*. Her mixed breed cat bounded up. "Hey, Goliath. It's good to see you too." She smiled as she reached down to scratch between the feline's ears.

He purred his approval, and she set her purse on the foyer table and shed her coat. As she made her way to the coat closet, located down a short hallway past the living room of her condo, Goliath followed. Exchanging her heels for slippers, she moved into the kitchen and gifted him with a few cat treats, then poured a glass of wine. Last night's lasagna would have to do for dinner, so she placed the leftovers into the microwave.

Goliath stared up at her, his blue eyes accusatory. "Yes, I know I'm a home later than usual." She stooped to pet him again, but he stalked off. Just like a cat to demand attention only to shun it when offered.

Lena rested against the counter and watched her meal rotating in the microwave. It had been a long day, and her body craved bed. Her mind drifted to Devlin, who had been so sweet a week ago, bringing over the gel cold packs and a two chimichangas from Guajillo. Sadly, they'd missed each other at the mailboxes in the intervening days.

She took out her reheated lasagna and carried it to the table. As she ate, thoughts of what Devlin had shared about his background during their brief time together flitted through her mind. He and his three older sisters had grown up in Lancaster, Pennsylvania. After attending medical school at Georgetown, he'd stayed in the DC area to do research work on treatments for liver cancer at the National Institutes of Health in Bethesda, Maryland.

In short, he had an upbringing she had longed to experience herself, instead of feeling isolated and alone as an only child. She'd sketched the bare minimum of her own backstory, preferring to hear him speak of his childhood shenanigans as they ate dinner.

When she'd finished her solitary meal, she washed up the dishes, then connected her iPhone into the Bose audio system. The *Hamilton* soundtrack would help ease the transition from work to sleep. Someone knocked on her door in the middle of Jefferson's "What Did I Miss?".

Silencing the music with a swipe of her finger on the phone, she padded over to the door. Surely it wasn't an overly ambitious solicitor trying to sell her windows. She wished the condo association would figure out a way to enclose the entire the property instead of only the stretch along Wilson Boulevard. Just last week, she'd had to shoo away a salesman who'd knocked on her door despite the signs saying *no solicitors* posted in prominent places around the complex.

A quick glance through the peephole revealed Devlin on the other side. Her heart leapt as she unlocked the deadbolt and opened the door. "Devlin, what a pleasant surprise."

He smiled. "I'm sorry to drop by unannounced, but we keep missing each other at the mailbox. May I get your number?"

"Sure, come on in." As he entered the apartment, she grabbed her phone from the entryway table. "Ready?" At his nod, she rattled off her number, which he keyed into his phone. Then he did the same for her. "That was easy." She saved the new contact.

"Thanks." Devlin returned his phone to his pocket and shifted his feet. "I also wanted to see if you're okay after the near-miss last Tuesday. I've been working late and had to go out of town over the weekend, so didn't get a chance to check until now."

Lena rubbed the back of her neck. "I'm still a tiny bit sore. The past few nights I've slept without waking up from a bad dream about the incident." The Incident. Good grief, she sounded like the heroine in a gothic melodrama. "I probably overreacted about the whole thing. I mean, who would want to run me down?"

Goliath jumped onto the table beside Devlin, butting his head into Devlin's arm. "Hey, boy. Remember me?" He scratched the cat under his chin, eliciting a loud purr from Goliath. The cat suddenly pivoted, then leaped from the table onto the floor, his hind legs scattering the mail Lena had placed there.

"Goliath! That cat definitely has a mind of his own." She started toward the pile of paper on the floor, but Devlin waved her off.

"I'll pick it up."

Lena smiled at him. "Thank you." His thoughtfulness could certainly grow on her. "Would you like some coffee?"

He nodded.

"Great. I got a one-cup Keurig for my birthday, and I love it."

"Those machines make a good cup of coffee. We have one in the break room, although we only get the generic pods."

She left him to gather the mail while she went into the kitchen and turned on the machine. When she returned to the living room with a selection of pods for Devlin to pick his brew, he had placed the mail back on the table but held a postcard in his hand. "I've always wanted to visit Bryce Canyon."

"Bryce Canyon? Where is that?" Lena peered at a photo showing a sun-washed vista of towering red rock formations dotted with evergreen scrub brush and trees.

"Utah." Devlin flipped the postcard over. "The photo is, to quote the text, 'A view from Sunrise Point, which shows the Boat Mesa and the Sinking Ship, set against the stark Pine Cliffs of the Aquarius Plateau.'" He handed her the postcard.

She studied her name and address printed in block lettering, then at the message scrawled on the left side of the back. No signature, just a short note written in German.

"Earth to Lena.?"

Lena glanced at Devlin, her cheeks warming. "Sorry, I was puzzling over the strangeness of the card. There's no signature on it, just my name and address, and one sentence." Lena read the words. *"Ihre letzten ärztlichen Rat war falsch-es ist immer noch ein Leben zu führen."*

"Is that German?"

She frowned. "I'm sorry, what?"

He pointed to the words on the postcard. "It sounded like German."

Understanding dawned. "I didn't realize I'd spoken them out loud. Yes, it's German."

"What's it mean?"

She translated the sentence in her head, then shared it out loud. "Your past medical advice was wrong—there is still a life to lead." Lena flipped through her mental German-English dictionary but couldn't come up with a different translation. Both the German and the English words said the same, strange sentence.

Your past medical advice was wrong... Whatever the words meant, they reminded her of the idiomatic expression her mother used to say. *Der Schein trügt.* Things are not always as they look like.

THREE

"What do you think it means?" Devlin's question grabbed Lena's attention.

"I don't know." She put the postcard back on the table and gestured toward the basket of coffee pods. "Maybe coffee will give us a mental jolt to help us figure it out. What flavor would you like?"

He selected pumpkin spice decaf and handed her the pod.

"One of my favorites." She measured water into the Keurig.

Devlin trailed her and stood in the doorway. "I like what you've done with the kitchen. Mine's still mired in the 1970s with lovely avocado coloring on the appliances."

She inserted the pod into the Keurig and pressed the start button, then placed a twin of his pod on the counter to make her own cup. "I remember that. Renovating the kitchen was the first thing I did after I bought the unit six years ago."

"I keep meaning to do something about my kitchen too, but, well," he shrugged, "I don't spend much time cooking."

"Surely you know how to cook." She handed him the steaming mug before starting her own. "Do you want anything in your coffee?"

"Nah, I drink it black most of the time." He blew across the surface of the hot liquid. "I can cook but just don't have time."

"I imagine your line of work means long hours." She added a packet of raw sugar to her mug and stirred.

"Sometimes." He sipped his coffee, then grinned at her. "To be honest, on the cooking front, I'm probably more lazy than anything. Takeout is much easier, and microwave dinners easier still."

The smile triggered a warm glow around her heart. It had been way too long since a man's smile turned her insides to mush. "That's so true. I usually cook one big pot or casserole on Sunday evening to last the entire week."

Lena picked up her mug and moved to the couch. She spied the postcard she'd laid on the end table. The missive made her uneasy, but she couldn't exactly say why. Devlin's brown eyes twinkled as he settled on the sofa beside her. How good it felt to share something as casual as a cup of coffee with this man.

She read the translated text out loud again. "'Your past medical advice was wrong—there is still a life to lead.' It doesn't make any sense."

Devlin tapped a finger on the side of his mug. "Sounds like an infomercial for a magic elixir to cure all that ails you."

Lena laughed. "It is rather stilted wording."

"Hmm." He furrowed his brow.

"I can't imagine how it would apply to me. I'm rarely sick."

"Maybe it's about someone you know?"

"That's even more confusing. I don't know anyone who was given bad medical advice." She slipped off her shoes and tucked her feet underneath her. "I have no idea why someone would send me an anonymous postcard with a nonsense message."

"I might have read too many Hardy Boys mysteries as a kid, but it doesn't seem normal for someone to write so carefully—see the neat block letters?—and send a cryptic message. It must mean something."

"Hardy Boys, eh?" Lena smiled. "While I loved Nancy Drew, I

admit to reading quite a few Hardy Boys myself. Okay, Frank Hardy, how do you think we should tackle cracking the code, assuming there's a code to crack?"

"Let's see if we can come up with alternative meanings from the translated words." He set his mug on the coffee table. "What phrase should we start with?"

Lena stared at the postcard. "Past medical advice."

"What could that mean beyond the surface?"

"A misdiagnosis?"

"Or the patient discharged themselves too early from treatment," Devlin offered.

They bantered several more possibilities around, but none seemed remotely plausible. "We're grasping at straws," she said.

He crossed his ankle on the opposite knee. "Perhaps, but what about if we started by assuming what the *past medical advice* was instead of what the phrase itself could mean?"

Thoughts jumbled together in her brain as she explored the suggestion. "Such as assuming the diagnosis was wrong?"

"What could be the outcome of that?" His eyes met hers, the intensity of his gaze quickening her heart rate. For a moment, she forgot the question as she allowed herself to fully experience the connection between them. Then he blinked, and the electricity that had been zipping from him to her snapped.

"I think it could mean the patient would die," he said, tipping his mug back to finish the coffee.

She mentally shook her head to get her mind back on the post-card and not on Devlin's handsome face. "And if we take the word *past* and apply it to *die*, we get *dead*."

"That's what I was thinking." He straightened on the couch, his eyes bright. "Then we get to the last phrase. *There is still a life to lead.* It could mean the patient we thought was dead has some life left in him."

Lena pondered for a moment, then shook her head. "But why the subterfuge? Why not tell me, 'Hey, someone you thought was dead is alive?' I mean, it's not like we're actually in a Hardy Boys novel."

"You're probably right. I guess we all want a bit of mystery in our lives. You really have no clue who sent it?"

She studied the postcard more closely. There, under the word *rat*, which was advice in English, the imprint of the letters *DR* appeared in faint outline as if they had been added in pencil before being erased nearly all the way. She handed the postcard to Devlin. "Do you see anything beneath the word that looks like *rat?*"

He examined the card. "It looks like 'DR' or the abbreviation for doctor."

"That's what I thought. Do you see any other words like that?"

As he bent over the postcard, his dark brown hair flopped onto his forehead. She had a sudden desire to smooth it back for him.

His words brought her back to the mystery at hand. "I think there's an H and an O. There's possibly double Fs under the word spelled f-a-l-s-c-h. Then the word *man* behind the next set of letters." Devlin raised his head. "It could spell your last name: Hoff-man. You're not a doctor, are you?"

"No, of course not, but I..." She suppressed a shudder.

"Lena? Are you okay?" Devlin tossed the postcard onto the coffee table. "You're awfully pale."

Surely she was imagining a boogeyman when someone simply made a mistake. She sucked in a breath. "It's absurd because he's dead."

"Who's dead?"

Lena focused her eyes on Devlin's face. "My grandfather."

"Did that happen recently?" His forehead creased in concern.

"No, years ago. Since I don't believe in ghosts or communication from the other side, there has to be a rational explanation for someone sending me a postcard with his name hidden behind the message." Because if her grandfather was alive, it would mean yet another thing her parents had concealed from her.

"You never knew your grandfather?"

She shook her head. "I haven't thought about him in years. My mother said her parents had died before I was born. My father said he had no close relatives living. I presumed that meant my paternal grandparents were also deceased."

Devlin leaned forward, his attention squarely on her.

More memories spilled over. "My dad said his mom died right before he emigrated from Germany to the United States. He never talked about my grandfather, and I only know he was a doctor because I overheard my parents arguing about him one time as a kid." Another recollection slammed into her. "It's strange now that I think about it, but my parents had frequent discussions with the radio turned up really loud."

"To avoid being overheard?"

Lena nodded. "Looking back, it reminds me of those Hollywood spy thrillers set behind the Iron Curtain, with the hero and heroine having secret talks to avoid enemy agents hearing their plans." She shivered. "But my father was a janitor, not a secret agent."

"Maybe they didn't want you to hear them."

"Possibly." A wave of tiredness swept over her despite the coffee. Her hip twinged, reminding her of last week's pavement dive.

Devlin raised his eyebrows. "I can tell you're inspired by this conversation."

Lena's cheeks warmed. "I am, but I think the day is beginning to catch up to me."

Devlin's cell phone chimed, and he pulled it out of his pocket. "That's my alarm for bed. You're not the only one who needs to call it a night."

"And you must get your beauty sleep?" Lena rose and gathered the mugs, then deposited them in the kitchen.

He waited by the couch for her return. "I suspect you're the one who gets more beautiful with each passing day."

Lena blushed. "You're quite the charmer. I can see I'll have to keep an eye on you."

Devlin's smile stretched wider. "I'd like that very much."

She waggled a finger at him. "Enough, Dr. Mills."

Devlin's eyes crinkled at her mock reproof. He paused near her front door. "Maybe we should have dinner together one night soon, since you want to keep tabs on me."

"Perhaps that would be wise." Lena fought to keep the corners of her mouth from turning up but failed.

He pulled out his phone and scrolled through it. "What about Friday?"

Lena got her phone and clicked through to her calendar. Friday loomed wide open. "That should work for me."

"Meet you by the mailboxes after work?" Devlin raised his eyebrows.

"Perfect." She managed to keep her voice level when she really wanted to jump up and down. A real date with her hunky neighbor. Belinda was not going to believe this. Maybe she wouldn't tell her until Saturday. Then again, Belinda could ferret out a secret faster than Nancy Drew. "Good night."

"Sweet dreams, Lena." Devlin turned and slipped out. She closed the door behind him to keep her cat from escaping but pressed her ear against it to hear him open the door across the hall. She slipped the deadbolt home, then, with a bounce in her step, headed off to tidy up the kitchen.

Just before she clicked off the lights in the living room, her eyes spotted the postcard on the coffee table. The euphoria of a date with Devlin had temporarily overshadowed the mysterious message. If her grandfather had figuratively come back from the dead, it would mean revisiting her past.

And she had no desire to reopen that painful chapter.

FOUR

"It appears Dr. Hoffman has risen from the dead."

Dr. Tatiana Dern didn't look up from the microscope at the words spoken by Carl Schuler. The National Security agent moved closer to where she worked at a corner counter in a bustling lab.

She adjusted the focus and peered intently at the now-magnified cells. "Carl, you've been bringing me rumors of his resurrection for years." She removed the slide and snapped another one in its place.

From the corner of her eye, Carl shifted on his feet. Good. He was still rattled enough by who she was to not be easy in her presence.

"True, but this time, he called the *number*."

This bit of information broke Tatiana's concentration and she raised her eyes to his. His discomfort at her steady gaze showed in the slight flush on his cheeks.

"Did he indeed." Tatiana regarded him thoughtfully, the information about Dr. Hoffman swirling in her mind along with possibilities of what should come next. She always knew this day would come but wished it hadn't arrived so soon. There was much work left to be done, work Dr. Hoffman could assist with if given the right motivation.

She gave a crisp nod. "I think it's time to bring Dr. Hoffman in from the cold." She turned back to her microscope. "The next time I see you, he'd better be with you."

"Yes, ma'am." He was nearly out of the door when she called his name.

Tatiana hesitated only an instant. The possibility of Dr. Hoffman refusing to help was slim, but she couldn't take the chance he had developed a conscience after all these years. "If he won't come willingly, use any means necessary."

Without flinching, he nodded.

She'd measured his commitment by how he took the order. After his departure, she stared at the cells illuminated by the microscope's bright light. She had long admired Dr. Hoffman, but his cooperation was far from assured. Unfortunately, time could soften as well as harden. The years might have given him too much time to think. And a man contemplating his own morality was one who would be hard to control.

WOLFGANG HOFFMAN STARED AT THE ENVELOPE SLIPPED UNDER HIS DOOR while he was out to dinner with friends. He bent to pick up the slim padded mailer and shut the door behind him. Slitting it open, he tipped the envelope. Into his palm dropped a small thumb drive.

He hadn't stayed alive this long by making stupid mistakes like inserting unknown devices into his home computer. He had no desire to be found until he was ready to be found. He even regretted making that phone call last week, but what was done was done. He headed to the community library in the clubhouse complex.

After finding an empty computer terminal, he surfed a few news websites and the AARP website before surreptitiously inserting the drive into a USB port. Only one file appeared to be on the drive, a video file if he read the extension correctly. With a sense of trepidation, he clicked on it and, after selecting the appropriate media program, he watched a young woman nearly fall into the path of a SUV. The footage froze on a screen shot of the woman's face, tendrils from her long blonde hair framing her face, her terrified blue eyes beseeching.

Lena Hoffman, his granddaughter.

Wolfgang yanked out the thumb drive, sweat breaking out on his forehead. An icy hand clutched his heart. Somehow, the wrong person had discovered his connection to Lena—and had tried to kill her.

He flashed back to the phone call. Had that been a mistake, one that led to the attempt on Lena's life? He had purposefully stayed far away from his family when arriving in the United States. Followed from a discrete distance the lives of his only son and daughter-in-law. Rejoiced from afar at the birth of his sole grandchild. When his son and daughter-in-law died, he hadn't contacted their daughter in the hopes of keeping Lena safe. Now it seemed she was in danger despite his best efforts.

"Lenny, what are you doing here?"

A hearty voice jolted him back to the present. Slipping the drive into his pocket, he turned to see Max, a robust former two-star army general dressed in his usual attire: plaid shorts, a Hawaiian shirt, and sandals with knee-high socks.

Wolfgang, or Lenny, as he was known these days, stood. "Hey, Max. Just checking out some things on the computer. Trying to avoid the slow internet in our building today."

"You missed our golf outing this morning."

Wolfgang groaned. "I'm sorry. I woke up with a migraine, and the medication makes me so sleepy, I forgot to let you know I couldn't make it today."

"Are you feeling better?"

"Some, but I think I need a little more peace and quiet."

Max regarded him with a penetrating gaze, then shrugged. "Okay. Are you planning on going on the Sedona trip tomorrow?"

"No, I've got something else to do. Maybe I'll see you at the Old Timer's Grille Saturday night."

After exchanging goodbyes with Max, Wolfgang erased the search history and left the library. Someone knew Lena was his granddaughter. All he had worked for, all the sacrifices he had made, all he had done to ensure his family's safety, had been for naught.

AT THE NIH'S CENTER FOR CANCER RESEARCH, DEVLIN EXAMINED THE contents of a petri dish in one of the bio-hazard labs. The cells of JX-642 were replicating nicely and needed to be separated into several petri dishes to encourage more growth. With slow, precise movements, he performed the separation and placed the three petri dishes back into their sealed and locked container. He cleaned the work area with disinfectant, then checked again to ensure the container with the samples had been secured. Satisfied he had followed all the protocols, he walked over to his colleague, Dr. Nancy Orleans, who had been working on her own batch of JX-642 cells.

"Finished already?" Dr. Orleans transferred her petri dishes into a similar container, shutting the safe door and entering the access code, which locked it with a soft whirr.

"Yes. I'm ready to get out of this pressure cooker of a hazmat suit." As if to emphasize his point, a drop of sweat trickled down his face. "I really wish they would fix the heating and air conditioning in this room so we can keep it colder. I'm roasting."

She laughed and tossed her bleach wipe into a receptacle marked for waste. "There, all done." She too gave her area a careful perusal before nodding her head. "Let's get out of these."

Devlin walked beside Dr. Orleans as they made their way to the decontamination room attached to the lab. She pressed the buzzer to signal their entrance and the door slid open.

Devlin followed her inside and punched the button to close the door behind them, immediately sealing the room and releasing a whoosh of air to clean off anything attached to their suits. After sixty seconds, the air decreased, and he pulled a bleach wipe from a container attached to the wall. Each of them used the disposable cloths go over the outside of their suits.

The two worked in tandem to complete the arduous task of safely removing their hazmat suits. Once they had finished the process, Delvin stepped out of the decontamination room to a sealed locker room with single showers to scrub down with special soap. As Devlin let the hot water wash over his skin, he groaned. He'd forgotten to bring his cologne in and now would go to his date with Lena smelling like antiseptic. Not a romantic scent by any stretch of the imagination.

He toweled off and donned a robe to walk down the hallway to where he'd left his clothes before the suiting up. Once dressed, he strapped on his watch and checked the time. Three-forty-eight. Just over three hours until his date with Lena. But he had a lot of work to get through before their seven-thirty dinner reservation.

Back in his office, he tugged a binder off the shelf and paged through it. While working with JX-642 today, something he'd read in graduate school had tickled his subconscious. Delvin enjoyed the combination of lab work and book learning as he and his colleagues searched for new protocols, treatments, and vaccines for cancers.

The binder contained obscure journal articles his virology professor had handed out in class. Devlin extracted the article written four decades ago by a German scientist on the chicken pox virus and liver cancer. Firing up his laptop, he opened a document to take notes while he slowly read the article. He could barely make out the text on the original, so faded was the copy, but the attached short English translation gave a synopsis.

The German scientist had conducted clinical trials that showed early promise in using an altered chicken pox virus to attack cancer cells. The solution containing the virus had been injected into liver cancers, allowing the virus to enter the cancer cells. In theory, this would cause the cancer cells to die or to make proteins that resulted in them being attacked by the body's immune system. According to the research, this initially happened during the clinical trials, but the gains then reversed themselves, and the liver cancer cells roared back to life stronger than before.

He scrubbed a hand over his face. He and Dr. Orleans worked on the same type of thing. They'd found a similar problem. The chicken pox virus entered the cancer cells, causing the cells to die initially, but after forty-eight to seventy-two hours, the cancer cells started to rebound and overtake the chicken pox virus, rendering the virus impotent within a week's time.

The author's name had been smeared by the copier. Squinting at the paper, he made out a W as the initial of his first name and an H as the initial of his last name. No help at all. He sent an email to his Georgetown University professor to request a cleaner copy of the original source material. Maybe he could get a better translation that would provide some answers to the perplexing questions he and Dr. Orleans were trying to unravel.

Standing to replace the binder on the shelf, he groaned as he caught site of the wall clock. Six-eighteen. He should have left before six if he had any hope of being on time for his date. He shut down his laptop and secured it in a locked drawer before shrugging into his coat. The weather had turned cold again after a mild January week. At least the restaurant he'd picked was within easy walking distance of their complex. As he chirped open his car and settled inside, the feeling of being watched washed over him. Strange, he'd never had that thought before. Shrugging it off, he merged into traffic and headed for home.

CHAPTER

FIVE

Lena wrote the phrase from the postcard on a slip of paper and walked down the hallway to her colleague's cubicle. Gillian Drewyer had been translating documents from German to English for more than three decades. Perhaps the older woman would have another interpretation of the sentence that had been plaguing her all week.

She rapped on the cubicle frame. Gillian removed her head-phones. "Hello, Lena. How are you doing?"

"I'm okay." She moved into the cubicle. "I came across this phrase while reading some German magazines my aunt sent me, but I'm not sure I'm translating it correctly. I think it might be colloquial and that's what's throwing me off."

"Let me take a peek."

Lena handed Gillian the piece of paper. *"Ihre letzten ärztlichen Rat war falsch-es ist immer noch ein Leben zu führen."* She looked up at Lena. "What did you translate it as?"

"Your past medical advice was wrong—there is still a life to lead."

Gillian snorted. "I can see why you're confused. It's idiomatic in nature."

Lena frowned. "I checked my favorite German idiomatic expressions website, and nothing came back."

"That's because it's something a German in post-World War I Germany would have said." She patted Lena's hand. "Don't worry, *sehr geehrter*. You didn't miss anything in German class. The phrase wouldn't have been taught in school."

"But what does it mean?" Lena held her breath, as if hearing the reply would answer all of her questions about the postcard and its sender.

The older woman stared at the slip of paper. "It reminds me of what Mark Twain quipped so eloquently. 'The reports of my death are greatly exaggerated.'"

Lena struggled to keep her shock from showing. "It's an expression that means the person you thought was dead isn't?"

"Yes, at least that's as close to an English translation as I can get." Gillian handed back the paper. "The phrase entered the vernacular because of all the missing World War I soldiers who were presumed dead but then turned up one, two, or more years later and gave Mom and Dad the shock of their lives."

"I see." Lena folded the piece of paper. "Thank you. I guess you do learn something new every day."

"Especially when you're young," Gillian chuckled. "What article had that phrase in it? I'd be surprised if young Germans today would know that wording."

"It was a magazine geared toward senior Germans." The lie tumbled off her lips without a conscious thought. Lena hadn't considered herself able to tell fibs, but for some reason, she hadn't wanted to share the contents of her postcard with anyone besides Delvin. "Thanks again."

"Sure." Gillian put on her headphones.

Lena returned to her own cubicle. She studied the wording on the piece of paper. The person who was thought dead isn't dead after all. It looked like she might have a close living relative—her grandfather, Dr. Wolfgang Hoffman.

~

DELVIN SMOOTHED BACK HIS HAIR, THEN KNOCKED ON LENA'S DOOR. THE single pink rose surrounded by baby's breath suddenly looked tawdry in his hand. What had he been thinking? This wasn't the Bachelor. He should have gone with the bouquet of mixed blossoms instead. At least he'd splashed on some cologne to mask the smell of disinfectant before crossing to her condo.

The door opened, and Lena grinned at him. "Come on in. I just need to find my other shoe."

He glanced down, noting one foot encased in an ankle-high boot, while the other sported—he squinted—a Harry Potter sock?

"I love Harry Potter," she said as he entered.

"Who doesn't? It's, er, cute." He sounded like a schoolboy on his first date, not a thirty-year-old man. Thrusting out the rose to cover his blunder, he said, "For you."

"Thank you." She accepted the flower and sniffed the bud. "It's lovely. Let me put it in water, then find my other boot." Lena placed the rose in a vase and added water. "I'll be right back." She disappeared down the short hallway.

Goliath jumped onto the small end table and butted his hand with his head. Delvin scratched the cat's chin. "It's good to see you too."

Lean appeared, shoes on both feet. She slipped into her coat. "Ready?"

He nodded and followed her outside. "I thought we'd walk to that new Italian restaurant at Courthouse Plaza."

"I've been wanting to try it." She drew in a deep breath. "And a walk sounds lovely. I love cold, clear nights like this, don't you?"

"I don't know." He opened the security gate to exit the complex grounds. "I guess I hadn't really thought of it one way or another."

"My parents gave me a telescope for my tenth birthday, and I used to spend hours staring at the stars from my second-story bedroom window. On a night like this, I'd even climb onto the roof with a thermos of hot chocolate, an old quilt, and my telescope." She sighed. "I still have the telescope, but," she gestured to the street lights, "there's no good place to stargaze this close to the city."

The walk to the restaurant ended sooner than Devlin wanted. He'd been gathering his courage to take her hand in his as they strolled along, but that would have to wait until their return trip.

"Here we are." Devlin gave their names to the hostess, and she seated them in a corner at a table with a trio of small tea candles flickering on the snowy white tablecloth. He helped her out of her coat, then seated her across from him. His stomach rumbled in response to the scent of oregano, basil, and tomato sauce. "I think they do northern Italian cuisine here."

Lena picked up her menu. "I'm starving, and it smells delicious."

After placing their orders, the conversation drifted along familiar, first-date topics. Devlin shared a bit more about his research work while Lena entertained him with stories of translations that went horribly—and hilariously—wrong in her job as a translator with the U.S. State Department.

Their meals arrived, and talk shifted to their families. Lena was an only child whose immigrant parents had died in a car accident her freshman year of college, leaving her alone except for a distant relative in Germany. Devlin shared about his father's busy family medical practice, his mother's pottery, and one of his sister's recent marriage. Over coffee, Devlin moved the conversation toward more personal lines. "What are your weekend plans?"

Lena shrugged. "Housecleaning."

Her desultory tone brought a smile to his lips. "Not your favorite Saturday activity then?"

"Nope, but it's long overdue. Since my calendar's wide open for tomorrow, figured I'd better get on it." She hitched her eyebrows. "What about you?"

"I have a basketball game with some of the guys in the morning, then I should fit in a grocery run. My fridge is bare." The waitress dropped off their bill, and Devlin laid his credit card on top of the tray. After the server left to run his card, he ventured, "I've been meaning to visit the International Spy Museum in DC."

"That's always been on my list too, but I never seem to make it there." She took another sip of coffee.

"Want to go tomorrow afternoon?" He blurted out the question before he could second-guess himself. This was a first—asking a woman on a second date while on their first.

"Don't you need to make a reservation for timed tickets?"

His face fell at her question. "Yeah, I think you're right. Probably none left for a Saturday."

She briefly touched his hand with hers. "I'm sure we could check online to see if any tickets remain available."

Relief coursed through him. "I'll do it now." He pulled out his phone and found the spy museum's website. Quickly navigating through the screens, he located a few options. "Looks like we could go at three-thirty or four tomorrow."

"Doesn't it close at five?"

He consulted the website. "Yep."

"Then three-thirty would give us more time, if that works for you."

"I'll place the ticket order." He made the purchase, then pocketed his phone. "Done. We can take the Metro from Rosslyn to L'Enfant Plaza, and I think the museum's pretty close to the Metro stop."

"Sounds good." She smiled.

The waitress returned his card along with her wishes for them to enjoy the rest of their evening. Devlin put his card into his wallet. "Ready to go?"

Lena nodded. Outside the restaurant, a light breeze kicked up, turning the cold evening chillier.

"*Brr.*" Lena hunched into her coat as the wind ruffled her blonde hair.

"Here, maybe this will help." Devlin eased an arm around her waist, drawing her close to his body. She responded by tucking her left hand into the right-hand pocket of his coat.

"Much better."

His temperature shot up at her nearness, filling him with thoughts of his lips pressed to hers. As much as he desired to kiss her, a first date was way too soon for such a move. Instead, he would content himself with breathing in the floral scent of her shampoo and the way her body fit so nicely against his own. They walked in companionable silence toward their building.

"Let me get the gate." Devlin released Lena to step ahead. Swinging it open, he turned back to usher Lena through to the pathway leading into the complex.

Lena started to take a step when she glanced at the ground. "Hey, a penny." Bending, she plucked the coin from the sidewalk.

Something smacked into the brick post with a *thwunk*. The crack of a rifle echoed. The threat of danger galvanized Devlin into action.

"Stay down!" He yanked Lena through the gate as another projectile pinged off the iron railing.

Someone was shooting at them.

CHAPTER

SIX

S hots ricocheted off the iron gate. Lena stifled a scream. Devlin's firm grip propelled her through the opening. He shoved her behind a tree trunk, his body further shielding hers as more bullets smacked into the pavement and brick pillars of the fence.

After several minutes of only the sound of traffic on Wilson Boulevard, Devlin eased up to a crouch beside her. "You okay?"

She nodded. "What just happened?" Her voice cracked.

Devlin's jaw firmed. "Clearly, someone was shooting at us. What's not clear is why." He pointed to a building in the courtyard. "Let's move to safer spot."

Lena crouched alongside Devlin as they ran the few feet to the building and slipped inside. He pulled out his phone and dialed, putting it on speaker.

"911, where's your emergency?"

"We're at Colonial Village condos along Wilson Boulevard. Someone was shooting at us." Devlin sounded more angry than scared, while Lena wrapped her arms tightly around her body to stop from shaking.

"Sir, are you in a safe place? Is anyone injured?"

"We weren't hit, and my friend and I are inside 1721 Queens Lane." He glanced at Lena, then held out his hand.

She grasped it, and he tugged her to his side. With her head against his shoulder, she concentrated on the beat of his heart. The steady rhythm helped her own heart rate return to normal.

Devlin spoke a few more minutes to the dispatcher, then ended the call. "Help will be here soon." He smoothed back a strand of hair from her face. "You sure you're okay?"

"I think so." Tears pricked the backs of her eyes.

"Hey, I believe we're safe now." He put his other arm around her, rubbing her back.

Lena buried her face into his chest, breathing in the subtle scent of his cedar cologne. Her breathing calmed as they stood together. Sirens blaring filtered into the building, but neither of them moved. She didn't want to leave until the police told her it was safe to do so.

After another ten or so minutes passed, she stirred. "Why would someone shoot at us?"

"Do you think it has anything to do with the SUV that nearly ran you down last week?"

"That seems preposterous. If that were true, then..." She nodded toward the entrance as someone knocked before opening the door.

A uniformed police officer and a man dressed in a dark blue suit entered the building. The man flipped open a badge holder. "Dr. Mills? Ms. Hoffman? I'm Detective Bryan Geoly with the Arlington County Police Department. We've secured the grounds. Please walk me through what happened."

The detective removed a pen and a small notebook from an inside pocket of his suit jacket. Then he listened closely as Devlin outlined their evening, ending with shots fired at them as they entered the gate off Wilson Boulevard. After asking some clarifying questions, Geoly said, "Any idea if the shooter was aiming at one of you?"

Lena shuddered. "Why would someone try to shoot me or Devlin?"

"Ms. Hoffman, you said you work as a translator for the State Department. Do you handle sensitive documents?" Geoly tapped the notebook with his pen.

"No. It's ninety-nine percent translating run-of-the-mill government documents from German to English," Lena said. "And before you ask, the other one percent is doing in-person translations during trade negotiations and other meetings, which I haven't done in quite a while."

The detective jotted something down. "What about your work, Dr. Mills?"

Devlin leaned his shoulder against the wall. "I'm a medical researcher, working on finding a cure for liver cancer on a team of five others. But there's nothing we've discovered that would put a target on my back."

The outside door opened, and a uniformed cop poked his head inside. "Detective?"

"Wait here. I'll be right back." Geoly left the building. Through the window half of the door, a uniform cop stood guard outside.

Alone in the foyer, Devlin took her hands in his. "This wasn't quite how I pictured the ending of our date."

"Me, either." She tried to smile but her mouth quivered. "Do you think this is a random shooting?"

"Maybe." He didn't sound convinced.

Memories of her father's warning, "You never know who is listening," and her mother's hysteria every time a cop car drove down their street flooded her mind.

"Lena?"

She blinked hard, realizing Devlin had said something. "Sorry, lost in my thoughts. What did you say?"

"I asked if you still wanted to go to the spy museum tomorrow."

"Why wouldn't I?" Maybe he was having second thoughts about

being around someone who might have a target on her back. Or perhaps it was Devlin the shooter had been gunning for.

"I thought perhaps you'd rather stick closer to home after tonight's, um, adventure."

She shook her head.

"Good." He squeezed her hands.

Detective Geoly came back inside. "We identified three of the bullets buried in the brick pillars. We've cordoned off the area until the forensics team arrives. They'll get the bullets to the lab for analysis."

"Any idea where the shooter fired from?" Devlin let go of her left hand while keeping her right snug in his own.

"We're canvassing the buildings across the street but don't have any answers yet. We'll be in touch if we have any more questions and as we get more information from the scene." Geoly exited the building.

"What time is it?" Lena stifled a yawn as a wave of tiredness crashed over her.

Devlin pulled out his phone. "Nearly midnight." He studied her face. "You look done in. Let's go home."

"Good thing we have only a short walk. I feel like someone pulled the plug on me." She yawned again. "And now I'm circling the drain."

"I'll keep you afloat." He gave a little bow, then drew her arm through his and escorted her to their building. Outside her door, he paused. "Despite the dramatic ending, I had a very nice time with you, Lena."

"I did too."

Devlin leaned down and kissed her cheek, the gesture so quick she barely had time to register his intentions. The kiss warmed her from the inside out.

"Sleep well, and I'll see you tomorrow afternoon."

"Bye." Lena inserted her key into the lock and entered her apartment. As she closed the door, she could hear Devlin going into his condo opposite hers. Scratching Goliath's head as he mewed for attention, she couldn't remember a time when a date—not the aftermath—had held so much promise.

TATIANA DOTTED SWEAT FROM HER FOREHEAD WITH A TOWEL AS SHE SLOWED the treadmill to a fast walking speed. Her phone rang, disrupting her morning workout. Inserting her earpiece, she groaned at the caller ID. This would not be good news. "Hello?"

"Dr. Dern, it's Carl."

Of course, she knew it was Carl. "Yes?"

The man cleared his throat. "Last night, someone took a shot at Lena Hoffman and her date, a Dr. Devlin Mills."

Tatiana stumbled on the treadmill, then punched the stop button. "Tell me exactly what happened."

As Carl succinctly relayed the shooting, her mind considered and discarded multiple reasons behind the incident, none of them good. "Is she all right?"

"Yes. Apparently she bent down to look at something on the ground when the first shot was fired, thus missing her entirely."

"Who's this Dr. Mills?" She stepped off the machine and unscrewed the top of her reusable water bottle.

"He's a medical researcher at the NIH."

"That's a huge facility. Where exactly does Dr. Mills work?"

"In cancer research."

Tatiana paused, the water bottle halfway to her lips. She slowly lowered the bottle. "What's he researching?"

"Cures for liver cancer."

She set the water down hard into treadmill's cupholder, not caring that some sloshed over her hand. "Get me a full dossier on Dr. Mills immediately. And keep me posted on what the police find out about the shooting. You'll conduct your own investigation on the quiet."

"Yes, ma'am."

"I expect an update this afternoon." She ended the call, then drank water as she paced the room with short, quick steps. She needed Lena alive to get Dr. Hoffman back in the lab.

"Mom?" Her ten-year-old son, Kyle, scampered into the room, his blue eyes round with dismay. "Selana won't let me have the remote. It's my turn to pick the show."

His eleven-year-old sister waved the remote in her hand. "He's gonna pick Teen Titans. Again."

Tatiana allowed herself to be pulled into the sibling squabble. "Selana, it is his turn. You don't have to watch Teen Titans if you don't like what he picks."

Selana huffed, then slapped the remote into her brother's hand. "Fine." She stomped off while Kyle raced past her to the family room. She left them downstairs fighting over the snowman fleece blanket and headed to the kitchen.

At the stove, her husband pulled a crispy strip of bacon off the pan and onto a paper towel-lined plate. "How was your workout?"

"Good." She kissed his cheek and pinched off the corner of a bacon strip. "Hmmm. Bacon and eggs with toast. My favorite."

Tom laughed as he laid another strip of raw bacon into the sizzling grease. "You always say that."

"I always mean it." She rotated her shoulders, trying to recapture the relaxation her workout had induced before Carl's call. "I love being married to a man who can cook." She surveyed the table set for two, a single red candle in the middle.

"Do I have time for a quick shower before we eat?" She finished her water, then rinsed out the bottle.

"I think so." He pointed the tongs at her. "But if you take too long, there might not be any bacon left."

"I'll be quick." She hurried to their main floor master suite. Eleven minutes later, she re-entered the kitchen. Tom had set a platter of bacon and a bowl of eggs on the table. "I see I timed this right."

"You did indeed." He waited by her chair, always the gentleman.

On impulse, she took his face in her hands and kissed him with all the love in her heart before dropping into the seat.

"Wow. What did I do to deserve that?" Tom scooted in her chair, then sat across from her.

"Oh, this and that," she said. Her husband never complained about her long hours in the lab. He understood her commitment to her work and had willingly adjusted his own around the family schedule. A talented cartoonist, he drew from a home studio so he could easily take care of the children—and her.

Over breakfast, Tom told her a funny story about one of their neighbors, a windy day, and a trash can lid. She laughed, but her thoughts kept returning to Carl's phone call.

"The kids are excited about the trip to the zoo today," Tom said as he rose to clear the table.

"That's today?" Dismay washed over her. She needed to go into the office to check on things as well as figure out what to do about this unexpected development.

"Yes." Tom put the dishes in the sink, his back to her. "It's been on the family calendar for weeks."

"I know. I just lost track of the date." Her voice sounded weak to her own ears.

"I sense a *but* in there somewhere." Tom stacked the plates in the dishwasher.

Tatiana sighed. "I'm sorry, but work called. I have to go into the office for a little bit this morning. Can we go to the zoo after lunch?"

Tom squirted soap into the skillet. "Tatiana, I know how important your work is. I'll explain to the kids."

Her heart sank at his unspoken disappointment.

"I know how dedicated you are to finding a cure for liver cancer, especially after your mom's death."

He had no idea, not really, but she didn't interrupt him.

"However, I have to say one thing," he resumed in a more serious tone. "The kids are getting older, and they need their mother, espe-

39

cially Selana. She's at that age where her body's starting to change and," he put the washed pan in the drainer, "she doesn't want to talk about that stuff with her dad."

"What are you saying?" Her pulse quickened. She blindly reached for her coffee to wet her dry mouth while hanging on his every word.

An awkward silence hung in the air. At last he turned to face her, and his eyes searched hers. The sadness in his expression punched her in the gut. In the nearly twenty years they'd been together, she'd never seen that look before. "I'm saying things need to change. We need you home more."

Her heart hammered in her chest. "I'll try to do better."

Tom shook his head. "You'll have to do more than try."

Tatiana rose to her feet slowly, but fear at losing him made her knees buckle, and she retook her seat. "It sounds like you're giving me an ultimatum. Are you?"

He raked his fingers through his hair, sending the strands every which way. "No, I'm not, but things cannot go on the way they have, with you working eighty-plus hour weeks and the kids and I barely seeing you. And when we carefully plan something you assured me works with *your* schedule, you blow it up."

His words cut through her defenses with the accuracy of a surgical knife. "Tom, I need you to understand—"

"I'll tell the kids why you can't go, but we're heading to the zoo this morning as planned. They both want to see the penguin feeding at eleven. If you change your mind, we're leaving at ten." Tom stalked out of the kitchen and into their bedroom, shutting the door with a loud click.

CHAPTER

SEVEN

Monday morning, Devlin found it difficult to follow the thread of the conversation as the weekly staff meeting droned on and on. His mind bounced between speculating who had been shooting at them Friday night and his two dates with Lena. The Saturday afternoon trip to the spy museum had been followed by Chinese takeout at his place. While he hadn't ginned up courage to kiss her, he'd taken advantage of the cold temperatures to hold her hand and put his arm around her shoulders.

"Dr. Mills? Are you with us?"

With a jerk, Devlin brought his thoughts back to the present and discovered nine people staring at him. "My apologies. I was considering a possible solution to a tricky situation." He kept to himself the situation involved a lovely young woman and when he could kiss her.

Dr. Walter Shan, the head of the virus therapy department at the NIH Center for Cancer Research Division of Cancer Epidemiology & Genetics, raised his eyebrows. "I hope the solution outweighs your inattention."

Devlin lowered his chin, his pride wounded by the rebuke. Dr.

Shan hadn't raised his voice, but the chastisement came across loud and clear. He hated disappointing his mentor as well as his boss.

Dr. Shan leaned back in the leather chair at the head of the oblong conference table, his head cocked to one side. "Do you have an updated on JX-642?"

"Not as promising as we'd initially hoped." Devlin woke up his tablet, then accessed an app to project his findings onto the wall screen. "As you can see here, JX-642 replicates easily. When we inject a viral solution into samples of liver infected with hepatocellular carcinoma cells," he swiped to bring up another slide, "during the first few hours, the solution attacks the cancer cells, killing them off."

"Dr. Mills, how much of the viral solution did you inject in the first round?" One of his colleagues, Dr. Joan Buckley, asked.

"The usual 5 CCs." Devlin pulled up the third slide. "By the next morning, the cancer cells had stopped dying. The viral solution still had active cells, but for some reason we haven't been able to determine, the effectiveness of the solution, while starting out as a killing machine, ended up being able to simply co-exist alongside the cancer cells. The virus is neither killing nor being killed by the cancer cells."

The group of scientists, oncologists, and researchers studied the last slide in silence, then Dr. Shan opened the discussion to help Devlin solve the problem. Devlin took furious notes on his tablet as suggestions flew at him nearly as fast as JX-642 replicated in the lab. By the end of the meeting, Devlin had three or four solid ideas of where to go next in his research.

Dr. Shan dismissed the group. Devlin gathered his tablet and headed for the door, reaching it at the same time as Dr. Shan.

His supervisor motioned Devlin through first, then laid a hand on Devlin's shoulder. "Walk with me back to my office."

It might have sounded like a request to others, but Devlin recognized it as a command. He fell into step beside Dr. Shan as the older man made his way down the hallway, merely acknowledging greetings with the wave of his hand and not stopping to chat with anyone. At his office door, Dr. Shan unlocked it with the swipe of his ID badge and entered, Devlin coming in behind him.

"Shut the door." Dr. Shan took a seat behind his massive mission-style oak desk.

Devlin did as requested, then seated himself in one of the heavy club chairs in front of the desk.

"I'm impressed with what you've been able to accomplish so far with the viral therapy, and the suggestions your colleagues provided will be useful going forward in your research."

"Thank you, sir." Devlin puzzled over why his boss felt the need to have a closed-door meeting to tell him what he'd basically said in the conference room.

Dr. Shan eyed him with a thoughtful expression. "How much do you know about what went on in the medical community behind the Iron Curtain?"

Devlin couldn't keep the astonishment from his face. Whatever he had expected Dr. Shan to say, it hadn't been this. "The Iron Curtain?"

"Yes, surely George Mason University covered the events of the Cold War in your history undergrad studies."

Devlin nodded. "I took a class on the subject, but it didn't touch on medicine in depth at all. I only remember the difficulty average citizens had in gaining treatment and medications."

"Those were tough times in Soviet countries, but there were some interesting experiments going on in East Germany." Dr. Shan regarded him, then nodded, as if making up his mind about something. "Your advisor at Georgetown was Dr. Knox Edgerton?"

"That's right." Devlin was still trying to figure out what East Germany decades ago had to do with his viral therapy research.

Dr. Shan extracted a key from a chain hanging around his neck and leaned down to insert it into one of the desk drawers. He placed folders on the edge of the desk but misjudged their placement, and the stack toppled to the floor.

"I'll get those for you." Devlin knelt by the side of the desk and gathered the papers. As he did, he noted his mentor running his hand along the bottom seam before removing a false bottom. Inside lay a battered notebook. Devlin restacked the folders securely on the desk and returned to his chair as Dr. Shan removed the notebook from its hiding place.

Looking intently at him, Dr. Shan placed his hand on top of the notebook on his desk. "I had an uncle who worked as a janitor in Charité, the premiere medical research facility in East Berlin."

Devlin had heard of Charité but wasn't sure what a Cold War research facility had to do with the here and now. However, Dr. Shan wasn't one to waste time with irrelevant stories, so he listened.

Dr. Shan tapped the notebook. "My uncle saved this because it had a few blank pages in the back and his daughter liked to draw. On his meager salary, he couldn't afford to buy her paper, so he took it and a few others like it home instead of burning them in the incinerator as instructed."

"How did you get it?" Despite himself, Devlin was intrigued by the scenario being described. He had an inkling that the notebook contained medical information, but what good could decades old information be today?

"My uncle passed it along to my father with its mates for safe keeping, and eventually on to me." Dr. Shan paused, his eyes serious. "I keep them locked away for good reason."

Devlin asked the obvious question. "What's in them?"

Dr. Shan leaned forward. "Details of clinical trials and other medical experiments."

Devlin eyed the notebook. "Unpublished material?"

"Of course unpublished. Some would even consider it bad science because it hasn't been peer reviewed. As if peer review is all something needs to be right." Dr. Shan thumped the notebook. "It's written in German, so it's taken me a long time to translate the material. You don't read German, do you?"

"No, sir." Lena came immediately to Devlin's mind. "But I know someone who does. She's a translator with the State Department."

"I could not let anyone else read these, not until I know all of their secrets." Dr. Shan frowned. "Perhaps I shouldn't have even told you about them."

Devlin detected fear underneath Dr. Shan's words. The older man was genuinely worried about the notebooks. Although Dr. Shan had crested the mid-point in his career, he still had visions of making a breakthrough in cancer research, finding the elusive moonshot to cure one of the world's major diseases. His thick head of dark hair had no gray, and he kept his figure trim from regular squash matches. Dr. Shan must be in his mid-fifties. Many doctors practiced well into their eighties, depending on the specialty, so Dr. Shan should have plenty more years left to work in his lab.

"Dr. Mills, I must ask you not to mention these notebooks to anyone."

"Of course, but may I ask why you told me about them?"

Dr. Shan looked as if he wasn't going to answer, then he shrugged. "One of the words I learned early on in translating the notes was *leberkrebs*."

"Liver cancer." Devlin too had seen that German word in the article from his Georgetown professor.

"Right." Dr. Shan looked down at the notebook. "I think whoever wrote this was working on a cure for liver cancer using viral therapy."

"Wow. But I didn't think anyone used that until recently." Excitement filled him as he stared at the book on his mentor's desk. If someone forty or fifty years ago had had success—or even documented failures—with viral therapy against liver cancer, it could help him immensely in his own research.

"There is nothing new under the sun, eh?"

"I guess not." The quote from Ecclesiastes startled him. Then again, that saying popped up all over the place without its biblical connection noted. "There's very few documented trials related to viral therapy and liver cancer. We're all starting basically from scratch. To have access to previous trials and errors would be of immense help."

"I agree." Dr. Shan patted the notebook. "I have a feeling there's more to this than simple clinical trials on a new treatment for liver cancer. Until I discover what that is, I have to keep the existence of the notebooks a secret."

"I don't understand. Would someone try to steal the data?" That, Devlin could believe. Unpublished data related to cancer research would be a gold mine for any medical researcher.

"Steal it, perhaps." Dr. Shan returned the notebook to the bottom drawer and relocked it, then placed the key chain around his neck. It dropped underneath his shirt, hiding it from view. "To answer your question more fully, I'm concerned the data would be destroyed. People have died because of these notebooks."

His words chilled the air. "Who died?"

Dr. Shan shook his head. "I've said too much already, but I've felt for some time the need to share their existence with you. We will talk about this again soon, but for now, we should return to work."

Devlin stood. "Thank you for telling me about the notebooks. If you want a translator, let me know. My friend is trustworthy."

"I'm sure she is." Dr. Shan threw him a shrewd look. "And pretty too, am I right?"

His cheeks hot, Devlin chose not to respond to the comment. "Is there anything else, Dr. Shan?"

"I hope you're not spending too much time in the lab and not enough time with your pretty girl." A pensive look crossed Dr. Shan's face. "I wish I hadn't gotten so focused on my career that I ignored those around me." He looked at a photo on his desk. "I should have spent more time with my dear wife."

The melancholy in his boss's voice was palatable. When Dr. Shan's wife of thirty-three years died last summer, he hadn't revealed this much emotion.

"I'll do my best to remember that."

Dr. Shan, his eyes still on his wife's photo, sighed. "You're a wise young man."

"That means a lot coming from you." Devlin had his hand on the door when he turned back to ask a final question. "Do you know who wrote the notebooks?"

"The signature scrawled on the inside front cover of every one of them reads Dr. Wolfgang Hoffman."

Devlin couldn't hide his audible intake of breath at hearing that name again, but Dr. Shan didn't seem to notice his reaction. He slipped into the hallway, closing the door behind him. As he walked to his office, he turned the name over and over in his mind. What if Dr. Shan's Hoffman was the same as Lena's grandfather? On the heels of that question came another. If that proved true, why was Hoffman contacting Lena again after years of pretending to be dead?

How could a dead man keep cropping up? For decades, not a whisper of Dr. Wolfgang Hoffman could be heard from any of his excellent sources. But within the space of a fortnight, rumors of the man reached his ears from several usually reliable sources.

He banged his fist on the desk surface with such force a paperweight crashed to the hardwood floor, shattering upon impact. The noise brought his secretary to the door.

"Sir? Is everything all right?" The young woman's eyes widened at the glass littering the floor. "I'll get that cleaned up right away."

"Leave it for now," he barked, waving her out of his office. "I need to make some calls. Helga can clean it up when I leave for my luncheon appointment."

"Very well, sir." The secretary left with a backward glance at the mess, her high heels clicking on the floor with a staccato rhythm.

Once the door shut behind her, he lifted a square of carpet from underneath his desk and pulled up on a small trap door to reveal a buried safe. He placed his index finger on the sensor pad to release the lock. Once opened, he picked up a burner cell phone.

The person on the other end answered the call after one ring. "Yes."

"I hear the good doctor is not dead after all." He leaned back in his leather chair, trying to project an air of calmness he hoped would transfer to his voice.

"That appears correct."

"How can this be? I was assured of his demise." All his work could disappear in an instant if Dr. Hoffman came back from the grave.

"We verified his death as best we could, given the circumstances." The other person cleared their throat. "The doctor has not chosen to reappear. Someone else is pushing his return to the land of the living."

He hadn't considered that possibility. "Find out who that is and report back to me."

"Consider it done."

He started to hang up, but something in other person's voice made him ask, "What else?"

"He's contacted his granddaughter, Lena Hoffman."

His granddaughter? "Why wasn't I informed?"

"We've been keeping an eye on her. She knew very little about her grandfather apart from his name and that he's supposed to be deceased. Her parents had no information about Dr. Hoffman in their apartment, so there was no way she could compromise the situation."

The explanation made sense, but being kept in the dark infuriated him. He was the one taking all the risks. He should have all the relevant information. "What else haven't you been telling me?"

"Someone's targeting the granddaughter."

"How?"

"By running her down with an SUV and by shooting at her. We

48

think there are two operatives at work because the vehicle incident was designed to scare her but whoever shot at her wanted her dead."

"I expect an update tomorrow." He ended the call and replaced the phone. Someone wanted Dr. Hoffman unearthed, and someone else wanted him to stay underground. Either way, it spelled trouble.

CHAPTER
EIGHT

Lena tucked her feet into her favorite slippers, wishing she could as transform her thoughts as easily as the fuzzy comfort of her footwear soothed the aches in her toes. After a long day translating a hefty trade document, the lure of snuggling on the couch with Goliath nearly overcame her desire to learn more about her grandfather. She compromised by settling down with her cat and computer.

Little was known about the man. If it hadn't been for an overheard conversation between Mom and Dad, her grandfather's name might have remained a mystery. When Lena had asked who Dr. Wolfgang Hoffman was, Mom bit back a cry and lunged for the radio to jack up the volume while Dad snapped *his* father was dead and to never mention his name again. The blaring classical music did little to camouflage her parents' ensuing argument.

As she now opened Google and keyed the words *Dr. Wolfgang Hoffman* into the search engine, her finger hovered over the enter key. She shivered as if her next move would push her past the point of no return. But that was silly. How could looking into her deceased grandfather's background cause any trouble? She pressed the key.

Instantly, hundreds of hits appeared on the screen. The first dozen or so were quickly dismissed as contemporary medical professionals, much too young to be Grandfather.

Halfway down the page, an article from *Bild*, one of Germany's biggest tabloids, caught her eye. *DDR-Wissenschaftler Fehlende oder in Verstecken?* She translated the headline. "East German Scientist Missing or in Hiding?" The deck provided more information. *Ist Dr. Wolfgang Hoffman tot oder lebendig und arbeiten noch an streng geheimen Regierungs Experimente?* "Is Dr. Wolfgang Hoffman dead or alive and still working on top-secret government experiments?"

She glanced at the date. August 4, 1993. She skimmed the piece, but wrapped up in sensational language, it only provided the bare facts about the man her parents refused to discuss. Dr. Hoffman had worked for a top-secret research facility in East Berlin and had gone missing without a trace ten years earlier. Sources from the former East German government disavowed all knowledge of where the eminent researcher reportedly working on a promising cure for cancer had gone. Speculation that the doctor had been killed by East German officials was patently untrue, those same sources said. "Dr. Hoffman had been a trusted member of the East German medical community for many years, and his disappearance in 1983 shocked everyone," said one anonymous source. The article concluded that no one knew for sure where the doctor was today, but many believed he had tried to go to South America and perished on the journey.

Lena copied and pasted the article into a Word document, then returned to the newspaper's page. Johan Attmanstacher, the writer, had a clickable link for his name, so she followed the trail and discovered he was still with the *Bild*, having moved up the editorial food chain to become its national news managing editor. She book-marked the staff page, then entered *Dr. Wolfgang Hoffman* into the newspaper's online search engine. Nothing came up other than that one 1993 article.

Strange. The salacious nature of the first piece practically screamed for a follow up story. Belinda, a TV producer with the local

ABC affiliate, said often after a news story about a missing person or an unsolved crime ran, viewers would contact the station with information. Lena figured it worked the same way in print journalism. Maybe the follow up stories didn't migrate online. She could try contacting Attmanstacher directly. Lena quickly composed a message from the generic email account she used to anonymously sign up for newsletters or subscriptions.

After deleting several drafts, she chose to shield her relationship with Dr. Hoffman by signing only her middle name. She also wrote in German.

Dear Mr. Attmanstacher,

I recently came across your 1993 article on Dr. Wolfgang Hoffman and his possible disappearance but didn't see any follow up articles posted online. By chance did you write other pieces on the topic?

Sincerely,

Maike

Short and to the point. Germans tended to appreciate efficiency over flowery words or subterfuge. She hit send, then re-read the original article. Her parents, Andrea and Stefan Hoffman, had talked very little about their life before they emigrated to the United States. She had always assumed they had come from West Germany, but what if she had been wrong?

She went to her bedroom and tugged the weighty fireproof and water-tight security box from under the bed. Lena knelt over the box. She was being silly. Opening it was not like opening Pandora's box. Nothing sinister would happen. But the feeling she was crossing the point of no return wouldn't leave her.

She turned the key and lifted the lid. Sifting through the documents, she fished out her parents' birth and death certificates. She had never examined them closely. There had been no need. Losing both to a car crash when she was a freshman in college had been overwhelming, and it had taken all her strength to make it through those dark days and keep up with her studies. Her mom and dad, while not overly warm or demonstrative in their affection, had loved her—of that, she had no doubt. But she'd always sensed something cautious about them, as if they were constantly on alert to an unseen danger.

Now she unfolded the documents. *Andrea Maike Mulherin, born December 3, 1965, Charité Hospital, East Berlin, German Democratic Republic.*

Lena blinked hard. East Berlin? Mother had been born behind the Iron Curtain and never said a word. She quickly picked up her father's birth certificate. *Stefan Wolfgang Hoffman, born March 11, 1964, East Berlin, German Democratic Republic.* Father had mentioned he'd been born at home during a late snowstorm but implied it was in West Germany, not East Berlin. She shuffled the papers to their marriage certificate.

Andrea and Stefan had married on July 5, 1985, in an East Berlin civil registry office. They told everyone they'd emigrated separately to the United States and met while students at a university. She rubbed her forehead as another lie came to mind. Five years ago, an elderly aunt conducting genealogy research on the Hoffman family tree had contacted her from Germany. Despite the realization both parents hadn't told the truth about having no living relatives, she'd been thrilled to learn an entire branch of Father's family still lived in Germany.

Great-aunt Hilda Hoffman Berkemeyer had provided a basic family tree for Lena, noting the births, deaths, and marriages of a host of Hoffman relatives. Lena pulled the chart from the pile of papers in the metal box and examined it more closely. Above her father's name, were the birth, death, and marriage dates of his parents, Ida Louise Braun and Dr. Wolfgang Henrick Hoffman. Ida's death was listed as April 27, 1979, while Wolfgang was marked as having died in August 1985. No date, just the month and year. No other family member had missing information. That missing day for her grandfather's death niggled at her.

She returned the documents to the fireproof box and pushed it under the bed. Back in the living room, she emailed Aunt Hilda to ask if the death date for Grandfather had been incomplete on accident.

With a sigh, she shut down her laptop and got ready for bed. She'd hoped for more answers, and all she'd ended up with were more questions.

DEVLIN SWIPED HIS ID BADGE THROUGH THE SECURITY SLOT AND WAITED FOR the sliding doors to admit him. He caught himself whistling some long-forgotten show tune. Was it from *Brigadoon* or *Seven Brides for Seven Brothers*? His sisters forced him to watch a lot of musicals when he was a boy. He'd learned early on it was much easier to submit than to fight them on which movie they would watch for the weekly Saturday matinee on the couch with a big bowl of popcorn. If he didn't protest the choice, he got to hold the popcorn bowl. The memory made him smile.

"Hey, Dr. Mills? Have you seen Dr. Shan?"

Devlin stopped at the desk of Penny Wong, one of the department's research assistants. "I just got in myself. Dr. Shan usually starts work around seven. Did you try his office line?"

Penny nodded. "And his home and cell phones. No answer."

Devlin itched to get to his office to start his jam-packed day. If he worked straight through lunch, he'd have a fighting chance of running into Lena at the mailboxes—and might be able to coax her into having an impromptu movie night with him. The thought warmed him all the way from his head to his toes. He checked the time on his watch. "It's just after eight. Maybe he's running late."

"Maybe." Penny, a young woman with glossy black hair and a hesitant way of talking, frowned.

"What's wrong?"

"Dr. Shan and I had a seven-thirty meeting to go over my notes from yesterday's experiment." Penny chewed on the cap of a pen.

"He's never late. Even when his wife died last year, he didn't miss a single appointment."

Devlin remembered how Dr. Shan had thrown himself into his work as a way of coping with his grief. "Are you sure he remembered today's meeting?"

"He mentioned it last night when he stopped by my desk around six."

She was right. That didn't sound like Dr. Shan. "Come on. I'll walk with you to his office and see what's up. He probably stepped out for a minute and is back in his office waiting impatiently for you to arrive."

Penny gave him a sheepish grin.

Devlin waited while she grabbed a file folder and her cup of Starbucks coffee, then led the way to Dr. Shan's office.

Once there, Devlin contemplated the closed door before rapping on the surface. Silence. He knocked again. Still nothing. On impulse, he tried the handle, and it turned.

Pushing open the door, Devlin peered into the darkened room. The blinds drawn tightly across the windows shut out any natural light, and his body blocked the light from the hallway.

"Dr. Shan?" No answer. Concern inched up his spine as a coppery scent assailed his nostrils.

He fumbled for the light switch, and brightness flooded the room. Papers strewn onto the floor stopped Devlin in his tracks. Several bookcases had been overturned. Books with their spines broken and pages ripped littered the carpet. The two guest chairs had been slashed, foam spilling out like fish guts.

Penny tapped him on his shoulder. "Is he there?" She jostled Devlin from behind, trying to peer around him.

"Stay back. Something's wrong." Devlin stepped backward, forcing Penny out of the doorway and back into the hall. "Please get security. I'll stay here to make sure no one goes inside."

When Penny didn't move, he asked in a firmer tone, "Did you hear me?"

"Yeah, I'm going." With a final glance toward Dr. Shan's office, she turned and made her way down the hallway.

Devlin started to close the door but reconsidered. He hadn't looked around enough to see whether Dr. Shan was inside or not. Once he'd seen the damage, he hadn't wanted to contaminate a potential crime scene. But that smell reminded him of blood. He'd better check to be sure Dr. Shan wasn't laying hurt under the debris.

Devlin slipped inside, then closed the door behind him. He left the light on, not wanting to touch the switch again in case he smeared fingerprints. Maybe he'd been watching too many crime shows because he was starting to act like he was a cop. But he still stepped to avoid as much of the mess on the floor as he could, moving toward the massive desk, its polished surface invisible under the mountain of papers strewn all over it. The high-backed desk chair faced the shuttered window. He went around the desk, his eyes on the floor. A foot leaned against one of the chair's wheels. The sight of the penny loafer made him forgot about preserving evidence, and he rushed forward.

Dr. Shan sat slumped in the chair, a bullet hole in his right temple and a gun on the floor.

CHAPTER

NINE

Devlin touched his fingers to the carotid artery at Dr. Shan's neck. The cold skin told him the man had long departed this earth. The lack of pulse confirmed it. Devlin backed out of the room and shut the door just as Penny and a security guard arrived. His heart pounding, Devlin stood with his back to the door to block any attempt to enter. While the death scene indicated suicide at first glance, the office destruction screamed intruder.

"What's going on?" The Guard Force Operations Branch security officer barked, impatience stamped in every line of his hang-dog face.

"You need to call the police. There's been an accident," Devlin replied, not wanting to elaborate his suspicions. "Dr. Shan is dead, and his office has been ransacked. Penny, please contact the administration."

The guard, whose name tag read *Littleman*, made a move as if to enter the room, but Devlin shifted his stance. "This is a crime scene. You can't go in there."

"Who are you to tell me what I can and can't do?" Littleman tried to bully his way past Devlin, but Devlin didn't budge.

Instead, Devlin took out his cell phone and dialed 911, keeping his eyes hard on Littleman's. The other man huffed but didn't try to gain access to the room again. Succinctly, Devlin explained to the dispatcher what had happened. Ending the call, he turned to Littleman. "The police will be here shortly. No one is to enter the office until law enforcement or the paramedics arrive."

Littleman didn't argue but stepped back and made a phone call of his own. Devlin tried not to picture Dr. Shan, blood pooled from a head wound and lifeless eyes staring at the ceiling. The notebooks carried an ominous weight to them as the man had warned. *People have already died because of these notebooks.*

He'd chalked up Dr. Shan's words to a man mired in grief, but with his death, Devlin had an uneasy feeling the notebooks would be missing.

"Dr. Mills, the police are here," Littleman said, his eyes frosty. The guard wouldn't forget Devlin's actions anytime soon.

A man and woman stepped forward, both dressed in dark blue suits with crisp white shirts. "I'm Lieutenant Thomas Carter and this is Sergeant Glenda Quader with the NIH Division of Police Criminal Investigations section. Can you tell me what happened?"

Devlin explained to the National Institute of Health's own police force about Penny's appointment and his finding the room ransacked and Dr. Shan dead. Carter entered the room, leaving his partner to ask Devlin for more details. A few minutes later, Carter exited the room, his face grim.

"Take me through your movements once more," he directed Devlin.

Devlin did, reiterating the circumstances that led to his finding Dr. Shan.

"Let me through," a male voice yelled from down the hallway where uniformed police had blocked access to the crime scene.

The officer shook his head.

"I am the director of this center. I demand to talk to whoever's in charge," he huffed.

Quader turned to Devlin. "Is that the director?"

"Maybe," Devlin replied, eying the man's florid face and pinstriped suit. "I only met the man once at a meeting right after I was hired. He doesn't generally come to the lab floor."

Carter motioned to the officer to let the director through, and the man marched down the hall. In front of Carter, the man stopped. "Who are you?"

Carter made the introductions, ending with, "This is Dr. Mills."

Devlin nodded at the director, scrambling to recall the man's first name. All that came to mind was Tightwad Timms, the nickname the staff had given him because of his parsimonious nature.

"Dr. Edward Timms." The director aimed his gaze at Devlin. "What has happened?"

Carter stepped in before Devlin could answer. "Dr. Shan is dead."

"That's preposterous." Timms stepped forward as if to access the situation for himself.

Quader held up her hand. "The doctor's office is a crime scene."

Timms frowned. "How did he die?"

"That's for the chief medical examiner to determine," Carter said. "When was the last time you saw Dr. Shan?"

"At last week's staff meeting." Timms crossed his arms.

"Have you spoken to him since then?" Quader asked.

"Yes." Timms's forehead creased. "He left me a voice mail message last night, something about a missing notebook."

Devlin's heart rate accelerated. He wanted to ask what notebook, but decided if he kept silent, maybe the detectives wouldn't notice he was still hanging about. He tried to recall if the secret compartment had been opened in the bottom desk drawer but could only recall the slumped body of Dr. Shan.

"Do you still have that message?" Carter said.

"I didn't actually get it until this morning because he left it on my office number." Timms glanced around, then pointed to a closed office door. "If I can access the phone in that office, I can play it for you."

The detectives and Timms moved across the hall, Devlin discretely following. He lingered outside the office as the three crowded around the desk. Soon, the voice of Dr. Shan filled the air.

"Dr. Timms, I have asked repeatedly that the cleaning staff not be allowed in my office."

Devlin inched closer to the door.

Dr. Shan's message continued. "They keep moving things around, and it's unacceptable. My work must be left as I've organized it. Now I have to sort through these papers for the third time this week. I intend to file a formal complaint in the morning."

The message ended, and a mechanical voice intoned, "Message received at eleven-fifty-eight p.m., on Monday, January twenty-fifth."

Dr. Shan didn't sound like a man about to commit suicide. Devlin hastily stepped back into the hall and pulled out his phone to give the appearance of checking something. When the detectives and Timms exited the office, he didn't look up until Carter said his name.

"Yes?" Devlin asked, slipping the phone back into his pocket.

"Dr. Timms said you worked with Dr. Shan. When we're finished processing the scene, we'd like you to check to see if anything's missing in his office."

Devlin nearly said Dr. Shan hardly invited anyone into his inner sanctum, preferring to discuss issues with staff in the lab, but he wanted to see if the notebooks were still there, so he nodded.

"Where will you be?" Carter asked.

Devlin mentally reviewed his day. He needed to check on his experiments in the lab, but that would take at least three hours. "How long would they need?"

"Probably a couple of hours," Carter said.

Not long enough to suit up for lab work, so catching up on paperwork it would be. "I'll be in my office."

"We'll let you know when to come back to Dr. Shan's office," Carter said.

Devlin took the statement as a dismissal and hurried away from the crime scene. He managed to avoid a handful of colleagues and shut himself into his office without anyone asking what was going on. Devlin booted up his laptop while one thought looped through his mind.

Who had killed Dr. Shan?

~

TATIANA PICKED UP THE CALL ON THE DISPOSABLE CELL PHONE ON THE second ring. "Hello?"

"One leak has been plugged." The voice on the other end had a scratchy quality to it, as if the speaker had a frog in his throat, but the words were clear enough.

"Good." She sat ramrod straight, even though her desk chair had a very comfortable high back to it. Her petite frame kept her feet from touching the ground, hence they rested on a short stool kept hidden under her desk for just that purpose. "Will there be any problems with the suicide verdict?"

"Shouldn't be. The drug we used wouldn't show up in any normal tox screen. You'd have to specifically look for it, and that's only within the first forty-eight or so hours after death."

"No more details."

"Of course, wouldn't want to dirty your lily-white hands, now would we?"

"That's enough." Tatiana halted, considering whether to voice another concern. It had been a week since she'd last seen Dr. Shan, and his troubled expression would forever haunt her. That's when the plan for his demise began. Had there been another way versus ending the life of such an eminent physician, it would have been chosen. However, if Dr. Shan had even an inkling about what she was attempting, he wouldn't stop until he knew the whole story.

"Did you discover what happened with the shooting?" Impatience clipped her tone.

A short pause. "That wasn't our doing."

"I know that." She paused. "I want to know who else is interested."

"That wasn't part of our original agreement."

"How much extra will this cost?"

"Another fifty thousand dollars. In cash."

Tatiana calculated the amount of slush fund money she still had available and concurred. "I'll need a few days to gather that amount without suspicion."

"You have until Sunday."

"Where should I leave it?"

"I'll contact you on Saturday with instructions."

"Okay." Tatiana tapped her fingers on the desk softly. The rhythmic nature of the motion calmed her inner being and allowed her thoughts to crystalize. "Anything else from our Winter Bird?"

A short laugh. "No. He's pretty much stayed true to his normal activities. I doubt he suspects anyone is following him."

"I wouldn't be so sure." Tatiana heard confidence in the man's voice. The young were always so cocky, so full of themselves, always underestimating a person because of his or her age. "He's had a lot of experience with eluding undercover agents, or have you forgotten where he grew up?"

"That was a long time ago. He's gone soft in his old age."

"Perhaps." She disconnected the call. Time would reveal what the man could accomplish, but his arrogance might prove costly. She picked up her office phone and dialed Agent Schuler. Eyes on the ground to ensure nothing was revealed had become a necessity.

"It's Dr. Dern."

"What can I do for you, ma'am?"

"I need you to discretely monitor the investigation into the death of Dr. Shan over at NIH." Tatiana drummed her fingers. Best to trust him with only a sliver of truth. "He may have had a connection with the other matter we discussed. Please make sure that doesn't come to light or become the focus of the investigation."

She hung up without waiting for confirmation. Now, back to the lab and the project that would bring her worldwide recognition.

DEVLIN GAZED AROUND DR. SHAN'S OFFICE, HIS HEART HEAVY WITH THE LOSS of a man who had done so much to advance the science of cancer research. Carter had asked him to touch as little as possible in his assessment of whether anything was missing. Devlin started to the right of the door and made his way carefully around the room, leaving the desk for last. By the time he reached the desk, anger had supplanted sorrow at the destruction of Dr. Shan's extensive notes, papers, and books. The desk chair had been removed, as well as part of the carpet underneath the chair where Devlin recalled blood stains had been.

On top of the desk and on the floor near it lay the contents of the drawers. Pens, highlighters, sticky notes, and a staple remover lay jumbled amidst more papers and file folders. He glanced up to see if Carter had entered the office, but the detective remained outside talking softly to Quader.

Pulling out the bottom right-hand drawer, he sucked in a sigh of relief at the sight of the intact false bottom. Kneeling, he felt along the seam for the release mechanism he'd assumed Dr. Shan had accessed the day before. The spring popped open with a soft plunk, revealing a single notebook resting in the space that had held at least half a dozen yesterday. Devlin removed the notebook. Dr. Shan must have been looking through the other notebooks, which were now missing. If he alerted the police, they would confiscate this one.

He hesitated as the conviction that someone had killed Dr. Shan for those notebooks grew. Until he knew what was in the notebook, he wouldn't tell the police of its existence. Besides, no one would believe a nearly fifty-year-old notebook would have any relevance to a death today. Devlin tucked the notebook into the waistband at the small of his back and tugged down his lab coat over it. Then he informed Carter and Quader he didn't see anything missing from the office. His conscience twinged at the white lie, but he consoled himself with the fact that he didn't know for sure Dr. Shan had the notebooks still in his office. Bringing them up would only muddy the waters. And might focus the attention of Dr. Shan's killer on himself.

CHAPTER

TEN

Lena stretched and looked for the third time that morning at the clock on her computer. Eleven-fifteen. Even though she was busy with a large trade document to translate, she couldn't concentrate on the work at hand. Her mind kept returning to the mystery of her grandfather. Maybe she would see Devlin at the mailboxes tonight and could discuss the situation with him.

She leaned back as an image of the handsome neighbor filled her thoughts. A ping from her smartphone alerted her to an incoming email. She usually tucked the phone away in a drawer to avoid being distracted by texts or emails during the workday. Today she'd forgotten to do so and rationalized a quick check wouldn't hurt.

She entered her passcode and pulled up the email. The *Bild* writer had responded to her inquiry already. As she read the short message, she translated the German to English.

Dear Maike,

Unfortunately, that was the only article I wrote about the disappearance of Dr. Wolfgang Hoffman in 1983.

J. Attmanstacher

Lena stared at her phone. Someone prominent enough to

warrant a news article a decade after his disappearance would surely have garnered more attention than one story. The first piece read like a set up for a series on the subject, but this man said he'd written nothing else after the one story. Which implied he might have information that hadn't warranted a follow-up story.

She calculated the time difference between Washington, DC, and Germany. Six hours ahead. She could call the *Bild* newspaper office during her lunch break. Hopefully German journalists stayed at their desks past five o'clock like their American counterparts.

Eleven-twenty. Forty more minutes to tackle the latest trade agreement from Germany, then she could phone Attmanstacher and ask him what he had that wasn't published.

"Dr. Mills?" Carter stood in the office doorway.

Devlin bit back a groan. "Yes, detective?"

"We'd like to go over your statement once more." Carter entered with Quader behind him.

"Sure, have a seat." Devlin closed his laptop and stacked some reports on his desk. He'd learned early on to keep a close eye on his research.

Carter trained his gaze on Devlin. "What do you think happened to Dr. Shan?"

"It certainly looked like Dr. Shan had shot himself in the head." Devlin chose his words carefully.

Carter rested his elbows on the arms of the club chair. "You don't think he committed suicide?"

Devlin winced. "Although Dr. Shan was still grieving the death of his wife, he didn't seem emotionally unstable. He loved his wife, and getting used to someone you loved not being around anymore has to be a difficult adjustment."

"Would you say he was depressed?" Quader asked.

Devlin recalled his strange conversation with Dr. Shan less than twenty-four hours ago. Again, the niggling doubt about mentioning the notebooks assailed him.

Carter leaned forward. "No answer?"

"I don't believe Dr. Shan was depressed to the point of considering suicide." Devlin resisted glancing toward his messenger bag, where he had put the notebook from the secret drawer. It appeared someone had taken the rest of the notebooks, which meant that could have been the reason for Dr. Shan's death. On the chance he was right about the cause of his mentor's demise, Devlin had to tell the detectives about the missing notebooks. But he'd keep silent about the one he'd found —for now.

"I do recall that yesterday morning, when I talked with him after the staff meeting, he mentioned some old scientific notebooks. He kept them in a locked drawer of his desk, the bottom right-hand drawer."

Quader looked up from her tablet. "What kind of notebooks?"

"The old black-and-white composition style with the thick cardboard covers. He didn't actually let me look at it."

"Was there more than one?" Carter queried.

"I only saw one, but Dr. Shan stated there were several. He didn't give a specific number."

"Were any notebooks on the evidence forms?" Carter turned to his partner.

She tapped on her tablet, then shook her head. "I don't see any listed. Did you find any of them in your search, Dr. Mills?"

"There weren't any among the papers and books scattered around the office." He consoled himself that he had told the truth—just not all the truth.

"Why do you think Dr. Shan was so interested in these notebooks?" Carter said.

Devlin shrugged. "He said something about them being a record of old clinical trials related to liver cancer."

Quader's forehead wrinkled. "Wouldn't that information be

entered into a database or something? I thought older scientific data was shared among researchers."

"It is for the most part, unless it's proprietary, such as early formulas for medicines."

"What did Dr. Shan tell you about these notebooks?" Quader rested the tablet on her lap.

"That at least one contained unpublished material related to studies conducted on a treatment for liver cancer."

"What is the significance of that?" Carter regarded Devlin steadily.

There was no way the detectives knew about the pilfered notebook. *Stay calm.* "Liver cancer incidence has more than tripled since 1980. It's one of the most common cancers, so any new discoveries related to its treatment would be very important."

"Why do you think Dr. Shan shared that information with you?" Quader's expression held interest and a hint of a challenge.

"Because I'm working on finding a cure for liver cancer." Devlin returned her gaze as openly as he could. "Specifically, my area of study is on viral therapy."

Carter's cell phone jangled with a Star Wars-themed ring tone.

Quader said to Devlin, "I keep telling him to change the ring tone, but he refuses. Says it makes him feel like the Force is with him."

Devlin chuckled.

Carter held his phone against his chest. "Dr. Mills, we're finished with you for now. Please let us know if you have any travel plans out of the area."

Quader passed Devlin a card, and Carter did the same. Devlin pocketed the business cards, glad to leave the questioning behind for now. As he watched them leave his office, unanswered questions swirled in his mind like a whirlpool, sending them around and around without coming to any conclusions.

~

At one, Lena shut her office door and pulled out her cell phone to call Attmanstacher at the magazine office, the only number she could find. After circumnavigating the phone menu, she selected Attmanstacher's extension and waited as the call connected.

"*Hallo, Attmanstacher Apropos.*" The man's voice conveyed impatience.

"*Guten Abend, ich bin Maike.*" Lena introduced herself, then continued the conversation in German. "I emailed you about Dr. Wolfgang Hoffman."

A short pause ensued. Lena prayed she hadn't lost the connection.

"*Gib mir deine Nummer und ich rufe Sie auf eine bessere Linie zurück.*"

Lena rattled off her cell phone number and hung up, wondering why the man couldn't talk on his office line. Five minutes later, her phone buzzed, and an unfamiliar number appeared with the prefix forty-nine. She recognized the German country code and answered.

"*Hallo?*"

"*Maike, das ist Attmanstacher.*"

A car horn blared in the background.

"*Ja, vielen dank* for calling me back. I want to know more about Dr. Wolfgang Hoffman." Lean decided the direct approach would be best.

"*Warum?*"

Good question. Why did she want to know? She couldn't tell him she was Hoffman's granddaughter, but she hadn't considered what to say. Stupid of her not to have come up with a cover story ahead of time. She'd just have to wing it with a bit of truth wrapped in generalities.

"An aunt is compiling a family tree. Since she's not computer savvy, she asked me to check some of the more distant connections online. I had a hard time finding anything about Dr. Hoffman, but I did see your article about his disappearance."

"I see."

She ploughed on. "It seemed like a juicy story, so I was surprised to find no follow ups in your paper." That was the truth. A prominent man's disappearance revisited a decade later with no additional coverage from a newspaper that thrived on titillation and scandals was indeed a puzzlement.

"Why does an American want to know about a former East German doctor's disappearance?" Attmanstacher switched to accented English.

She had rattled off her cell number without thinking it would tie her to the United States. So much for cloaking her identity as an American. "I told you," she replied, also in English, "I'm asking for my aunt, who's doing genealogical research on the family. Dr. Hoffman is connected distantly through my mother's sister's brother, or something equally convoluted. You know how tangled the family tree branches can get."

"I'm afraid your aunt will have to find another source for her family tree. I can't help you."

"Why didn't your paper write a follow up story?" Lena kept her voice curious even as frustration built. She had been so sure this would lead to more information about her grandfather.

"I'm sorry. There's nothing more I can tell you."

Sensing he was about to hang up, she interjected a note of pleading into her voice. "Please, I—"

His voice, harsh and low, cut across hers. "*Manchmal ist die Vergangenheit nicht so weit zurück, wie es scheint. Auf Wiedersehen.*" The line went dead.

She hit end and leaned back in her chair, mulling over the last phrase. *Sometimes, the past isn't as far back as it seems.* Was he saying someone still wanted to keep what happened to Dr. Hoffman a secret? Her heart raced as another question chased the first one. What was her grandfather involved with that still mattered four decades after his disappearance?

CHAPTER

ELEVEN

Devlin waited at the restaurant for Lena. He'd arrived fifteen minutes early, having been told to go home early. Finding the body of Dr. Shan had been surreal in many ways. Devlin couldn't believe the head of their department would take his own life. He'd wanted to let Lena know about his eventful day, but sending a text with the information his boss was dead seemed callous.

He sipped his water, wishing he'd ordered something warm to drink instead. A biting January wind had chilled him during the short walk to the restaurant, which was unusually quiet. Or at least that's what he told himself to avoid the truth that the morning's events had shaken him.

All afternoon, he'd wrestled with the notebook, trying to decipher its secret, but while some of the sketches looked familiar, the fact he couldn't read German hindered his progress. Like Dr. Shan, Devlin had recognized the German word for liver cancer, which had been scattered tantalizingly throughout the pages.

He glanced at his watch. Five minutes until the appointed time of their date. The connection of the notebooks to Lena frightened him.

First she'd nearly been run over by a SUV, then she received a post-card that might be from her supposedly dead grandfather. At the same time, Devlin heard Dr. Hoffman's name in connection with handwritten notebooks detailing a clinical trial or experiment related to liver cancer.

Devlin couldn't shake the memory of the fear in Dr. Shan's eyes when he warned Devlin to be careful. Maybe Devlin shouldn't have mentioned the notebooks to the police. He certainly shouldn't have kept the lone notebook to himself.

"Devlin?"

He smiled, then stood to help Lena out of her wool coat. "Hello, I'm glad you made it."

"Me too." She slid into the booth while he hung her coat over his on the hooks at the end of the booth.

She looked tired, her skin a bit pale in the warm light.

"Are you okay?" Maybe he should offer to reschedule, but he didn't want to be alone after the terrible events of the day.

"I'm fine. Just a busy day." She gave him a bright smile, which faded as she studied his face. "But you don't look so good yourself. I mean, you look good, but, um, well..." A blush stained her cheeks as she ducked her head.

"Something happened at work today, but if you don't mind, I'll wait to tell you after we've ordered. I could use a hot meal, and you look like you could too." Devlin definitely didn't want to start their date by telling her about finding Dr. Shan and have the waiter interrupt with the day's specials.

Just then, the server approached. "Good evening. May I tell you the specials?" Without waiting for their reply, she launched into a dizzying array of off-the-menu items.

When the waitress finally wound down, Lena said, "I'll have a glass of water with lemon and a bowl of your clam chowder."

"You only want a bowl of soup?" The waitress wrote down the order, but her tone implied she wasn't impressed.

"I might order something else, but that will do for now." Lena softened the statement with a smile.

"And for you, sir?" The server turned to Devlin.

"I'll have the chicken quesadilla appetizer and a cup of decaf coffee."

The waitress jotted down his order, then gathered their menus. "I'll be back with your drinks shortly." She departed with a flounce that sent her short bob swinging across her cheeks.

"I don't think we made her day," Lena said.

"Maybe not." Devlin fiddled with his wrapped silverware, not wanting to spoil the mood quite yet with his news. "Why don't you tell me how you filled your hours?"

Lena threw him a knowing look. "I'm guessing your news isn't good."

"You could say that. I'd rather hear from you first." Devlin fastened his gaze on her, enjoying the site of her creamy skin and blue eyes.

"My workday was meh." She scrunched up her nose, looking even more adorable.

To distract himself from staring, he asked, "I know you said you're a translator with the State Department, but what does your day-to-day work look like?"

"I translate German documents related to the U.S. government into English."

"Sounds interesting."

"It can be, although some of the documents can be rather boring." Lena paused as the waitress returned with their beverages.

She set water down in front of Lena and placed Devlin's coffee on the table, along with a small pitcher of cream. "Sweetener's on the table."

"Thanks," Devlin said. The server nodded and walked away. "I guess every job has its boring components."

"You've got that right." Lena squeezed her lemon into her water.

He sipped his coffee, glancing about the near-empty restaurant.

At least no one would be likely to overhear their conversation. "Did you do any more research on the postcard?"

Lena nodded. "Last night, I Googled Dr. Wolfgang Hoffman and came across an article from the *Bild* newspaper from 1993. That's a national tabloid covering mostly sensational stories and celebrity news."

"What did the article say?"

"Not much, actually. The gist of it was Dr. Wolfgang Hoffman worked for a top-secret research facility in East Berlin. In 1983, he vanished without a trace. Unnamed sources in the former East German government told the reporter they had no idea what happened to the doctor."

Devlin cupped his hands around the mug, trying to capture some of its warmth. "Why would they write a story about a ten-year-old disappearance?"

"I wondered that too, until I read Dr. Hoffman apparently had been working on a promising cure for cancer. My grandfather, if this is indeed the same Dr. Hoffman, had been a trusted member of the East German medical community."

"What did the article say might have happened to him?" Devlin took another sip of his coffee.

"The writer reported many believed the doctor took off for South America but died somewhere along the way." A sadness crossed Lena's face. "I thought maybe that's what my father believed, but now I'm not so sure."

"Why do you say that?" Devlin leaned back as the waitress approached with their food.

"Clam chowder for you," she placed the steaming bowl down, "and chicken quesadillas for you." After placing the food down, she turned to Devlin. "Is there anything else you need?"

"Lena?" Devlin asked, but she shook her head. "I think we're good for now."

"Enjoy." The waitress moved away to check on the couple in the booth next to theirs.

"Shall I ask the blessing?" Devlin reached across the table and took Lena's hand in his. "Dear Heavenly Father, please bless our food and our conversation. In your Son's precious name, Amen."

"Amen." Lena toyed with her spoon. "My parents weren't the warm and fuzzy type. They always seemed to be afraid, of what I never knew. Then last night I think I figured out what might have been the behind the way they lived."

Devlin picked up a triangle of quesadilla and dipped it into the sour cream on the side of his plate. "What did you find out?"

"They were both born in East Berlin. In fact, that's where they got married." Lena spooned soup into her mouth, a thoughtful expression on her face.

"They never told you where they were born?" Devlin smeared guacamole on the rest of the triangle and popped it into his mouth.

"Only that they were born in Germany. East Germany was never mentioned at all. They spoke German at home exclusively. I used to think it was because German made them feel more comfortable, more connected with their homeland." She paused, then added, "They had a phrase they often said that didn't make sense to me as a child, but now that I know the East Berlin connection, it explains a lot."

"What was it?" Devlin selected another triangle. The food tasted good, and he realized he had skipped lunch in the commotion of the day. No wonder he was hungry.

"*Die Wände haben Ohren,* which means *the walls have ears.*" She tapped her spoon against the side of her bowl. "My mom or dad used to say it whenever the other one started getting angry. It always made them stop yelling and start whispering, usually with the stereo volume turned up." She winced. "When I heard the loud rock station blaring, I knew they were fighting. I thought they didn't want me to know they were arguing. But maybe it was because they were afraid."

Devlin finished a second triangle and drank some coffee. "I took a class on the Cold War in my undergrad studies at George Mason

University. My professor used to talk about how the Stasi, the East German secret police, used informants to monitor the populace. But the thing was, those informants were normal people themselves. Their entire system of fear and intimidation ran on the fact that neighbors would inform on neighbors, relatives on each other, for Western goods or special treatment or just to stay on the good side of the Stasi."

"It seems so unreal, doesn't it? To think that's the way my parents grew up. And my grandfather was part of it somehow."

LENA NOTED THE PALENESS OF DEVLIN'S CHEEKS AS HE SIPPED HIS COFFEE. Something terrible must have happened at work for him to look so disconcerted. He'd made a valiant effort to focus on her, but she could tell something was bothering him, a big something. "Devlin, are you really okay?"

"I don't know." Devlin twisted his coffee cup around. "Something happened today at work, something very disturbing."

She sucked in a breath, her appetite fleeing at the seriousness of his expression. Her body tensed as if preparing for a blow.

"There's no easy way to say this." He blew out a breath. "This morning, I found Dr. Shan, the head of our department at the NIH, dead in his office."

Lena gasped, her hand reaching out to touch his briefly. "That's awful! What happened?"

"The police seem to think it's suicide, that he shot himself." Devlin winced as if the memory pained him.

Lena studied his face, which bore a trace of uncertainty. "But you don't."

"I'm not sure." He sighed.

"More coffee?" The waitress hefted a pot of decaf coffee like a sword above the table.

Devlin nodded, and she poured him a fresh cup. "Anything else I can get you?"

They both shook their heads. She reached into her apron pocket and brought out the bill, placing it face down on the table. "I'll take that whenever you're ready."

As she moved away, Devlin continued, "While it's true Dr. Shan's been sad about his wife's death last spring, I have a hard time believing he would take his own life. Not to be morbid, but Dr. Shan always talked about leaving his body to science, and shooting himself in the head would mean no one could study his brain."

"That does sound out of character." Lena set down her spoon.

"There's more."

Lena listened as he relayed the events of the morning, starting with the missed meeting with Dr. Shan's research assistant and ending with the interrogation with the detectives and the missing notebooks. "Do the police think that there's a connection between the notebooks and the break in and Dr. Shan's death?"

"I'm not sure." Devlin pushed away his plate. "But I didn't tell you the strangest part of the entire thing."

"What's that?" Lena wiped her mouth with her napkin, then dropped it beside her soup bowl.

"Dr. Shan told me the notebooks originally belonged to Dr. Wolfgang Hoffman."

Lena blinked, disbelief welling up inside her. "Dr. Shan had notebooks from my grandfather?"

Devlin shrugged. "Maybe. Dr. Shan showed me one of those black and white composition notebooks, you know the ones without the spiral?"

She nodded.

"He said it contained notes on a clinical study Dr. Hoffman had conducted related to a treatment for liver cancer."

Lena frowned. "The article said Dr. Hoffman worked for the East German government at some sort of research hospital."

"The notebooks were written in German, and Dr. Shan was

translating them very slowly on his own because he didn't know German." Devlin gave her a half smile. "He was using a German-English dictionary, I think. I offered to contact you about translating, but he said he didn't think it would be safe to do so."

She toyed with her napkin. "How was Dr. Shan's demeanor?"

"The police asked me that very question. At one point, he seemed afraid of something. He also was very territorial about the notebooks."

"Territorial? I would think cancer researchers would share their information readily so a cure would be found more quickly."

He grimaced. "Ah, but then who would get the glory—and the research dollars that come with such a discovery? Medical researchers are just as likely as anyone else to want to take sole credit for a major breakthrough, and that means they jealously guard their data and sources for as long as possible."

She raised her eyebrows. "Who knew you were such a cutthroat bunch." Then she sobered. "So it's probable Dr. Shan was waiting until he knew exactly what he had before allowing anyone else to see those notebooks."

"Entirely possible."

"How did he get the notebooks in the first place?"

Devlin leaned forward. "Dr. Shan told me his uncle was a janitor at the research facility where Dr. Hoffman worked and took the notebooks out of the trash for the blank pages. According to Dr. Shan, it was difficult to get blank paper in the German Democratic Republic."

The server returned with Devlin's card and credit card slips. "Thank you and enjoy your evening."

"Ready?"

Lena scooted out of the booth. Devlin held her coat for her. His hands brushed her neck as he smoothed the collar of her coat down. The touch sent a shiver of desire down her spine. Something about this man drew her, and, unless she'd misread the look in his eyes as she turned around, he felt the same.

He placed his hand on small of her back as they exited the restaurant and into the cold January evening. Once outside, she picked up the conversation thread again. "Do you find it puzzling this Dr. Hoffman would simply toss medical notes in the trash?"

"That caught my attention as well. I had planned on asking Dr. Shan about it today."

"And he was killed, ostensibly by his own hand, before you could do so, and the notebooks went missing."

Devlin drew her arm through his, nestling her closer to him as they walked down the sidewalk toward their condo building. On impulse, she rested her head against his shoulder. His height fit her five-foot-nine perfectly. She couldn't remember the last time walking with a man had made her feel so safe and cherished.

As they approached their building, a dog barked, followed by the outraged snarl of a cat. Lena froze. She knew that meow. Straightening, she peered into the shadows cast by the lamps along the walkway. A flash of gray-white fur caught her eye as an animal darted into the bushes in front of their building.

"Goliath?" A strident hiss, then a meow followed her question. "Goliath!" Lena slipped out from under Devlin's arm and raced for the shrubbery.

"Lena? What's wrong?" Devlin called after her.

"I think Goliath got outside somehow." She dropped to her knees in front of the bushes. "Goliath? Hey, there."

A golden retriever nosed in beside her, emitting a low woof. She pushed the dog back, then used the flashlight function on her phone to see into the inky blackness. "Where are you?"

The canine shoved against her body. "No, you're not going to frighten the cat anymore. Let's get you back," Devlin said over her shoulder.

Lena didn't acknowledge his assistance, her focus on finding her cat. Her flashlight picked up a pair of blue eyes. Goliath huddled against the brick of the condo, plaintively meowing. "Come on." She slipped her glove off and held out her hand, stretching her fingertips as close to the cat as she could amidst the branches. Goliath sniffed, then crept forward enough to butt his head against her fingers. Scratching his chin, she moved her hand to the scruff of his neck and grabbed a handful of fur.

Goliath meowed as she dragged him out from under the bushes, but he quickly settled into her arms once she regained her feet. "It's okay." She stroked him, murmuring soothing sounds.

Devlin stood a few feet away, talking to a neighbor who had leashed the retriever. Now that her pet was safe, one question loomed large. How had Goliath gotten outside of her condo?

CHAPTER

TWELVE

Wolfgang tucked an extra pair of pants into the small overnight bag. He had to travel light to avoid suspicion, but it was time to leave. He'd always known this day would come, had made contingencies related to it, so taking up his new identity in a new location would be simple. He had done it often enough in the nearly four decades since he'd slipped out from under his East German handlers. His only moment of true panic had come in 1993 when the *Bild* had run a story about his disappearance. But his former colleagues had quickly quashed any follow up. They had reasons of their own for keeping Dr. Wolfgang Hoffman hidden.

Then six years ago, someone had made him an offer to resume his medical research work. At first, he'd been thrilled to once again battle cancer cells in the lab, but then he'd learned the true nature of the project. There was no way he would be part of destroying lives in order to save future ones. As it was, he slept little because the young trial volunteers haunted his dreams. No, he refused to be part of that again, so he'd escaped a second time.

It had been easier to slip into the ether this time because his American handlers so easily dismissed him as an old man with scientific knowledge but not physical agility. In his retirement, he had taken special care to stay fit. He'd also set up numerous safe houses and new identities to ease the transitions.

With a sigh, he closed the bag, not eager to leave Florida and the comfortable life he'd created. But the threat to his granddaughter meant he once more had to disappear.

Opening his safe room, he removed a few personal effects and tucked his laptop into his bag. He then placed the homemade bomb on the desk and closed the door. The resulting explosion would destroy his apartment and hopefully convince everyone he had died too.

A quick peek into the hallway confirmed his earlier reconnaissance. Empty. He made a final sweep of the units on his floor, using a high-powered listening device to detect any sound behind closed doors. Silence. Good. He didn't want any casualties on his conscience —he had enough souls for which to repent.

Now he slipped silently down the stairs and to the back entrance to the building. He paused by the door, checking his watch. Thirty seconds to impact. With a gloved hand, he pulled the fire alarm and left the building, walking briskly to a waiting taxi, his baseball cap pulled low over his face. The taxi had rounded the corner when a plume of smoke shot up to the sky.

The driver tapped the brakes. "Hey, what's happening?"

"Keep driving. I'm late to an appointment," he growled as the driver slowed the cab to gawk at the smoke rising into the air.

"Sure, sure." The driver returned his attention to the road.

When the cab stopped for a red light several blocks away, Wolfgang slid a twenty through the money slot in the plexiglass partition and opened the door. Ignoring the shouts of the driver that he couldn't leave the car at an intersection, Wolfgang melted into the crowd.

~

Tatiana slapped shut the report and glared at the intruders. Why couldn't people leave her alone? These interruptions took her away from her important work. "Yes?" She allowed the full weight of her disapproval radiate over the somber man and woman who stood in her office.

"Dr. Dern, I'm FBI Special Agent Sy Lofton and this is Special Agent Emory Erdman," the tall man said.

In response, she raised her eyebrows, a gesture that usually sent her subordinates scurrying to do her bidding. The FBI agents appeared unimpressed by her stern expression.

"Did you know Agent Carl Schuler with Homeland Security?" Lofton asked.

"Yes, he was assigned to my security detail. I'm involved in highly classified research on behalf of the U.S. government." Her tone implied that the interruption had better be worth her time.

"Yes, ma'am, we understand the basics of your work." Erdman kept her voice soft. "Do you know where Schuler is at this moment?"

Tatiana hadn't gotten to where she was by allowing fear or intimidation rule her emotions. "I believe he took some personal time off."

"Do you have any idea why he would be at a retirement community in Boca Raton, Florida?" Lofton's voice had steel behind it.

She'd better be careful with how she responded to his questions. "No."

Both agents stared at her for several seconds before the woman asked, "Do you have any knowledge of why Schuler would be in the apartment of an elderly gentleman?"

Only years of training kept Tatiana's composure in place. She plastered a puzzled expression on her face. "I don't understand. Has something happened to Schuler?"

"There was an explosion in an apartment on the third floor of Deerfield Estates. The apartment had been purchased by Raymond Carver five years earlier," Lofton said.

Icy fingers danced along her spine. Tatiana drew in a breath. "And Schuler?"

Erdman's grave face told her the answer before her lips formed the words. "Schuler was found dead in the living room of that apartment."

Tatiana allowed her shock to show. They had been so close, so very close to bringing in Hoffman. "And the owner of the apartment?"

"It appears he was killed by the blast as well, although it will be several days or weeks before the forensic team will sift through all the debris to make sure." Lofton eyed her, his expression unreadable. "You don't have any idea why Schuler would have visited Carver's apartment?"

"Schuler never mentioned knowing anyone named Raymond Carver. But then again, we rarely spoke of personal things." She schooled herself to show concern. "I'm so very sorry he died."

"How long had he been on your detail?" Erdman asked.

"About four years." She paused. "Will there be anything else? I should call his family."

"His family has been informed of his death," Lofton said.

"Nevertheless, it is my duty to offer condolences." Tatiana reflected she hadn't a clue about his family, whether he was married or had children. Shame heated her cheeks. She had been so focused on her work, so convinced of her own importance that she had ceased to be a decent human being. But she knew she wouldn't have changed her decisions, not when she was so close to the fruition of her life's work.

"Dr. Dern, thank you for your time. If we have further questions, we'll let you know," Erdman said, then she and her partner left.

Tatiana opened the folder, but the words swam on the page. Schuler's death meant either the agent had gotten careless or someone else was after Hoffman and his secrets.

~

DEVLIN SMILED AS GOLIATH RAN FIGURE EIGHTS AROUND LENA'S ANKLES. "Someone's happy to be home."

Lena sidestepped the cat to place a bowl of wet food on the floor. "Yes, and hungry too."

Goliath meowed, then began to eat.

She exited the kitchen, her brow furrowed. "I still don't know how he got out. My door was locked."

"Maybe he ran out after work and you didn't notice?"

"Maybe." Her raised eyebrows indicated how unlikely she thought that scenario was. "I was rather focused on getting to the restaurant on time."

"Hold still." He plucked a twig from her ponytail, then held it out for her to see. "From diving under the bush to rescue Goliath, I guess."

"Probably." She smiled.

His heart thumped faster.

"I had a nice time tonight." She sidled closer to him.

"I did too." He dared to reach for her hand, rubbing his thumb on the top. She squeezed his hand, her response giving him boldness. "Lena, I'd really like to kiss you."

Something sparked in her eyes, and she tilted her head. "Devlin, I'd really like to kiss you too."

Her parroting his statement brought a chuckle to his lips, but all laughter faded as he gazed down into her blue eyes. "Well, then."

"Hmm."

He inched closer until his lips hovered over hers. How long had it been since he'd wanted to kiss a woman this much? Her eyelids fluttered shut, and she leaned into his body. Dropping her hand, he wrapped his arms around her and touched his lips to hers. He slid one hand up her back as the kiss deepened.

Then she broke contact. "I think your phone's ringing."

Her breathless statement didn't immediately register, but then his ringtone trilled into the silence. "Oh." He released her, even though every fiber of his being wanted to tug her closer and kiss her again. Wow.

"Devlin?"

Right, the phone. Yanking it from his back pants pocket, he answered. "Hello?"

"Dr. Mills?"

Devlin frowned, not recognizing the voice. "Yes?"

"This is Dr. Timms."

Why was the head of the cancer research center calling him after hours? "Yes, sir?"

"I hate to add to your already tough day, but I need you to come back to the office." Timms sounded anything but regretful. However, his wasn't a command Devlin could ignore and hope to keep his job.

"First thing tomorrow morning?" He ran his hand through his hair, turning slightly away from Lena. If he kept looking at her, he'd drop the phone and kiss her again. Not a smart career move.

"No, right now."

Devlin wasn't sure he'd heard correctly. "This can't wait until the morning?"

"How soon can you come?" Timms snapped back.

Devlin glanced at his watch. Eight-fifty-three. "I'm in Arlington, so I'm probably at least half an hour away, maybe more depending on traffic."

"I'll be in my office." Timms hung up without another word.

Devlin disconnected the call. He had no idea why Timms wanted to see him ASAP, but he had to go. The underlying threat behind the director's words indicated Devlin would be in major trouble if he didn't show.

"Bad news?"

"I'm not sure." He tapped his phone against the palm of his hand. "That was my boss's boss. Apparently he needs me to come into the office right away."

Concern etched fine lines into her features. "Tonight?"

He smoothed his fingers over her forehead. "I need to leave now."

She kissed his cheek. "Then you'd better go."

He hurried to the door, then paused to glance back at Lena. "See you tomorrow night?"

Her answering smile and nod sent him on his way with a spring to his step. Only when he merged onto the Beltway did his thoughts return to why Timms had summoned him into the office after hours. Whatever it was, it wouldn't be good news.

CHAPTER
THIRTEEN

At a public computer at a large branch of the public library several states removed from Florida, Wolfgang stared at headline from the *Washington Post* on the computer screen.

Dr. Shan Found Dead of Apparent Suicide

Wolfgang skimmed the short piece, noting the bare facts. Police were investigating his death, but a source said the scene looked like Dr. Shan had shot himself. The only other piece of salient information was a note about his office being ransacked.

He logged out of the site and erased the browser history, then left the library. He had known for years Dr. Shan had his notebooks. Wolfgang had planned on taking them with him when he slipped out of East Germany. However, two days before his scheduled departure, he'd gotten home twenty minutes later than usual. Entering his building from the back entrance, he'd caught a glimpse of four men in dark suits and stern expressions climbing the stairs to his seventh-floor apartment.

He hadn't survived living in East Germany as long as he had without knowing when to leave. With a sigh of regret, Wolfgang had caught a bus to the train station to retrieve a small bag packed with a change of clothes and his new identity. In the crowded station, he asked a man about his height to exchange overcoats. The stranger's threadbare one sported a missing collar and a half-undone hem— enough of a change from the cashmere one he'd loved wearing.

After purchasing a ticket on the next train out of East Berlin, he'd enough time to grab a meat pie from a street vendor before boarding. Once in his compartment, he'd plotted his next moves very carefully.

Six weeks later, he'd arrived in California, welcomed by the open arms of the United States military. However, that relationship had soured, as he'd suspected it might, and so Wolfgang had once again disappeared.

On the street, a woman, her head bent over her phone, bumped into his shoulder. She glanced up, flashing him an apologetic smile. Wolfgang nodded in return, but the woman's dark eyes reminded him of Ida. If only she had lived, his life might have turned out differently.

But regret only made one careless. Shoving all thoughts of Ida back into the recesses of his mind, Wolfgang slid behind the wheel of the rental car and started the engine. Soon he would be able to stop running. The only question was would he have time to tell his story.

Or would he be dead?

DEVLIN SWIPED HIS BADGE THROUGH THE SECURITY CHECKPOINT AND entered the building. Despite the quietness of the late hour, a few labs had lights on with scientists working the overnight shift. He briskly walked to Dr. Timm's office, apprehension roiling the chicken quesadillas from dinner in his stomach. He paused outside the office to take a deep breath to try to clear some of the fatigue from his mind, then rapped on the door.

"Come in."

Devlin pushed open the door and stepped inside.

Timms sat behind his desk, his fingers rolling a pen back and forth, a nervous tick that put Devlin on high alert. "Close the door, Dr. Mills."

Devlin did as requested. Only when he turned back to Timms did he notice the third person in the room, a man dressed in a dark gray suit and highly polished wingtip black shoes standing near the window.

"This is Venedict Calkins with the Department of Homeland Security."

Devlin held out his hand to the man, who crossed to shake it in a firm grip. "Mr. Calkins."

"Dr. Mills." The man selected one of the club chairs in front of Timm's desk and sat, crossing his legs.

"Please have a seat, Dr. Mills." The director indicated the opposite chair.

Devlin took his seat.

"We're all very concerned about what happened with Dr. Shan this morning." Timm's tone was serious and somber. "But there are some additional considerations in this matter."

When Timms didn't elaborate, Devlin gave him a level look. "Such as?"

"There are sensitive issues surrounding some of work Dr. Shan was conducting," Calkins said, his voice as oily as canned sardines.

That explained exactly nothing, given most of the work done at NIH could be labeled as sensitive. "I don't follow you." Devlin wondered if he'd stepped into an alternative universe, where people alluded to things but never spoke plainly enough to be understood.

"May I be frank?" Timms asked. "Dr. Shan's research of late delved into things not sanctioned by the National Institutes of Health."

Devlin raised his eyebrows. "Dr. Shan always followed protocol. He was a stickler for rules."

"That may be, but he was conducting his own, separate research." Timms leaned forward. "What did you know about that?"

"Nothing." Which was perfectly true. Dr. Shan had said something about the research in the notebooks, but not a thing about any offline work of his own.

"Hmm." Timms seemed disappointed with his answer.

"Did he ever talk about someone named Hoffman?" Calkins asked in such a bland way that Devlin immediately knew it was important.

Devlin summoned an equally blank expression on his own face. Since he had mentioned Hoffman's name to the police earlier, he decided it was best to keep as close to the facts as possible. "As I told the police this morning, on Tuesday Dr. Shan mentioned interesting clinical trial research he'd found in some old notebooks. I didn't look at the notebooks myself and only saw one with my own eyes. But Dr. Shan said a Dr. Wolfgang Hoffman had written them."

Calkins nodded. "And did he tell you anything more about Dr. Hoffman?"

"No." That was easy to answer truthfully.

"I see." Calkins relaxed in his chair.

Devlin had the feeling he had passed some sort of test.

"It appears Dr. Shan had some highly confidential research, which is now missing. That has created an issue of national security. I'd appreciate if you didn't mention those notebooks to anyone else." Calkins fixed a steely gaze on Devlin.

Oops, he'd already told Lena about them, but he wasn't about to confess that to this man. "Okay."

Timms smiled. "Thanks for coming in so late, Dr. Mills. I've let your team know you'll be taking tomorrow off. You deserve a day of rest after the ordeal you've been through."

"Thank you, Dr. Timms." Devlin stood and walked to the door, leaving with more questions than answers. He nodded to the security guard on duty in the lobby. Once back in his car, the hairs of his neck tingled as the sensation of being watched washed over him. Surreptitiously checking his mirrors, he thought he could see someone stepping back into the shadows behind his vehicle.

Trying to act normal, he buckled his seatbelt, then pulled out of the parking spot. All the way home, he checked his mirrors to see if anyone followed him. To his untrained eyes, no vehicle appeared to have done so. But the unease of his conversation with Calkins and Timms didn't leave him. Even in the relative safety of his condo, sleep eluded him long into the night. Maybe tomorrow he'd ask Lena to translate the notebook he'd taken from Dr. Shan's hiding place. For the life of him, he couldn't fathom why the Department of Homeland Security would consider decades-old medical research a matter of national security.

LENA POWERED DOWN HER EREADER, THE LATEST ROMANTIC SUSPENSE BY Lynette Eason not holding her attention through no fault of the author. Her attempt to wind down and fall sleep hadn't worked. She touched fingers to her lips. Much better to relieve that kiss. Talk about flying sparks. Her mind on Devlin's mouth on hers, she wasn't paying close attention when she set the ereader on the bedside table and knocked the postcard sent by Dr. Hoffman to the floor.

She picked it up, studying the correspondence presumably from her long-dead grandfather. The postcard's message couldn't have been more obscure. *Your past medical advice was wrong—there is still a life to lead.* If everyone thought he was dead, maybe this was his way of telling her he was alive. After all, no one from East Germany would be pursuing him these days. The Soviet Union had dissolved years ago.

She rubbed her head. The trouble was she had so little information about her grandfather to see if he was this Dr. Hoffman. The journalist Attmanstacher must know more, but for some reason, he wouldn't tell her. However, she had other sources to mine for info on Dr. Wolfgang Hoffman. Through her translations, she had developed a network of contacts in Germany. She mentally ran through the list.

Sylvia Fuchs at the German Embassy in Washington, DC, would be an excellent place to start.

Lena spent the next hour emailing Sylvia and a dozen other contacts she'd made through her work with the State Department.

Yawning, she clicked out of the email program just as her phone pinged an incoming text from Sylvia.

Hey, Lena. I'm on furlough in Germany right now. Got your email RE Dr. H.

Eat a Berliner for me.

I've already had a dozen. . I asked around @ Dr. H.

And??

My cousin works as a researcher for Stasi-Unterlagen-Behörde. She entered the name into its database. No records came back.

Nothing? That's strange.

For the Stasi Records Agency to have no information about an East German citizen was unheard of, especially for someone in the medical field. The higher up a person was in East German society, the more digging Stasi agents did to ensure that person stayed true to the regime.

What's even weirder is that my cousin told me not to ask her to do such a thing again.

Why?

I pressed her for an explanation. She said the words Diese Person existiert nicht *appeared on the screen, but underneath was listed another phrase:* hoch eingestuft.

Lena considered what it meant. *This person does not exist* seemed pretty clear, but why add *highly classified* to the search return of someone who didn't exist?

That doesn't make sense.

Anyway, gotta get going. Let's do lunch when I'm back in DC.

Sure! And thanks.

Lena set her phone on top of the postcard. The urge to double-check the front door propelled her out of bed. She had secured the deadbolt, chain, and knob lock. After climbing back into bed, she turned off the light and snuggled down, Goliath purring at her back.

How could Dr. Wolfgang Hoffman both not exist and be highly classified in Stasi records? That explained everything and nothing, all at the same time. Maybe tomorrow things would make more sense. Better to think about more pleasant things, like seeing Devlin again and perhaps, if she was very lucky, kissing him again.

CHAPTER

FOURTEEN

Devlin stepped outside during his lunch break on Friday to call Lena. He had buckled down trying to make up for two lost days of work and hadn't noticed the time until two o'clock.

"Lena, how are you?" The weather might be gloomy and overcast with rain in the forecast for the evening's commute, but there was sunshine in his heart at hearing her voice.

"I'm okay." Lena sounded distracted.

"Did I catch you at a bad time?"

"No." She blew out a breath. "Yes. Can I call you back in a couple of minutes?"

"Sure."

While he waited for Lena to call back, Devlin stepped closer to the building. A blustery wind stirred the bare tree branches. He should have shrugged on his overcoat instead of relying on his office fleece jacket for warmth.

His cell rang. "Hello again."

"Dr. Mills?" a woman said, adding after a short pause, "This is Dr. Tatiana Dern."

Devlin immediately recognized the name. Although only in her early forties, Dr. Dern had achieved legendary status in cancer research. She had been the youngest recipient of the Paul Marks Prize for Cancer Research from the Memorial Sloan Kettering Cancer Center, and this year, had been nominated for the Oliver R. Grace Award for distinguished service in advancing cancer research from the Cancer Research Institute.

"My apologies for bothering you on your lunch break."

A gust of wind sliced through his fleece, and he inched closer to the building. "How did you get this number?"

The woman laughed. "I'm afraid I wouldn't take no for an answer from your assistant about your whereabouts."

"Why are you calling me?" Devlin blurted, then mentally smacked his forehead at his bluntness.

"To offer my condolences on the death of Dr. Shan." Something in her voice made him even more suspicious about the real reason for the call. He couldn't quite believe she knew Dr. Shan personally, as his boss had never mentioned any previous interaction with Dern, although Dr. Shan had discussed some of her research papers.

"I didn't realize you knew Dr. Shan."

"He was my advisor for a time during my post-doctorate work."

"I see." Her words did nothing to allay his concern. "Thank you for calling."

"Dr. Mills, I think we might be of assistance to each other."

Curiosity drove him to ask the expected question when Dr. Dern paused. "In what way?"

"Dr. Shan said you're working on viral therapy solutions to liver cancer."

His area of research wasn't a secret. "Yes."

"That's similar to what I'm working on."

Devlin's earlier suspicion this wasn't merely a condolence call returned.

"I think we should meet and discuss our research. Perhaps we can help each other find a breakthrough."

"That's a very generous offer, Dr. Dern, but I can't discuss my work with anyone outside of NIH."

"I'm not asking you to share data, just a cup of coffee between two medical researchers." Sincerity rimmed her words, but still he hesitated.

"My work leaves me with very little free time," he said.

"If you change your mind, you have my private cell number."

"Thank you for calling. Good-bye, Dr. Dern."

"Bye, Dr. Mills."

He ended the call, and his phone immediately rang. Lena's number flashed on the screen. "Hey, there."

"Hi, sorry about earlier. I was right in the middle of straightening out a snafu in a translation and needed to finish it."

"No problem. It's been a crazy couple of days around here, so I've been working late." He stamped his feet to keep circulation flowing as the cold seeped deeper into his body. "And I've missed seeing you at the mailboxes."

"I know what you mean. My department has a new translator, fresh out of school, and he knows the language, but he hasn't figured out the office politics yet."

"That can be quite the learning curve."

"Tell me about it. His rather abrasive attitude isn't helping matters. For some reason, I've been tasked with helping to smooth things over between ruffled parties." Her exasperation came through loud and clear in her tone.

"Not your favorite thing to do?"

She laughed, the sound easing the tension from his call with Dr. Dern. "Not even in the top one hundred. But are you all right? You sound a little stressed."

He blew out a breath, watching the puff of air disappear into the cold. "I had a rather interesting call." He recapped the conversation with Dr. Dern.

"You think she was fishing for something?"

"That's the impression I got, but what, I don't know." The notebook he'd taken from Dr. Shan's office flashed into his mind, but how could Dr. Dern know about that? He really was beginning to see spies behind every bush. "Probably just one of those awkward encounters between scientists who spend more time in the lab than with real people."

"You could be right."

He mentally switched gears back to more pleasant topics. "Any chance you're free tonight? I could bring dinner to you."

"That would be lovely."

"Great." He checked his watch. "I'll have to work a bit late. Is seven okay?"

"Seven would work."

"Any food dislikes I should know about?"

"Oh, no." She chuckled again. He liked the airy but warm sound. He'd have to make her laugh more often. "I like just about everything, except for really spicy foods."

"I'll bring Vindaloo pork then."

"What is it?" The caution in her voice brought a smile to his lips.

"It's a very hot in-every-since-of-the-word Indian dish."

Her laughed warmed his insides. "Don't worry. I'll also bring something nice and bland for you. See you at seven."

"I'm counting the hours."

As he hurried to his office, he hummed "It's Almost Like Being in Love" from the 1954 musical *Brigadoon*. Sometimes he almost didn't hate his older sisters for subjecting him to hours of old Hollywood musicals. He quickly locked his phone in his desk and exchanged his fleece for his lab coat. Less than five hours before he could see Lena again.

Tatiana pushed away the remains of the salad at her desk. She should have gone with the turkey club with extra bacon. Or better yet, a juicy cheeseburger with the works plus a double order of fries. Lab work always made her ravenous.

Today, though, her appetite had been off due to the phone call with Dr. Mills. She had been sure her charm, coupled with her reputation, would make him eager to meet. The certainty that Dr. Shan had shared something about those notebooks with Mills had driven her to contact the younger scientist directly. But either Mills hadn't a clue or he had more integrity than the average researcher. In her experience, if you dangled the right incentive, most researchers would be all too happy to collaborate or share unpublished results. Maybe she needed to find a different carrot.

She returned her attention to an electronic report on her laptop. Hoffman had gone underground. No trail had been found yet, and no second body in the ruble of his apartment. Too bad he had scented the hunt was on and vanished. Hoffman had eliminated any evidence in his apartment of his true identity with that bomb and killed Schuler in the process. She doubted Hoffman had meant to kill him, although she'd been wrong on that score before.

An incoming email drew her attention away from the report. Interesting. She picked up her disposable cell and dialed a number.

"Hello?" The male voice had the same gruff edge to it that it had twenty years ago, though perhaps with a little more hoarseness from smoking cigars.

"Hello yourself." Even though it had been two decades since they'd last spoken, Tatiana was confident the general would recognize her voice.

"Ah, Dr. Dern. I thought you might be in touch soon."

"Did you?" Tatiana had no doubt he had been expecting her call ever since the explosion at Hoffman's former residence. "You know how I hate to disappoint."

A chuckle warmed her toes. General Marvin Pettigrew had much to recommend him, but his sense of humor especially made him attractive, even as he pushed sixty. "Yes, I do know that, yet my reports tell me you bungled the grab."

Tatiana allowed herself to sigh, playing up the general's disposition to treat a woman with kid gloves. "I'm calling to apologize for that. I had no idea he would leave in such a dramatic fashion." She paused, thinking of Schuler, whom she had liked. "I lost one of my best agents in that blast."

"One of the tragedies of the situation. I heard Homeland Security has horned in, sticking their nose into the investigation of the explosion."

"Yes, but I doubt they will figure out who really owned the apartment. Our friend was much too careful to leave anything behind to identify him as the occupant." Tatiana leaned back in her chair. "But there might be a way to bring him in without exerting ourselves too much."

"I knew you would have something up your sleeve." Pettigrew coughed, then cleared his throat. "What is it?"

"Schuler discovered the man still has family living."

"Of course he does—in Germany. Some ancient cousin or aunt. We know he hasn't been in touch with her for decades." His impatience brought a smile to her lips.

"There's a closer relation than that, living right here in the Washington, DC, area."

"Who's that then?" Suspicion with a touch of eagerness colored his tone.

Tatiana smiled. She did enjoy making a big reveal. "His granddaughter."

THE BUSTLING CAFÉ OFFERED THE PERFECT PLACE TO SIT UNNOTICED AND think. Wolfgang spooned the last of the soup into his mouth, swallowed, then blotted his lips. He offered the waitress a small smile as she cleared his dishes and refilled his coffee. He had been on the road for twenty-four hours, putting good distance between him and his former home, but he knew it wasn't quite far enough. Not yet.

He stared at the fake wooden table, its sleek surface brushed free of crumbs. The utilitarian nature of it reminded him of the boxy architecture of the German Democratic Republic. Only the beauty of the human body and his attempts to combat interlopers with ever-changing treatments had kept him from losing the last bit of his humanity in the grayness of the world around him. He might have worked in a building devoid of personality or even warmth, but in his lab, he could create a thing of such intricacy that it took his breath away.

Running his hand over the smoothness of the table top—what was it? Formica, or some other manmade substance?—the irony of running from the very thing that had sustained him in East Germany amused him. Funny how life had a way of coming full circle without one even realizing it until it was too late. He had a chance, though a slim one, to change, to not be sucked back into that way of looking at life. He could become the man his wife always thought he was. Ida had not let the potential good of something outweigh the means with which it was accomplished. She had firm ideas about using one's God-given abilities for the good of all, not just for the advancement of science or the future.

Ida had kept him on the path of doing the right thing, but upon her death, it was as if the floodgates had opened. His anger at how science and medicine had failed her drove him to ignore the warnings of his conscience and dive deep into the murky waters of the end justifying the means. Swimming in that ocean had cost him more than his integrity. It had cost him his son, daughter-in-law, and granddaughter too. But nearly forty years ago, he'd suddenly realized how wrong he had been and how right his dear, departed wife had been. At first, he'd thought removing himself from the work was enough. Lately, though, he knew Ida expected better of him.

So he went about collecting evidence—proof that would indict him along with scores of others—in order to bring to light what had been operating in darkness far too long. He also wanted to reconnect with his granddaughter but protect her at the same time. Cryptic postcards might seem melodramatic, but Ida had loved her postcard collection. Sending the missives to a granddaughter she'd never met provided another connection with the love of his life.

He tapped the blank postcard of scientist Louis Pasteur on the tabletop, thinking about what to write. Then he smiled. He would hide a number in plain sight to direct her to his old friend, Wilson Shamblin. Pulling out his handkerchief, he tugged on latex gloves, then carefully wiped the postcard to eliminate his fingerprints.

Only when he was satisfied he'd done a thorough job did he pick up the pen and write her address in block letters, then added his nonsensical message in the same method to disguise his handwriting: *Jib a box. Abuzz, jazzy, quick. Furzy, gauzy, buxom, jupon.* He only hoped she enjoyed word puzzles and would be able to decipher his simple code.

He affixed a stamp, then gathered his things. Leaving the restaurant, he dropped the postcard into the blue mailbox across the street. He stripped off his gloves and tossed them into a garbage can nearby before walking briskly to his rental car. Time to get back on the road. With any luck, he'd soon be able to stop running.

CHAPTER

FIFTEEN

Lena pushed open the door, sidestepping Goliath as he meowed his welcome. "Nice to see you too." The cat stalked her as she deposited her purse on the entryway table, then hung up her coat. "*Brr.* I think the temperature dropped again."

Goliath rubbed his head against her calf. "I know you're hungry. Give a girl a chance. I'm going to the kitchen now." Lena smiled as the cat darted ahead, meowing from the kitchen doorway as if to hurry Lena along.

After feeding Goliath, she plugged in the electric kettle. A nice cup of herbal tea might take the edge off her hectic day before Devlin arrived with dinner. Carrying the mug into the living room, she kicked off her shoes and tucked her feet underneath her. Breathing in the scent of peppermint, she leaned against the back of the couch. The stress of the day faded as her mind drifted.

Her cell phone chimed an incoming text. The noise jolted Lena, who started and nearly spilled the now-cooled tea. Setting the mug on the end table, she read the text from Devlin. *Running a little late. On my way. Be there with food in 20.*

She sent a quick thumbs-up emoticon reply, then checked the

time. Goodness. She'd slept for nearly an hour. Goliath lay curled up beside her, and she scratched his head while scrolling through her email on her phone. One of her German contacts had responded to the inquiry about Dr. Hoffman.

Liebe Lena. Gut von euch zu hören.

Ich konnte einige der Informationen finden, die Sie gesucht haben.

Mila Weber, who Lena met during a semester abroad at the University of Munich, had found some information. Mila included a list of six names along with a note.

These names were connected with Dr. Hoffman's clinical trials conducted in the early 1980s. That's all I could find before I was warned to stop looking into Dr. Hoffman because it could prove dangerous to my health. I'm passing along the same warning to you. I beg you to take care.

Now she had six more leads to find out information about Dr. Hoffman, but Mila's warning troubled her. Mila wasn't easily scared or overly concerned. She was one of the most commonsense people Lena had ever met.

She focused on what she'd been told about her grandfather. Her father had said his dad had died in the early 1980s. That tallied with Hoffman's disappearance in 1983. If only she'd pressed her father more about her grandparents. Closing her eyes, she dredged her memory for any mention of Hoffman from her childhood. A snippet of a conversation her parents had had a few months before their deaths filtered into her mind.

Coming down the stairs on her way to meet some friends, she'd been putting in her earrings when she dropped one. Stopping to find the stud on the carpeted stairs, her parents' raised voices made her freeze. Always when they argued, the radio blasted at a volume that sometimes had the neighbors banging on the walls of their apartment.

"It's always about his work, his precious life-saving work!" her mother yelled in German. They had insisted on speaking only German at home, although both parents knew more than enough English to communicate in that language.

"But his work is important. I can't let all those years simply vanish into the night. People need to know," her father pleaded.

"Does it matter that if you do this, we will be haunted by it for the rest of our lives? He's not around. He won't have to deal with the fall out. You and I and Lena will take the brunt. It won't stop with some notebooks. It will go on and on. You know that!" Desperation colored her mother's tone.

"I know, *meine Geliebte*." Her father's voice softened. "As long as we keep the notebooks, we are in danger too. Giving them to *Der Doktorwissenschaftler* is our best hope for a more normal life."

Lena's mom sobbed. "I wish you had never found those notebooks."

"But I did find them. I think he wanted me to find them, wanted his work to have meaning."

Lena stayed on the stairs, her body tense. She didn't understand the conversation, but she picked up on the despair in her mother's voice and the resignation in her father's.

"You old *die Sau*." Her mother sniffed, then blew her nose. "Your father doesn't have the right to demand from beyond the grave that you give meaning for his life."

"He entrusted them to my care."

Her mother sighed. "That troubles me more than anything, Stefan. You kept this a secret for so many years."

Lena crept down the stairs a few more steps. Her parents stood in the middle of the living room, a stack of composition notebooks nestled inside an open cardboard box.

"My father's work was the harbinger of things to come. His work focused on treatments that are beginning to be studied today. I was looking for the right man to give them to. They are too precious to hand over to just anyone."

"You have read these notebooks?" Her mother moved closer to the box and touched the top notebook.

"Only the first part of one. But you shouldn't read them. This is for your protection. If anyone asks, you know nothing about the notebooks or where they came from." He tugged his wife close, his hands stroking her back. "I thought we could leave this behind us, but we can't."

"But why now?"

Lena's presence must have been detected because her parents fell silent.

"Lena?" Her father called.

She walked down the stairs. "I'm going out with my friends." She smiled at her parents and nonchalantly moved to the door, avoiding the box on the coffee table. "Be back by eleven."

Lena opened her eyes as vestiges of the long-forgotten scene ceased to rumble through her mind. Her father had worked as a janitor at a government building, but which one? And why had he chosen janitorial work when he'd been a professor in Germany? At least she thought he had been a professor in Germany.

Her mother worked at a small insurance office not far from their Falls Church, Virginia, home. What were the odds that these notebooks were the same ones Devlin had told her about?

Maybe she could verify if her father worked for the National Institutes of Health. If he had, then that could be how the notebooks got to Dr. Shan. She opened her browser and Googled *How to find out if someone worked for the federal government.*

Skimming the results, she sighed. She would have to request a copy of his records in writing—mail only—from the National Archives and Records Administration. Might as well compose a letter and see what she could find out. First she needed his full name, Social Security number, date of birth, name and location of the employing agency, and the beginning and end dates of service.

Dislodging Goliath, she went to her bedroom and tugged the heavy fireproof box out from under her bed. She sifted through the papers to find her father's Social Security number. She would have to fudge the dates of service and hope she was in the ballpark. She'd ask Devlin if Dr. Shan had worked for the National Institutes of Health in the late 1990s. She finished the letter and hit print, then copied the address onto an envelope.

A knock on the door signaled Devlin's arrival.

DEVLIN RAPPED LIGHTLY ON THE DOOR TO LENA'S CONDO, A BAG OF INDIAN takeout in his other hand. The aroma of chicken tikka masala, butter chicken, and garlic naan bread teased his nostrils and fired up his taste buds.

Lena opened the door, Goliath meowing at her ankle. "Hello."

"Hi. Sorry I'm late."

She smiled and pulled the door open wider. "Since you're bringing something that smells so delicious, I forgive you."

He returned her smile as he stepped into the apartment. "Where should I put this?"

"Come on into the kitchen."

After a companionable meal, they settled in the living room. Goliath immediately jumped up beside him on the couch, head butting his hand for attention. Rubbing the cat's head, Devlin said softly, "I like your mistress." The cat purred and moved to his lap, circling several times before settling down.

"Goliath likes you." Lena handed him a mug.

"He's certainly very friendly for a cat." He sipped the coffee, then set it on a coaster.

They shared a smile, then Lena's faded. She cupped the mug in her hands as if needing its warmth. "In my translation work, I've developed a network of people in Germany who do a similar job to mine. I found early on that there are many colloquial and business phrases that can be clunky or not quite right with a straight German-to-English translation. It's amazing what a difference a word out of place can mean on some of these treatises."

"I can imagine." Devlin stroked the cat's fur, giving Lena space to say what was on her mind.

"I emailed several of them to ask about information related to Dr. Hoffman. One of them replied with a list of six names she said was connected with Hoffman's research work in East Berlin in the late 1970s and early 1980s."

"Did you recognize any of the names?"

Lena shook her head. "No, and when I entered the names into a search engine, too many hits returned. I couldn't decipher which ones connected to the names on the list."

"The contact didn't give you any more information to point you in the right direction?"

"The contact said it was too risky to provide anything else."

Devlin should be concentrating on her words, but he couldn't stop staring at her face, with its smooth skin, arched eyebrows, and slight flush on her cheeks.

"She did say all the names had a connection to Dr. Wolfgang Hoffman, so I tried entering my grandfather's name along with each name in the search engine, but still nothing useful at all."

"Sounds like it might be a dead end."

"Maybe." Lena sipped her coffee. "But I'm not done yet. I have a contact who works in the East German archives. That's where all the papers from the German Democratic Republic are stored. He might be able to help. I have his number at the office, so I'll call him during my lunch break on Monday."

"Be careful. Someone's shot at you and tried to run you off the road already." If he had anything to do with it, he'd keep her safe and secure for many years to come.

CHAPTER

SIXTEEN

Lena's brow furrowed. Devlin gripped his mug tighter to keep his hands occupied instead of reaching out to smooth away the wrinkles on her forehead. His feelings for Lena grew each time they were together, but he didn't want to scare her off by moving too quickly. Better to take things slowly.

"You think those incidents are connected?" She bit her bottom lip. "I thought we figured the first was merely a distracted driver who —thank goodness—corrected his course at the last second."

"Maybe, but someone did shoot at us." Devlin drank his coffee. "Since we haven't heard anything from the police, I'll give the detective a call tomorrow morning to see if there's an update."

"Thanks. I was going to call this week myself, but work was rather crazy." Her eyes widened. "Although not as bad as your week. I'm so sorry again about Dr. Shan's death. How are you holding up?"

"I'm okay. I hope they're able to figure out how he died, but the autopsy will take a while." Sorrow over his mentor's passing tightened his stomach. Maybe Indian food, followed by decaf coffee, wasn't such a good idea after all.

"Well, to change the subject, I remembered something from when I was a teenager related to my grandfather."

Grateful for the distraction from thoughts of finding Dr. Shan's body, Devlin asked, "What's that?"

"My parents weren't very forthcoming about their lives, like I've already told you. But I recalled hearing them arguing about some notebooks my dad wanted to give to someone where he worked."

His body tensed. "Notebooks?"

Lena scrunched up her nose in an expression he found adorable. "I saw only the top of one, but it looked like one of those old composition notebooks with a black and white cover. There was an entire box of probably seven or eight total, based on the size of the box and what my dad said to my mom."

"Where did your father work?"

"He was a janitor at a government agency. I can't remember which one, but it certainly could have been the National Institutes of Health. We used to live in Falls Church, and he would take the Metro to work. It was a long commute."

"A janitor?" Devlin shivered, and Goliath repositioned himself on his lap. Dr. Shan told him he'd gotten the notebooks from his uncle who had been a janitor. Truth wrapped in lies was always more believable than pure fabrications. "Dr. Shan said he'd gotten the notebooks from a janitor."

"I tried to find out of if my dad had worked at the NIH, but it takes a while to retrieve old employment records. I have to mail in a request to the National Archives and Records Administration with his information and employment dates. I hope I guessed right on when he might have worked there."

He finished his coffee, his mind trying to fit together all the pieces of disparate data into a coherent picture.

"Enough about the past." Lena eyed him over the rim of her mug. "Let's talk about Dr. Devlin Mills."

His heartbeat quickened at the playful light in her blue eyes. "Okay, what do you want to know?"

"What made you go into research rather than general practice?"

That he could answer easily. "I realized that talking to new people all the time wasn't for me. I would freeze up or I'd be too gruff and practically ignore the patient entirely. My advisor, ahem, advised me to think about medical research." His play on words brought a smile to Lena's face. "Working on finding a cure for cancer —or at least a more affordable or effective treatment—appealed to me."

"Kind of how I got into translation." She set down her mug. "My parents insisted on speaking German at home, so I easily picked up the spoken language. My mom would give me lessons in reading and writing German after school, then I took classes in high school and college."

"Is German the only language you know?"

"No. I also studied Spanish and French in college, but I'm not good enough to work as a translator in those languages."

"That's quite impressive."

"Wait, there's more." Her eyes twinkled. "I also know a smattering of Russian and Portuguese. I've been wanting to study Chinese but haven't found a class that works with my work schedule."

He raised his eyebrows. "Now I'm really, really impressed."

She shrugged. "I have an aptitude for languages."

"I should say so." He finished his coffee. "Since I wanted to be a doctor, I took Latin, which did come in handy when learning all those terms in medical school."

"Well..."

He shook his head. "Don't tell me you studied Latin too."

She nodded, then slapped a hand over her mouth as if to keep in her laughter.

"Sure, laugh at my expense. I concede the language round to you." He pointed a finger at her in mock annoyance. "But I bet you can't tell the difference between cancer cells and healthy cells."

"Nope, I can't." Her eyes danced as a laugh bubbled out.

Devlin's breath caught at the joy on her face. This time, he gave into the urge to brush a stray lock of hair from her cheek. She stopped laughing, her smile fading as their eyes locked.

"You're so beautiful."

"I am?" A light flush stained her cheeks.

His gaze dropped to her lips. "Yes, especially when you look at me like that."

"Like what?" Her lips parted.

"Like you want me to kiss you again." Devlin's heart pounded.

"I didn't realize you were a mind reader." Her eyes softened, and she swayed closer to him.

"Mind reader?" As his senses went into overdrive, Devlin had trouble following the conversation.

Lena chuckled softly. "Yes, because I was thinking how nice it would be if you kissed me."

Devlin sucked in his breath at the invitation he read in her gaze. "Well, then."

"Well, then." She repeated, sliding her eyelids closed and tilting her head upward toward him.

He closed the gap and pressed his lips on hers. Lena's fingers tangled with the hair at the back of his neck. "Lena," he whispered before kissing her more deeply.

Raised voices penetrated the warm cocoon of holding—and kissing—Lena. Devlin broke off the kiss.

"What's going on?" Lena wiggled out of his embrace. "What's that scrabbling noise?"

"I don't know." He headed to the trio of windows facing the courtyard. Moving the shade on the middle window aside to peer out, he saw a man and a woman calling for Baxter to come out from under the boxwood bushes in front of Lena's living room windows. "Looks like their dog is after something in the shrubbery."

She joined him at the windows. "It's probably a chipmunk or squirrel."

The man succeeded in grabbing Baxter's leash. "Come on, boy."

With a tug, he managed to get the dog out of the bushes. Baxter danced farther away from the boxwoods.

"What's that in Baxter's mouth?" Lena asked. "Is that a package?"

Devlin registered her words as his mind latched onto the potential danger. "No!"

He tugged Lena down, covering her body with his own seconds before an explosion rocked the building and blew out the windows, raining glass over them.

THE BUILDING SHOOK. GLASS SHATTERED, STRIKING LENA'S LEGS AND exposed arm. Devlin's body shielded her from most of the falling debris. Cold air blew in through the now open windows.

"Devlin?" Lena whispered, then nudged him with her elbow. "Are you okay?"

He slowly eased up on his elbows, his body still prone over hers. Shards of glass slid off his shoulders and onto the carpet. "I think so. How about you?"

She assessed her situation, noting stinging pain from cuts and some aches where her knees had hit the carpet hard. "No serious injuries, thanks to your quick action."

"I don't want to move too quickly, given all the glass." He winced. "I feel like I have a million paper cuts."

"Me too." She lay still as he gingerly raised up and away from her. Once he'd gained his feet, his face paled.

"What is it?" She wanted to scramble up but with glass everywhere, she needed to take her time as well.

"The couple with the dog..." His voice trailed off. He glanced down, his eyes filled with pain. A siren pierced the night, then another joined the chorus. "Let me help you up."

She took his proffered hand, and he gently pulled her to his feet. The sight outside her shattered windows nearly brought her dinner back up. A patch of the common area lawn resembled photographs of war zones, a burnt circle with smoke rising to the sky. A crowd of onlookers had gathered outside adjacent buildings, their voices indistinct. Lena couldn't stop looking for the couple and the dog, even though she knew they couldn't have survived such a blast.

Firefighters ran forward, hoses aimed at the smoldering earth. Police officers and EMTs joined them. A pair of EMTs headed toward their building while the cops herded people back inside buildings.

"Anyone else in your apartment?" A burly EMT, his head shaved, asked through the shattered window before entering the building.

"Just us in this unit," Devlin answered. "I live across the hall in 104, the occupant of 101 is out of the country, and I don't know about 103 or the upstairs units."

"Thanks. Then we'd better start with you two." The EMT and his partner, a slim woman with long black cornrows, pulled open the outer door.

"You wait here. I'll let them in." Devlin left her side.

A meow redirected her attention from the carnage outside. "Goliath!" She spotted her cat in the hallway. Quickly, she side-stepped as much glass as possible to reach him. "Come on, let's get you safe." She used her feet to shoo him to the spare room she used as an office and then closed the door.

"Lena?" Devlin called down the hallway.

"Just locking Goliath in the room so he won't try to escape through the windows." She winced as a piece of glass grazed her cheek as it tumbled from her hair.

"The EMTs want to take us to the hospital to check us out and get all of this glass off of us," Devlin said.

"It's easier under the bright lights and magnifying glasses we have there to make sure we don't overlook anything," the female EMT said.

"Okay, I guess." Lena looked around at the debris covering her living room.

Detective Bryan Geoly, who'd taken their statements about the shooting, stepped into the apartment. "Trouble seems to follow you two around. First that shooting last week, now a bomb goes off yards from your apartment."

Lena shuddered at the memory of bullets flying. For thirty-one years, she'd lived a fairly quiet life. In the span of a fortnight, she'd been nearly run over, shot at, received a mysterious postcard, and now had a bomb blow out her windows.

"Tell me what happened." Geoly poised a pen over his slim notebook.

Devlin explained about dinner, then hearing the couple's voices near the windows calling for the dog, Baxter. "I peeked out and saw the dog had dragged a small, odd-shaped package that had been underneath the shrubbery right by Lena's windows. I can't explain it, but I knew it was a bomb and dragged Lena down with me seconds before it exploded." He swallowed, his eyes misting.

Lena touched his arm gently, wishing she could hold him tight. But with both of them coated with glass fragments, comforting him would have to wait.

"The couple and the dog—they didn't make it." Devlin didn't pose it as a question. The flatness in his voice tugged at Lena's heart.

She longed to reassure him it wasn't his fault, that even if he had been able to shout a warning, it wouldn't have mattered.

"No, they didn't." Geoly tapped his pen against the notebook. "Your building and 1812 had windows blown out on the first and second floors facing the courtyard, but very few people were home, so other injuries appear to be minimal."

"Thank God." Devlin said out loud what Lena had been thinking.

"Ms. Hoffman, do you have anything to add?"

"Devlin gave an accurate account of our evening." She hesitated, wondering if she should mention the postcard.

"Are you sure?" The detective's eyes bored into hers.

But Lena had a lifetime of distrust of authorities drilled into her by her parents and nodded without saying more. "I just can't think of why someone would want to hurt me."

"Why do you think this is directed at you?" Geoly asked.

"The shooting, and now someone apparently placed a bomb underneath my windows. I'd say that's pretty personal," Lena replied.

"It could be argued that Dr. Mills was the target, not you," Geoly pointed out.

She exchanged a look with Devlin. "There is one more thing." At the detective's raised eyebrows, she hurriedly explained about the SUV nearly running her down.

Geoly looked from her to Devlin. "And you didn't think to mention this after the shooting because...?"

"I didn't think it was relevant." She started to cross her arms, then winced as a piece of glass cut into her forearm. "It looked like the SUV was heading directly toward me, but it could have been a distracted driver."

"Give me a description of the vehicle."

Lena relayed what she could, then Devlin chimed in with what he remembered, including a couple of letters from the license plate.

Geoly replaced his notebook. "Head to the hospital. We'll go over your statements tomorrow."

The EMTs, who had been hovering in the background, hustled forward to direct Lena and Devlin to one of the waiting ambulances. The question looping through her mind was one for which she had no answer. Why was all this happening to her—and would she live long enough to find out?

CHAPTER

SEVENTEEN

Wolfgang uttered a German curse he hadn't said in forty years after reading about the bomb outside Lena's condo on a news site. His exclamation barely caused a ripple in the packed coffee shop. How dare they target his granddaughter in order to send him a message. Didn't they know the lengths he would go to protect his family? Hadn't he proven that over and over again?

The buzz of the coffee shop receded as a memory of his son's anguished face surfaced in his mind.

"*Vati*, please. They detained Andrea yesterday, questioned her for hours." Stefan hunched his shoulders against the biting wind.

Wolfgang barely registered the slicing cold of February in East Berlin. He leaned closer to his son. "What did she say?"

Stefan's eyes narrowed. "What could she say? She knows nothing about what you do, as do I. You said that would protect us, but it hasn't."

"Then she—and you—will be all right." Wolfgang had been careful not to let his son and daughter-in-law know more than the bare facts of what he did. Even his beloved Ida didn't know the true extent of his work. How he would miss her. Each day, the cancer took a little bit more until soon, there would be nothing left of the beautiful blonde girl he had married all those years ago.

"Andrea's pregnant."

Stefan's statement yanked Wolfgang back into the conversation. For a moment, father and son stared at one another. Pain and adulation vied for prominence in Wolfgang's heart. This changed everything. The child—his grandchild—must be protected. He placed a hand on Stefan's shoulder. "How long?"

"Maybe nine or ten weeks." Stefan correctly interpreted Wolfgang's question. "Then it will be too obvious, especially in the spring." He sighed. "Andrea's such a little thing. No extra weight to hide the pregnancy."

Wolfgang nodded. "Then we will have to move faster than I anticipated."

"*Vielen dank.*" Stefan pulled the collar of his coat tighter around his neck. "I'd better go before Andrea starts to worry." He walked briskly away before his father could say goodbye.

"*Auf Wiedersehen, mein Sohn,*" Wolfgang said into the wind. Despite the cold, he didn't move until he could no longer see Stefan, knowing it would be the last time he ever saw his only child.

Someone bumped into his chair, drawing him back to the present.

"Sorry, man," said a young man wearing a knit cap and carrying a large insulated cup. The man settled into the table behind Wolfgang, joining three other young men. All four bent their heads over their phones as they talked.

He would not let his hard work of getting Andrea and Stefan out of East Berlin and to America before anyone knew about her pregnancy be for naught now. Sliding the burner phone from his pocket, he dialed the general.

"Pettigrew."

"We had an agreement," Wolfgang said.

"We might have had an agreement, but then an agent turned up dead in your apartment."

"And you think I had something to do with that?" Wolfgang regretted Schuler's death, but he hadn't made the man break into his apartment just before a bomb exploded.

"You're telling me you had nothing to do with the bomb that destroyed the place?"

"There was no one in my apartment building when I left."

"You always were scrupulously careful about that sort of thing. Schuler wasn't killed by the explosion. He was already dead before the bomb detonated."

Wolfgang glanced around the shop, but no one appeared to pay him the least bit of attention. The young men at the table behind him carried on their boisterous conversation.

"But you're calling because you heard about the package bomb that went off yesterday in Arlington, Virginia, nearly killing your granddaughter."

Wolfgang shouldn't have been surprised that Pettigrew knew about Lena. "Yes."

"That wasn't us." Pettigrew sighed. "Listen, do we want you back on our team? Yes. Would we send an agent to convince you? Possibly. But you know we would never harm your family. This isn't the former Soviet Union. We aren't like that."

The general's words had a ring of truth in them, but Wolfgang hadn't outfoxed Stasi agents without being able to read between the lines. Pettigrew might not have ordered someone to hurt Lena to get to Wolfgang, but the general had an idea of who was behind the attacks on his granddaughter. Time to change tactics to see if he could find out the other piece of information he wanted from the general.

"How is Dr. Dern these days? I hear she's close to finding the elusive cure she's been after for years."

Pettigrew barked a laugh. "And here I was thinking you weren't in the game at all."

Wolfgang smiled. While the other man hadn't answered his question, he had given away by his deflection that Dr. Dern was still searching for answers—and still in touch with Pettigrew.

~

LENA GINGERLY LOWERED HERSELF INTO THE CHURCH PEW BESIDE DEVLIN, her body still stiff and sore from aftereffects of the explosion Friday night. At least they had both only suffered minor cuts from the flying glass, thanks to Devlin's quick thinking. Yesterday had been largely spent at the police station, answering the same questions over and over again from Detective Geoly and Captain Barry Sparks from the Arlington County Fire Department Bomb Squad. The condo association's maintenance crew had cleaned up the glass and secured her windows with plywood until she could replace them. Then she'd called Belinda to reassure her friend she was okay.

Devlin flashed her a smile as the pastor called the congregation to worship. She had been surprised when he'd invited her to attend the early service with him, and even more surprised at the small congregation. Devlin explained it was a church plant just a few years old but that the pastor's challenging sermons coupled with the friendliness of his fellow worshipers had made him feel at home.

He had warned her the music was low-key and hymns made up the bulk of the song service, but standing beside Devlin and sharing a hymnal as they sang "How Firm a Foundation" to the accompaniment of a keyboard and violin brought a peace to her heart. How long had she simply attended church without really participating? Hearing the other voices raised with hers helped to center her soul on why she was here—to worship her Savior.

The sermon on the doctrine of providence made her think about how circumstances had thrown her together with Devlin in a way that connected her past with his present. That couldn't be a coincidence. For some reason, God had orchestrated these disparate things to come together at this point. Twice, Devlin had saved her life. But it was more than that. Her heart beat faster when she was around him. Her nerves tingled with anticipation of a glance from him. Her lips longed for another kiss. With an effort, she refocused on the closing hymn instead of reflecting on how much she cared for the man at her side.

"What did you think?" Devlin asked after they had reached his car.

"I can see why you come. Everyone's very friendly." It had taken them more than fifteen minutes to walk the few feet from their seats to the door because it seemed like everyone had wanted to say hello to Devlin. "Or were all the greetings because of me?"

"I'm sure you were a big draw, but those are people I usually talk with too." He waved to a couple chasing after a toddler, a baby in the woman's arms. "We're grateful we've been able to share this building with another congregation. The first few years of the plant, we had to set up and take down chairs and stuff at a local school."

"How long has this been a congregation?" She settled into the passenger seat.

In the driver's seat, Devlin answered her question. "Five years. We've been in this building for only nine months. How about a walk on one of the Lubber Run trails since the weather is fine?"

"That sounds like a good idea, if we can stop by my condo for a change in shoes." She indicated her heels.

After a quick stop to change, Devlin drove them to the park. They'd only started down one of the paved walkways when his phone trilled "No More Mr. Nice Guy."

Lena raised her eyebrows. "That's an interesting ring tone."

He grinned. "Like it?" He picked up the phone and glanced at the screen. "It's from a friend at the NIH. I asked him about employment records yesterday. Maybe he's found something out."

"Go ahead and take it."

They ambled along while Devlin carried on a muted conversation. A family with three kids approached from the opposite direction, the children loudly squabbling over who had the longest stick.

Their noise drowned out Devlin's side of the conversation. His expression projected concern as the lines on his forehead deepened the longer he listened. He ended the call as the family passed them.

"What's up?"

Devlin frowned. "Dr. Shan has been at the NIH since the mid-nineties, which was what I expected. During that time, Stefan Hoffman worked there as a janitor."

"I was right about my father being there at the same time." Lena stepped over a tree root pushing up a portion of the pathway.

"Yes, it does put them in proximity."

His tone of voice prepared her for more to come. "But?"

"But the strange thing is your father's employment record disappeared."

"Disappeared?" Lena repeated, sure she hadn't him right. Records didn't go poof.

"My friend went back in today to check another record, but when he logged in, the last record he accessed, which the program always brings up if you don't manually close out of it, was Dr. Shan's, not Stefan's. Thinking it strange since he hadn't closed Stefan's record, he searched for it again and came up blank. No record for Stefan Hoffman at all." Devlin placed a hand on her back to guide her in front of him as a pack of runners overtook them.

"That is strange." Lena liked that he grabbed her hand as he came alongside her again. "What do you think it means?"

"I don't know. My friend speculates the system could be set to archive older employment records automatically."

"Has it happened before, a record vanishing?"

"Occasionally for older records, but he's always been able to find it."

She met his eyes. "But not Stefan's."

He shook his head. "However, there is some good news. He did print out Stefan's file, so he's going to take a photo and text the pages to me."

Another group of people came toward them, and by unspoken

agreement, they discussed other things until they were alone again. But to Lena, the walk had lost its appeal. Too many coincidences were piling up for her to attribute them to chance. Someone was deliberately targeting her, and by extension, Devlin, because of something that had happened in the past.

"Do you have a busy work week coming up?" Devlin asked as they looped back around to the parking lot.

"Yes, this time of year is always crazy because of the trade agreements needing to be finalized for the year."

"You're not going to keep asking about Dr. Hoffman, are you?" Devlin held the car door open for her.

Lena buckled her seatbelt. "Don't worry, I'll be careful."

"Please don't take any chances. You've had too many close calls lately for my comfort."

Lena caught a serious expression on his face. Trying to lighten the mood, she playfully said, "You'd miss me?"

He studied her for a long moment before starting the car. "Yes, I would." Then he leaned closer and kissed her lightly on the lips. "I would miss you very much."

CHAPTER
EIGHTEEN

Tatiana shut her front door as silently as possible. Shrugging out of her coat, she hung it on the rack, then slipped off her stylish knee-high leather boots. In her sock feet, she padded to the kitchen in search of dinner.

Rotating her stiff neck, she mentally reminded herself to schedule a massage. Too much time bent over a microscope played havoc with her posture and created sore muscles. Opening the fridge, she smiled at the sight of a plastic wrap-covered plate. For all his fussing about her hours, Tom always took care of her.

She popped the dinner in the microwave and hit start. Wine. She needed a glass to unwind from the day's disappointment. Uncorking an already open bottle of pinot noir, she poured a generous glass. The cultures, which had started out so promising, had turned out the same way dozens of others had. Which meant she had to start over from scratch. Again. Frustration coiled her muscles even tighter.

This was why she needed those notebooks. Dr. Hoffman had gotten so much farther in viral therapy. Having access to that research could shave days, weeks, or even months off her own quest. She wouldn't be spinning her wheels, trying experiments he had probably already done. The microwave dinged, and she pulled out her dinner. Sitting at the kitchen bar, she lifted the plastic wrap. Zucchini noodles with Tom's homemade pasta sauce and crispy green beans. Digging in, she contemplated how to address her latest failure. Maybe if she kept the cultures at a warmer temperature? No, she'd tried that already, hadn't she? She'd check her notes and see what variables were left to alter in the hopes of getting a different result.

After loading her plate in the dishwasher, she topped off her glass.

"Another late night at the lab?"

Tatiana fumbled with her glass at her husband's question, nearly spilling the wine. Her hand on her chest, she turned to find him standing in the doorway. "You startled me. Want a glass?" She held up the wine bottle.

He shook his head. "No, I fell asleep waiting for you to come home."

"I said I'd be late." She heard the defensive tone in her voice and pasted a smile on her lips. "But it's nice that you waited up for me. How are the kids?"

For a moment, he didn't answer. With a sigh, he said, "They're with my parents."

Her mind scrambled to pull up the day of the week. "But it's Sunday. Don't they have school tomorrow?" Then she noticed her husband wasn't wearing pajamas but jeans and a bulky sweater. Her heart hammered in her chest. "Tom, what's going on?"

"Do you remember what you said last Saturday when you went to the lab instead of the zoo with us like you promised?" He crossed his arms over his chest.

She sipped her wine, needing its courage to brazen this out. He was angry she hadn't been home for dinner at all this week. He'd been upset before about her work hours, but she always charmed him out of his bad mood. She could do it again tonight. "I had to work long hours so I could clear my calendar for this week."

Tom didn't reply. With only the light above the sink on, she couldn't see his expression clearly to know if her words had any impact.

"Maybe Daphne could come over and watch the kids next weekend." She hated the pleading in her voice but pressed on. "We could get away to that little B&B we love in the Shenandoah Valley."

Still no reaction from her husband of fourteen years. She set down the wine glass and moved toward him, stopping a foot away. "You know I love you, and—"

"Love isn't enough, Tatiana." Tom's words cracked like a whip in the air. "All the love in the world can't take the place of you actually being here, participating fully in our life and the lives of our children."

The sadness in his eyes cut her more than his words. "I explained why I wasn't home much this week. I had to finish up a few projects so we could spend next weekend together."

"Stop. Just stop."

She fell silent, swallowing the rest of her lies and pleas. Tom reached out and brushed a tear she hadn't realized she'd shed off her cheek.

"I loved you so much, Tatiana. I kept hoping you would realize what you had with me, with our children, before it was too late."

She gripped his hand between both of hers, the finality of his tone tearing her heart into bits. It couldn't be too late. "What are you saying?"

He gently extracted his hand. "I'm leaving, and I'm taking the children. You never have time for them anyway." Stepping back, Tom slipped the strap of a bag over his shoulder. Only then did she see the two suitcases behind him.

"Leaving? When will you be back?"

"We're not coming back. It's over."

What he was saying made no sense. He couldn't actually mean it. "A break is probably a good idea. We can talk when you've calmed down, and—"

"Calmed down?" Tom's eyes flashed, breaking through his placid exterior. "You think this is me in a snit about what...? Your precious work?"

Anger rose up inside her like a tsunami, and she let all the frustration of her work, the death of Schuler, and the missing Dr. Hoffman feed it. "You've always resented my work ethic. It's my job that's put this very nice roof over our heads. My job that sends our children to private school. My job that pays for your Jaguar."

He pointed a finger at her. "Don't."

She ignored his warning, flinging out her last shot in an effort to quiet the voice in her head screaming he was right. "My job that allows you to draw cartoons all day."

Instead of countering her arguments or making snide remarks about her lab hours, Tom directed his gaze to the floor, not moving or saying anything as the seconds ticked by. Then he raised his head to look straight into her eyes. "Well, your job won't have to do some of those things anymore. I've decided to homeschool the kids for the rest of the year."

The change in topic startled her. "Why?" She thought the kids loved their school.

"Selana's having a hard time this year, and Kyle is starting to cut up more in class."

"Why wasn't I informed about this?"

He snorted. "You were. I forwarded every email from the school about this. I even put the meeting we had with the principal and the children's teachers on Friday afternoon on your personal calendar, but I guess you were too busy to come."

She frowned, flipping through Friday in her mind. Her phone had pinged a reminder about the meeting, but she'd been knee deep in cell extraction and had chosen to finish the task. "I, uh, couldn't get away."

"So I withdrew the kids from school." He continued as if she hadn't spoken. "Tomorrow we're packing up my aunt and uncle's RV and hitting the road."

"You're doing what?" She rubbed the back of her neck, trying to keep up with all the information Tom was throwing at her.

"I've lined up a list of art shows across the country. The kids will see some of America as part of their education, and I'll get to see if anyone likes my paintings."

Tom painted? He drew a one-panel syndicated comic strip, but she couldn't recall seeing him paint. "Why didn't you tell me about your paintings?"

He winced. "Seriously? You really haven't heard a word I've said about my work over the past year. I suspected you tuned me out sometimes once you asked the obligatory question about how my day went, but to find out you never listened at all?" He shook his head. "That certainly sums up exactly how you feel about me and our marriage."

"Tom, I—"

"I can't do this anymore. I wasn't going to tell you now, but I see no need to spare your feelings." He squared his shoulders. "I've started divorce proceedings, and I'm seeking full custody of the children."

The words sucked the air from her lungs. For one horrible second, she couldn't catch her breath at all. Then the blood rushed through her body, reigniting her anger. "You cannot take my children away from me! I will fight you, I will—"

"Go for it," he spat back. "You know how you used to tease me about how organized I am? Because of my OCD tendencies, I have documentation for every instance of maternal neglect, every missed school event, every missed meeting, every missed family outing. So knock yourself out on that front. If you can even remember to attend the court dates." He turned and walked to the front door, pushing the suitcases in front of him.

She trailed behind him, wondering whether shouting at him to stop or begging him not to go would change his mind. But her pride wouldn't let her find out.

He opened the front door and moved onto the porch. Finally, he turned, the tears on his cheeks surprising her. "Goodbye, Tatiana."

She slumped against the door frame, watching as he loaded the luggage into his Jag, then climbed in. Not once did he look back toward the house. She didn't move until the darkness swallowed up his taillights. Stirring, she shivered as her body registered the cold. Back inside, she padded to the kitchen and poured another glass of wine to drown out the relief that vied with sadness over the demise of her marriage. Without Tom and the kids waiting for her, she could devote even more hours to her research and prove her worth to the world.

❧

DEVLIN SAT BACK FROM THE MICROSCOPE, DISAPPOINTMENT TRIGGERING A long sigh. The virus had had little impact on the cancer cells. Maybe if he switched the process order and used undiluted samples of the virus, the results would be more positive. Energized to try something different, he set about conducting the experiment.

"Going home anytime tonight?" Nancy asked, pointing to the wall clock that read five-forty-five.

"It's that late already?" Devlin rotated his shoulders, noticing the stiffness in them for the first time.

Nancy glanced at his workstation. "Trying something new?"

"More a variation on the same theme, but now that it's set up, it's time to let those little cells do their thing." He usually wasn't so circumvent with his colleague, but something held him back from divulging the details of his experiment.

"Need any help finishing up?"

He shook his head. "I just need to lock these away."

She watched him lift the petri dishes one by one into his secure safe, curiosity reflected in her eyes. "I've never known someone who cleans up as they go."

He inserted the last dish, then closed the safe, tugging to ensure the latch caught. "My mom taught me to cook, and part of my education was washing pots and pans along the way so the person doing the dishes didn't have a mountain of dirty dishes to do." He shrugged as they headed to the decontamination room. "Guess I transferred that training to the lab."

"So you cook too."

"Sometimes." Lately, Nancy had been weaving in more personal comments during their lab interactions. While he thought she was attractive, he only had eyes for Lena, and he didn't want to encourage his colleague. "I've got to hurry, as I'm running late. I meant to leave the lab closer to five."

"Hot date?"

He hadn't planned on seeing Lena tonight but needed to make sure Nancy knew he was interested in someone else. "Don't know about hot, but yeah, a date." He pretended not to see the hurt flash in her eyes but instead worked on changing back into his street clothes as quickly as possible.

Back in his office, he unlocked the small safe everyone had to secure their phones and other valuables when working in the lab. Checking his phone, he saw Justin Glacon, the friend who had looked for Stefan Hoffman's employment records, on the call log, although he hadn't left a voicemail message. Justin had also texted only half an hour ago. Devlin opened the text.

What's going on?

I don't know what you mean.

I've had the administration higher ups breathing down my neck about those searches I conduced on Hoffman and Shan over the weekend.

What happened?

Not here. Are you leaving soon?

Yes.

Meet you by your car in five minutes.

Okay.

Six minutes later, Devlin walked across the garage to his vehicle, spotting Justin leaning against the passenger side front door.

"Hey, what's with the cloak and dagger routine?" Devlin chirped open the locks.

Justin glanced around, then opened the door and got in. A fissure of fear snaked its way down Devlin's spine as he rounded the hood and climbed into the driver's seat. "Justin—"

"Just drive." His friend hunched down in the seat as Devlin started the car and pulled out of the parking space.

He drove out of the garage and off the NIH campus with Justin slumped in the seat not saying a word. A few miles down the road, he spotted a convenience store on the right. Once parked in a space away from the entrance, he twisted in his seat to face Justin. "What's going on?"

Justin straightened to look around, then retreated to his former position. "I did the searches at work Sunday morning." He spoke in his rapid-fire way. "We've been updating the personnel records system, which is supposed to be ready to go by Wednesday, not that it will be ready. There's a bug in the system, and my boss had approved me to work the weekend to try to figure out what was going on. I decided to use the names you gave me as part of my test. I needed to see whether the system would pull up both current and former employees, so your names were perfect."

When Justin paused, Devlin said, "But then Hoffman's record disappeared."

"Yeah. I initially thought maybe older employment records had been flagged for archiving, so I checked the electronic archive. No Hoffman record."

"You said you printed out the records and would send me a scan or photo, but I don't think I received it."

"I was going to send them, but then thought better of creating an electronic trail." Justin reached into an inside pocket of his coat. "Here." He held out a white envelope.

Devlin took it and started to break the seal, but Justin's sharp intake of breath made him pause. "What is it?"

"Go! Now!" Justin yelled, his hand thumping on the dashboard.

Devlin punched the car's engine to life, then reversed out of the parking space. The urgency in his colleague's voice spurred him into action, even though he didn't know the danger.

"Hurry!" Justin's eyes cut to the passenger side mirror.

Throwing the car into drive, Devlin gunned the engine and peeled out of the parking lot, swerving to miss colliding with an incoming vehicle. Once on the road, Devlin glanced in the rearview mirror, his heart rate accelerating even faster at the sight of a black SUV with tinted windows screeching out of the parking lot after them.

He pressed down on the pedal harder, pushing his Kia Sportage faster as he weaved in and out of rush hour traffic.

The black SUV mirrored his every move. The car was the same make and model of the vehicle that had nearly run down Lena a few weeks ago. "Can you get the license plate of the black SUV?"

Justin peered between the seats out the back window. "There is no front license plate."

Not registered in Virginia or Maryland, which both required front and back plates. Devlin took the 495 North entrance ramp as the SUV closed the distance. Merging onto the Capital Beltway, he shot into an opening between two semis, then squeezed into the left lane just ahead of a BMW. The driver honked, but Devlin ignored him.

"Do you see the SUV?" He checked his speed as traffic thickened.

Justin craned his neck. "No, but I have the feeling he's still behind us, waiting."

"Keep your eyes out. There's no way he can run us off the road in this heavy traffic." Devlin flicked his gaze from the rearview mirror to the windshield. "What made you suspicious at the convenience store?"

"The gun I saw under the passenger's jacket."

Devlin whipped his head to stare briefly at Justin's white face. "What?"

"I glanced over your shoulder at the SUV parked two spots down. The passenger got out, and the wind caught his unzipped jacket, blowing it back a bit. I saw the gun in a belt holster. Then he looked our way without appearing to look our way. He stared at the window in front of our car, and I could see we were reflected in the glass."

"Could he have been a cop?" Devlin checked the rearview mirror again. No black SUV in sight. His shoulders relaxed a fraction.

"I don't think so."

They crossed the American Legion Bridge into Virginia with no sign of the SUV. Maybe the driver had given up, but somehow, Devlin didn't think so. "Looks like we've lost him for now."

"What did you drag me into?"

"What do you mean?"

"I mean the favor of looking up Stefan Hoffman's personnel records." Justin shot his hand through his hair. "This morning I get a call from Timms, asking me for an in-person update on the system pronto. I head to his office only to be ambushed by Timms and two other men who didn't bother to introduce themselves."

"Ambushed?" Devlin took the Dulles Access Road left exit.

"That's how it felt. They kept asking me questions about why was I looking at Dr. Shan and Hoffman's records. I explained about the glitches and how I was checking to see if my fix worked."

"Did they buy it?"

"Maybe. One of the men abruptly ended the questioning, thanked me for my time, and dismissed me."

"I'm sorry to put you in that position."

"Are you going to tell me what this is all about?"

Devlin hesitated. His gut told him that the fewer people who knew about the notebooks and the other things going on, the better. He settled on being honest—up to a point. "I don't know. I'm as in the dark as you are about why those names triggered such a response."

Justin huffed. "Right. But the Hoffman name had to come from somewhere."

Again, Devlin split the truth. "This girl I've started dating thinks her father might have worked at the NIH years ago, so I said I'd find out. Both of her parents died in a car crash when she was in college, and she's an only child. She wants to know more about them. Apparently, neither one shared much, so there are huge swaths of information she simply doesn't know."

Something bumped the back right side of his vehicle. Devlin managed to hang onto the wheel and avoid being driven into the fence separating the road from the Metro rail line.

"Our friend is back," Justin said.

Devlin hit the gas, sending his vehicle leaping forward. Traffic was lighter than on the Beltway, but not enough that Devlin could outrun the other vehicle. He changed lanes several times, eliciting honks from other drivers, but the SUV stayed on his bumper. Taking the I-66 West exit ramp, he merged onto the interstate, his progress slowing in the heavier traffic. "Is the SUV still there?"

"Yep." Justin held up his phone. "I think we should call in the calvary."

Before Devlin could respond, Justin had dialed 911 on speaker.

"911, where's your emergency?"

"I'm a passenger on I-66 West, and there's a black SUV with no front license plate driving in an unsafe manner."

"Where is your current location?"

Justin rattled off the mile marker as they moved forward at a much slower speed. The black SUV hung two cars back in the middle lane.

"The vehicle had been on Route 267, weaving in and out of traffic before taking the I-66 West exit as we did."

139

"There's a state trooper just past the Sycamore Street exit finishing up a minor fender bender. I'll alert him to the situation. May I get your name?"

Justin disconnected the call without providing the requested info. "Hopefully, she'll be able to connect with the trooper before the SUV passes him."

"We're coming up on the Sycamore exit ramp." Devlin checked his mirrors once more. The black SUV had moved closer. "I think the SUV's trying to come alongside us."

"There's the cop's car." Justin pointed to the left-hand verge. As they passed, the SUV drew up level with Devlin's Sportage.

Traffic slowed even more as they passed the Sycamore exit, which was backed up nearly the entire length of the ramp. No sense trying to get off the highway there.

"Look out!" Justin cried.

Devlin turned his head to see the black tinted window lowering. The passenger, a man wearing a leather jacket, dark shades, and gloves, raised his arm.

In his hand, he held a gun pointed straight at Devlin.

CHAPTER

NINETEEN

Flashing police lights and a siren split the air as a Virginia state trooper raced up the left shoulder. For a second, the SUV passenger kept the gun aimed at Devlin. Then the man powered up the window and sped off with the trooper in hot pursuit.

Devlin exchanged a glance with Justin, whose white face probably mirrored his own. "That was close."

"Too close." Justin wiped his hands on his pants. "Should we report this to the police?"

"We already reported the SUV's unsafe driving. Would anyone believe it if we said the passenger had a gun aimed out the window at us? The police would ask us why. What would we tell them?"

Justin's face drained of its remaining color. "Are you saying it's because of the records search I did for you?"

Devlin slipped into the right lane, his hands still shaking from the close call. "I don't see why asking about the employment record of a deceased janitor and a dead colleague would warrant someone preparing to shoot us."

"What else could it be?"

Devlin had no answer.

"I'm done with this cloak and dagger stuff. Drop me at West Falls Church Metro."

"Are you sure? I can take you home." Devlin turned on his right blinker ahead of the next exit.

"No offense, but I'd rather face a long Metro ride than spend one more minute in your vehicle."

"No offense taken." Devlin negotiated the exit ramp, then drove to the Metro station. "Thanks. I think you might have saved my life back there."

"Mine too." Justin opened the door. "But please don't ask me for any more favors."

"I won't. Stay safe." Devlin didn't pull away from the Kiss & Ride curb until Justin had disappeared into the station. All the way home, he replayed the events of the evening in his mind. The chances of it being the same black SUV in Lena's near hit-and-run were slim, given the popularity of the make and model. He hadn't imagined the gun in the passenger's hand—had he? Now that the immediate danger had passed, the entire scenario seemed far-fetched and more the stuff of fiction than reality.

At the mailbox, he dropped a grocery store flyer, his hands still unsteady after the close call. Maybe Lena was home, but no one answered his knock on her door. Pulling out his phone, he started to write a text to her before remembering that she attended a women's Bible study on Monday night. He'd send her a text later and make plans to see her tomorrow night.

A restless night punctuated by dreams of being chased through a forest had Devlin making multiple trips to the break room for coffee throughout Tuesday morning. With a mid-morning staff meeting each Tuesday, he generally spent the hours before lunch catching up on email and typing his research notes. Clutching his third cup of coffee of the day, he returned to his office to find it occupied by a man dressed in a dark suit and wearing sunglasses who stood with his back to the door.

"Can I help you?" Devlin hovered in the doorway, not sure he wanted to enter his own office.

"Dr. Mills?"

"Yes?" He sipped his coffee while he studied the man.

"I'd like to ask you a few questions."

Devlin moved around his desk, then gestured to one of the guest chairs. "Have a seat."

The other man sat down, still wearing the dark sunglasses and thus obscuring the man's expression. The affectation irritated Devlin. "Something wrong with your eyes?"

"Pardon?"

Devlin pointed to the sunglasses. "You're wearing sunglasses inside. On a cloudy day."

The other man barked a laugh, then pulled them off. Dark brown eyes bore into Devlin's with a hint of amusement. "Better, Dr. Mills?"

"Yes. I like to see who I'm talking to." He paused. "I also like to know the name of the person to whom I'm conversing."

"So formal." The other man folded his hands on his lap. "My name is Enno Kurimsky."

Devlin waited a beat to see if Kurimsky would offer anything more, but the man stayed silent. "Mr. Kurimsky, where do you fit in?"

Kurimsky appeared to consider the question. "Why don't you tell me where you think I fit in, as you put it?"

Devlin leaned back in his chair. "You're not a doctor or a researcher."

"Why do you conclude that?"

"Because you don't have the demeaner. I've been around enough of both to spot the telltale signs."

The other man raised his eyebrows, the amusement in his gaze growing. "Go on."

"I'm guessing you're in law enforcement, but not with the police or the FBI. They love to flash their badges, and you'd rather not be too showy. No." Devlin warmed up to his analysis. "If I had to guess, I'd say you were with Homeland Security."

"Not CIA?" The man queried with a lifted eyebrow. Just the one in a very insolent manner. Devlin had never been able to master the one-eyebrow lift, no matter how many hours he'd practiced as a kid in front of the mirror.

Devlin shook his head. "I don't think so."

Kurimsky reached into his breast pocket and held up an ID folder with the Homeland Security seal.

Devlin smiled at the confirmation of his correct guess.

Pocketing the badge, Kurimsky said, "I've heard you're a good medical researcher and that you're on track to find an effective treatment for liver cancer."

Devlin smiled. "I'm figuring out what doesn't work. It's too early in my research to say whether the treatment will be effective or not."

"Point taken." The man studied him. "What interests me is why you asked to see the employment records of Dr. Shan and Stefan Hoffman."

Devlin kept his expression neutral. He'd known the man would ask about Dr. Shan and perhaps the Hoffmans, but he hadn't expected it to be so directly. "I'm the one who found Dr. Shan." Pain clenched his gut at the loss of his mentor.

Kurimsky didn't reply, letting the silence build.

Devlin debated whether or not to mention Lena's connection to Hoffman but decided he wouldn't. Not until he had answers to why Kurimsky was here. "Why are you asking these questions?"

"I don't think you understand the gravity of the situation."

Devlin crossed his arms. "Why do I have the feeling you're going to enlighten me?"

"This is a matter of national—"

"Security. Yeah, I thought you'd say that. Just like your colleague Venedict Calkins told me. Am I under arrest?"

Kurimsky lifted his eyebrow again. "No."

"Then I'm under no obligation to answer your questions." Devlin stood. "I have work to do. Please leave my office. Now."

The door opened, and Dr. Timms stepped inside. The director's eyes flicked to Kurimsky, then back to Devlin. "Dr. Mills, I assured Agent Kurimsky of your full cooperation with his questions."

Devlin shot a tight smile at Kurimsky. "Tattle telling to the principal, huh."

Kurimsky spread his hands in a who-me gesture, but Devlin detected a hint of amusement behind those dark eyes.

"I would be more than happy to cooperate with Mr. Kurimsky as soon as he explains his interest in this line of questioning," Devlin said.

Timms thinned his lips. "Mr. Kurimsky assured me this was a matter of national security."

"I'm sure he did." Devlin wouldn't budge. Too many coincidences had piled up for him to merely take the word of this man sitting in his office. "But that's not really an answer."

The tension in the office rose like a cloud of dust ahead of a storm. Timms glared at Devlin, while Kurimsky studied Devlin.

"Dr. Mills, need I remind you that I am your direct supervisor, and I'm ordering you to answer Mr. Kurimsky's questions?" Timms's voice was tight with anger.

"And I respectfully refuse," Devlin countered.

"Then please clear your desk. I am suspending you effective immediately." Triumph colored Timms's words.

Devlin decided to call his superior's bluff. "Okay, I could use some time off." He turned off his laptop. "Since you said suspended, I will be unable to answer any questions about the current state of my experiments. A pity, as I just started what might turn out to be a very promising one yesterday."

He put his computer into the secure drawer, locked it, and gathered his messenger bag. Timms stared at him, his face an unflattering shade of purple.

"You can't leave," Timms spluttered.

"Yes, I can." Devlin slung the bag strap over his shoulder. "You just said I was suspended. Immediately."

~

LENA SAVED AND THEN CLOSED HER TRANSLATION DOCUMENTS BEFORE putting the computer to sleep. Stretching her arms over her head, she rotated her upper torso to loosen the tight muscles. She'd worked through lunch, munching on a sandwich as she finished a rush job on a document.

She checked the time. One-thirty, which meant seven-thirty in Berlin. Lara Becker should be home from the Stasi Records Agency. She'd take her lunch break now and call her. After closing—and locking—her office door, Lena dialed her friend's cell.

"*Guten Abend, darf ich bitte mit Lara sprechen?*"

"*Sprechen.*" The female voice sounded harried.

"*Es ist Lena Hoffman.*"

"Lena!" Lara exclaimed. "It's been a long time," she said in English. Lara always enjoyed practicing her English with Lena.

"Yes, it has." For the next several minutes, Lena and Lara caught each other up on the happenings in their lives since they'd last spoken a few months prior.

"I wish I could talk longer, *mein freund*, but I have dinner reservations awaiting me."

"Oo, did Jannick finally ask you out?"

Lara laughed. "No, I asked him to dinner."

"That's great." Lena paused, not sure if she should tell Lara why she'd called or let her get ready for a date with a man she'd been after for nearly a year.

"I do not think you called just to catch up," Lara said. "So please tell me."

"I was calling to ask a favor."

"Then ask."

Lena didn't take Lara's abruptness to heart, knowing her friend's bluntness was one of her quirks. "Okay. I have a list of names."

Before she could say more, Lara jumped in, "And you want me to check for them in the archives?"

"Yes." Lena shouldn't have been startled by Lara's perception. Her friend often leapt two steps ahead in their conversation.

"Oo, it sounds mysterious. Like James Bond or Jason Bourne, eh?" Lara tried to brush everything with a hint of intrigue.

"Probably nothing that exciting."

"Frankly, anything other than what I'm currently doing would be exciting. Scanning and labeling old documents is so boring, but it's *alle mann an deck* at the moment. Text me the names."

"Will do."

"Give me a call Saturday, and I should have found out something."

"Okay, have fun with Jannick, and thanks," Lena said.

"*Bis später.*"

After disconnecting, Lena texted the six names Mila Weber had given her in connection with Dr. Hoffman's clinical trials in East Berlin: Sebastian Neumann, Jan Becker, Nadine Brown, Klaus Lange, Felicity Mayer, and Hans Vogel.

She had hit send just as someone knocked on the door.

"Lena?" Her supervisor called. The door handle rattled as someone, presumably Jenny Wells, tried to enter.

"Coming." Lena hurried to open the door. Ms. Wells stood on the other side with a man dressed in a dark blue suit. Sunglasses hid his eyes. "Yes?"

"Lena, this is Enno Kurimsky with Homeland Security." Ms. Wells made the introductions, her fluttering hands indicative of her unease. The more her supervisor's hands moved, the more upset or concerned the woman was.

"How can I help you?" Even as she said the expected response, Lena couldn't imagine why someone from Homeland Security wanted to talk with her. Her mind went over the last month's translation documents. All of those had been fairly straightforward trade agreements related to tariffs and import and export duties. Nothing about those documents should have triggered interest from the U.S. Department of Homeland Security.

Kurimsky turned to Ms. Wells. "We'll talk in Ms. Hoffman's office. If I need anything else from you, I'll let you know."

Ms. Wells nodded. "Lena, did you send me task TD543?"

"It should be in your inbox."

Ms. Wells thanked Lena, then left.

Lena stepped back to allow the man to enter her office. Not for the first time was she grateful that her security clearance netted her an office with a door, rather than a cubicle. The sometimes sensitive nature of the documents she translated required the work be done away from prying eyes.

Kurimsky moved into her office with the air of someone used to getting his own way. His first words confirmed that. "Why don't you close the door, Ms. Hoffman." The man might have phrased it as a question, but his inflection made it a statement.

Lena complied, then returned to her desk. "Please, have a seat."

The man straightened his sleeve cuffs under his suit coat and crossed his right leg over his left, projecting the image of a man at ease. Lena wasn't buying the relaxed stance for an instant. The man seemed too alert for this to be as casual a conversation as he apparently wanted her to believe. She waited for him to begin. Her translation work had taught her the value of patience.

"It has come to our attention you have been inquiring about your father's work at the National Institute of Health." Kurimsky removed his sunglasses.

The phrasing amused her. Translating from English to German and vice versa had strengthened her sense of obscuration. Mentally, she translated the sentence into German: *Es ist uns aufgefallen, dass Sie sich nach der Arbeit Ihres Vaters am National Institute of Health erkundigt haben.* Yep, still didn't say much at all.

When she didn't respond, he let silence fill the air. But she wasn't one of those people who needed to talk to avoid the quiet. She waited, meeting his stare with her own.

Finally, a faint smile crossed his lips as he spoke. "What exactly are you trying to find out about your father?"

"Why does that concern you?" She figured he was on a fishing expedition, although why Homeland Security cared about a long-dead janitor, she had no idea. But her parents' paranoia had taught her one very important lesson. Don't reveal more than you absolutely have to.

Again, a smile nearly crossed his lips, but he quashed it before it could fully tilt up the corners of his mouth. "I'm afraid that's a matter of national security."

Although he gave the expected answer, a stab of disappointment hit her. Lately, memories of her parents had been dodging her thoughts, and she longed to find out more about both of her parents. "Ah, I see." She folded her hands on top of her desk and waited. She wasn't about to reveal anything more until she knew exactly why this man was in her office. Since he was hiding behind the national security wall, she would have to find answers about her father elsewhere.

After several minutes had ticked by without either one talking, she allowed impatience to tinge her voice. "As much as I'm enjoying this scintillating conversation, I'd like you to leave now. I have work to do."

Kurimsky didn't budge, his dark eyes assessing her. She didn't waver under his scrutiny. "Have you heard from your grandfather, Dr. Wolfgang Hoffman?"

Lena had been waiting for him to ask about her grandfather, so was prepared for the query. "My father told me his father was dead. Why would you ask if a dead man had contacted me? Do you mean to tell me my grandfather is alive?" She leaned forward. "Or is that information a matter of national security too?"

"Thank you for your time, Ms. Hoffman." Kurimsky rose to his feet. Then he was gone, closing the door behind him. Lena sat back in her chair, thoughts swirling in her mind like leaves being blown about in a gust of wind. She'd learned two important things. The United States government knew her grandfather was alive, and whatever Hoffman had been involved with, they didn't want it coming to light now.

CHAPTER
TWENTY

"How was your day?" Devlin flopped onto his recliner, his cell phone to his ear.

"Okay." Lena sighed.

"I'm sorry I missed our mailbox meeting."

As he suspected would happen, Timms had called Devlin's cell half an hour after Devlin had walked out of his office, revoking the suspension. Devlin had returned to the lab and wrestled with a vexing problem with his experiment. He'd nuked a cup of noodles for dinner at the office as he poured over his research notes. In theory, the virus should have attacked the cancer cells, causing them to die or make proteins that triggered the body's own autoimmune response, which would then invade the cells and stop the spread. But he couldn't seem to get the solution right.

"It would have been nice to see you."

"Did you hear anything about replacing your windows?"

"The condo association secretary sent me a list of acceptable vendors, and I have someone scheduled to come out tomorrow to measure and give me an estimate. At least my insurance should cover most of the work."

"That's good." He toed off his shoes and sank down on the couch.

She cleared her throat. "I had a visitor today."

"Oh?" He leaned back to bring up the footrest, enjoying the relaxing position.

"Some man called Kurimsky with Homeland Security."

Her words jolted him. "Really? Sounds like the same man who ran me to the ground today as well." Devlin quickly related the encounter to Lena. "What did he ask you?"

"What information I was after about my father."

"What did you say?"

"Nothing. I asked him why it concerned him, and he said it was a matter of national security."

"Did he say anything else?" Devlin's stomach rumbled. It was after eight. Maybe he'd fix himself a snack before going to bed.

"He asked if I'd heard from my grandfather. I said my father had told me Dr. Hoffman was dead, so why was Kurimsky asking me about a dead man contacting me?"

The indignation in Lena's voice brought a smile to Devlin's lips. "What did he say to that?"

"Nothing. He thanked me for my time and left."

"Very strange." His stomach made another noise. Devlin rose and padded to the kitchen. "There must be something else going on to bring a Homeland Security agent to ask us about your father. Are you sure your dad was a janitor?"

"Yes. I mean, as sure as I can be. But," she said slowly, "I think he might have had a medical background. My parents argued about a lot of things, including money, and one time I recall my mom shouting that my father could have gotten a better job if he would only use his training. I wish I could remember more, but they turned the music up so loud when they argued, I couldn't decipher much of their conversations."

Devlin filed the information away to ponder another time. For now, he asked the question burning in his own mind. "What would a former East German scientist have to do with the security of the United States?"

"That's been puzzling me as well. Every time I think I've found answers, I'm left with more questions."

"Me too." He paused. "We need to find out more information about your grandfather. Did I tell you about the article I found written by a Dr. Hoffman?"

"No, when was this?"

Devlin filled her in, adding, "Would you mind translating it for me? I have a synopsis in English but would like to have the entire piece to examine."

"Sure, drop if off anytime."

Her offer to translate the article reminded him he'd yet to tell her about the notebook squirreled away in his apartment. "I have a confession to make."

"That sounds ominous."

"I have one of the notebooks." He held his breath, hoping she wouldn't be upset he hadn't told her sooner. He rushed to explain how he found it in the locked drawer after he discovered Dr. Shan. "When I told the police about the missing notebooks, I didn't say I had one."

"Where is the notebook now?"

"In my apartment."

"Open your door."

Devlin moved to the door and peered through the peephole. Lena stood there, phone to her ear. He pulled open the door. "Hey there."

She smiled and lowered her phone. "Hey."

He put his in his pocket, then swept an appreciative eye over her body, stifling a laugh at the sight of her slippers, which had bunny ears flopping over the top. "Love your footwear."

"One of the perks of living across from you. I don't have to put on actual shoes to drop by." She brushed past him, and a scent of something floral teased his nostrils. Closing the door, he followed her into his living room.

"Pretty neat for a bachelor." She slid her phone into her back pocket. "Where's the notebook?"

Beckoning her to follow him, he opened the oven and removed the it. "Here."

She accepted the notebook, setting it on her lap. "You think my grandfather wrote this?"

"That's what Dr. Shan said." Devlin pointed to the book. "Look on the inside cover."

She did so. "It definitely says 'Dr. Wolfgang Hoffman.'"

"Can you read it? Dr. Shan said he was translating it but that it was slow going because he didn't know German."

Lena bent over the notebook's first page. After a few minutes, she looked at him, her brow furrowed. "Devlin, this isn't only in German."

"What do you mean?" He scooted closer to her on the couch until their thighs touched.

Her finger tapped the words scrawled on the page. "There are German words, but there are parts I'm unable to decipher because the words aren't complete."

"But you can read it since it's in German, right?"

She shook her head. "Not entirely. I can translate the German words, but it's mostly written in abbreviations and symbols." She studied the page for a few more seconds. "Almost like it's in a personal code."

Devlin leaned back against the cushions. "Which means only Dr. Hoffman can decipher what he wrote."

"I think so. I'm sorry."

"Not as sorry as I am. I think these contain his notes from the clinical trials he cited in that paper. That's why Dr. Shan kept them a secret. He wanted to figure out what Hoffman had done in order to use that for his own gain somehow."

She closed the notebook and handed it back to Devlin. "You said someone had taken the rest of the notebooks. I still don't understand how notes about decades-old clinical trials could still have relevance today."

"Usually you'd be right to think scientific endeavors had outpaced previous methods. But Dr. Shan thought Hoffman had conducted research into viral therapy, which is what our team is working on under Dr. Shan's guidance. Actual clinical trial data—even from that long ago—would be like finding a long-lost treasure."

"It's that important?"

"Yep." Devlin tapped the notebook against his thigh. "I could use some help figuring out what's in German and what's not."

She grinned. "I thought you'd never ask."

THE NEXT MORNING, DEVLIN STARTED HIS WORKDAY BY REVIEWING HIS email. Spending time with Lena last night had been the perfect way to end his day. They'd ended up swapping funny work stories. Her sparkling eyes as she told a particularly humorous tale of a translation gone horribly wrong had sent his pulse racing. At her door, he'd stolen a kiss. Less than twelve hours later, he could feel her soft lips on his, the touch of her hand on the back of his neck.

But he had a very busy day, so he reluctantly yanked his thoughts from his beautiful neighbor and back to the task at hand. After all, he would see her tonight. He opened his email, eager to get the administrative part of his job out of the way so he could return to the lab and his experiments with the viral therapy. He made short work of the messages related to the entire NIH Center for Cancer Research, noting on his calendar the required all-staff meeting, a retirement party for a senior administrator, and a memo about the upcoming time off related to President's Day. He skimmed the rest, filing the ones about his colleagues' work for future reference.

Then an email from his former undergraduate history professor—and now friend—made him pause. Dr. Henry Silverton had replied to his email from the previous week about translating the original German article written by Dr. Wolfgang Hoffman. Devlin had nearly forgotten about passing along the scientific journal piece to Henry to translate.

Hey, Devlin,

Here's the translation. There were a couple of scientific words for which I wasn't sure of the English equivalent, so I put those in parenthesis. Maybe someone who's a native German speaker would have a better idea what those should be. I hope you can make more sense of it than I can. It was rather technical and chockfull of medical terms and explanations.

Violet's been asking when we can get together. A little mutual bird told me you might be seeing someone. Bring her along to dinner, perhaps next week? I'll check with Violet and give you a few dates we're free.

Henry

Devlin smiled. It would be good to see Henry and Violet, who had only been married a few months. Lena would like them, and Henry would be thrilled to meet someone with ties to the Cold War in East Germany, his specialty.

Clicking open the document with the paper's translation, he soon lost track of time as he read about Dr. Hoffman's clinical trials with the chicken pox viral therapy on liver cancer patients. An hour later Devlin hit print, then sat back to digest what he'd just read. The earlier translation had been way off, leaving out or glossing over huge chunks of the author's findings and relevant notes. Now that he had a fuller picture, he couldn't believe no one else had followed up on what could be a huge breakthrough in the treatment of liver cancer. Why hadn't anyone tried to duplicate Dr. Hoffman's clinical trials in the intervening years?

Maybe because Dr. Hoffman had done his work behind the Iron Curtain, and, as Devlin himself knew, discovering any information about the scientist himself was nigh on impossible. Devlin had only come across this one scientific journal paper. But the research, the clinical trials, and the procedures developed by Dr. Hoffman could revolutionize the cancer world. It wasn't a moonshot cancer drug, but, from the report in this paper, it came pretty darn close.

Dr. Shan knew Dr. Hoffman's research had involved viral therapy, which was why he attempted to translate the notebooks on his own. Those scribblings could be the key to finding a less invasive and more successful cancer treatment. But with only one of those notebooks—and that one written in some sort of code—then only Dr. Hoffman himself could shed light on his discoveries. And how could a dead man tell them anything?

IN THE QUIET OF HER LAB, TATIANA RAN HER HAND OVER THE TOP NOTEBOOK, its mottled black-and-white cover warped with age. Hoffman was still missing, but she had confidence he soon would be brought to heel. Then they could get on with the important work he'd started at Charité in East Berlin forty-odd years ago. Why the doctor had developed a conscience, jeopardizing years of work, she couldn't fathom. The man had been brilliant in his cancer research and ruthless in his application of that research for the good of future generations. Yes, some in the medical and scientific communities couldn't understand that single-minded pursuit of a cure, spouting off about informed consent and doing no harm nonsense. Silly people who didn't have the foresight to realize the importance of what work like hers and Dr. Hoffman's entailed.

She opened the notebook with a number one circled in bold, black ink in the upper right-hand corner. Skimming the notations in German, she smiled. Yes, good, good. This explained so much. She flipped ahead several pages, then stopped. The notebook, which had started out in comprehensive German, had degenerated into some kind of shorthand. She grabbed another notebook, labeled number two. Fanning the book open, the same half words and strange symbols adorned the entire notebook. With a cry of rage, she slammed the notebook down on her desk and yanked a third one out of the box. The same writing in the same unreadable text filled the pages.

Furious, she picked up a disposable cell phone and punched in a number. "Have you found him yet?"

"No, he's still in the wind."

"I need him found. Now." She hit the end button and tossed the phone onto her desk. Dr. Hoffman would be found and brought to see the wisdom in continuing his research. A slow smile slid across her lips. He had shown a chink in his armor—his granddaughter. Maybe it was time to turn up the heat on that score and remind Hoffman just who he was dealing with.

CHAPTER
TWENTY-ONE

Lena dropped her bag on the ground beside her mailbox and inserted her key. Inside was the usual junk mail and jumble of bills. Picking up her bag, she moved down the short hall to her condo and entered, the door swinging shut behind her. Immediate mewing greeted her as the cat executed a figure eight around her ankles.

"Hey, don't trip me up, Goliath." She laughed. "Then who would get your food?"

"Who indeed?" A male voice came from the darkness.

Lena froze, her hand on the light switch. She yanked open the door to escape but was confronted by another man standing in front of her with his arms crossed.

"Ms. Hoffman, please," the man behind her said. "I only want to a little chat."

Having little choice, Lena slammed the door shut, then flipped on the light on and stepped out of the small vestibule into the living-dining room area to see a man on her couch, his legs crossed. He rested his left arm along the back of the couch. The way he sat, so smug and self-assured, as if he had every right to be in her apartment, pushed anger ahead of the fear. "Who are you and what are you doing in my apartment?"

"Please have a seat, Ms. Hoffman."

Irritated at the way he'd spoken as if she were the interloper and not himself, Lena sank down into the comfy chair positioned at a ninety-degree angle to the couch.

"Those are very good questions, but first, an introduction is in order." The man extracted a badge folder from his inside breast pocket and held it open.

She leaned forward, first matching the photo with the man sitting on her couch, then reading the name. Nathan Bradley, an agent with the Defense Intelligence Agency. "That answers the who, but not the why."

The man eyed her. "You don't look at all like your grandfather."

Lena nearly rolled her eyes at the absurdity of the statement. "Why would I?" Goliath jumped up on her lap, and she rubbed his head to quell the uneasiness still coursing through her veins. He might be from the government, but he'd still gained access to her apartment without her permission.

"Oh, there are some hereditary traits, such as persistence in pursuing a line of unwise questioning, but no physical resemblance that I can see."

"Really? You've met my grandfather?" Her voice sounded steady even as her nerves did a tango along her limbs.

"Oh, yes. We've met, although I doubt he'd remember me."

"Which one?" Lena tossed out the question like lobbing a softball to a teammate.

Bradley blinked. Lena was pleased her question had thrown him off his game, even if for only a moment.

Then his countenance hardened. "Let's not play games, Ms. Hoffman. There's only one grandfather who matters to this conversation. Dr. Wolfgang Hoffman. Do you know where he is?"

Lena gaped at the man, letting her astonishment show. "Why are you asking me? I've never met the man, who, as far as I know, is dead."

The man shook his head. "Come now. We both know you've been searching for information about Dr. Hoffman."

"Maybe because the more questions I ask, the more questions I'm asked." She straightened in her chair, hoping the fear rising inside her wasn't reflected on her face. "Why should it bother the government that his granddaughter would want to know more about him? After all, he is family, and searching for one's roots is all the rage these days."

"I think you know more than you're saying. If you don't tell me, you'll only succeed in making some very important people very angry." Bradley delivered this in an almost gentle tone, but Lena caught the steel that glided underneath.

"I am not being flippant." She jumped to her feet, dislodging Goliath, who meowed his displeasure. "You break into my home and start grilling me about my dead grandfather, wanting answers I can't give you. I think you're the one playing games here, not me."

Her phone buzzed. Without waiting to see what the man would do, she picked up the call. "Hello?"

"Lena?" Devlin's voice never sounded so good. "Are you all right? You sound kind of funny."

"I have an unexpected visitor, a Nathan Bradley with the Defense Intelligence Agency." There, at least Bradley would hear her give his name to someone else.

"I'm still at work but am leaving now. Do I need to call the police? Are you in danger?"

"Let me ask." She lowered the receiver and turned to Bradley. "Am I in danger?"

His lips twitched as if he suppressed a smile. "Not from me."

"I don't think so. Come by when you get home." She ended the call. "How did you get into my apartment?"

He shrugged as if the question held no importance to him.

She tried another query. "Why is the Defense Intelligence Agency interested in me and my family?"

Bradley stood. "That's a conversation for another day."

"I have a secret security clearance," Lena pointed out, although she suspected this man knew most everything about her.

"I'm afraid it's not high enough for this information. But I believe you when you say you don't know anything else about Dr. Hoffman." He started for the door.

Lena swallowed a sudden lump in her throat. "You mean he is alive?"

Bradley paused, his hand on the doorknob. "I'm afraid I can neither confirm or deny that." He looked over his shoulder at her. "But I do strongly advise you to stop looking into his past. You've already had two close calls. Your luck may be running out."

Then he nodded to her and left. Lena locked the deadbolt and handle, then secured the chain. Knowing Devlin was on his way home, she sent him a quick text to let him know the man had gone and she was okay.

If Bradley's intent had been to talk her into stopping her search into her grandfather's past, he failed. His visit had confirmed the very real possibility Dr. Hoffman was still alive. She would continue asking questions, but she would be more careful. And she would get a locksmith out tomorrow to change the locks on her front door and add a second deadbolt. No sense in making it easy if Bradley had any future visits planned.

CHAPTER

TWENTY-TWO

After work the next evening, Devlin knocked on Lena's door, a bag of takeout from Five Guys in one hand. He'd checked on her the night before when he arrived home later than he'd wanted to because of an accident on the Beltway but hadn't stayed long, as both had been exhausted. However, they'd made plans to share dinner at her place tonight.

Lena opened the door. "Devlin, come in." She sniffed. "I love Five Guys burgers."

"I'm glad." He came inside, and immediately walked to the kitchen to deposit the food. He then hung up his coat in the hall closet. He turned to find Lena staring at him, an odd expression in her eyes. "What?"

"I see you know your way around my apartment."

"Well, it is exactly the same layout as my own." He winked.

A fleeting smile crossed her lips at his lame joke. His experience growing up with older sisters had made him able to pick up when things weren't copacetic. "Hey, are you okay?"

Her eyes filled with tears. "I thought I was, but seeing you, I, oh, bother." A tear splashed down her cheek. Devlin pulled her into his arms, pressing her head against his shoulder.

"It's okay. I should have stayed longer last night." Devlin wanted to punch that Defense Intelligence Agency guy for scaring her. What was up with all the cloak and dagger stuff anyway? Her grandfather wasn't a nuclear scientist, just a man in pursuit of a cure or treatment for liver cancer. He stroked her hair, breathing in the citrusy scent of her shampoo.

She raised her head, a few tears still on her cheeks. He brushed away the wetness, the softness of her skin heightening his senses. Her lips parted and her head tilted up toward his in an unspoken invitation he couldn't ignore. Slowly, he lowered his lips to meet hers. She tasted of coffee and cherry lip balm, a combination he hadn't considered sexy before now. Gathering her closer, he deepened the kiss, his hand at the back of her head so his fingers could tangle in her hair. She slid her hands up his chest and clutched his shirt.

A light nip at his ankle broke his concentration, and he pulled back as a very distinctive meow rent the air. And broke the mood. Devlin had never been so grateful for a cat in his life. If the feline hadn't interrupted, he wasn't sure he would have come to his senses before their food was stone cold.

"Oh, my." Lena leaned back in his arms. "That was, well, simply incredible."

He released her. "I agree." The cat meowed again, and Devlin looked down into a pair of brilliant blue eyes. "And you," he said to Goliath, "have impeccable timing."

Lena laughed. "That he does."

The cat meowed again and butted against Lena's boot. She bent down to scratch under his chin. "He's a bit of a pest, but definitely entertaining."

"We'd better eat before the food gets even colder." Devlin's stomach growled loudly. "Although I much prefer what we were doing, I need some substance."

Lena blushed, the delicate pink on her cheeks adding to her appeal. "Sure." She moved to the dining room table, then held out her hand. "Shall I ask the blessing?"

In answer, Devlin slid his hand into hers and bowed his head. He hadn't realized how precious it was to have a woman who prayed. His own parents believed in a heavenly Father, and their example had spurred him to search for a godly woman. He had been longing to have someone with which to share not just his life, but his faith as well. As Lena said grace, he knew he had found someone special, perhaps even someone with whom he could plan a future.

"Devlin?"

At her query, Devlin snapped open his eyes, his face warming. "Sorry, a bit of daydreaming." He dropped her hand and grabbed his burger, hoping she wouldn't ask just where his mind had wandered.

She smiled at him in a way that made him think she might just have an inkling of what he had been thinking about. But she didn't say anything, thank goodness. The two ate in silence until most of the food had been consumed.

"I was hungrier than I thought." Lena dragged a french fry through the remaining ketchup on her plate. "I practically inhaled my food."

Devlin grunted. "Me too." He looked down at the few straggling fries that remained. "I guess I worked up an appetite."

Lena tossed a fry onto his plate. "What are you saying? That kissing me was the equivalent of a workout?"

"The best workout I've ever had." He wiggled his eyebrows as he ate the fry. Then he sobered. "I was so worried about you."

"Oh." She finished her fries. "Stress can increase your appetite, I'm told."

"I'll say." Devlin cleaned his plate as well, then stood to clear the table. "I was really scared last night after you told me a man was in your apartment."

Lena wadded up the burger wrappers and put them in the takeout bag before carrying the bag to the kitchen trashcan. "You know, at first I was frightened by the fact he had gotten into my apartment. Then I got good and mad because he wouldn't tell me anything. He hinted I should be careful, but even then I didn't think I had anything to fear from him."

Lena tucked her feet underneath her, and patted the couch cushion beside her. "What have we stumbled onto? I have no idea about anything except that I've been nearly run over by a car, shot at, had a bomb explode in my front yard, received a postcard I think is from my supposedly dead grandfather, and been warned to stop looking for him."

"Then there's the NIH side of things with Dr. Shan's death and the missing notebooks written by someone named Dr. Hoffman," Devlin added. "There's something more. I got a better translation of a 1981 article by Dr. Hoffman in which he discussed an initial clinical trial on virus therapy for liver cancer treatment that showed real promise. But the article only talked vaguely about results without providing concrete evidence. Dr. Hoffman hinted another article would be forthcoming after he duplicated the first clinical trial, but I can find nothing more in European medical journals or any other scientific journals from that time period."

Lena frowned, the movement making an adorable vee on the bridge of her nose. The desire to kiss that area had Devlin leaning forward, but he halted himself in time as she asked, "Is that unusual?"

"Yes, which got me wondering if Dr. Hoffman might have been conducting the trials under the table."

"What do you mean by *under the table*?"

Devlin spread his hands out. "There are certain protocols medical researchers are supposed to follow when conducting clinical trials on human beings. Usually, researchers start in the lab and hone the procedure and hypothesis of how it would work. Then they try it on mice first, progressing up to other animals depending on the disease and procedure. Finally, after years of research and modifications, they're ready to start clinical trials on people. They'd have to have three subgroups: a control group, a placebo group, and a treatment group. The placebo and treatment groups wouldn't know which one they were in. That's important. There are a lot of other hoops to jump through in regard to disclosures and regulations, but that's the gist of it."

"You think Dr. Hoffman might have bypassed some of those steps?"

"He might have."

"Why would that matter now?" Lena cocked her head to one side. "It might mean his research couldn't be trusted, but why would someone from the Defense Intelligence Agency warn me to stop looking for my grandfather?"

"And why would someone steal his notebooks? It doesn't make any sense."

The two sat in silence for a few minutes, then another question Devlin had wanted to ask Lena surfaced in his mind. "Have you received any other communications from your grandfather? Another postcard perhaps?"

Lena started to shake her head, then paused. "Wait a minute. I think I might have gotten a postcard in yesterday's mail, but I completely forgot all about it when I found Mr. Defense Intelligence Agency in my living room."

She rose and grab a stack of mail from the table by the door. Fanning through it, she tugged something out and held it up. "Here it is. A postcard of Louis Pasteur."

Devlin hurried over to her and peered over her shoulder as she flipped it over to see her name. "It's the same lettering as the first one, right?"

"It looks the same." Lena read the message, this time written in English, aloud: "Jib a box. Abuzz, jazzy, quick. Furzy, gauzy, buxom, jupon." She looked up at Devlin. "That makes absolutely no sense at all."

Devlin frowned. "Wait a minute. Some of those words are familiar to me. Let me think of where I heard them before." He closed his eyes to concentrate, then popped them open. "I've got it. They are high-point Scrabble words."

"As in the word game?" Lena sounded more puzzled than ever.

"I know it sounds crazy, but *jib* is a great three-letter word. I had a roommate in medical school who used to play in Scrabble tournaments, and I used to practice with him. He had notecards with high-point value words for various lengths, such as three, four, five, and six letters long."

Lena scrunched her nose. "Do you think Hoffman wrote this postcard to help us with Scrabble?"

Devlin laughed. "Probably not, so he must have a different meaning."

"The words themselves can't have meaning in their normal sense." She stared at Devlin, her blue eyes sparkling. "Is it a code?"

"Maybe." Devlin studied the words again. "But I can't discern a pattern at all."

"For Scrabble, aren't their points associated with certain tiles?"

"Yes. Do you have some scratch paper? I have Scrabble in my condo, so I'll go get it."

Lena nodded, then she disappeared down the hallway. He quickly grabbed the game from his living room bookshelf and returned to her apartment. The two of them hunkered over the dining room table, tallying up the points for each word. But no matter how they added up the points, the message still made no sense.

After half an hour, Devlin threw down his pencil. "This is useless."

She tapped her pencil against the table. "Let's try to see if it's in a code."

"I heard there's an app that can break some codes." Devlin searched the app store. "Here it is. Cryptoy." He downloaded it and entered the words. But while the app managed to rearrange the letters into words that made more sense, there was no coherent message.

Lena ran her finger along the postcard. "What if we're making it harder than it needs to be?"

"What else could we try?" Devlin rubbed his eyes.

"If we count the number of letters each word has, we'd have: three, one, three, five, five, five, five, five, five, five."

Devlin squared his shoulders. "Read those numbers again, slowly."

Lena complied. Her eyes met his. "It's a phone number."

CHAPTER
TWENTY-THREE

Once again, Wolfgang dialed the number he had sent in code to Lena. *Please, let Wilson Shamblin answer this time.* The prayer startled him. As a doctor and scientist, he had eschewed religion, agreeing with East Germany's state-sponsored atheism. But now, in the twilight of his years, he found prayers to a higher power slipping into his thoughts more and more often.

"Hello?" Shamblin's greeting redirected Wolfgang to the difficult conversation ahead of him.

"*Guten Morgen, mein alter Freund. Es ist lange her.*" The understatement of the year. It had indeed been a long time since they had last spoken.

Silence stretched for thirty, then forty seconds. Finally, Shamblin replied in German, "So you call me at last, old friend."

Wolfgang ignored the less than cordial tone in Shamblin's voice. He knew it would be difficult to reconnect with his former rival, but he had no choice.

"*Bist du gekommen, um Vergebung für die Vergangenheit zu bitten?*" Shamblin's voice held an edge to it reminiscent of their old, heated exchanges.

If only it were that simple and he could ask forgiveness from this man for the past. Wolfgang continued in the language of their youth, although both spoke English well. "No, I know the past can't be forgiven as easily as that." Wolfgang's own drive for fame and glory had robbed him of this true friend. "But I would like to make amends."

"Amends. You think you can erase the past with good works now?" Shamblin chuckled, but the sound held little mirth.

"Not erase the past, but ensure a better future." Wolfgang had been thinking about how to accomplish this for years. Only now he had the courage to put his plan into action taken hold of him. It would likely cost him his life and the companionship of a grand-daughter he'd never known, but he could no longer live with the guilt and the knowledge he had disappointed his dear Ida.

"You are talking in riddles. I'm an old man and have no patience for your games. Why have you called me?"

"I will speak plainly." Wolfgang drew in a breath and let the words ride on the exhale. "I let my ambition and arrogance cloud my judgment. You were right to speak up for those who I used in my quest. My success only fueled my greed to be the one who found the cure. But you, *mein alter Freund*, were the true hero. You stood for what was right, despite the cost."

"Now you talk of right." Shamblin dropped his voice. Sadness crept into his tone like fog settling on a mountain top. "You had no time for righteousness, and you had no patience for those who stood in your way. You talk of cost. What cost did you pay? You slipped away and left the rest of us to clean up your mess, to succor those you left behind. You weren't demoted and shunted off to some god-forsaken place. If the Berlin Wall hadn't come crashing down, I'd be in that little village still, eking out a living among a people so poor and ignorant, I might as well have been practicing in the Dark Ages. Don't talk to me of sacrifice."

Wolfgang remained silent. He had known, of course, that his actions would have repercussions on his fellow physicians and medical researchers. Shamblin had correctly assessed that Hoffman had only cared about the research, not the lives ruined along the way. And for what? He hadn't achieved glory but had come close to a breakthrough treatment for liver cancer. "We both know I would be lying if I'd said I would do it differently. I was an arrogant *das Schwein* back then. But you know I was also onto something special, something that could one day revolutionize how we treat one of the deadliest cancers in the world."

"Ah, I wondered when the real Dr. Hoffman would come out." Shamblin sighed. "In your voice, I still hear the younger version, the one who believed he would cure liver cancer in his lifetime if only he could do things quicker, faster, without following protocols that only slowed things down."

Wolfgang hung his head. He had never been able to fool Shamblin. The man who had been his supervisor during his residency had seen right through him into his very soul and still could, even over the phone. Wolfgang might be searching for redemption, but he wasn't entirely repentant. His work had been important, and he wanted to carry it on, but this time adhering to the rules. But one couldn't explain to those who had aided in his escape from East Germany the acquirement of an inconvenient conscience.

"If you didn't call to apologize for the past, why did you call?" Shamblin coughed, a racking sound that prickled the back of Wolfgang's neck. He would ask about the cough later. Better to focus on the reason for his call.

"I have a granddaughter, Lena Hoffman, whom I have never met. It was best for her parents to believe I was dead, and so she did as well. But I find in my twilight years, I miss the companionship of family and wish to know her. To do so, I must reconcile with the past and make amends from my formerly wicked ways."

"You sound like you've found God."

Wolfgang considered the question, so similar to his own musings. "Not exactly. Let's just say I have warmed to the idea there likely is a God."

Shamblin's chuckle turned into another hacking cough. "An honest man at last, eh, Dr. Hoffman?"

Wolfgang paced the small hotel room, his disposable cell phone pressed to his ear. "For various reasons, I'm not able to visit her right now and tell her about my time in East Berlin."

"On the run again, are you?"

Wolfgang let the question slide by without replying. "I gave her your number."

"What on earth for?"

"I want you to tell her the truth."

A longer pause, another cough, then Shamblin said slowly, "You want me to tell your granddaughter what a monster her grandfather was?"

Wolfgang screwed up his courage. "Yes."

LENA HAD NO TIME TO THINK ABOUT POSTCARDS, HER GRANDFATHER, OR much of anything else the next day, as her department received a rush translation job related to the U.S. president's upcoming visit with the German chancellor. The entire day had flown by in a flurry of activity. Once home, she flopped on the couch after eating a bowl of soup, Goliath curled up beside her, glad to be home in her snug apartment. The window repairman had finished installing her new windows, which had sturdy locks. She'd also had a locksmith out to change the front door handle and deadbolt on the off chance the Defense Intelligence agent had gotten hold of a key.

Devlin had texted he would be out that evening with friends. Thoughts of his brown eyes and dark brown hair worn a little too long filled her mind. She stroked her cat, wishing Devlin was sharing the couch with her instead of Goliath. It had been a long time since she had felt so much joy and anticipation in a relationship. Maybe this would lead to something more permanent.

With a great meow, Goliath leapt up and shot across the end table, scattering a stack of mail she hadn't sorted yet.

"Sorry, boy." Guess she'd tangled her fingers too tightly in his fur while thinking of Devlin. She leaned over and gathered the mess together. Separating junk mail from the few flyers for local restaurants, she found the postcard with the strange words in the mix. Maybe she should call the number—if it was indeed a phone number from her grandfather. The numbers had the correct digits for a US number, even though the area code wasn't a local one. Somehow, she couldn't quite believe that he was alive but she also couldn't stop from grabbing her cell phone and dialing the number just in case.

The number rang and rang, then the voicemail kicked on, reciting the number she'd dialed in a generic voice, adding "Please leave a message after the tone."

Lena hesitated, then punched the end call button. She wasn't about to leave a message for someone she didn't know, but at least they knew their hunch might have been correct. It was indeed a phone number. Whether it was someone connected with her grandfather, she'd have to find out another day.

Her cell phone rang from an unfamiliar number with the German country code. Frowning, she answered cautiously in German. "*Allo?*"

"Lena? It's Lara."

"Ah, how are you? It's late for you to be calling." It had to be after two in the morning in Berlin.

"I'm fine." Lara's voice dropped even lower. "I'm at a call box."

"I didn't realize they still had pay phones." Something in her friend's voice sounded akin to fear, but it must be a bad connection.

"There are still a few left. I didn't want to call from the office or my apartment or use my mobile. This seemed the safest option."

This time, Lena definitely noticed a tremor in her voice. "Has something happened?"

"I'm being followed, and I suspect my phone at home has been tapped. I don't know about my cell phone, but I managed to lose my tail tonight with the help of a friend." Lara must have pressed her mouth closer to the receiver because Lena heard her more clearly, although her voice was still very low. "I think I put in enough money for this call, but I'd better talk fast. I found out information on each of the names. Ready?"

Lena wanted to ask more questions about why her friend thought she was being followed, but instead hit the record button, put the call on speaker, and opened the notes section of her phone. "Go ahead."

"Felicity Mayer is a native of Dusseldorf. She moved to Berlin after the war as an orphan, then was in the Eastern sector when the city divided. She trained as a nurse and worked in Charité during the 1960s through the 1980s before retiring in 1985. She's still alive and in an old folks' home in Erfurt." Lara rattled off the telephone number to the home. "Got all that?"

"Yes."

"Hans Vogel worked as a medic on the Eastern front in Russia during the final year of the war. He was young, barely in his twenties, when the war ended. He returned to Berlin after the armistice and got a job in the same hospital, completed his medical studies and eventually working his way up to head surgeon. In the late 1970s, Vogel resigned to work as a consultant in the medical research part of the hospital. He died after falling down a flight of stairs at his Berlin apartment in 1985."

Lena keyed in the information as fast as she could, praying the recording app was working.

"Sebastian Neumann had a murky childhood, an orphan by all accounts, growing up rather wild and in and out of reform schools in the late 1960s. He worked as an orderly in the research part of the hospital and died from alcohol poisoning in 1984."

Lena did the math in her head. "That seems rather young for such a death."

"Thirty-eight. And before you ask, that was the official cause of death on the death certificate." Lara cleared her throat. "Jan Becker was another nurse, this one with extensive oncology training. She was in her late 30s in the early 1980s and worked almost exclusively in the medical research side of Charité. She died twenty years ago from lung cancer."

Three dead so far, one alive. The odds weren't good for this group.

"Nadine Braun wasn't a medical professional nor did she work for the hospital in any capacity. She was the daughter of a woman who died in 1984 during treatment for liver cancer at the hospital. Nadine left East Germany when the wall came down in 1989 and hasn't been heard from since. I can't find anything more about her, but here are her vital stats." Lara rattled off the birth date, deceased parents' names, and hometown. "Her file lists her friends as saying she was headed for South America, possible Argentina."

"And Klaus Lange?"

"He was an oncologist, who worked at the hospital during the same time frame—1970s to early 1980s—in both the patient side and the research side. He kind of floated between both worlds. He was murdered in 1984. Gunshot wound to the head. Body dumped in the Havel River. No one ever charged with his murder." Lara paused. "I managed to track down an old police officer who found his body as a young cop. The officer said that his seniors, what you would call detectives in America, took one look at the body and evident gunshot wound in the back of his head, and simply shrugged. They didn't even try to solve it. In fact, someone told him *Es war seinen Job nicht wert, den Mörder zu finden*."

"What does that mean?" Lena finished entering the notes about Klaus.

"I forget that you speak German like a native but haven't lived here." Lara blew out a breath. "It means they knew perfectly well who killed him and they weren't about to get involved."

"Who killed him?"

"Lena, this was East Berlin in the early 1980s. Who would an East Berliner not want to cross?"

Immediately Lena flashed on her parents and the hushed conversations they had with the stereo going full blast. "The Stasi."

"Right, the secret German police. Even today, the old policeman spoke in a whisper when he mentioned the circumstances of Lange's death, as if the Stasi were still listening."

Maybe they still were—or whoever had taken their place. "Thanks, Lara. I owe you."

"You do indeed. That's all I can give you on this. I had to be very careful during my searches, as no one wants to talk about the old days anymore, especially what went on in that hospital on the research side."

"Why? It's been four decades." Lena didn't think it would matter after all that time had passed, but she was beginning to believe she was wrong. Somehow, it mattered very much.

"Because some secrets have a long life."

CHAPTER
TWENTY-FOUR

Tatiana leveled her gaze at the man prowling her home office. He had been waiting for her when she'd arrived home after another long, frustrating day in the lab. She'd known someone was in the house the moment she stepped inside. For one, brief glorious moment, her heart quickened. Tom couldn't stay away. He'd come back to apologize and to resume their life together. Rushing down the hallway, she'd glanced in rooms on her way to the kitchen. No Tom. Now her pulse beat faster, not in anticipation of a reconciliation with her husband, but with a fissure of fear.

"Dr. Dern, why don't you join me?"

At the familiar male voice coming from the study, the fear resolved into relief. She had been expecting him to contact her by phone but should have known he'd try to keep her off balance with a surprise in-person visit.

He leaned against the desk, the lamp behind him casting his face in shadows. "Sorry to disappoint you that I wasn't your husband returning to the nest."

"Why are you here?" Despite her resolve to not give the man the satisfaction of seeing her rattled, his remark stung. So he knew about her marriage troubles. The *Butzemann*—what she privately called the man since he'd never revealed his real name—gave her a smile that despite its joyful appearance struck fear in her heart. Maybe calling him the German boogeyman of her childhood had been more apt than she realized.

"You know I wouldn't be here unless it was important."

Or unless you wanted to insure I wasn't going rogue on you. She merely crossed her arms across her chest, trying to project an air of impatient indifference.

Amusement danced in his dark eyes. "Hoffman has managed to stay one step ahead, but I'm confident we'll run him to ground soon. However, he did contact Dr. Shamblin, as we had suspected he might."

Tatiana stayed silent, knowing from previous experience with the *Butzemann* that he liked to dole out information as if he were dealing cards in a casino—slow and steady.

"You were right to be concerned about Hoffman. He instructed Shamblin to reveal all should his granddaughter call."

Vindication for being correct in her assessment of Hoffman's change of heart overrode her intention to play it cool. "I was right."

"And yet you still haven't been able to duplicate Hoffman's success, even with his notebooks."

The taunting tone broke her resolve to keep her frustration out of sight. "He wrote them in some kind of personal shorthand. We need Dr. Hoffman himself to interpret them."

The *Butzemann's* impassive eyes never left hers. "If you can't get the job done..." The implication hung in the air between them.

Gathering the tattered remains of her control, she refocused on what the *Butzemann* had said about Hoffman. "How would his granddaughter know to call Shamblin?"

The *Butzemann* pushed himself to a standing position and rebuttoned his wool coat. "My guess is Hoffman sent another cryptic postcard."

A chink in his armor she could explore. "You didn't find such a postcard when you were in her apartment?" Tatiana cocked her head. "I thought you were a professional."

The *Butzemann* had the gall to laugh rather than get angry at her dig. The man donned leather gloves. "I will let you know when Hoffman has been located. Do you still think you can turn him around from his current faulty thinking?"

Tatiana considered what she knew of the scientist and his work. "I think with the proper enticement, the good doctor will see the error of his ways and return to what he does best."

DEVLIN JOGGED TO CATCH UP WITH DR. RON LANKFORD, WHO HAD BEEN AT the NIH for more than three decades and had a reputation of remembering more studies than anyone else in the center. "Hey, Ron, do you have a minute?"

Ron slowed to let Devlin walk beside him. "Sure, what's up?"

"I have a bit of a sticky problem." Devlin kept pace as the older man charged down the hallway, his white lab coat floating out behind him. "I've come across some older research that is similar to what I'm working on, but I can't locate any additional info. That seemed strange to me, given the promising results of the clinical study cited."

"What's the name of the author and study?" Ron paused outside a locked laboratory.

"Dr. Wolfgang Hoffman. The study's on virus therapy in the treatment of liver cancer."

Ron paused with his hand hovering over the keypad to gain access to the lab. He turned to look Devlin straight in the eye. "What was so promising about it?"

"The article purported he had successfully conducted a clinical trial on humans."

"That's impossible. No one has ever done that. Virus therapy has shown promise, but it's nowhere near ready for human trials." Ron raised his eyebrows. "Where did you say this study took place?"

Devlin swallowed, then plunged ahead. "Behind the Iron Curtain in East Berlin."

Ron stared at him. "What year was the paper published?"

"In 1981, in a small German journal called *The Krebsjournal*." Devlin waited while Ron raised his head to stare at the ceiling in his colleague's typical thinking pose.

"Has this Hoffman published any follow ups?"

Devlin shook his head. "None that I could find."

Ron rubbed his chin. "Tell me more about his findings."

"He somehow—he doesn't reveal how—got the chickenpox virus to attack cancer cells without giving the patient chickenpox. The therapy was ninety-nine percent effective."

"How many patients?"

"The paper said 161."

Ron gaped at him, echoing Devlin's reaction to the number. "161?"

"That was only for the trial listed in the paper. The author alluded to previous trials with similar results on more patients."

"That would indeed be amazing." Ron keyed in his code and pushed open the lab door. "Send me an email with the details, and I'll see what I can find out. If the research was true, this Dr. Hoffman might have found a cure for cancer."

DEVLIN IDLED HIS CAR BEHIND A TAXI WAITING FOR A FARE OUTSIDE THE Metro. When he had texted Lena about seeing her tonight, she'd said she had an appointment at home between seven and eight but could do dinner beforehand. He had offered to pick her up from the Metro on her way home to save time.

A text popped up on his screen. *On my way up.*

He smiled and studied the passengers exiting the Courthouse

Metro station. He finally spotted Lena weaving her way among the throng, and he opened his door to half rise from his seat to wave her over. She saw him and hurried to his car.

"Hi." She slid inside, dumping her bags at her feet and clicking her seatbelt before rubbing her hands together. "I forgot my gloves this morning."

"I'll turn up the heat." He did so, then pulled out into traffic onto Wilson Boulevard.

"Thanks for picking me up." She rested against the back of the car seat. "I have a lot to tell you."

"Me too." Devlin hung a left on Adams Street. Traffic was heavy like usual, but Fire Works Pizza was just ahead on the left. "I thought pizza sounded good."

He snagged a parking spot on street and pulled up his phone's parking app to pay the meter. "Let me get your door." He circled the car to the passenger side. "Here you go." He held out his hand to Lena, who took it in her own. "Your fingers are cold."

"Told you." She hitched her purse on her shoulder, leaving her larger bag in the car.

Devlin tucked her hand in the crook of his arm and pushed the door closed. He was glad she wasn't wearing gloves because he liked the feel of her bare skin against his own. "We won't be out in the cold long since I got a Doris Day parking spot."

"What?" She paused as he reached around her to open the door of the pizzeria. The warm scent of rising dough reminded him lunch was too long in the past.

"That's what my grandmother used to say whenever she found a parking spot right in front or near the entrance. In Doris Day movies, especially the ones with Rock Hudson, her character would zoom up to easily park in front of whatever New York City building she was visiting, no need to circle the block or squeeze into a tight space. Hence, when you get a really sweet spot, it's a Doris Day parking spot."

Lena laughed. "Your grandmother sounds like someone I'd love to meet."

"I wish you could have, but Nana died when I was twenty-one." Devlin pointed to a table in the corner of the seat-yourself restaurant. "How about that one?"

Lena agreed, and they made their way over to claim it. As she picked up a menu, Devlin returned to the topic of his grandmother. "It was because of Nana I decided to go into research medicine rather than practice."

"Sounds like there's a story there." Lena gave him one of her shy smiles.

Devlin's heart flip-flopped. The sensation was becoming quite familiar to him, as it happened every time he was around a certain blue-eyed blonde. "Let's order first, and I'll tell you."

A waiter sauntered over, and they decided on raspberry Italian soda and a large Margherita pizza.

Lena removed the paper roll around her silverware and napkin. "Now, about your Nana?"

"She died of liver cancer. They caught it late, probably because she never complained about anything. But the late diagnoses meant she had few options. She went quickly, only a few months after learning she had cancer. I had always been interested in research, so it seemed natural to turn my attention to cancer research."

"Oh, I'm sorry. Sounds like it was tough on you and your family." Lena looked down at the table. "At least you had family to comfort you. I felt so alone when my parents were killed in a car accident when I was a freshman in college. I'm just beginning to realize there were whole swaths of their lives they kept hidden from me."

The waiter returned bearing iced bottles of Italian soda. "Here you go."

Devlin took a pull of his, letting the fruity fizziness drizzle down his throat. "Sometimes we never really know the people with whom we should be close."

She turned the bottle around in her hands. "But that's just it. It's not that there are things my parents didn't tell me. I get that grownups have their secrets. What hurts the most is the lies."

"What kind of lies?"

"For starters, where they came from. All those stories about their idyllic childhoods in the countryside of West Germany were falsehoods. They were both born and lived in East Berlin, not outside of Luebeck in West Germany." She sipped her soda.

He covered her hand with his. "I'm sorry."

The waiter returned, bearing a pizza on a stand and two plates. "One Margherita pizza." He put down the pizza in the middle of the table and distributed the plates. "Anything else you need?"

"No, we're good." Devlin reached for her hand and bowed his head to say grace. He served Lena a slice of the steaming basil, tomato, and mozzarella cheese pizza made New York style, then himself. "Did you call the number from the postcard?"

Lena used her knife and fork to cut a triangle off the end of the hot slice. "Yes, but no one answered, and the voicemail message was one of those generic responses that simply repeat the phone number. Since I wasn't sure who I was calling, I didn't leave a message." She popped the bite in her mouth and chewed. "Delicious." She rested her cutlery against her plate. "Then this morning, a man calls my cell phone before seven and demands to know who I am. Naturally, I refused to tell him anything and hung up. A minute later, my cell buzzes again, but this time it's a police detective from Alexandria, apologizing for the earlier call and explaining he's investigating a homicide."

Devlin nearly choked on his mouthful of pizza. He quickly finished chewing and swallowed the food. "Murder? Who?"

Lena cut another piece off her slice. "I don't know. Detective Olsen wanted to know why I was calling, but I couldn't tell him. I didn't know even the person's name. Then all the detective wanted to know was whether I had spoken with the person whose number I called. I said I hadn't."

He washed down another bite with soda and wiped his mouth with a paper napkin. "Did you tell the detective about the postcard?"

"I didn't yet, but he's coming by my apartment tonight to ask more questions. I can't imagine it has any bearing on his murder, but I have to give an explanation as to why I was calling the number of someone I don't know at all." She picked up her slice.

"I see you like to eat your pizza with a knife, fork, and your hands?" Everything about this woman fascinated Devlin, from the way she scrunched up her forehead when she was puzzling over something to her eating habits. If he wasn't careful, he might be falling for her hard. Maybe he should start being more careless.

"Are you making fun of the way I eat?" She shook a finger at him. "I'll have you know I'm a very neat eater. I hate the way the end of the pizza slice flops over, and so I cut and eat that part to make it easier to pick up and eat the rest."

Devlin laughed. "I've never heard something so silly—and so sensible—in my life."

She made a face at him and took a huge bite of her pizza.

CHAPTER
TWENTY-FIVE

Thirty minutes later, Lena inserted the key into her door lock, Devlin right behind her. "Thanks for agreeing to be here when the police come." She pushed the door open, Goliath mewing his welcome, and stepped into the tiny foyer.

"No problem." He crowded against her, swinging the door closed. He leaned closer, a scent of pizza and cedar tickling her nostrils. "Always looking for an excuse to spend more time with you."

"Really?" As her heart rate accelerated, her voice came out breathlessly. She swayed toward him.

Devlin leaned down, his lips hovering over hers. But instead of his anticipated kiss, the force of the door being opened slammed his body into hers and sent both of them sprawling onto the floor.

Before Lena could register what had happened, a man in a dark jacket jerked Devlin up, twisting his right arm behind his back. Another man wearing a tan overcoat closed the door behind him.

"Devlin!" Lena scrambled to her feet. "Let him go!"

The second man, a bit taller and thinner than the one who held Devlin, spoke in German to his companion. "Let him go. The woman will not be any trouble."

Instinctively, Lena didn't react to his words, not knowing if the intruders knew she spoke German. If they didn't, it could be to her advantage to understand what they said to each other.

The man pushed Devlin forward hard. Devlin fell to his knees on the carpet at her feet. She reached down and helped him up. "You okay?"

Devlin nodded, pain flaring briefly in his eyes. He stood beside her, massaging his right arm and shoulder. "What do you want?"

The taller man ignored him, his eyes on Lena. "*Fraulein*, you must stop this search for Dr. Hoffman," he told her in perfect German. So much for him not knowing she understood the language. "It will do you no good this poking and prodding into the past."

She raised her eyebrows. "Oh? If it will do me no good, then why are you telling me to stop?" Her German was just as good as his.

A smile that held no mirth crossed his face. "You speak our language like a native."

She inclined her head to accept the compliment. Beside her, Devlin wrapped his arm around her shoulders but didn't say a word. She knew he didn't understand, but she trusted he would let her try to string this out long enough for the police to arrive. Her small mantle clock chimed the seven o'clock hour.

"You have not taken seriously your warnings to leave this alone." The taller man eyed her. "Now we will have to make a—how do you Americans put it?—a big impression. Hans?"

Lena shrank back against Devlin, who tightened his hold as Hans approached them. But the man stooped to sweep up Goliath, who had been sitting near her feet. With a sharp meow, Goliath sank his teeth into the man's wrist. The man yelped and dropped the cat, who scampered off in the direction of the bedrooms. The man started after him.

"*Verlasse die katze*." The taller man snapped.

Lena sagged against Devlin at the command to leave her cat alone.

"We will be watching you closely." The taller man walked to the door, his minion behind him. "We are through with warnings."

The two disappeared out the front door. A sob escaped her lips. "Do you think he was going to hurt Goliath?"

Before Devlin could answer, another knock sounded on the door. Lena closed her eyes, then opened them. "That's probably the detective."

"Here, you sit down." Devlin guided her to the couch. "I'll check first before opening the door."

She sank onto the cushions and pressed shaking fingers to her temples. Devlin's voice sounded as if from far away. As the room began to spin, she shoved her head down between her knees to avoid passing out. A hand rested on her shoulder as the murmur of male voices buzzed above her.

"Lena?" The concern in Devlin's voice brought her head up.

The pictures above the fireplace on the wall opposite the couch stayed in place. Lena blinked but nothing moved. Devlin pressed a glass of water into her hand and she took a long drink, handing the nearly empty glass back to him. "Thanks, I'm better now."

"Ms. Hoffman?"

Lena turned her head to see a short man wearing a rumpled navy suit, his tie pulled away from his neck. "Yes?"

"I'm Detective Olsen." The detective gestured to someone standing partially behind him. The person moved into Lena's line of vision, and she registered a middle-age woman with cropped black hair shot with gray. "This is my partner, Detective Burlington."

Lena nodded and reached for the water glass Devlin had put on the coffee table. She took a sip, then leaned back on the couch. "Sorry about that. I felt rather faint for a minute or two."

"Understandable, given the circumstances," Burlington said. "Dr. Mills told us what happened right before we arrived. Olsen informed the Arlington police about it, since it's out of our jurisdiction, and we'll follow up with them if it has any bearing on our investigation. Mind if we sit down and go over what happened?"

"Please do." Lena massaged her temples as Detective Burlington pulled up one of the dining room chairs while her partner settled into the recliner. Devlin sat beside Lena on the couch.

"Tell us what happened."

Lena recounted the incident, then shivered as Goliath jumped up and began making muffins on her stomach. "I think the shorter one was going to kill my cat."

Olsen barked a laugh. "From what Dr. Mills said, I don't think he would have gotten the chance."

"Maybe not." She hugged Goliath, suddenly cold. Devlin slung his arm around her shoulders again, and she gave in to the urge to snuggle into his embrace.

The two detectives questioned her further until Olsen tapped his pencil against his notebook. "You've given good descriptions of the two men." He turned to Lena. "You're sure they knew you spoke German?"

Lena nodded. "From the way he looked directly at me and didn't hesitate when he talked. He spoke like a native, probably a Berliner, if I had to guess."

Burlington raised her eyebrows. "That's pretty specific."

"I talk to a lot of Germans in my line of work, and just like someone from the Big Apple could pick out a fellow New Yorker by their accent and speech pattern, for example, I can do the same fairly accurately with German speakers."

"I know that Burlington hails from the great state of Texas by her idiomatic expressions," Olsen said, a grin on his face.

"Don't get me started, or I'll hog tie you quicker than you can say Jack Rabbit," his partner replied, her eyes twinkling.

Lena brought the conversation back to the point at hand. "Do you think you'll catch those two men?"

"We'll pass it along to our colleagues in Arlington County," Olsen replied. "Or you could phone your local precinct yourself."

Lena would think about doing just that once the two Alexandria City cops left. "Thank you."

"When we spoke on the phone, you said you couldn't name who you were calling." Olsen flipped some pages in his notebook. "Why were you calling someone you didn't know?"

Lena exchanged a glance with Devlin, who nodded at her. She sucked in some air, then told the detectives about receiving the two postcards and how they had decoded the second one into numbers that resembled a phone number. The detectives didn't say much during her recitation.

"Do you have the postcards?" Burlington didn't look like she believed Lena but at least she wasn't dismissing it outright.

"Yes." Lena turned to Devlin. "Would you please hand me that print off the wall, the one with the Chinese writing?" At his questioning glance, she pointed to the cat curled up on her lap. "GOL—Goliath on lap."

"Sure." Devlin rose to remove the framed pen and ink drawing of a boat with Chinese lettering down the right hand on the side. He handed the square picture to Lena, who turned it over and inserted her fingernail under a small flap on the corner without disturbing the feline. The three of them watched her remove part of the backing and tug out the two postcards.

"That's a good hiding place," Olsen said.

Lena blushed at the amusement in his voice. "It's from a mystery book." She handed each detective one of the postcards.

They each examined them, then exchanged the cards. Finally, Burlington gazed at Lena. "Walk us through these."

Lena pointed to the first one she'd received. "That's German, and it translates as: *Your past medical advice was wrong—there is still a life to lead.* Look at the words carefully."

She waited as the pair studied the words.

Burlington spotted it first. "Behind the word *Rat*, it looks like the faint outline of the letters DR." She looked at Lena. "Is that what you mean?"

"Keep looking," Devlin urged, squeezing Lena's hand, then interlacing his fingers in hers and holding her hand on his lap.

It felt good to hold his hand, and she returned the pressure. Relief at sharing this bit of what had been happening made her shoulders sag against the back of the couch.

Olsen nudged his partner. "Look at this." They hunched over the postcard, talking quietly.

"Sitting here with you, I can almost imagine we're here to watch a movie, not be interrogated by the police." Devlin stroked her hand, while his arm cocooned her in a warm embrace.

With a sigh, Lena relaxed into the crook of Devlin's arm, the solidness of his frame soothing her frayed nerves after the encounter with the two Germans.

Burlington tapped the Bryce Canyon postcard. "It appears that the lettering behind the German writing spells *Dr. Hoffman*."

"That's what we thought too." Lena didn't move from the embrace of Devlin's arm and body.

The two detectives exchanged a glance as the tension in the room shifted.

"Any relation to you?" Olsen's voice tried for a casual tone, but Lena caught the undertones of something else.

Lena pulled out of Devlin's embrace, removing her hand from his. Something wasn't quite right here. "Dr. Hoffman is my grandfather."

Olsen raised his eyebrows. "How did you not know you were calling your grandfather last night?"

Lena's jaw sagged as surprise coursed through her faster than rising flood waters. "The number was for Dr. Hoffman?"

Both detectives nodded, their expressions grave.

Lena leaned forward, dumping Goliath to the floor as she tried to make sense of this new information. "Until I received the Bryce Canyon postcard last week, I thought my grandfather was dead."

Skepticism rimmed Burlington's eyes. "I think you'd better fill in the gaps."

"My parents emigrated from what I thought was West Germany back in the early 1980s. I was an only child of only children who was told we had no living close relatives at all. I always thought both sets of grandparents were dead." She rose, unable to stay seated a moment longer. "My parents were killed in a car accident by a drunk driver when I was a freshman in college."

"So you never met Hoffman?" Burlington said.

"No. I assumed my father's father was dead, but when I got the first postcard, I realized my parents never came right out and said Hoffman was deceased. They said things like, 'He's no longer with us,' that I took to mean death."

"And the Bryce Canyon postcard changed your mind?" Olsen interjected.

Lena nodded. "I became curious about this grandfather of whom I knew next to nothing. When I Googled his name, I found an article from the early 1990s that said Hoffman had disappeared in 1983 from East Berlin and was presumed dead. That's when I examined the papers from my parents and realized they had lied about their own background."

"In what way?" Olsen asked.

"That they emigrated not from West Germany as they led me to believe but from East Germany." Lena pivoted on her heel to avoid walking into her dining room table. Her small living room left little space for pacing, but she couldn't sit still. "I thought the second postcard and its phone number would lead me to Hoffman."

"It did." Burlington's somber tone stopped Lena in her tracks.

Her heart pounding, Lena licked her lips, then forced out the question. "It was his number, wasn't it?"

The compassion in Olsen's eyes brought tears to Lena's. "I'm sorry. The homicide we're investigating is Dr. Hoffman's."

CHAPTER
TWENTY-SIX

At the detective's words, Devlin leaped to his feet to wrap his arms around Lena, not caring what the detectives thought. His only wish was to comfort her. She leaned into his embrace, her hands fisting in the fabric of his dress shirt. He blocked out the two detectives sitting close by and concentrated on soothing Lena's pain. "Shh, it will be okay."

With a shuddering sigh, she pulled back just enough to face the detectives, twisting her body to stay within his embrace. "What happened?"

Burlington ignored the question. "Have you ever spoken to your grandfather?"

Lena brushed off a tear from her cheek. "No, I've never spoken to him. I never even thought he was alive until recently." She sucked in a deep breath. "And now I never will be able to meet him."

Devlin rubbed her back. "What happened to Dr. Hoffman? His death must be suspicious if you're investigating it."

"He was murdered," Olsen said.

Lena gasped. "Murdered?"

"He was hit over the head with a blunt object." Burlington leaned forward, her eyes intent on Lena. "Ms. Hoffman, where were you last night between seven and ten o'clock?"

Devlin bristled. "You can't possibly think Lena had anything to do with Dr. Hoffman's death."

"Dr. Mills, let us do our job," Olsen said in a smooth tone. "Ms. Hoffman, answer the question."

"Last night, I was home. Alone." She pinched the bridge of her nose. "I sent some emails and made a few calls."

Olsen jotted something in his notebook. "On your landline or cell phone?"

"Cell phone." Lena rested more of her weight on him. "I sent the emails from my laptop using my WiFi."

As Burlington jotted something down in her notebook, Devlin noted the exhaustion rimming Lena's eyes like a smudge of black ink. When the detectives didn't ask yet another question, he did. "How do you know Hoffman was killed?"

The two detectives shared a glance. "Because we've seen the body." Olsen's raised eyebrows suggested he thought the question inane.

Devlin shook his head. "I assumed there was a body. I meant how do you know the man you found was Dr. Wolfgang Hoffman?"

Olsen's brows now nearly met together on his forehead as the man frowned. "The man had a DC driver's license stating that as his name. Other documents in the home indicated that was his name. A neighbor positively identified him as Dr. Hoffman."

"How long had he lived in the District?" Devlin pressed.

"Property records indicate it's been at least fifteen years." Burlington consulted her notes. "Is it Ms. Hoffman's grandfather? We can't answer that at this stage of the investigation."

"Strange he would send postcards with a Florida postmark if he lived in DC," Devlin said.

Olsen glanced over at the postcards lying on the coffee table. "That does seem a bit odd. But maybe he took a trip down south."

"Easy enough to check." Devlin still wasn't convinced this man was Lena's grandfather.

"Did you find books or papers in German?" Lena asked.

"German? I don't know. We'll have to look at the inventory list," Burlington said. "But all the papers on the desk were in English. Why do you ask?"

"German is my grandfather's native language. He probably speaks and writes English very well, but he would more than likely still jot notes to himself in German." Devlin noted she still used the present tense, as if she too had doubts that this Hoffman was related to her.

Another question occurred to Devlin. "What kind of doctor was he?"

Olsen flipped through his books. "He retired from a general practice seven years ago at the age of sixty-four."

Lena shook her head. "My grandfather was a medical researcher, not a general practitioner."

"He might have changed his specialty," Burlington said.

But Devlin interrupted before she could continue. "You don't change specialties late in life. You stick with one path in medicine. You have to because you spend so much time gaining knowledge and expertise."

Olsen closed his notebook. "Whether this man was related to you or not, he has been identified as Dr. Wolfgang Hoffman."

"Do you have any suspects?" Lena asked.

"His apartment had been ransacked, his flat screen TV and other portable objects of worth taken," Burlington said. "It appears he came home and surprised a burglar."

"Is that what you think happened?" Devlin looked from one detective to the other, but neither gave anything away by their facial expressions.

"Thank you for your time." Olsen handed Devlin and Lena business cards. "If you think of anything else, please don't hesitate to give me or Detective Burlington a call."

Devlin tucked the card into his wallet, while Lena placed hers on the end table. The two detectives rose. "We'll be in touch of there's any developments you need to know."

Olsen turned before following his partner outside. "We'll pass along the details of the two men breaking in, but it would be good for you to follow up with the Arlington police too."

"We will," Devlin promised as the man slipped out.

Lena closed and bolted the door behind him. Devlin touched her shoulder. "You okay?"

"I don't know." She tucked a strand of hair behind her ear. "It's hard to think my grandfather could be dead before I've had a chance to meet him. I've gone from thinking he's been long dead to thinking I might have some family still alive to hearing he's been murdered."

"It does seem very strange." He ran a hand down her arm before intertwining his fingers with hers. "I feel like we're trying to put the puzzle pieces together upside down, that we're not seeing the picture at all, just the blank shapes."

Tatiana hated to rely on others. If she could take care of all the details herself, she would, but sometimes, she didn't have the requisite expertise. The notebooks lay scattered on her desk, each one taunting her with their secrets. The crude start Dr. Shan had attempted only showed her that using a German-English dictionary would do little good. The writer's own personal shorthand meant feeding the pages into Google Translator would only result in some English words along with gobbledygook. Besides, one tiny mistake would likely spell failure in the laboratory and endless redoes to see what went wrong. She needed the author to translate his work.

Her burner cell rang. "This had better be good."

"Dr. Wolfgang Hoffman has been found murdered in a Georgetown townhouse."

The man on the other end of the line sounded downright

cheerful in reporting such a grisly fact. Tatiana rolled her eyes. Deliver her from such imbeciles who thought she would be glad of such news. "And why do you think such news would be of interest to me?"

The man's voice faltered. "He's the man we've been looking for. They are the same age. I checked."

"Listen carefully. That is not the real Hoffman. I've known about this imposter for years." *And dismissed him as knowing nothing about the man I seek.*

"But the police went to see Lena Hoffman, his granddaughter."

Tatiana sat up in her chair, adrenaline coursing through her body. "Did they?"

"Yes, ma'am. They stayed for about an hour."

She considered her next move very carefully. Maybe it was time to tighten the noose around Hoffman, and she knew just the way to do it.

IF YOU WANTED SOMETHING DONE, YOU HAD TO DO IT YOURSELF. THE MAN Tatiana called the *Butzemann* had ignored that adage to his detriment. Hiring that fool to kill Dr. Hoffman had been a colossal mistake. The idiot had killed the wrong Hoffman. Sure, the dead Hoffman was the right age, a doctor, and had identification saying he was Wolfgang Hoffman. However, he wasn't the German medical researcher, but instead a close family friend, Wilson Shamblin. The *Butzemann* slammed his fist on his desk, sending papers flying. Rising, the man stalked to the window, a plan formulating in his mind.

Yet this might work to flush the real Hoffman out of hiding.

Returning to his desk, he selected one of his burner cells and dialed. "Any updates on the whereabouts of Hoffman?"

"We think he's on the move toward DC, but he's staying below the radar, paying in cash and staying off toll roads, etc." The man on the other end huffed. "For an old guy, he sure knows how to avoid detection."

"He learned from the best."

"What does a doctor know about evading a tail?"

The *Butzemann* decided to sate the man's curiosity. "He survived living in East Germany, and he got out on his own terms."

That silenced his employee. "I see we'll need to up our game then."

"You'd better, or the old guy will be breathing down your neck." The *Butzemann* switched topics. "I don't have time to wait for you to get a bead on Hoffman. It's time to put plan B into action."

"Copy that."

The *Butzemann* added, "And I don't want the merchandise ruffled or broken."

The other man sighed. "You take all the fun out of a good kidnapping."

The sorrow in his employee's voice elicited a laugh. "Don't worry. When we're finished, you can have your bit of fun."

The *Butzemann* laid the phone on a piece of stone on the floor beside his desk, then took a hammer and smashed it. Using a small broom and dustpan, he swept up the pieces and deposited them into the trashcan. With any luck, plan B would bring in Hoffman within the week. Then the real work could begin in earnest.

CHAPTER

TWENTY-SEVEN

id-morning, Lena closed her office door. Calculating the time difference for Erfurt, Germany, she figured four o'clock wouldn't be a bad time to call Felicity Mayer, a former nurse who had worked with Lena's grandfather and the only name on the list for whom Lara had located a current number. Last night, she'd worked out how she could elicit the information she sought about Dr. Hoffman without letting Felicity know her personal connection with the man.

"*Guten Abend, Sonnenuntergang leben,*" a cheery voice said.

Sunset Living must be some sort of assisted care facility. "*Gutentag.* Felicity Mayer, please."

"One moment." Silence, then a series of clicks before the phone started ringing again.

"*Hallo?*" A frail female voice gave Lena a glimpse as to the age of the recipient.

"Is this Frau Felicity Mayer?" Lena spoke in very formal German, wanting to put the other woman at ease.

"*Ja,* who is calling?"

The wariness in the other woman's voice made Lena reconsider her carefully constructed script. On impulse, she hit the record button before revealing her identity. "I'm Dr. Wolfgang Hoffman's granddaughter."

Silence, a quietness that stretched so long, Lena worried the connection might have dropped. "Frau Mayer?"

The older woman sighed. "I haven't heard that name in *sehr lange zeit.*"

Nearly forty years would be a very long time. Lena waited, not wanting to hurry Felicity.

"His granddaughter, you say?"

"Yes, ma'am."

"What can I do for you, *fraulien?*" Felicity sounded stronger, more alert.

"I was hoping you can tell me about what my grandfather was working on right before his disappearance."

"*Nein!*" The strident *no* carried with it the voice of a much younger woman, giving Lena a glimpse of the nurse Felicity had been.

"I don't understand."

"Did you ever meet your grandfather?"

"No."

"Then you cannot know what you are asking. It is impossible. I cannot go back to that time, even in memory. So much hope lost and lives destroyed."

The pain in the former nurse's voice touched Lena's heart. "I'm sorry."

Felicity huffed. "It is not you who should be sorry. Your grandfather caused a lot of pain and suffering. He was an egotistical genius. We all feared and hated him but believed in his work."

Stunned by the vehemence in her voice, Lena ventured, "What work did he do?"

"You think you can trick an old lady into revealing that? Ha, I have refused to talk about it for close to forty years. I'm not about to do so now, even if you speak German like a native and claim a relationship with the man who was in charge."

"Please, I—"

"I have given my answer." Felicity coughed. "I might not like this place, but at least I am alive. Oh, yes, I know why I am still alive. I have endured because I took precautions others thought silly. I will not jeopardize my situation by spilling those secrets now."

Lena bit back a groan. This was going nowhere. She was so sure this former nurse would provide answers, not leave her with more questions. "I just want to know the truth about my grandfather."

"*Die Wahrheit ist zu groß für dich.*"

The truth is too big for you to handle. Lena wanted to ask what Felicity meant, but before she could form the question, the other woman continued.

"There are people who will do anything to keep the past from coming to light, and there are those who want the information Dr. Hoffman discovered. Be careful you don't find yourself caught in the middle."

The former nurse hung up. Lena pushed the end button on the recoding app. She emailed the recording to herself, then also secured the audio file in her cloud storage account for good measure. Later, she would ask Devlin just what her grandfather could have been working on that would stir such a reaction four decades later—and why fear had been the underlying emotion in Felicity Mayer's voice.

DEVLIN KNOCKED ON THE PARTIALLY OPEN DOOR OF DR. ISABELLE JACKSON. At the invitation to enter, he came inside the cramped office and pushed the door fully closed. The woman seated at the desk covered in papers looked up. "Hey, Devlin."

He smiled. "Isabelle, do you have a minute? I have a conundrum I'm hoping you might be able to shed some light on."

She glanced around at the organized chaos and let out a bark that passed for laughter. "Sure, why not. I'm already so far behind, I will be working the weekend anyway."

He sat down and handed her the translated article by Dr. Hoffman. "Read this and tell what you know about it."

Isabelle took the sheets and immediately started scanning them. He stayed silent, knowing she would digest the material at lightning speed. What she lacked in social skills, she made up for in research, one of the most brilliant scientists at the NIH. Not that she got much of the credit. She much preferred to stay in the shadows.

Five minutes later, she slapped the papers down on her desk and stared at him. "Tell me."

For ten minutes, he shared what he suspected and what he had found out. Then he stopped talking and waited.

"Hmm." She leaned back in her chair, her frizzy gray hair standing out from her head like porcupine quills. "You think this Dr. Hoffman developed a workable virus therapy for liver cancer."

Devlin nodded.

"If that's the case, where's the evidence? The clinical trial data?"

He drew in a deep breath. He had been speaking more in generalities before, now he would share what he and Lena had uncovered. "I think that information is contained in a series of notebooks."

"Unpublished—and therefore unverifiable—material."

"That's right."

"Where did this supposed clinical trial take place?"

"East Berlin in the 1980s."

She put a finger to her lips, tapping out a beat only she could hear. "Did I ever tell you I spent a semester abroad as part of my medical residency training?"

Devlin shook his head.

"Yes, in West Germany during the early 1980s."

He raised his eyebrows.

She laughed. "My maternal grandparents came from Germany in the 1930s. They'd seen the writing on the wall and realized what

Hitler would do to their beloved country. I spent summers with them at their upstate New York home and picked up the language."

"Impressive."

"I could converse but not read German." She shrugged. "But when I first arrived at a now-defunct West German medical research facility, my colleagues preferred to practice their English. After a time, none of them recalled I spoke their language."

Devlin tried not to allow impatience at the seemingly disconnected story show on his face.

"So I overheard things." She paused, her eyes focused on something beyond his right shoulders.

Devlin suspected she was lost in the past and gave her space to marshal her memories.

With a shake of her head, Isabelle continued. "Most was staff gossip I couldn't care less about, but one day I delivered some test results to the head of the cancer division. His secretary was away, so I was going to leave the papers on her desk when I heard raised voices coming from the director's office."

"What did you hear?" He leaned forward, anticipation making him want to shake the woman into spilling her story faster.

A wry smile crossed her face. "I wasn't above a little eavesdropping, and I inched closer to the partially open doorway. I couldn't see who the director spoke with, but the anger in his voice came through loud and clear. My German wasn't quite good enough to catch everything, but the gist was something about a hush-hush experiment in East Germany that involved test subjects being made sick in order to find a cure. And before you ask, I do not know what disease the men were talking about. His secretary came back before I could find out more."

Devlin's stomach dropped. He hadn't considered that as the reason why Hoffman hadn't published or broadcast his findings. "That's terrible."

Her eyes bored into his. "The Soviets, especially the East Germans, wanted to be the first at everything—space, medicine, the

Olympics. They certainly weren't concerned with minor things like consent. It can take decades to bring a new treatment or drug to market by following the rules."

"But those were only rumors, right?" He wished he could believe Dr. Hoffman hadn't crossed the ethical line with his research, but her statement had the ring of truth to it, especially in light of how secretive Dr. Shan had been with those notebooks. No matter how the trials had been conducted, the information would be extremely valuable, even decades later.

"Who knows? A lot of things went on behind the Iron Curtain about which we might never know the full story." Isabelle handed Devlin back the article. "But I do know that many people would kill for such a study or information. You know how valuable it would be to your own work." She studied him. "Dr. Shan had some notebooks written in German."

Devlin couldn't hide his astonishment that Isabelle knew of the notebooks.

"Oh, yes. I saw the notebooks with the German notations and the name Hoffman scribbled in the front. I know they are now missing."

"Did Dr. Shan show them to you?"

She shook her head. "No, I saw them on his desk one day. He tried to cover one of them up with some papers, but I saw enough to draw my own conclusions."

"So you never discussed them with Dr. Shan?"

"No, but you did." She met his gaze. "And I think that's why you believe Dr. Shan didn't kill himself."

"No, I don't." He stood. "Thank you for your time. I'd appreciate it if you didn't mention our talk to anyone else."

"Of course not." She shuffled some papers on her desk. "You be careful. If they are willing to kill a prominent researcher like Dr. Shan, they will not hesitate to silence you."

~

Wolfgang dialed a number he knew by heart. An unfamiliar male voice answered the phone.

"Hello?"

Suspicion made Wolfgang more cautious than usual. Dropping his voice down an octave to mask any identifying marks—he had no doubt the conversation would be recorded—he said briskly, "Is your superior on the premises?"

"No, sir." The man responded to the authority in Wolfgang's voice.

"What is your name and rank?" Wolfgang knew the presence of someone with a superior was likely with the police, which meant trouble at his old friend's home.

"Alexandria City Police Officer Brown, sir."

"How long have you been on the force, Officer Brown?"

"A little over a month, sir."

Good. "Ah, then we haven't met yet. I'm Detective Gordon Lively, just back from an extended leave taking care of my mother, who passed away a few weeks ago. Before I pop by the scene, would you bring me up to date?"

The young officer rushed to fill him in on the details. "The deceased was a Dr. Wolfgang Hoffman, age sixty-four, found dead yesterday morning by his housekeeper. Preliminary cause of death was from a hit on the back of the head by a blunt object. Medical examiner estimated time of death as between six-thirty and eleven-thirty Wednesday evening."

Wolfgang listened to the recitation of the facts with sadness. Shamblin had been willing to live another life—his life—in order to protect Wolfgang's secrets and for a price, of course. Not that it had fooled everyone who mattered. "Any suspects?"

"That I don't know, sir."

"Have they finished processing the crime scene?"

"I believe so, sir. I'm on duty until noon in case they needed to come back."

"Has the next of kin been notified?"

"I think the detectives went to his granddaughter's house last night, sir."

"Thank you, Officer Brown. Good bye." Wolfgang disconnected the burner cell phone and sighed.

Lena must have called the number he'd hidden in code on the second postcard. Bright girl. But she probably told the police about the postcards. Maybe it would be enough for them to question the identity of the dead Dr. Hoffman, but he couldn't count on that.

He smashed the SIM card in the burner cell and dropped the pieces into the pocket of his wool coat to deposit into a public trashcan during his morning walk. He slipped his arms into the garment, shivering a little in anticipation of the cool January morning. His blood had become too weak living in Florida, and his body had forgotten the biting temperatures of his younger years in East Germany.

Adding a scarf and knit cap, he pulled on his gloves before leaving his motel room. On the street, passersby hurried along, heads bent to avoid the breeze. At the corner, he turned right, then crossed the street to head to the public library. A block further along, he tossed the pieces into a trashcan.

Once inside the toasty library, he divested himself of his outer garments before sitting down at one of the computer terminals. The walk had cleared his head and crystalized his thoughts. The time had come to bring his work into the open. Such a move would have its risks, but at his age, he no longer viewed those risks in fear. The things he'd done had been sanctioned by the government for which he'd worked, and the proof of that still rested in a very safe place.

The faces of those he'd both helped and hurt had been visiting him more often during his dreams. His dear wife, Ida, had implored him before her untimely death to *mach die Dinge richtig*. At the time, anger, grief, and his own sense of infallibility had driven him to continue along the same path. But almost too late, he'd realized the danger to his son, daughter-in-law, and unborn grandchild. Moving quickly, he had managed to spirit the couple out of East Berlin to safety in America, following them himself. But he had merely exchanged one master for another and had not made things right, as Ida had asked.

His failure to do so had driven him underground to wait until he could make his move without endangering his loved ones even further. Quietly, slowly, he'd gathered the necessary evidence to rip the curtain back to expose the ugly underside of his life's work. Then his son and daughter-in-law had been killed in a car accident. Despite his careful investigation, he still didn't know if it truly had been an accident or a message to him to stay quiet.

Fearing for his granddaughter's life, he'd gone deeper underground until whispers of someone looking for him, someone who wanted him not silenced forever but back in the lab, reached him. Protecting his granddaughter became the only thing that mattered. But to do so, he would have to reveal himself for the monster he had been.

Opening his email, Wolfgang sat for several minutes, staring at the blinking cursor. *Vergib mir Lena.* Maybe Lena would find it in her heart to do so one day, but he couldn't bank on her forgiveness, not when the truth came out.

CHAPTER
TWENTY-EIGHT

Lena stifled a yawn as she looked away from her computer monitor. Sleep had been fitful after the police had left, with dreams of a tall, shadowy figure haunting her sleep. Her phone buzzed. A text from Belinda flashed on the screen.

Are we still on for lunch?

She checked the time and yelped. Eleven-fifty. She would barely make the lunch date. Replying to Belinda's text in the affirmative, Lena put her laptop to sleep, secured the paper copies of the trade document she had been translating in her locked desk drawer, and shrugged on her coat. Locking her office door, she waved to a few colleagues as she hustled down the hallway to the elevator. During the ride to the lobby, she pulled up the DC Metro and Bus app. The 31 Metro Bus running North to Friendship Heights would arrive at Virginia Avenue in five minutes. Perfect.

Once on the bus, she elected to stand for the short ride to Circa Bistro's Foggy Bottom location. Belinda loved its steak frites, a steak and french fries entrée, and often picked the restaurant when it was her choice to select their monthly lunch spot.

Her best friend had been working nearly around the clock getting a new program ready to air, so Lena hadn't been able to catch her up. She had only sent a few texts letting Belinda know about her date with Devlin, but the short replies from Belinda spelled out just how busy her friend had been. Lena had half-expected Belinda to cancel their standing lunch date but was glad she hadn't.

At the restaurant, Belinda waved at Lena from a table near the bar before the hostess could even ask for a name. Checking her coat with the hostess, Lena hurried over to Belinda.

"So good to see you." Lena gave her friend a hug before sitting down. "I've missed you but am glad things have settled down a bit at work so we could still have lunch."

After ordering—Belinda her beloved steak frites and Lena a veggie burger with sweet potato fries—Lena listened as her friend related a few funny stories from work.

The waiter delivered their food with a flourish. When he departed, Belinda said grace, then leaned across the table. "Spill it."

Lena chewed a bite of her burger, then swallowed. "Spill what?"

"Your date—or is it dates by this time?—with the hunky doctor." Belinda cut a piece of steak.

"There's not much to tell," Lena said, waiting until her friend had taken a bite before continuing, "other than we've been out a few times, he's been over to my condo a couple of times, and he kissed me."

Belinda coughed, grabbed her water glass, and took a sip. "Are you trying to make me choke? Girl, you've been holding out on me. Details. Now."

While they finished their meal, Lean doled out more information about her encounters with Devlin, leaving out everything to do with her search for Dr. Hoffman. When the waiter cleared their plates and left the check, Lena picked it up. "My treat this month." She laid her credit card on the bill tray. "Do you have to rush right back to the office?"

Belinda checked the time on her phone. "No, I can play hooky for a little longer."

"Would walking back to my office take you too far out of your way?" Lena replaced her card in her wallet and scribbled a tip on the receipt.

"No." Belinda shrugged into her coat, wrapping a scarf around her neck. "But it's kind of windy today. It might be a cold walk."

Lena bundled up herself and walked with her friend to the restaurant's door. "I have something I want to talk to you about, but I don't want anyone to overhear."

Pushing the door open, Belinda said over her shoulder, "I'm intrigued enough to brave the cold."

As they walked down 23rd Street NW, Lena told Belinda everything that had happened, starting with the first postcard. At the corner of 23rd and E streets, they waited for the crosswalk. "What do you think?"

Belinda frowned. "I think you need to stop whatever it is you're doing before you get hurt. Shooting at you? Breaking into your house? You could have been seriously hurt. Not to mention the bomb exploding in the courtyard."

Lena shuddered. "If that dog hadn't dragged it from the bushes, I might not be here." Tears filled her eyes at the memory of the couple. "And those poor neighbors. I think they had just moved into the building next door a few weeks ago."

Belinda pointed to the crosswalk signal. "We can go now." She stepped into the street, Lena right behind her.

Back on the sidewalk, Belinda asked, "What will you do next?"

"I thought you said I should stop." Lena gazed at her friend.

"I did, but I know you well enough to know you won't. Especially if it would shed some light on your parents." Belinda stopped in front of the State Department building, a sprawling limestone and concrete structure. "What can I do to help?"

"I'm not sure. I feel like we have too many missing pieces to make a coherent picture. If I think of anything, I'll let you know." Lena hugged her. "See you at Bible study next week?"

"Sure." Belinda glanced toward the street. "My Uber is here."

"Too cold to walk back to the TV station?"

"You've got that right. Take care." Belinda squeezed her arm. "I mean it. Don't take any chances."

"I won't." Lena waved as her friend got into the car, then hurried into the building. Back at her desk, she tried to immerse herself in her work, but her brain wouldn't compute the trade document she had been attempting to translate. Picking up her water bottle, she drained the last of it. Maybe a quick trip to the water cooler to refill it would help refocus her attention.

She filled the bottle and returned to her desk. A whopping four minutes had passed. Good grief, she had never been much of a clock watcher. Usually the workdays zipped by. She truly enjoyed her translation work and her colleagues, but she couldn't settle down today.

The puzzle of who the murdered Dr. Hoffman had really been nagging at her. She couldn't believe the dead man was her grandfather. The police had told her this Dr. Hoffman had resided in Alexandria for more than fifteen years. Why be so close and send postcards from Florida? Then the timing of his death coinciding with her receiving a postcard with that number made her doubt it was a coincidence.

Her cell phone chimed, dragging her from her thoughts. An unfamiliar number flashed on the screen. Frowning, she tapped the screen to read the text in German: *Operation Red Schuhe. Sei sehr vorsichtig.*

Operation Red Shoes. Be very careful.

She hit reply and typed in the same language: Who is this?

Nothing. Then up popped the words *Undeliverable message.*

How strange. Multiple tries resulted in the same status, almost as if the phone from where the text originated had been not just turned off but destroyed. Something pushed her to send the text message to Devlin and also forward it to her email as well as save it as a note in the cloud. Overkill, perhaps, but she figured it wouldn't hurt to be extra careful. The uncomfortable feeling her life depended on being extra vigilant wound its way through her mind. She shivered and reached for the cardigan she kept draped over the back of her chair. Wrapping the sweater around her shoulders, she wished she could dispel the feeling that answers to her questions might be coming soon.

And she wasn't sure she was ready to hear the truth.

DEVLIN STRETCHED HIS ARMS OVER HIS HEAD AND ROTATED HIS SHOULDERS to ease the tightness between his shoulders. Spending most of the day hunched over a microscope played havoc with one's back and shoulder muscles. Too bad he wouldn't have time to hit the gym tonight, but tomorrow's stiff muscles would be a small price to pay for dinner with Lena. He placed the slides back into a container and glanced at the wall clock. Four-fifty-eight. Nearly time to knock off for the day. At least he didn't need to go through the decontamination ritual since he hadn't worked in the secure lab. Instead he'd checked tissue slides to see how the liver cancer cells had reacted to other viral therapies.

If only he could read Hoffman's notebooks. Devlin was sure the scientist had stumbled onto some sort of solution or breakthrough related to virus therapy. Timms would not be pleased Devlin's work had stalled. While the chicken pox virus, JX-642, entered the cancer cells and initially killed some of them, the cancer cells soon reversed the gains and attacked the chicken pox virus, rendering it useless. His next step would be to get clearance to try the smallpox virus, or at least the version used to make the smallpox vaccine. Even though his biohazards certification were up to date, he lacked the necessary experience to handle such potent live viruses.

With a mental shrug, he finished putting away the slides and tidying the work area before leaving the lab. He stopped to wash his hands at the sink in the vestibule before the keyed outer door, his thoughts on when he would see Lena again. Perhaps he would have an opportunity to thread his hands through her hair to revel in its silkiness. If he wasn't careful, he'd be well on his way to falling in love with her. Who was he kidding? He already was heading down that pathway, and he didn't mind it one bit.

Back in his office, he woke up his computer and opened his email. A few minutes into cleaning out his inbox, a pinprick on the back of his neck made him swivel in his chair to find Timms and another man, who pocketed a cell phone as the pair entered the office without the courtesy of a knock.

Devlin quickly closed out of his email program and tamped down a fissure of unease. By the scowl on the director's face, Timms wasn't here to impart good news.

"Dr. Mills," Timms began, his unctuous voice cluing Devlin in that the man with him outranked the director, "this is Dr. Jerrod Waldrop."

At hearing the name of the head of the entire NIH, Devlin rose to his feet, struggling to keep his face in what he hoped was a neutral expression at the surprise. "Dr. Waldrop, it's a pleasure to meet you."

Waldrop nodded but didn't extend his hand. Devlin recalled the man was famous around the institute for not shaking hands, said it was a deplorable practice that did more to spread germs and sickness than any other social custom.

Timms shifted as Waldrop studied Devlin, who managed not to squirm under the scrutiny. Clearly, Waldrop had an agenda, and Devlin didn't mind waiting. Patience was something every good medical researcher needed. Many times, patience and perseverance led to both major and minor discoveries.

"Thank you for the introduction, Timms." Waldrop held Devlin's gaze as he dismissed the other man. "I have some things to discuss with Dr. Mills and don't want to take any more of your time."

Timms couldn't ignore the dismissal in his superior's words, but by the way his eyes darted from one to another, Devlin suspected he wanted to stay. "Dr. Waldrop, Dr. Mills. Good day to you both." He turned and left the office.

Waldrop closed the door and motioned Devlin to return to his seat. "I hope I'm not keeping you from anything." He took the office chair across from Devlin. "I realize it's after five on a Friday evening."

Devlin didn't want to discuss his after-work plans. "How can I help you?"

The older man steepled his fingers and regarded Devlin with a sharp eye. "I understand you're working on virus therapy as a potential cure for liver cancer."

Devlin nodded, not surprised the man knew that information. After all, he headed the sprawling institute and had access to any employee's files and data.

"How are you progressing?"

"Not as well as I'd hoped." Devlin relaxed. Talking about his work with someone of Waldrop's expertise was a chance he wasn't going to waste. "I'm using the chicken pox virus, but it's not aggressive enough to withstand the onslaught from the cancer cells." Devlin added some more details about his recent findings, the other doctor asking astute questions along the way.

"Have you thought about using another virus?"

"To be honest, the chicken pox virus wasn't my first choice."

"And what would you have started with?" Waldrop's demeanor didn't change outwardly, but Devlin sensed an inner sharpness behind the question.

"The *variola* virus."

"Hmm. Why do you think the smallpox virus would do better than its cousin varicella-zoster as the basis for your virus therapy to cure cancer?

Devlin didn't hesitate in his reply. "The varicella-zoster has the right properties and acts in the right manner—entering the cancer cells easily before either killing the cells or creating the proteins needed for the body's immune center to go after the cells more effectively."

"So your hypothesis is that a more aggressive form in the same virus family might be able to put up more of a fight against the cancer cells."

"That's right." Devlin wasn't surprised the director immediately latched onto his reasoning. The man had built his own reputation on out-of-the-box thinking on gene therapy for breast cancer, helping to identify the mutant genes that caused the cancer as well as leading a team that came up with a way to offer more effective treatment for the cancer.

"And as a junior scientist, you haven't the clearance to work with classified viruses like smallpox."

Devlin nodded. Perhaps Waldrop had dropped by to provide a way for Devlin's work to progress, but something told him discussion of his work was a preamble to the real reason for the director's visit.

"I heard you were the one who found Dr. Shan."

"Yes." Emotion thickened Devlin's voice, and he cleared his throat. "His passing grieves us all."

"Did you work closely with Dr. Shan?" Waldrop's demeanor expressed the correct amount of sympathy, but Devlin also detected a whiff of something else.

Treading carefully, he replied, "No, he supervised my work, but he had a more hands-off style of management. We mostly interacted at staff meetings."

"Dr. Timms said you had a closed-door meeting with Dr. Shan the day before his death."

Waldrop was either on a fishing expedition or trying to verify what he already knew. Either way, Devlin would repeat what he had told the police. "Dr. Shan had wanted to know how I was progressing on my work. He asked for more details than we normally give in the department meetings."

"That's all you discussed?"

"No." Devlin met the other man's gaze with candor. "He also asked me about some notebooks he was trying to translate from German."

"What notebooks?"

Devlin detected a slight tensing around the director's mouth. He suspected they had come to the true reason for the director's visit. It all circled back to those notebooks. The way no one wanted to talk about them but everyone asked about them meant they must be very valuable. The question in Devlin's mind was the sudden interest in them now that they were missing. Or was it only now because their existence had been confirmed?

Devlin spread his hands wide. "I don't know exactly. As I told the detectives, I only saw one resting on his desk. Dr. Shan didn't let me look at it more closely. I could tell they were old, in the school composition style, with a mottled black cover, and filled with writing and notations. Dr. Shan indicated he had more than one."

"Did you learn their origin?"

"No. Dr. Shan said he'd had them for years and only now started to translate them himself." That ought to satisfy Waldrop. Just enough information to make it appear he'd shared everything but not the important bits about East Berlin and the janitor who had passed them along to Dr. Shan.

"I wonder why Dr. Shan had them."

"I don't know. All I know is that I didn't see them in his office after his death."

"You looked for them?"

"Not exactly. Since the office appeared to have been ransacked, the police asked me to look around and see if I noticed anything missing."

Waldrop furrowed his brow.

"Since I had been in the office the day before, they thought I might have an idea if anything had been taken."

"And the notebooks were the only things missing?"

Devlin shrugged. "That's the only thing I noticed wasn't there that had been the day before." He threw caution to the wind, tired of dancing around the question. "May I ask what this is all about?"

Waldrop stayed silent, his dark eyes seeming to evaluate Devlin for several long moments.

Devlin ticked off the passage of sixty seconds in his head.

"The police seem satisfied Dr. Shan killed himself, but that conclusion doesn't sit well with me. Nothing in his regular portfolio would appear to warrant such a response. I wanted to probe a bit deeper to see if perhaps something connected with his current work might have precipitated his decision to end his life."

"And what have you found?"

"Nothing." The other man smiled briefly. "That surprises you."

"Yes." Looking at the candid expression in Waldrop's eyes, Devlin decided to take a chance. "You think someone might have murdered Dr. Shan."

"I think that's a more likely scenario than the man killing himself." Waldrop continued to hold Devlin's gaze. "Dr. Shan was a good friend and good scientist. I would like to clear his name of suicide if at all possible."

"I understand, sir." Devlin had known Waldrop was a man of deep convictions. It warmed his heart to hear him speak of Dr. Shan with such high regard. But that didn't mean Devlin could trust him completely with the truth. Not yet. "I wish I could be of more assistance."

Waldrop rose. "If you think of anything else that might help, please let me know. My door is always open to you."

"I will, Dr. Waldrop." Devlin watched the older man leave his office while mulling over the very interesting turn of events. He needed to figure out what exactly was in the notebook he had. But before he tackled that, he first had a date with Lena.

CHAPTER
TWENTY-NINE

L ena cut a bit of steak, cooked to perfection by Devlin. A snowy linen tablecloth, folded napkins, and fine china—albeit mismatched—graced the small table. A trio of fat candles flickered in the center, completing the transformation of his dining nook into a romantic space.

"Is your steak okay?"

She yanked herself out of her musings to look across at Devlin. "Yes, it's delicious."

His shoulders relaxed. "It's the one thing I feel I can say I've mastered in the kitchen."

She chewed and swallowed the meat, the slightly tangy taste of the beef lingering on her tongue. "What kind of seasoning did you use?"

As Devlin described the marinade, she let her gaze wander over his handsome face, drinking in the five o'clock shadow along his strong jawline, the way his hair brushed his forehead.

"And then I added eye of newt for that extra zing."

Lena blinked, then smiled. "Sorry, my thoughts went astray."

"What has you so preoccupied this evening?"

Not wanting to confess she'd been mooning over him, she redirected the conversation. "I had the strangest text today from an unknown number. When I texted back to ask who it was, I got one of those message-is-not-deliverable replies."

She had his complete attention now.

He leaned forward, his brown eyes intent on hers. "What did it say?"

"The message was in German, but the English translation is 'Operation Red Shoes. Be very careful.'"

"'Operation Red Shoes, be very careful?' That was it?"

"Yep, that's all she or he wrote. I tried to trace the number in those reverse lookup sights, but only got a *number does not exist* return."

"What do you think it means?"

Lena nibbled on her bottom lip. "I can't believe that it's random, so I have to think it's related to my grandfather. Maybe it's what he was working on at the time of his disappearance. But how I'm supposed to find out what it means?"

Devlin tapped his fingers against his glass, his brow furrowed. Lena wanted to reach across and smooth out the ruffled skin of his forehead. She wanted to talk about music and movies and how many children they wanted to have one day, not her grandfather, missing notebooks, and the fact that someone had nearly run her over, shot at them, and tried to bomb her apartment. "My former history professor might have an idea. His specialty is the Cold War in East Berlin and East Germany."

"Do you think it's a good idea to bring more people into this when we don't even know what this is?" Lena didn't want anyone else to get hurt helping her uncover the truth. The fear in Lara's voice when she'd told her what had happened to the six names connected with Dr. Hoffman made her shiver.

"He's not an ordinary history professor. Dr. Henry Silverton and his wife, Violet, had a dust-up with a former East Berlin spy last year.

If anyone would know of the potential danger of such an investigation, they would. And they would be very discrete. Besides, we're friends, and he's been asking me to bring you around, so this might be a good opportunity to get his expert opinion under the guise of a social call."

Lena's cheeks warmed. "Have you been talking about me? How come I didn't know about this Dr. Silverton and his wife before tonight?"

Devlin chuckled. "I guess there's a lot we don't know about each other." He reached across the table and took her hand. "But I'm eager to find out more." He rubbed the top of her hand, sending little slices of pleasure across her skin.

All thoughts of her grandfather, Operation Red Shoes, and all the other events happening lately flew out of her mind. She turned her hand over and laced her fingers through his. "What are we waiting for?"

DEVLIN WHISTLED AS HE WALKED DOWN THE HALLWAY TO HIS OFFICE Saturday mid-morning. Normally he didn't come to work on the weekend, but after the director's visit the night before, he had forgotten to prep for a Monday morning presentation. He had awakened with a song in his heart and ready for love, as Gene Kelly had so memorably sung in *Singin' in the Rain*. All because of a five-foot-nine, blue-eyed blonde named Lena. Now all those corny love songs were starting to make sense.

If he hurried, he could finish the PowerPoint in an hour, then still have plenty of time to relax before his date with Lena and the Silvertons. Outside of his office, he halted mid-whistle. The door, which he had locked the night before, wasn't completely closed. A chill danced down his spine, driving the euphoria of the previous moment away. Should he call the police or push open the door?

A memory of Dr. Shan's limp body propelled him backward a few steps, his cell phone in hand. He called the building's security department and waited for the guard on duty to pick up. The phone rang once, twice, three times. The phone clicked and rolled over to voicemail. Devlin hit the disconnect button without leaving a message. The uneasy feeling increased. Time to call in the pros, even if it turned out he had overreacted. Devlin punched in the number for one of the NIH detectives.

"Detective Carter speaking."

"Hello, this is Dr. Devlin Mills from the NIH Cancer Research Center. We met last week when you came about Dr. Shan." Devlin paced a few more steps away from his office.

"You're the one who found the body."

"That's right."

"What can I do for you, Dr. Mills?"

Devlin drew in a breath in an attempt to steady his nerves. "This may be nothing, but with what happened to Dr. Shan last week, I thought someone should know."

"Know what?"

"That I think my office has been broken into. The door isn't closed all the way. I know I checked it was locked last night before leaving. Overnight, security guards walk through the building to ensure all the doors are closed tight to the labs and office. Then when I called the security office just now, no one answered, which is a bit unusual. Even on the weekend." Devlin forced himself to stop talking to allow the detective to reply.

"Are you in a safe place?" The detective's voice had a sharp edge to it that, paradoxically, calmed Devlin immediately.

"I guess so, I mean I'm in the corridor outside my office." Devlin took a few more steps away from his office door.

"Dr. Mills, please walk to a more secure location, preferably one with several people in it."

"Okay, I'll go to the front entrance." Devlin put motion to his words and moved down the hallway toward the lobby area.

"I'm about fifteen minutes away. I'll meet you there. Do not, I repeat, do not attempt to enter your office or any other office."

The urgency in the other man's voice erased some of the calmness. "Okay, I won't. What's happened?"

The detective sighed. "You'll hear about it soon enough. The autopsy results show Dr. Shan was murdered."

WOLFGANG KEPT HIS NONDESCRIPT RENTAL CAR AT A DISCRETE DISTANCE from the tractor trailer in front of him on U.S. Highway 15 North as he crossed from Florida into Georgia. He'd been making the trip from Boca Raton, Florida, to his final destination in short stages. Driving for long stretches wasn't something he could accomplish easily at his age. Besides, he enjoyed talking with locals at the small towns he favored for stopovers. Larger cities did offer more anonymity, but he exercised caution, never revealing his real identity or travel plans.

The miles clicked by as his thoughts returned to his granddaughter. He had been so foolish to think he could keep her safe by sending those postcards. Instead, he'd drawn a bullseye on her back. Now they knew about her and his communications with her.

They would wonder what she knew, what he had told her, and what she might find out on her own. He struck the steering wheel with the heel of his hand at his stupidity. For years, he had kept his head down, writing his memoirs, and keeping an eye on the latest liver cancer treatment research. When word of promising tests reached his ears, he couldn't help himself. He had to find out more. His surreptitious inquiries had stirred the pot, alerting them he was still alive.

A flicker of regret touched his heart at the loss of his son and daughter-in-law. He had been right to make arrangements for Stefan and Andrea to leave right before he disappeared. But he had counted on his son to burn the notebooks when he purged the apartment of personal things. But Stefan had brought them to the United States, then handed them over to Dr. Shan years ago. Dr. Shan, that egotistical and foolish man who thought deciphering the notebooks would bring him glory. Ha, no one could read Hoffman's own special shorthand. He had taken such precautions to protect his work by recording the true results of the experiments in those notebooks while copying a sanitized version into the official record.

Whoever had the notebooks would need him to interpret the data. Which meant he probably had less time than he originally thought. A small part of him still believed in the work he had done behind closed doors. Sharing the results with the world would bring both accolades for his innovations and horror at his methods. More and more, the need to atone for his actions drove him forward along this path. But when the time for confession came, would he have the courage to bare his soul? He had practiced deception for so many years that truth had become as foreign to him as snow to an island native.

His stomach growled. 11:32. Close enough to lunchtime. He pulled off at the next exit and drove through the town of Wrens, Georgia. At a roadside diner, he ordered the daily special with country fried steak, mashed potatoes with gravy, and a side of green beans cooked in real bacon fat. The Saturday lunch crowd of families and travelers filled the diner to capacity. He noticed a steady stream of customers at a separate takeout area. Definitely a good spot for lunch.

The perky waitress, who retained a youthful air despite the crow's feet crinkling the corners of her eyes, refilled his sweet iced tea without his asking. "Got everything you need, hon?" She paused in front of him, pitcher in hand.

His mouth full of fried steak, he nodded. It wasn't every day a woman called him "hon," although he suspected she said that to all her customers.

"Give me a holler if you need anything." The waitress moved off to check on the other customers sitting elbow to elbow on the worn counter stools.

Wolfgang washed down his bite with a swallow of iced tea and had another forkful halfway to his mouth when a scream pierced the diner. Dropping the fork back onto his plate, he turned, along with others, to see an older woman slumped sideways in her chair. A younger woman grabbed her arm to keep her upright. Without thinking, Wolfgang made his way toward the pair, shouting over his shoulder for someone to call 9-1-1.

Before he reached the women, the older one slid out of her chair in a heap, her eyes closed and her breathing fast.

Wolfgang gently moving her head into position so he could check her pulse and breathing. As he did so, he spoke to the younger woman, who had dropped to her knees beside him. "I am a doctor. What is her name?"

The younger woman turned frightened eyes to his face. "It's, um, it's Josie. Josie Snyder."

Wolfgang nodded as his fingers registered Josie's pulse. Accelerated. "Josie." He shook the woman's shoulder, and her eyelids fluttered. "Open your eyes, Josie." The woman complied, her gaze unfocused. "Can you hear me?"

Josie slowly nodded.

"Can you smile for me?" Hoffman kept his voice soothing as he scanned the woman's face.

The woman stretched her lips into a smile, only the left side of her face drooped while the right side rose.

"Josie, I think you've had a stroke," Wolfgang said. "Can you move your left arm?"

Josie appeared to attempt the movement, then shook her head.

"Can you tell me your name?"

Josie's lips moved to form a word. "Geufe." Frustration lit her eyes.

Wolfgang placed a hand on her shoulder. "It's okay, Josie. The ambulance is on its way."

As if on cue, sirens wailed in the distance, growing louder as they came closer to the diner. The young woman clutched Josie's hand. "Mom, you'll be okay." Tears streamed down her cheeks.

"Sah, hoffy." Josie's words came out garbled.

Wolfgang made sure the woman was as comfortable as possible and waited for the EMTs. Less than a minute later, the door to the diner burst open and two EMTs hustled in, a stretcher beside them. The crowd parted to let them through.

"Sir, we'll take it from here." The burly man set down his kit beside Josie and reached for her wrist to check her pulse.

"I'm a doctor." Wolfgang moved aside to let the burly man examine Josie.

"What can you tell us about her condition?" The second EMT held a clipboard, pen poised above it.

"She's had a stroke." Wolfgang listed the symptoms and his observations succinctly.

"Thank you, doctor." The EMTs worked together to load Josie on to the stretcher. "Let's roll!" The two pushed the stretcher out of the diner, the woman's daughter hurrying after them. In seconds, they were gone, leaving a void in the now still diner.

A minute later, everyone started talking again. People drifted back to their tables or stools, the kitchen staff returned to the grill and waitresses resumed delivering food and drinks. Hoffman slid back on his stool, but his appetite had fled.

"Want a box for that?" The waitress asked, pointing to his half-eaten platter.

"No, thank you. Just the bill." He reached for his wallet.

"No charge. It's on the house for what you did to help Miss Josie." The waitress eyes were sad. "She's been coming to this diner since she was a little girl. Will she be all right?"

"I can't say but getting help right away is very important for those who have a stroke." Wolfgang stood. "Thank you for the meal."

He slipped out of the restaurant and headed to his car. The incident replayed in his mind. He should have stayed hunched over his meal, but a lifetime of helping people had driven him to his feet and over to Josie before his mind could question the wisdom of such a move. A shudder wound through him at the memory of younger customers holding their smartphones up, no doubt recording the incident. In saving Josie, he might have signed his own death warrant.

THIRTY

Devlin stared at what used to be his neat office. Paper littered the floor. Desk and filing cabinet drawers had been yanked out. His desk phone had been flung across the room and now lay shattered on the carpet. The two office chairs had been slit open, stuffing pulled out. Books lay on the floor, spines crushed and pages ripped out.

Detective Carter stood to the side. "Someone must have a grudge against you, Dr. Mills. This is beyond looking for something. Someone wanted to send you a message."

Devlin rubbed his jaw. "I have no idea what this could be about." He had been warned to not continue pursuing the Hoffman case, but beyond talking with Lena, he hadn't searched for anything more. He had set into motion some things before being warned off by Enno Kurimsky with Homeland Security, but he hadn't overtly done anything to trigger this sort of destruction. Not to his mind at least.

"I've called a forensics team to come sift through all of this," Carter said. "Is there someplace we could talk?"

"There are some chairs near Penny's desk, down the corridor."

His eyes swept over his office once more, then he led the way to the research assistant's workstation.

After settling into one of the two visitor's chairs positioned slightly to the side of her desk, Carter asked, "Is there anything else about Dr. Shan that's come to mind?"

Devlin shook his head. "No. I had my doubts about his committing suicide, but you already knew that."

"The autopsy showed the angle of the bullet's entrance could not have been achieved by his own hand. There was also evidence of a sedative administered by an injection to the back of his neck."

Devlin couldn't suppress a shudder at the confirmation someone had murdered Dr. Shan.

"Usually, this type of drug clears the system very fast. However, the medical examiner said something about Dr. Shan's metabolic rate being particularly sluggish and that hampered the drug's exit from his bloodstream."

The cold certainty that Dr. Shan had been killed for the Hoffman notebooks settled in the pit of Devlin's stomach. Before Carter could ask another question, Dr. Timms hustled up, his overcoat unbuttoned and a scarf trailing behind him.

"Dr. Mills, why are you here on a Saturday?" Dr. Timms fairly quivered with indignation.

Devlin pushed to his feet to face the director. "I had some work to do on a presentation I'm giving Monday morning."

Timms's gaze flicked to Carter. "Why is he here?"

"When I arrived, I found my office door ajar, so I called Detective Carter when I couldn't connect with someone in security. After what happened to Dr. Shan, I thought I should err on the side of caution."

"What do you mean? Dr. Shan killed himself. An unfortunate turn of events but nothing sinister about it." Timms bristled.

"Dr. Shan didn't shoot himself." Carter's statement silenced Timms. "We have the results of the autopsy. He had been drugged, then shot in a manner to make it look like suicide."

"Murdered?" Timms's eyes widened.

Carter's phone buzzed. "Crime scene techs are here to process the office. Dr. Mills, once they've finished, you'll need to look through the mess and see if anything's missing."

Devlin nodded his assent, hoping it wouldn't take too long. He had a dinner date he most certainly did not want to miss.

"Dr. Mills, my office now," Timms snapped.

"Just a minute, Dr. Timms." Carter's voice held a note of firmness Devlin's boss automatically heeded. "My partner and I will be back on Monday morning to question the staff again about Dr. Shan, now that we're dealing with a homicide. May we use the same conference room as before?"

Timms waved his hand, his fluster apparent by the flush on his cheeks. "My assistant will know the schedule for the conference room, so you can check with her Monday." He turned to Devlin. "Dr. Mills?"

Devlin followed him down the hallway to the director's office, his mind not on Timms but why his office had been trashed. It didn't make any sense unless... The notebook. Someone knew he had one of the notebooks. Thank goodness he hadn't left it in his supposedly secure office.

"Dr. Mills, have a seat." Timms closed his office door behind Devlin. "I was going to wait until Monday, but since you are here, I will address the situation now."

The director's serious expression warned Devlin this wasn't going to be a pleasant conversation. Devlin put aside the matter of the notebook and turned his attention to Timms.

"It has come to my attention that despite my direct command, you have been dabbling in things other than your assigned research."

Devlin bit back a retort. Timms had been riding Devlin hard ever since Devlin arrived at NIH four years ago. A colleague once observed that Devlin's success in viral therapy had made Timms jealous, since the director's own field work had produced so-so results, thus shunting the man from research into administration. Cold comfort when your supervisor nitpicked every move you made.

233

"What do you have to say for yourself?" Timms's voice had a decided bite to it.

Treading as if navigating through broken glass, Devlin said, "Of course I talk with my colleagues about things tangentially related to my work."

"Tangentially related to your work." Timms huffed out a breath. "I see I must be more direct. You asked Dr. Lankford to look into a Dr. Hoffman's research, which I've been informed is classified."

Devlin hid his shock, knowing Lankford wouldn't have mentioned it. Someone else had been shadowing his movements at the office.

"Then I received this." Timms opened a folder and extracted a photograph before handing it to Devlin.

Devlin took the picture cautiously, schooling his face to a bland countenance in preparation for seeing the image. The first one showed Devlin and Lena in the living room of her first-floor condo, the two foreign "visitors" conversing with them. His heartbeat thudded in his chest. Someone had indeed been spying on them. He flipped it over and read the short sticky note on the back: *Well-known associates of the Al-Zein Clan.* "I have no idea what this Al-Zein Clan is."

"The Al-Zein Clan is one of the most powerful crime families in Germany."

The information did little to clear up why Timms had such a photograph. "Okay, but why do you have this photo?"

"You had a conversation in a private residence with two known foot soldiers of organized crime."

First someone broke into his office, now this weird interrogation from his boss. Maybe explaining what had really happened would be enough to satisfy whatever bee Timms had in his bonnet. "Those two men were waiting for us in her apartment, trying to scare Lena for some reason. We didn't invite them in, for goodness sake."

"So you say." Timms's eyes grew cold and hard. "But nevertheless, you didn't report this to our security team as required under our employee handbook, section eighteen, part seven." He referenced a binder on his desk. "'All employees must report any interaction of any kind, no matter how minor, with foreign nationals considered dangerous to the United States or who have ties to groups deemed terrorist, to the NIH security team within twenty-four hours of the occurrence.' You didn't do that."

Devlin ran his hand through his hair, frustration boiling up inside him as the certainty that Timms had been waiting to reprimand Devlin. Why, Devlin hadn't a clue. But it didn't matter. With Dr. Shan gone as a buffer between Devlin and the director, Timms could impart whatever punishment he deemed fitting, and no one would contradict him.

"No, I didn't." Devlin struggled to keep his voice calm. "But then again, I had no idea who those men were. And we did report it to the two Arlington Police detectives who arrived after the men left. Since I did not know who those men were, it didn't occur to me their uninvited visit warranted officially reporting it to security."

Timms's half smile told Devlin all he needed to know. "You know ignorance is not a defense." He spread his hands out over his desk. "I have no choice but to put you on suspension until this matter is resolved. Please remove any personal effects you might need from your office and turn in your keys immediately."

Devlin swallowed a sarcastic response and settled for the bald truth. "My office was ransacked. Whatever personal effects I have, I can't remove."

Timms's shoulders slumped like a helium balloon losing its air. "Oh, I'd quite forgotten about that."

Devlin plunged forward. "The detectives asked me to be available for further questions and to see if anything's missing from my office when it's been released from their crime scene techs."

Timms recovered his indignation, his gaze stern as it fixed on Devlin. "Dr. Mills, you will wait in the reception area until the police have completed their investigation, then turn in your badge and keys to the security office, and leave the building immediately. Do not contact anyone on staff about any matter. Human resources will be in touch when this matter has been cleared up. Good day."

Devlin started to ask about his ongoing experiments, but one look at the stony face of the director, and he swallowed the questions. Rising, he stalked from the office, his mind whirring. Why were members of German organized crime trying to intimidate Lena into not looking for her supposedly dead grandfather? The notebooks held the key. He'd better figure out what the one he held said before something happened to him—or Lena.

～

Setting her coffee cup down on the table, Lena fished her phone out of her pocket. "Hello?"

"Lena, it's Devlin."

A warmth filled her body. "Hi." Then the tension in his voice registered. "Are you all right?"

"Yes, no." He paused. "I'm at the office. Had to finish something before an early Monday presentation but when I arrived, I noticed someone broke into my office and trashed it. They even busted up my computer. Thank goodness everything's backed up on the NIH's mainframe and in the secure cloud we all use."

"Devlin, that's terrible. Why would anyone do something like that?" Lena unwound her scarf and draped it across the back of her chair. On a Saturday afternoon, the small local coffee shop teemed with people. She'd been lucky to snag a table tucked into a corner.

"I don't know. There's more news. I knew something was wrong when my door wasn't closed all the way. With all that has happened with Dr. Shan, I immediately called Detective Carter. He came over to check it out and told me Dr. Shan was murdered. Someone gave him a sedative, then made him shoot himself."

"Murdered." She managed to keep her voice low, but her insides churned. "That's terrible."

"I know. I just spent most of the morning answering questions and seeing if anything's missing from my office. I honestly couldn't tell because nothing had been left untouched." He sighed. "And there's more."

"More? What possibly could there be after those bombshells?" Lena wanted to smooth out the wrinkle on his forehead that he got when agitated, but instead, injected as much warmth into her voice as possible.

"Timms hauled me into his office shortly after the detective arrived to inform me my security clearance has been compromised. He showed me a picture of you, me, and those men from Germany in your apartment. Apparently, those men are part of some big-time crime family there."

"Like the Mafia?"

"Yeah, but German. Al-something or other. I was in trouble for not reporting the encounter to the NIH security team within twenty-four hours as outlined in our employee handbook."

Lena couldn't keep the astonishment out of her voice. "But how were you to know the identity of those men?"

"I have no idea, but Timms has been looking for an excuse to ding me. He has been on my case even before I started asking around about Dr. Hoffman's research. Earlier this week, he insisted I focus exclusively on viral therapy and stop talking to others in the department about matters outside that purview."

"That seems weird. Wouldn't he want you to explore all possibilities?" Lena rubbed her neck.

"You'd think that would be the case, but since I've been asking questions about working with the smallpox vaccine, which is not my bailiwick, he's gotten a little more snarly."

"You can't ask questions?"

"I know it sounds strange, but medical researchers are a prickly lot. You are definitely supposed to stay in your lane. It's all about getting there first. There are no grants for second place."

"Ouch. And I thought you had a nice safe job." Lena sipped her coffee.

Devlin laughed, the rich sound filling her heart with warmth. "Nah, we scientists live dangerous lives, don't you know? All that subterfuge over Petri dishes in the laboratory."

She smiled at the lighthearted response. Good, she'd managed to get his mind off the office break-in for a few minutes. "What happens now?"

"I'm suspended effective immediately while the security office investigates my supposed infraction."

"Suspended? As in can't go into work?"

"That's right."

"Oh, Devlin. I'm so sorry. That's awful."

"It certainly is, but it will give me time to catch up on my reading. I have a stack of medical journal articles I've been meaning to get to, and maybe I'll figure out what I want to do with my kitchen."

His attempt to make light of the situation touched her heart. "Sounds like you've got it all planned out."

"Yeah, well, it's not ideal, but it could be worse. I checked our employee handbook, and they still have to pay me part of my salary when the suspension has to do with security, so I won't starve."

"Good to know."

"I will be in desperate need of mental stimulation, so daily inter-actions with my lovely next-door neighbor will be essential to my well-being."

Delight at his obvious flirting rippled through her. "Then I shall endeavor to be accommodating."

"Seriously, Lena." He dropped his voice. "I don't know what I'd do without you."

"The feeling's mutual." Emotion clogged her throat. Clearing it, she added, "Speaking of seeing you, are we still on for dinner tonight with the Silvertons?"

"Yes, confirmed it with Henry. We'll leave around six-thirty. They live in Old Town Alexandria, so it's not far away."

"Sounds good. I think we could use some outside advice on this very curious situation."

CHAPTER

THIRTY-ONE

Tatiana hated the way smartphones intruded on every aspect of life. Hers vibrated during the Queen of the Night's aria in the first act of Mozart's *The Magic Flute*. Since only a handful of people had the number, she gathered her purse and slipped silently out of the box at the Kennedy Center. Once in the corridor, she pulled her phone out of her purse and checked the incoming text. It simply asked her to call a number.

With a sigh, she dialed the number. When the man greeted her, she snapped, "This had better be important. I'm at the opera."

"Oh, I am sorry to drag you away from a cultured evening, but you'll want to hear this, I promise you." The thread of excitement in the man's voice jerked on her nerves.

"Well?" If she had been sitting across from the man, she would have simply stared him down with a perfectly raised eyebrow. Now she had to prompt him to spill the information he was eager to tell.

"We have a location on Dr. Hoffman. Or more precisely, we know where he was around noon today."

She sucked in a breath. This was a lucky break indeed. The notebooks had been giving her fits. She needed Hoffman, and she needed him yesterday. She could feel in her bones that the notebooks held the key to bridging her research with his. Fame, fortune, and the gratitude of all mankind lay within her grasp. "Where?"

"A small town in Georgia along Highway 1."

"How did you find him?"

"Using the few known photographs of Hoffman, we've been running facial recognition software on all social media sites as well as transportation terminals."

"And?" She prompted when the man fell silent.

"We got a hit. Someone posted a video of the good doctor helping a stroke victim at a diner."

The news stopped her pacing the corridor, her every nerve on high alert as the man continued.

"The video was posted as a live Facebook feed, so it happened in real time. We, of course, didn't discover it until some hours later, but I can send you the video if you'd like to take a look."

"Yes, do that." She paused, considering. Hoffman in Georgia. "Can you tell if he was heading north or south?"

"No. We did get boots on the ground at the diner, but while people remembered Hoffman, no one recalled if he'd said where he was going or where he had come from. There are no security cameras in the parking lot to tell us what kind of vehicle he was driving or which direction he turned when he left. The only thing we can confirm is the timing of his visit."

"Stay on it and keep me posted. You can send the video to this email." She rattled off her secret email address and disconnected the call. A few seconds later, her email program dinged. Moving down the hall to the restroom, she went into a stall and shut the door. Thankfully, intermission should be at least twenty to thirty minutes away, and she had the room to herself.

The slightly grainy video sharpened as it played, the camera work a bit shaky. At first, the scene portrayed chaos with a lot of shouting and people milling about, but soon the lens focused and

Hoffman came into view, kneeling beside a prone woman, his hand at the side of her throat as if to check her pulse.

Tatiana paused the video at a close up of Hoffman's face. Still a handsome man despite the obvious signs of age. A man of decision and character. A man who held the keys to finding a cure for liver cancer through viral therapy. Her grip tightened on the phone. And a man who had betrayed both his homeland and his adopted country.

She unfroze the frame and watched the rest of the video. Hoffman displayed a level of competence. He would be found and forced to see the error of abandoning the cause for an attack of the conscious. And if he wouldn't listen to reason, she had just the weapon to make him cooperate.

~

"It's good to see you again." Dr. Henry Silverton shook Devlin's hand as he and Lena entered the home. "You must be Lena Hoffman."

"It's nice to meet you," Lena said.

Devlin helped her out of her coat, resisting the urge to wrap his arm around her shoulders and pull her close.

"Just put the coats on the rack by the door, then come on through to the living room." Violet came to the end of the short hallway, a dishtowel in her hands.

"Violet, this is Lena. Lena, Violet." Devlin performed the introductions as the two women nodded greetings at each other. After hanging up their outwear, Devlin followed Henry and Lena to the cozy living room at the back of the townhouse. A fire blazed in the hearth, and several knitted afghans draped over the back of the sofa and club chairs.

"I see Violet's put her stamp on your former bachelor quarters," Devlin said.

Henry eased into a club chair, tucking his crutches in the space between the wall and chair. "Since she already had her stamp on my heart, it made sense to allow her free reign to redecorate the townhouse."

Devlin coughed as Henry winked at him. "I see the honeymoon continues." He turned to Lena. "Henry and Violet got married six months ago, then went on a very long honeymoon. They're only now coming up for air."

Henry laughed. "What can I say? We're in love." Violet perched on the arm of his chair, and he wrapped his arm around her waist. "She's the best thing that ever happened to me."

"Hey, if you two are going to be so darn lovey-dovey, then I might have to leave," Devlin joked.

"We'll behave." Violet poked her husband in the arm. "Hadn't you better check on dinner?"

"Yes, dear." Henry's eyeroll and exaggerated agreement made everyone laugh as he rose and slipped his arms into the cuffs of his crutches. "Devlin, want to give me a hand?"

Devlin followed his host into the kitchen. He couldn't remember seeing his former professor so happy and content.

"Married life agrees with you." Devlin tried to keep the envy from his voice, but it still peeked through in his tone.

Henry clapped his shoulder before slipping his hand back onto the crutch handle. "It does. You'll get there, sooner rather than later, if I'm not mistaking the way you look at Lena."

Devlin's cheeks grew hot. "She is a most attractive woman."

Henry shot him a knowing glance. "You are already head over heels in love with her. Confess."

Devlin thought about equivocating, then decided on the truth. "Henry, I've been in love with her from a distance for a long time. Now I find myself in very deep indeed."

"Violet will be pleased. She loves a happy ending." Henry shifted his weight.

Henry directed Devlin to putting the finishing touches on the salad while he inserted the meat thermometer into roast. "Done." He pulled the pan out of the oven and placed it on a hot pad on the counter. "You've got a bit of a mystery going on, haven't you?"

Devlin dumped the sliced cucumbers into the salad bowl. "We feel like we've jumped into the middle of a play in which we don't know the actors or the plot."

"Hopefully we can figure out some things tonight. Besides getting to know your lovely Lena." Henry grinned at Devlin. "Violet? Roast is ready."

Violet appeared in the doorway. "Okay, thanks. Devlin, what would you like to drink? I have unsweetened iced tea with sweetener available, plain or sparkling water, hot tea, or coffee."

Devlin choose sparkling water, and Violet left to get Lena's drink order. Once everyone was seated and after blessing the food, Henry started passing the dishes around, and conversation filtered around the good food and various mutual acquaintances.

Near the end of the meal, Henry put down his fork. "Devlin's told me about some of the strange things that have been happening and about your connection with Dr. Hoffman. I've done some research on my own."

Devlin leaned forward. Henry had numerous connections in the former East Germany. He'd hoped Henry could uncover something vital to their understanding of what Lena's grandfather had been doing and why people cared about it years later.

Henry exchanged a look with Violet, who nodded. He cleared his throat. "What I'm about to tell you is highly sensitive information. I only found out about it because a very good friend of mine works at the Stasi archives in Berlin and because I happened to know some ex-spies who were willing to do a little digging. But given everything going on with you two, this should help fill in some of the blanks."

VIOLET HAD SUGGESTED THEY MOVE TO THE LIVING ROOM FOR THE discussion, since everyone had finished eating. As they cleared the table and put away the food, Lena tried to keep her jitters under control at the delay. Violet made everyone a hot beverage. Lena leaned against the back of the couch, Devlin close beside her. The anticipation of what Henry would reveal twisted her insides into knots.

Devlin reached over and took her hand. Lena grasped it tightly. She had a feeling what Henry would tell them wouldn't put her grandfather into a positive light. She already suspected his work in East Berlin wasn't on the up and up, given the former nurse's reaction to her questions and Dr. Shan's secrecy with the notebooks. An inkling as to why people would care today formed in the back of her mind, but she didn't want to give voice to so hideous an idea.

Henry laid out the background his Stasi contact had found. Numerous references to Dr. Hoffman and his experiments on humans in the early 1980s. The files detailed how the Stasi found subjects for his experiments according to Dr. Hoffman's specific protocols. "These files are not kept with the declassified documents, which is why your Stasi connection couldn't locate them."

Lena nodded, her heart aching as her grandfather's dark deeds came to light.

"The file related to Dr. Hoffman's disappearance had been redacted with obvious pages missing. The official conclusion of emigration and death on a ship superseded the actual investigation notes, which appeared to point to defection to the United States. In other words, to save face, the East German government said he emigrated to Argentina to cover up the fact that he actually defected to America," Henry said.

"What exactly did your grandfather do in East Germany?" Violet added another log to the fire.

Lena frowned. "I'm not sure exactly. Devlin can probably explain better."

"According to the paper Henry translated for me, I think Hoffman was experimenting with virus therapy as a treatment for liver cancer. That involves introducing a virus into the cancer cells, which cause the cancer cells to either die or make proteins that trigger a more aggressive response from the body's immune system." Devlin paused, his eyes troubled. "It appears the missing notebooks Dr. Shan had were Dr. Hoffman's clinical notes, what he jotted down as he observed what occurred during the trial."

Violet tapped her finger against the arm of her chair. "So he was experimenting on rats in the lab?"

Devlin shook his head. "I don't think he was using rats. I think he was using humans in his trials."

"I thought it was illegal to use humans in such a trials," Violet said.

"It is and it isn't. Some people want to be part of a drug trial in order to get access to potentially life-saving medicines that won't be available for everyone's use for perhaps years." Devlin sat forward, the passion for his work evident by his rapid speech. "Nowadays, it takes a very long time, sometimes a decade or more, to bring a viable drug to market. Even forty-odd years ago, there would have been safeguards in place, at least in the United States, that would have made Dr. Hoffman's experiments on humans impossible."

"Why impossible?" Dr. Silverton asked.

"This is speculation, but I think he started the trial on humans too soon in the therapy's timeline. He should have spent more time in the laboratory with animals to prove his idea that using a virus to beat cancer cells would truly work. Human trials are the last step in a drug or treatment, not the first one." Devlin settled back in his chair.

"But using humans would speed up the process, right?" Henry asked.

"Yes, potentially saving hundreds of thousands of dollars by having the drug or therapy vetted quicker," Devlin replied. "But finding a large enough pool of willing subjects isn't the only potential problem. The reason trials of this magnitude take so long is finding enough people who have liver cancer and are willing to participate."

As the others continued the discussion, bits and pieces of forgotten conversations between her mother and father filtered back into Lena's mind. Something clicked into place, and she straightened, looking first at Devlin, then the Silvertons. "I don't think he defected on his own. I think someone brought my grandfather to the United States to continue those experiments."

CHAPTER

THIRTY-TWO

Devlin stared at Lena. "You mean that some mad scientist heard about Dr. Hoffman's work and wanted him to continue experimenting on humans in the United States?"

Lena met his gaze steadily. "Not a mad scientist. The U.S. government or military or some quasi-official branch."

"That's ludicrous and fanciful thinking." Devlin thought about all the hard work he and other scientist did at the NIH with all the protocols to protect the integrity of their work. Even back in the 1980s, those structures had been in place.

Henry cleared his throat. "But we do have a rather sad history of doing just that. The Tuskegee Syphilis Experiment is one example of subterfuge being used to hide the true intent of the doctors."

Violet chimed in. "After Henry told me a bit about Dr. Hoffman and what he'd found out, I Googled around to see what else had happened in the United States in terms of unethical experiments on humans." She shuddered. "Truly awful stuff, like injecting female prisoners with viral hepatitis and deliberately infecting people with syphilis to see if penicillin worked as a treatment."

"But that's all in the past. There are more safeguards in place to prevent such things from happening again." Devlin's voice rose, but he couldn't help himself. He thought they would understand how hard he worked under safety protocols. The stress of his suspension, his feelings for Lena, and the death of his mentor pressed down on him as it seemed like his friends were questioning the ethics of his livelihood.

Lena placed a hand on his arm. "Devlin, no one is saying that you or anyone at the NIH is involved in this type of thing. I'm only saying I think it's entirely possible my grandfather was and that's why he defected to America."

"To continue his experiments on humans without their knowledge as part of some government conspiracy." Devlin couldn't stop the words from boiling over. "I work with scientists and medical researchers very closely. The red tape we have to go through just to use certain viruses in the lab is unbelievable. None of us want to jeopardize our work by cutting corners with illegal human experimentation. To hear you talk, it's like we're all rogues after the fame and glory of finding a cure and haven't a care for the patients themselves."

Lena's brows knitted together. "That's not true. You're overacting, and—"

"Maybe, but frankly, I'm not interested in discussing this any longer. Henry, Violet, thank you for dinner. Lena, let's go." His voice was harsher than he wanted, but he couldn't pull back now as anger from his encounter with Timms earlier in the day spilled over.

He strode down the hall and snatched their coats off the rack, willing Lena to hurry up and join him. Lena arrived at the front door, Violet at her heels. Without another word, Devlin handed her the coat, then shrugged into his own. With a nod to Violet, he opened the front door and stepped into the frigid January air, Lena behind him. As Violet closed the door, Lena opened her mouth but closed it when he shot her a look. He really didn't want to talk. Not now. His blood still hummed in his veins. The fear he would say something he would truly regret kept his own voice silent.

Lena didn't speak until Devlin started the car and pulled out of the driveway. "What is going on, Devlin? You were very rude to the Silvertons."

Devlin fisted his hands on the steering wheel and negotiated a turn. "Maybe it's because I'm feeling a lot of heat at the office to stop poking my nose into whatever this is and I'm starting to see the point. I'm working hard to find a cure for cancer, and I'm getting very close to a breakthrough. I can't afford to jeopardize my position at the NIH with this wild goose chase."

"That can't be the only thing you're worried about." Lena's voice had a harder edge to it than Devlin had ever heard from her, but he ploughed on, ignoring the warning note.

"Let's see. My mentor and immediate supervisor was murdered." He slammed on the brakes at a four-way stop sign intersection he nearly blew through. "The head of my division—never a fan of mine —has put me on indefinite suspense because my security clearance might have been compromised due to my involvement with you. Oh, and things have not been going well in the lab. If I don't make significant progress soon, I will find myself out of a job, all of my research for naught. Not to mention I've been shot at, nearly exploded to bits with a bomb, and had my office trashed."

Lena wilted against the seat, her eyes staring out of the passenger windshield. "I see." Her voice had dropped to a near whisper.

"No, I don't think you do." Devlin could hear the hardness in his voice, but the anger and fear that had been building up inside him needed an outlet. "You've had your mind on conspiracies from the beginning, from the first postcard which may or may not have a secret message hidden in it."

"You saw the same letters I did."

Devlin put on his blinker and pulled to a stop in a left turn lane with a red arrow. "No, I saw what you wanted me to see."

"What about the phone number? The men who came to my apartment?" Lena turned to him, her eyes blazing in the reflected streetlights.

"It was because of two of those men I nearly lost my job. Still might."

"I had nothing to do with that!"

"How could I know? You spoke German to them. I hadn't a clue what you were saying. You could have planned the entire thing to get me on your side, pull me into your sick game to find a dead man." As soon as the words left his mouth, Devlin realized he'd gone too far. A beep behind them made him focus on the green arrow.

"Is that what you really think? That I somehow created all of this drama? To what end?" She choked on the last word.

The hurt in her voice doused the last of his anger. His voice softened. "I don't know. There could be innocent explanations for everything that doesn't involve some sort of government cover-up of human experiments."

"There's a Metro stop up ahead. Please drop me off there." She had her head turned toward her door, her posture stiff and unyielding.

"Look, I'm sorry. I shouldn't have taken my anger out on you." He pulled over to the curb and slid the car into park.

"You think maybe you overreacted?" Lena gathered her bag and put her hand on the door handle.

Devlin rubbed his hand over his jaw. "Yes, I admit to overreacting."

"But you still think there's a reasonable explanation to everything that's happened"

He couldn't help nodding.

"You also think I'm somehow to blame for everything that's happened to you since we met."

He opened his mouth to refute her statement but couldn't find the words.

She gave him a long look, her eyes shadowed. "I see."

Lena stepped from the car, closing the door with more force than necessary, and disappeared into the Metro station. Devlin merged back into traffic, regret dodging every mile. How could he have let his fear and anger soil the one good thing to come out of this mess, his relationship with the most wonderful girl in the world? More importantly, how on earth was he going to fix it?

CHAPTER
THIRTY-THREE

"You have good news for me?" Tatiana didn't like the sound of hope in her voice. It had been more than twenty-four hours since Hoffman had been in that Georgia diner. The notebooks continued to elude her translation efforts. Hoffman must be found to interpret his notes.

"We haven't picked up Hoffman's trail, but his granddaughter had a fight with Dr. Mills."

Tatiana perked up. This could be very good for business. "Tell me more."

"They were seen arguing outside the King Street Metro stop in Alexandria last night. Ms. Hoffman slammed the car door when she exited Dr. Mills's car. He didn't go after her."

"Hmm. Keep tabs on both of them. And find Hoffman." She ended the call. Her source would eventually find Hoffman. The only question was would it be before Hoffman arrived at his destination. The man hadn't eluded the authorities for more than a quarter century because he was stupid. He always had a plan. Look at how neatly he'd engineered his escape from East Berlin. The precision necessary for such a successful plan had astounded her. However, his real genius lay in knowing who would be willing to pay for his expertise and how to finagle that into a nice, comfortable life for himself.

Until that fateful day in the laboratory. She was never sure exactly what had triggered the awakening of his conscious. She had been but a young girl fascinated by science. Her parents shipped her off each summer to spend time with her mother's older brother and his wife, who had been childless. Her uncle, seeing her interest in his scientific work, let her tag along to his work in a facility deep in the hills of West Virginia. There she had met Hoffman, along with a handful of other carefully picked medical researchers. She had been in awe of the German doctor, with his precise methods and harsh dismissal of anyone not able to keep up with his brilliant mind.

Tatiana smiled as she recalled the first time Hoffman had noticed her potential. When a lab assistant had injured his hand when Tatiana was a young teen, her uncle had allowed her step into his role for the summer. Soon her adeptness at handling the petri dishes and their precious content won her the respect of the other scientists, but not Hoffman.

It wouldn't be until she'd graduated from college and had a paid internship at the facility that he deigned to speak to her. That glorious summer between her undergraduate and her graduate scholastic career, Hoffman had taken her under his wing and shown her how injecting viruses directly into the bloodstream of lab rats would impact the cancers the rats had been given. Fascinated by the immune system's rejection of each virus injection, her mind raced for possible ways to get around that to allow the virus to attack the cancer cells. Maybe cloaking the virus inside another virus, sort of a double dose, would work, especially if a common cold virus hid a more virulent virus.

One day, after completing her assigned experiments, Tatiana had worked hard on figuring out how to layer the cold virus on top of the chickenpox virus she had been using. Hoffman had approached her while making his final check of the laboratory before locking up for the night.

"*Fraulein* Tatiana. What is it you are doing here so late?" Hoffman swept his eyes over her messy workstation.

"Dr. Hoffman, I, uh..." Her voice trailed off as she realized there wasn't an explanation for what she was doing in the lab after hours. She straightened her shoulders and told the truth. "I finished my assigned work. I had wondered if attaching a virus to a virus would allow the embedded virus to escape detection long enough for the inside virus to attach to a cancer cell."

He hadn't flown off the handle at her blatant disregard to protocol, but instead had gazed at her intently. "And what have you concluded?"

She smiled sheepishly. "That I should have paid more attention in biology class when they talked about cells."

That had brought a guffaw from Hoffman. "Yes, I can see where that would have been helpful. Show me what you are doing."

She did. From then on, whenever she finished her assignments, she would work on this project. Hoffman would stop by once a week to check on her progress and offer suggestions, never taking over the experiment or making her feel foolish when things didn't work out the way she had theorized. By the end of the summer, she had gained enormous knowledge of cells and how they worked, while he had been rumored to be on the cusp of a major breakthrough.

However, when she asked her uncle about Hoffman over Christmas, he had tersely told her to never mention Hoffman's name again. Her uncle also said she could no longer intern at the facility. All through medical school and into her first positions as a medical researcher, she would subtly ask about what had happened to Hoffman. It took her years of careful questioning to discover Hoffman had balked at moving the trial to the human stage and had simply vanished, taking all his research. Hoffman had shared just enough with his colleagues to keep them informed but not enough for them to duplicate the final phase of the experiments. Without that crucial information, the virus therapy he had been developing couldn't move forward. After two or three years of attempting to recreate the protocol Hoffman had developed failed, the lab had been shuttered, and the personnel scattered to other projects.

Tatiana had been both bewildered by his leaving and devastated by his betrayal. She had idolized the man, basking in his praise and soaking up his knowledge. To have him simply go without a word hurt deeply. From what she pieced together later, Hoffman could have been the one to find a new treatment that would revolutionize cancer treatments. Through the years, she had learned enough about Hoffman's past in East Berlin to find his abrupt departure strange. He hadn't any scruples when it came to his East German test subjects, but somehow, he wouldn't do the same in America.

When she'd finally clawed her way to the top of the lab food chain, she determined she would find Hoffman and demand he finish the job. For ten long years, she had been searching, hiring private investigators who would pick up his trail, only to have it go cold soon thereafter. Then a few years ago, one of the private investigators brought her news about Hoffman's family—a son and daughter-in-law and granddaughter, who had been born in the United States. The son and daughter-in-law had died in a car accident, and the granddaughter had no idea her infamous grandfather lived.

When a rumor surfaced someone had discovered documents related to Hoffman's research in East Germany, she had been elated. It had taken her months to sift through the chatter to discover Dr. Shan's possession of the very notebooks Hoffman had used to record his experiments in East Germany.

She had carefully crafted her plan, called in her favors, and schemed with those of like mind, who embraced the same vision of a cure for cancer. Now those plans were coming to fruition. She opened a desk drawer and withdrew one of the notebooks. She kept the others in a safer, off-site location. Running her fingers over the smooth cover, now mottled with age, she flipped it open, resting her palm on the page filled with Dr. Hoffman's unreadable German shorthand. The answers were within her grasp. She would stop at nothing to find them.

~

LENA FLOPPED ONTO HER COUCH, WISHING SHE'D GONE TO LUNCH WITH Belinda and other friends after church. But last night's fight with Devlin gnawed at her, making her seek the solace of her quiet condo. While she'd sketched the bare outlines of the situation to Belinda, she had no desire to answer teasing remarks about her handsome doctor friend from the others.

She checked her phone. Still no calls or texts from Devlin. Tears pulsed at the back of her eyelids. The first guy she'd really liked in a long time, gone over a silly argument. Her fingers touched her lips, remembering the feel of his mouth on hers, the shiver of desire that had spread throughout her body like molten lava flowing down a hill. She pulled up his name in her contacts, her finger hovering over the call button. He should be the one calling her. She had done nothing for which to apologize.

Then her phone rang, startling her so much she nearly dropped it. Devlin at last. With a smile, she accepted the call without registering the number. "Hello?"

"Lena? *Sind Sie das?*" The quivery tones of an elderly person greeted her instead of Devlin's strong voice.

Mentally switching gears, Lena responded, *"Ja. Tante Hilda?"* Her distant aunt usually only called on Lena's birthday and at Christmas.

"Ja. How are you?" Hilda asked politely in German.

Lena replied, her mind busy with what news could have prompted Hilda to call so soon after Christmas.

"I am moving. I do not want to do this, but my son and my doctor insist it's for the best. I am too old to live in so remote a place. Since I do not want to share my home with a stranger, I am selling the farmhouse and moving into an apartment building near my son."

"Oh, I'm sorry to hear that. I know you loved that house."

"Ja, it has been in my family for several generations. But my son has no interest in the land or the house, so sell it I must." Hilda sighed. "But that's not the only reason I am calling. I have started to

257

go through the attic to see what must go and what I should toss. I had forgotten until now all about it."

Lena frowned at the abrupt change in topics. "Forgotten about what, Aunt Hilda?"

"Your grandfather. He married my husband's sister, you know. That's how we are distantly related."

"Grandfather Mulherin?" Lena couldn't recall exactly who had married whom, only that this elderly woman had been her only living relative, given a series of only children on both sides of the family tree.

"No, my dear. Hoffman. Wolfgang Hoffman, he was a doctor. Died trying to emigrate to Argentina."

Lena's heart began to race. "What about Grandfather Hoffman?"

The old woman coughed again, a long, drawn-out affair that had Lena concerned for Hilda's health. "A few months before he left, he sent some books to us, with a note to keep them in our attic until he could collect them. Since he died, I forgot about them until last week when I came across them in a trunk along with some family photos and other mementos. Do you want them?"

Without hesitation, Lena said, "Yes."

"Good, I will send them to you when I can."

"Aunt Hilda, if I pay for the shipping, would you send them sooner? I know so little about Grandfather Hoffman that I'd be most grateful to read his old books." Lena held her breath the old woman would agree.

"*Ja, Meine Liebste.*"

Lena heard some rustling.

Then Hilda cleared her throat. "I will call you tomorrow at this time from the post office, and you can talk to the clerk about sending the package."

Lena breathed a sigh of excitement. Finally, she would hold something of her grandfather's in her hand, read books he had read and possibly notes he had made in the margins. "*Danke.* I can't thank you enough. This means so much to me."

"It's only right that I pass on to you, his only direct descendant, these items. I will go pack them now and call my son to take me to the *Deutsche Post DHL* tomorrow."

After disconnecting, Lena nearly dialed Devlin's number to share the news, but she let the phone fall to her lap instead. Maybe she should make the first move, but the hurt of his words made her hesitate. Devlin would have to be the one to contact her.

CHAPTER

THIRTY-FOUR

With a sigh, Devlin sifted through another pile of torn paper in his office. Not how he wanted to spend his Sunday afternoon. When Timms had realized the full extent of the destruction, he had demanded Devlin come into the office today to see what could be salvaged. A security guard stood guard at the door, and Devlin had had to turn in his cell phone at the security department.

Several large, black trash bags bulged with unusable material—bits of chair stuffing, binders, book pages. A trio of bins held the remains of any sensitive documents for burning. Tying off another black bag, he moved it into the hallway outside his door.

Dr. Nancy Orleans walked by, a manila envelope in her hand. Most of the staff had been called in today to check their offices, but all had been warned of his probation pending a review of his security clearance and strictly forbidden from interacting with him. She slowed as she came parallel with his doorway. "Dr. Mills." Her voice low, she slid a sly glance his way. "Fancy meeting you here when you're on administrative leave."

"Nancy, you don't usually roam these hallways." Devlin suspected she was up to something.

"Since you couldn't come to me, I had to come to you." She raised her eyebrows. "Dr. Ron Lankford pigeonholed Timms and is subjecting him to a rambling discourse on an article in the latest *American Journal of the Medical Sciences.*" She grinned. "Lankford owed me a big favor."

"I see." Devlin wasn't sure he wanted to know what she had found, but since she went to so much trouble, he might as well listen.

She cocked her head. "Yes, I think you do." She peered around him to view the half-cleaned mess in his office. "Wow, that was some kind of ruckus in there. You must have ticked somebody off."

Devlin shrugged. "If I knew who or what, I would rectify it immediately. I doubt anything will be saved, not even my books."

"That's really destructive." She studied his face for a long moment. "I'd be extra careful if I were you."

"Believe me, I am." He looked beyond her down the quiet hallway. "You'd better get moving before someone spots you talking to the outcast." He smiled to take the sting out his words.

"You still drive a maroon Kia Sportage?"

He nodded.

"Did they let you park in the employee lot?"

"Nah, I had to schlep over from the visitors' parking garage today."

"I've always wondered how quickly those fill up." She tapped the envelope against her leg in a rhythm only she could hear.

He caught on and added, "I had to drive up to the fourth deck but managed to get a spot near the middle stairs."

She started down the hallway again. "Hope you get the security snafu cleared up soon."

"Yeah, me too. Thanks for stopping by."

She waved in answer and disappeared around the corner. If he wasn't very much mistaken, that envelope would end up under the windshield wipers of his car. He only wished he could gin up some enthusiasm for what she had uncovered, but thoughts of his fight with Lena took precedence. Turning back to his office, he continued sorting through the debris while the awful things he'd said to Lena last night looped through his mind. Tying off yet another black garbage bag, he faced the truth. He'd fallen in love with Lena, and he was very much afraid he had ruined his chances with her.

WOLFGANG STARED AT HIS IMAGE IN THE VIDEO AS HE BENT OVER THE WOMAN in the diner. With a sigh, he quickly closed the video and logged out of his email. If his friend found the video, so could others. And if they pinpointed where he had been so recently, he would be found before he reached his final destination unless he took additional precautionary methods. He exited the public library and walked briskly down the sidewalk to the parking lot at the back of the large building. He always picked big city libraries because his presence would never be noticed among the hundreds of patrons who streamed in the doors. The Birmingham, Alabama, library had served his purpose well.

Those looking for him would assume he had a car, so he needed to find alternative transportation. His library search revealed a Greyhound bus station and an Amtrak train station within a block of each other. He'd have to disguise his appearance to elude the cameras now gracing nearly every transportation hub in the United States. The price of security in a post-9/11 society.

He smiled and nodded as he passed a group of middle-aged women bunched together outside a restaurant. Good thing he'd had lots of practice living under the ever-watchful eye of the Stasi and its hordes of everyday informants. Eluding cameras to ensure no one spotted his face for facial recognition software would take planning.

Pausing beside his rental, the sensation of danger jolted through his body like a lightning strike. He would ditch the car here and make his way by foot to the stations. A longer walk than he'd like, but at least January in Birmingham wasn't nearly as cold as January in East Berlin. With quick movements, he repacked essentials into a smaller overnight bag and wiped down the vehicle with a microfiber cloth. He'd worn gloves while driving and interacting with the car, but being overly cautious always paid dividends.

He'd shredded the rental agreement shortly after picking up the car, leaving the bits of paper in a McDonald's trashcan. Now he walked briskly away from the vehicle. Outside of the parking lot, he pulled his knit cap further down his forehead and ducked his head, adopting a shuffling gate. By a busy shopping mall, he dropped the car fob wrapped in a paper napkin into a trashcan before making his way to the Greyhound bus station.

Across the street, he scanned the people entering and exiting the busy building until he spotted the perfect decoy—a man near his own age. Observing the man purchase a ticket and tuck the boarding pass into the dingy overcoat pocket, he settled back to wait for his opportunity. When station's PA system ran through the next list of upcoming departures, the man headed to the restroom. Hoffman followed, keeping his head down to avoid being seen by the station's security cameras. He waited for the man to finish and casually bumped into him as the man washed his hands.

"Hey, watch where you're going!" The man shook the water from his hands as he glared at Hoffman.

"My apologies." Wolfgang smiled, then exited. Leaving the building, he checked the paper boarding pass he'd lifted. Bus number 354 heading to Knoxville, Tennessee, leaving from spot ten in six minutes. Perfect. Hoffman limped toward the bus with about two dozen people in line to board. He exaggerated his non-existent limp, wincing as he approached the front of the line. He paused as if to catch his breath, then asked the driver standing by the open door, "Is this the bus to Knoxville?"

The driver glanced his way. "Yeah, you'll need to go to the back of the line."

Wolfgang drew in a ragged breath. "Way back there?" He turned to go, his steps faltering.

He'd only moved past a couple of people when the driver called him back. "Sir?"

Wolfgang turned. "Yes?"

"Come on, you can get on board." The driver waved him back to the front of the line.

"No, no. I do not want to cut in front of these nice people who are waiting so patiently for their turn to board." Wolfgang nodded at the woman next in line with three young children in tow.

She smiled. "It's okay. Go ahead."

With a shrug and another smile, Wolfgang handed the driver his purloined boarding pass.

"Your ID?"

Wolfgang patted his pockets. "I have it right here."

One of the kids behind him began to wail, and the driver gestured for him to board. Settling into a seat near the back, he slouched down, turning up the collar of his coat to further hide his face. Five minutes later, the driver boarded, and the bus left the station. Hoffman fleetingly thought of the man whose ticket he'd stolen, but hopefully the four hundred-dollar bills he'd left in its place would compensate for the inconvenience of having his travel plans disrupted.

Late that afternoon, the bus pulled into Atlanta, where Wolfgang disembarked, then purchased a new burner cell phone from an unmanned kiosk using a prepaid credit card.

The other man picked up on the first ring. "Hello."

"There's been a change of plans. I may have been spotted, but I'm taking evasive maneuvers. I'll be out of touch for a while."

The other man grunted his acceptance. "And the girl?"

Wolfgang's heart tightened at the mention of his granddaughter. "Continue to keep an eye on her. We may have to move faster than expected."

He ended the call and slipped the phone back into his pocket as he hailed a taxi. "The train station, please."

Leaning back, a prayer for Lena's safety rose to his lips, but he quashed the impulse. He'd disregarded God his entire life, spitting on the very idea of an omnipotent being ruling the universe and judging men. Better to put his trust in science. *Where has that gotten you?* The question whispered through his mind. Down into a deep, dark pit of despair and agony with the other monsters.

His ambition most certainly killed his son and daughter-in-law, and what he had set in motion decades ago now greedily reached for his granddaughter. Shaking off the desire to throw himself on the mercy of God, Wolfgang stared out of the window. He alone had evaded the Stasi. He alone would have to be in time to save Lena as well.

CHAPTER
THIRTY-FIVE

Lena pushed back a strand of hair behind her ear and sighed. The words on the trade document kept swimming together. The legalese and pedantic nature of the document strained her patience and her eyes. A headache pulsed behind her left eye, hammers chiming in along the base of her neck, while the muscles in her shoulders contracted as if playing harmony. First she rubbed her left temple, then her neck, and finally her shoulders, but self-massage didn't work out the kinks or reduce the throbbing in her head.

Devlin still hadn't called her. It had been two days now, her phone silent as a mime. Maybe she shouldn't have pushed so hard to find out about her grandfather, but something kept pressing her forward toward the truth. Dr. Hoffman's secrets had torn her parents apart like a fourth person in their family, never acknowledged but always present.

Now the drive to uncover what had happened and why Dr. Hoffman had contacted her so cryptically filled her waking hours. Reaching into her purse, she found her homeopathic headache tabs and popped one under her tongue.

A knock at the door jolted her upright in her chair. She must have dozed off for a minute or two. Her head didn't ache as much. The person sharply rapped a second time. Lena pulled herself together. "Come in."

The door opened, and the unit admin walked in with a small box in his hand. "This came overnight from Germany."

"Thank you." Lena accepted the package with a smile. After closing her office door, Lena glanced at the return address. Aunt Hilda had overnighted the package as requested. Lena had set up an account with an international shipper to provide an easy way for Hilda to send the books to her. Not wanting to wait for airmail, Lena had recklessly splurged on overnight shipping. She didn't even want to see how much that cost her.

Open it here or wait until she went home? Curiosity got the better of her, and she sliced the tape holding the flaps closed. Inside was a small envelope and four slim books wrapped in brown paper. Hilda's shaky handwriting adorned the outside of the envelope with the words *For Lena*. Lena slit open the envelope and extracted a single piece of paper.

Liebe Lena,

As I mentioned on the phone, your grandfather, Dr. Wolfgang Hoffman, left these volumes with my husband for safe keeping. I only discovered them a week ago when cleaning out our attic. My husband had the books in a paper sack with a note that simply said: From Wolfgang Hoffman to hold until he returns. *Since your grandfather never came back for them, I am sending them to you, his only living relative. I have no idea what's in them, as my eyesight isn't what it used to be and the handwriting is very precise and small. However, I think you will find them interesting because they are a link to your grandfather.*

I will write to let you know of my new address soon.

Mit freundlichen Grüßen,

Hilda

Lena frowned. When she'd spoken to Hilda on the phone, her aunt hadn't said the books had been placed there by her husband, who had died in the early 1990s. Why had Hoffman given the books to him? Back then, there would have been closer blood relatives still living and nearer to Berlin than the farm's location. The other salient point in the letter was the allusion to the books being handwritten. On the phone, Hilda had led her to believe the volumes were part of her grandfather's library.

With trembling fingers, she tugged the first book free. She gently eased it from its brittle brown paper wrapping and rubbed her hand across the cracked leather. Opening the book slowly, she bit back a gasp as she read the neat handwriting. *Dies ist ein Tagebuch der Entdeckung. Dr. Wolfgang Hoffman. April 1981 bis Dezember 1981.*

A journal of discovery written by her grandfather? She flipped to the first entry, written in German in the same precise hand.

4 April 1981. Heute überschritt ich den Rubicon.

Lena frowned as she translated the German into English. *Today I crossed the Rubicon.* What a strange way to begin a journal. She searched her memory for why the Rubicon should have significance and came up blank. That's what Google was for. She entered *crossing the Rubicon,* then read the Wikipedia entry. The idiom 'Crossing the Rubicon' means to pass a point of no return, and refers to Julius Caesar's army's crossing of the Rubicon River (in the north of Italy) in 49 BC, which was considered an act of insurrection and treason. Julius Caesar uttered the famous phrase '*alea iacta est*'—the die is cast—as his army marched through the shallow river.

What point of no return had her grandfather crossed in 1981? She shook her head and read on, translating in her head as she skimmed the first entry.

I did so joyfully, willingly, cocooned in the rightness of my journey. One day, the world will know what I've done and applaud me for taking the courageous first step.

Pausing, she suppressed a shudder, as if a cold breeze had wafted around her. The words, written so nonchalantly, bespoke of a man who had made his decision and plunged forward, the rest of the world be damned. She skimmed, noting many unfamiliar terms, then stopped at a 6 May 1981 entry.

The boy, barely into his teens, had the hard look of a career criminal despite his tender years. He was the best patient, though, answering my questions and not even wincing when the nurse drew blood. Back in the lab, I was heartened to see his blood had high levels of AFP already. Since I had injected his liver with cancer cells, I did not need to run more tests. But to be thorough, I ordered an MRI to confirm the cancer had taken hold of his liver.

Lena's stomach churned. No wonder he spoke of crossing a point of no return. After the horror of the Nazi experiments, she couldn't believe any German government would condone such actions. Certainly, even in the 1980s, no respectable scientist would bend the rules so blatantly. Fanning the pages, she paused at a 4 December 1981 entry, one of the last in the volume.

Things are progressing better than I had dared to hope. We divided the 90 patients participating in our trial into three even groups—a control group that received no treatment except for pain medication, one that received the current recommended treatment of chemo and radiation, and one that received my new treatment. All of them developed the disease nicely. One in the control group died this morning, much quicker than I had anticipated, but we did use a particularly strong form of liver cancer to test my theory.

With a sob, she slammed the book closed and shoved it, along with the other three volumes, into her bag in the bottom drawer of her desk and locked it. She needed some fresh air, and she needed it now.

Once outside, she pulled her coat tighter around her to ward off the stiff breeze stirring mild temperatures into frigid air and took a turn around the inner courtyard of the building. Avoiding eye contact with co-workers taking a smoke break—fewer of them these days but still a core group—she sank down onto a stone bench underneath a crape myrtle tree. Her grandfather had been the worst kind of medical researcher, deliberately infecting people with a dreadful disease just to test his new treatment. Those poor people must have suffered greatly.

She pulled out her cell phone and punched up Devlin's number. Her finger hovered over the send button. To make heads or tails of the medical jargon in those journals, she would need help. Swallowing hard, she hit send, praying he would answer. Despite their argument, the longing to be safe in his arms overwhelmed her.

DEVLIN STRETCHED HIS SHOULDERS AND TURNED OFF THE TV. TWO O'CLOCK, and already he was bored out of his mind. He had spent the morning surfing his favorite websites and catching up on Twitter conversations. After lunch, he'd plopped down to watch Netflix, but after binging on several episodes of "Young Wallander," he'd grown restless.

He had his cell phone out and Lena's contact info pulled up before remembering their stormy parting two day earlier. His anger over his suspension had faded, but he couldn't stop thinking his connection to Lena had resulted in his clearance being compromised. If he hadn't been involved with her, he wouldn't have been in her apartment with those German men. He only had Lena's word for it what they said. He certainly didn't speak German.

Tossing his phone onto the coffee table, the gist of their argument resurfaced in his mind. How could she believe the United States would be so underhanded in the pursuit of a cure for cancer? Sure, shortcuts and deception happened in the past, but there were more rules and guidelines and oversight nowadays. It was just too crazy to think things like that went on in the twenty-first century. Maybe in developing countries, but not America.

"There is Nothing Like a Dame" from South Pacific pierced the air. He grabbed his phone, his heart hammering as the ring tone he'd assigned to Lena's number continued to warble. He should probably change that, but for now, the song's exuberance reminded him of Lena. "Hello?"

"Devlin, it's Lena."

The breathless quality to her voice jacked up his pulse, but he sucked in air to slow it down. "Yes?"

"I, uh, you see, there's these diaries, and a lot of medical terms, and well, I was hoping..." Her words sputtered to a halt.

He couldn't make sense of what she was saying but steeled himself against being drawn in by the utter adorableness of her confusion. It didn't sound like she was apologizing, which she needed to do. Because of her, he sat in his apartment bored out his mind. "Why are you calling?" The question cracked out before he had time to consider how it would sound to Lena.

For several seconds, she didn't reply. Then she blew out a breath. "Sorry to have bothered you. I thought..." Again her voice trailed off, and in the silence, he thought he detected a sniffle. "But my mistake. Don't worry, Dr. Mills. I won't bother you again."

"Lena." But he was too late. She had disconnected the call. Devlin slumped back against the couch cushions. *Idiot.*

The rest of the afternoon, Devlin vacillated between anger at himself for his callous behavior toward Lena and frustration with the entire situation. By four, his better self had prevailed, and he'd run to the store for dinner ingredients. By six, a pot of chili simmered on the stove and a pan of golden cornbread cooled on the counter.

He cracked open his door to listen for Lena to come home. At 6:35, he caught a glimpse of Lena's fair head as she approached her door. Stepping into the hallway, he spoke before she could disappear into her condo. "Lena?"

She froze, her key in the lock. For a moment, he feared she would turn the key and enter before he could apologize.

"I've been an utter fool." His words fell like chunks of ice to the floor. "I jumped to erroneous conclusions. I said hurtful things. In short, I was a big, colossal moron. I'm so sorry, especially for how I acted when you called today. Do you think you could find it in your heart to forgive me?"

"Just a minute." Without waiting for a reply, Lena shoved open her door, then closed it behind her.

Devlin waited, silently counting the seconds. One, two, three. Maybe she wouldn't come back out. Eight, nine, ten. Maybe she wanted to see how long he would wait for her. Thirteen, fourteen, fifteen. Maybe she had an urgent call of nature. Nineteen, twenty. At thirty seconds, he stopped marking the passage of time. When he judged she'd been gone for more than a minute, he nipped inside, leaving his door partially open, to turn off the burner under the chili.

Stepping out of the kitchen, he froze at the sight of Lena standing in the middle of his living room, a bag in her hands.

"Hi." Her soft greeting eased some of the tension from his shoulders.

"Hi." She never looked more beautiful, her golden hair in a thick braid over one shoulder, and her blue eyes sparkling. He closed the distance between them until they stood nearly toe-to-toe. "What's in the bag?" So not what he had planned to say, but his nerves got the better of him.

In response, she set it on the coffee table, then laced her fingers together. "Later." Her eyes sought his, and he gazed into their depths. "Did you mean it?"

His apology. Right. "Yes, every word." He traced the outline of her jaw with one finger, her skin as soft as he remembered. "I missed you."

"I missed you too." Her breath hitched, and she caught her bottom lip in her teeth, drawing his attention to her mouth. "I'm sorry too."

Brushing the back of his fingers across her cheek, he inched closer. "So we're good?"

"I think so." Her breath fanned his face.

"Then I can kiss you." Sliding his hand to the back of her neck, he touched his lips to her.

Her body swayed into his as her hands clasped his shoulders. Desire shot through him at her enthusiastic response. Deepening the kiss, his thoughts spiraled toward a place a single Christian guy shouldn't go. He broke the kiss and moved a few steps back, his heart pounding and his breath as ragged as if he'd run a sprint.

Lena's chest rose and fell rapidly, and her eyes had a slightly glazed look. "I'm not sure we should do that again."

"You didn't like it?" Devlin tried to interject a teasing note in his tone, but his voice came out not quite steady.

A hand to her mouth, she stared at him. "Maybe a little too much."

"Me too." Time to switch gears. "Hungry? I cooked you dinner. I hoped I would be able to convince you to eat with me."

She sniffed. "Now that I'm not distracted, something does smell delicious."

"Good thing I turned off the burner before you, we, er..." He wasn't sure what to say after their explosive kiss. "Let me get the bowls and we can eat."

"What can I do to help?" Lean trailed him to the kitchen. Within minutes, they were sitting across from each other at Devlin's small table with steaming bowls of chili and thick slabs of cornbread.

While eating, they talked about anything and everything not related to her grandfather. He told her about watching musicals with his sisters, two of whom were married and expecting their first children in the summer. "Darla's due in June, while Deborah's due in August. Mom thinks they'll both have July babies."

Lena laughed. "What, meet in the middle?"

"Something like that." He scooped the last bite from his bowl. "At least the anticipation of two grandbabies has her attention firmly fixed on my sisters and not me."

"And you're okay with that?" The teasing note in her voice brought a smile to his lips.

"Yeah, considering she had been dropping more than a few hints about my single status." Devlin wanted to smack his forehead. He hadn't meant to reveal his mother's penchant for matchmaking. "Let me clear the dishes."

"Oh, no, you don't. You're going to have to explain that." Lena's hand on his arm arrested him in his seat. "What has your mom been up to?"

He sighed. "She sends me articles about online dating sites or tries to set me up with a friend of a friend of a friend who just 'happens to be in DC this weekend.' You know, the usual gotta-get-my-bachelor-son-a-wife stuff. Never mind that I'm a grown man perfectly capable of finding my own mate."

Instead of sharing a laugh with him about his matchmaking mama, a wistful look crossed her face. "Must be nice to have a mom who cares that much."

All at once, he recalled her orphan state. "Lena, I'm sorry, I—"

"Don't worry about it. It's times like this I realize how much I missed out. Even if my parents were still alive, I doubt my mom would concern herself with finding a spouse for me." She gathered their bowls, then pushed to her feet. "You cooked, so that means I'm on kitchen duty."

Devlin started to protest but caught a sheen of moisture in her eyes. He'd let her recover her composure over the kitchen sink, then they could discuss their next steps. Maybe he should send his mom a text to say she could stop trying to set up her bachelor son. He'd manage to find someone all on his own.

CHAPTER

THIRTY-SIX

By nine a.m. on Tuesday, the entire condo building had emptied as residents left for work, leaving Devlin in a cocoon of silence. Lena's revelation last night about her grandfather deliberately infecting people with liver cancer in order to test his theory that viral therapy would cure them both horrified and fascinated him. She'd translated a few passages from the first diary with his assistance on the medical terms. His scientific mind raced with the possibilities Hoffman's audacity had unleashed. Combined with Hoffman's article about the promising early results, Devlin considered tweaks to his own research.

Lena had promised to return after work tonight to decode more of the diaries. Since Devlin had no knowledge of German, he didn't ask her to leave them with him. He spent a good portion of the morning reading the Psalms and praying for wisdom and strength. Wisdom to know how to proceed and strength to resist the lure of using Hoffman's research to bolster his own.

At eleven-thirty, he drained his third cup of coffee and debated a run before lunch. The fickle Virginia weather had decided to warm up to the low fifties with clear skies, although meteorologists were already salivating about the possibility of snow by Saturday. Changing into his running gear, he slipped his phone into an arm band and adjusted his wireless earbuds. Picking a 1980s rock station on Spotify, he yanked open his door and nearly plowed into a woman standing in front of it, her hand raised as if to knock.

"Dr. Mills?" The woman's voice sounded familiar, but he couldn't place it.

After he stopped the music, he leaned against the door jam, his left foot keeping his door open. "Yes."

A smile crossed the woman's lips. Auburn hair cut in a bob drew attention to her green eyes sparkling with intelligence. "I'm Dr. Tatiana Dern."

Devlin gaped. "What are you doing here?" His rude question barely registered as his mind scrambled to find the meaning of why such an imminent medical researcher would come to his condo. "How did you know my home address?"

"May I come in?" She took a step toward him.

He stood his ground, crossing his arms across his chest. "Not until you answer my questions."

For a few seconds, she regarded him. "Fair enough. I want to talk to you about your viral therapy research. You weren't hard to find."

"I told you earlier I wasn't going to discuss my work with anyone outside of NIH."

She shifted her feet. "But you're no longer working at NIH."

His eyes narrowed as he considered which one of his colleagues had spilled the beans about his suspension. "That doesn't negate my obligation to NIH in relation to my work there. If that's why you came, then you might as well leave." He pulled his door closed behind him, forcing Dern to take a step back into the hallway.

When she didn't say anything else, he moved around her and headed for the outside door when she spoke to his back.

"I have the notebooks."

TATIANA HAD BEEN GOING TO SLOWLY REVEAL THIS FACT TO DR. MILLS ONCE she had extracted more information about Mills' own experiments, but she hadn't counted on his integrity. His suspension should have made him angry enough to be indiscrete, especially with a senior scientist of her caliber. But instead, he'd held fast. She had seen the implacable look in his eyes and had known all the usual inducements would not work on this man.

Her words stopped him in his tracks, but he didn't turn around. Tamping down her delight in grabbing his full attention, she slowly reeled him in. "Yes, the very notebooks Dr. Shan had in his office."

He faced her, his expression closed. "Did you murder him?"

She widened her eyes. "No, of course not."

"Then how did you get the notebooks?"

"Dr. Shan gave them to me." True as far as it went. He had given them to her emissary in a vain attempt to hang onto his own life. When he didn't respond, she lowered her voice. "He wanted help in deciphering what Dr. Hoffman had written."

Mills came closer.

"Hoffman had been working on a new drug that would cure, not just fight, cancer." Tatiana couldn't keep the excitement from her voice. "Imagine the hope that would bring to millions of people."

"Why come to me? I'm a lowly researcher working on the same thing as dozens of other researchers across the country."

Because you're the boyfriend of Hoffman's granddaughter, and I think she might be able to decipher the notebooks or help me get to Hoffman. But she couldn't tell him that, so she settled on the partial truth. "Because Dr. Shan was your mentor."

"And you think that means I can decipher the notebooks."

His words sent a shockwave through her. She hadn't mentioned not being able to figure out what the notebooks contained. Dr. Shan must have shown them to his protégé. She slipped the notebook she'd brought out of her bag. Holding it up, she asked, "Can you?"

Before he could answer, the outer door opened. Two burly men in wool dress coats entered, followed by a third man. The first two men stationed themselves on either side of the door while the third man paused in front of Mills.

"Dr. Mills, we meet again." A slight accent made the words sound menacing. "Why am I not surprised? Join Dr. Dern."

The gun in the speaker's hand must have convinced Mills to obey because the young doctor crowded next to Tatiana in the small space at the back of the hallway near a trio of doors leading to his own apartment and two others. Her heart beat faster as the man came closer.

"Dr. Dern, the notebook if you please." He held out his other hand, the gun pointed at her now.

She gripped the notebook. She'd only brought one, but she didn't want to give it up, not until she knew its secrets.

The man sighed, then jerked his head toward her. One of the men walked swiftly from his post by the outer door and paused in front of Tatiana.

"The notebook?" The first man's tone was as implacable as granite.

Tatiana glanced down but still couldn't bring herself to hand it over. The blow to the side of her head caught her off guard, slamming her body into Mills's front door.

"Hey!" Mills cried out.

Vaguely, she heard the grunts and sounds of fists connecting with flesh, then the fight was over. The man had Mills pinned against a door, his arm twisted up behind him. Blood dripped from Mills's nose.

As Tatiana regained her feet, she noted the man holding Mills had a busted lip. Straightening, her own head swam, and she blinked to bring the world back in focus.

"I will not ask a third time." The man snatched the book from her hand, then slapped her face hard, throwing her against the wall a second time. "Where are the others?"

"I don't know." She managed to get the words out, her hand on her stinging cheek.

Snapping a command in German, the second man grabbed her bag and dumped the contents on the floor. Lipstick, hand lotion, wallet, smartphone, keys, and other objects bounced on the carpet. The speaker grabbed a fistful of her collar, yanking her close. "Give me the notebooks. I will not ask again."

She banked the fear rising in her gut at the hard expression in the man's eyes, but she wouldn't hand over her future so easily.

Then he smiled, loosening his grip slightly. "Let's take a trip to your lab."

Her heart stuttered, fear leaping into her throat, making it hard to breath.

"Ah, yes. Your precious lab." The man said over his shoulder, "*Ins Labor und bringen Sie den Arzt.*"

She recognized the German language from hearing Dr. Hoffman mutter to himself around the lab, but not the meaning. The man holding Dr. Mills frog-marched the doctor to the door, which the third man opened.

"After you, Dr. Dern." Her captor waved his arm as if escorting her to a black-tie event. He pocketed the gun as they circled the building and moved through a gate to a waiting SUV idling in the parking lot of the adjacent apartment building.

The two henchmen bracketed Tatiana and Dr. Mills in the back seat. The tight fit pressed one of the men against her right shoulder and Mills against her left. Tatiana gazed at Mills, noting the bruise darkening his left temple. "Are you okay?"

Mills nodded.

She lowered her voice. "What did he mean by meeting you again?"

"No talking," the leader snapped from the passenger seat. He murmured something in German to the driver, who put the vehicle in gear.

Frustration vied with concern as the SUV sped away. Questions swirled around her mind, but one kept rising to the surface. What would happen when they got to the lab?

~

WOLFGANG STARED OUT AT THE PASSING SCENERY AS THE TRAIN CHUGGED ITS way through the countryside. He never tired of viewing America's vastness, so open and big compared to the cramped existence he'd once lived behind the Iron Curtain. Then, his world had been reduced to three or four city blocks—Charité, where he worked, and the drab apartment building where he lived with Ida. Giving in to the need to see her face, he opened his wallet and extracted the only picture he had left of her. The radiance shining from the faded photo strengthened his resolve. He would end this. He would finally be free to get to know his granddaughter. The truth had been buried for too many years.

But his success was not guaranteed. Failure loomed on the horizon. A prayer spilled over his lips before he could stop the words. *God, help me to put this right.* He had no right to pray, no right to ask the God of the universe for anything. Not after what he'd done. But maybe God would answer such a prayer, given it wasn't for him but for Lena. His life had been over when he stepped across the Rubicon and injected a young man with liver cancer.

A buzzing yanked him out of the past. He frowned as he checked the disposable cell. An unfamiliar number blinked on the screen. Wrong number, most likely. The way the phone company recycled numbers, it was a wonder he didn't get more of them on the various burner phones he'd had over the years.

The phone pinged, indicated the caller left a message. Probably a hang up recording, but Wolfgang accessed the message anyway.

"We have a problem." The caller didn't bother identifying himself. "Members of the Al-Zein Clan have kidnapped Dr. Mills and Dr. Dern. I'm following them. It's possible they're headed for Dern's lab."

Wolfgang deleted the short message, his mind whirring with possibilities. Tapping the phone against his leg, he considered and discarded half a dozen responses before circling back to the first one. Call General Pettigrew.

The general answered on the first ring. "Pettigrew."

Without identifying himself, Wolfgang relayed the message he'd been given.

For a moment, Pettigrew said nothing. "Your information is reliable?"

"Yes." The man keeping an eye on Mills had been one of the best Stasi agents until Wolfgang had managed to convince him that freedom awaited him in America.

"Thank you for letting me know." Pettigrew disconnected.

Wolfgang itched to call back and demand to know what Pettigrew would do with the information, but resisted. Already, he'd taken a risk calling the general, even with a burner phone. He phoned his contact back.

"What's the status of the package?"

"We're on the Dulles Toll Road, heading towards Leesburg."

"How much farther to the delivery point?"

"Probably forty minutes."

"Keep me posted." Wolfgang stared out at the Alabama countryside as the train huffed into Tuscaloosa. He would need to accelerate his timetable if he wanted to keep Lena safe. Pulling out a tablet, he accessed flight information from New Orleans. The urge to pray that a dead man hadn't been put on the no-fly list rose to his lips. This time, he consciously gave in to the impulse. *Dear God, please let me get to my final destination safely. Watch over Lena and Dr. Mills.*

THE BUTZEMANN SLAMMED HIS FIST DOWN, JOUNCING A DELICATE paperweight onto the carpeted floor. He should have known hiring the Al-Zein Clan to recover the notebooks would be risky, but kidnapping Dern and Mills hadn't been part of the bargain. His operations ran with precision, every contingency checked and rechecked.

The men assured him the transfer to the vehicle had gone unremarked and that they would have the notebooks in hand shortly. The Butzemann drew in a deep breath, letting it out slowly. His heart rate had settled back to its normal rhythm by the time his assistant buzzed to remind him about a meeting starting in five minutes.

He acknowledged the reminder, then picked up the paperweight from the floor. When his vice presidents of marketing, and research and development came into his office, he had regained his legendary composure.

"Mr. Doty, Dr. Whitman." He nodded to each as they sat in the chairs facing his massive desk. "I hope you have good news for me."

His subordinates exchanged glances before Dr. Whitman took the lead. "We had to stop the trial at Phase 3."

The Butzemann narrowed his eyes. "What happened?"

The doctor's fingers tugged at his busy eyebrows, a nervous habit that grated on the Butzemann's nerves. "While participants in Phase 2 had relatively low incidents of side effects, more participants in Phase 3 developed side effects, which included a higher percentage of adverse effects."

Doty sat straight in his chair. "Six people have died, and ten have been hospitalized with severe reactions to the drug. That was after only one of the three proscribed doses."

The Butzemann didn't respond for a full minute, slowly counting out the seconds to avoid exploding at these numbskulls. "That's still a very low percentage of the trial participants, isn't it?"

"If that was all that had happened, maybe we could press on, since our sample pool was quite large, as you point out," Whitman said. "But one of the participants who died made social media videos of her participation in the trial and posted only minutes before her death."

"Why didn't you find out about these videos before now?" The Butzemann turned his steely gaze on Doty.

"We, uh, had a lot of people to monitor," the VP of marketing stammered.

"And yet you couldn't manage to find the one person whose postings would do the most damage to this company." The Butzemann dropped his voice to a near whisper.

Doty blinked rapidly. "The participant posted the videos on her sister's social media sites. We couldn't have known she would be that sneaky."

"You know how much money we have spent developing this particular drug? Billions. Your sole job once Dr. Whitman started these trials was to ensure we didn't get any bad publicity. And you failed." The Butzemann buzzed his assistant. "Have security escort Doty from the building. He no longer works here."

Doty rose, anger splotching his face red. "I've worked here for twenty years. I know—"

"I suggest you read your employment contract very carefully before you threaten me," the Butzemann said softly. "You wouldn't want to jeopardize your exit package with scurrilous accusations."

Doty opened and closed his mouth like a fish gasping for air, then stalked from the room, slamming the office door behind him. The Butzemann allowed himself a brief smile before turning his attention to the medical researcher. "Now tell me why you think the drug triggered such reactions."

CHAPTER

THIRTY-SEVEN

Devlin gaped at the state-of-the-art, level 3 biosecure lab tucked inside a nondescript warehouse near the Virginia-West Virginia border close to the town of Wilson Gap, Virginia. Guarded on the perimeter by men and women in combat fatigues and automatic weapons, the lab had several checkpoints. Dr. Dern's presence guaranteed entry onto the facility grounds. Entry into the building had been relatively easy, but Dern used her handprint to unlock the other door to the lab, then a retinal scan to go deeper into the building.

The closer to her lab she got, the straighter Dern stood, her movements surer. No one had questioned her entrance with an entourage of four strange men in tow.

"I must admit that I'm impressed, Dr. Dern," the leader said, his gun hidden in a hip holster. He gestured toward the glass walls from the second-story office area, which provided a birds-eye view of the scientists and lab assistants bent over petri dishes and microscopes. With their biohazard gear on, Devlin couldn't decipher gender but counted at least thirty people working as well as several rooms with cages of mice, hamsters, and monkeys. "This is quite a set up. And so secretive. Are you only working on viral therapy?"

Dern raised her perfectly plucked eyebrows—his sisters would be envious of their symmetrical shape—before replying. "That's my area of focus. Others are working on vaccines for variations of COVID-19 and other viruses, while some even work on quicker responses to potential biowarfare attacks."

Devlin tried to catch her eye as she continued to outline what went on in this secret lab. Surely she shouldn't freely share what must amount to state secrets with these men, who had ties to the German mob.

One of the men snapped something in German, and the leader held up his hand. "That's enough for now, doctor. Hand over the notebooks, and we'll be on our way."

"No." Dern crossed her arms, her gaze steely.

Devlin couldn't believe her reaction.

The leader didn't even blink at her rebellion. "I know you think those stalwart young men and women with their M4 carbines will race to your rescue, but they're out there and we're in here." He nodded toward the windows. "Your colleagues down there won't notice anything's wrong until you and Dr. Mills are dead."

"Then it's a good thing we're here, isn't it?" Venedict Calkins stepped into the room, a handgun aimed at the leader. Entering behind him, Homeland Security Agent Enno Kurimsky had his weapon raised too. Several more men dressed in dark suits and grim expressions stationed themselves on either side of the door, their guns on display.

"Put the gun down slowly and raise your hands," Calkins directed.

The leader complied, as did his two accomplices. Agents patted down the trio, extracting weapons. Within minutes, the three Germans had been handcuffed and led from the room, leaving only Calkins and Kurimsky with Devlin and Dern.

The two Homeland Security agents holstered their weapons.

Devlin sagged against the wall, relief pouring over him at the denouement of a very sticky situation. Beside him, Dern moved as if to follow the men from the room.

"Dr. Dern, a moment if you will." Calkins's voice cracked through the room. Dern jolted to a stop.

Calkins came closer to her. "The notebooks."

Her mouth firmed into a thin line. "I don't know what you're talking about."

Calkins sighed. "Arrest her."

Kurimsky spun the doctor around and yanked her arms behind her back, handcuffs in his hand.

"You can't arrest me!" Dern struggled but the agent had her cuffed within seconds. "I haven't done anything—"

"Wrong?" Calkins inserted. "My dear doctor, you most certainly have broken quite a few laws in your quest for glory." He flicked a glance at Devlin, then back to Dern. "But we don't have to air your dirty laundry here. Now do we have to ransack your office, or will you hand them over nicely?"

Her flushed face and snapping eyes told Devlin the doctor would have slapped Calkins if her hands had been free. Instead, she spat out, "There's a safe behind the molecule picture."

Calkins removed the indicated frame, revealing a wall safe. He studied it for a couple of seconds. "Uncuff her."

Kurimsky did so. Dern rubbed her wrists, her eyes darting toward the door. "Don't even think about it," the agent growled.

"Come here and lend me a hand, Dr. Dern," Calkins demanded.

For a second, Devlin thought she would refuse, then she shrugged and crossed to where the agent stood in front of the safe. Calkins stepped to the side, and she raised her palm, placing it on the screen. At an audible click, she dropped her hand.

Calkins opened the safe. From his position a few feet away, Devlin spotted a stack of notebooks. The agent grabbed them and put them on a nearby desk. Running his fingers along the spines, he frowned. "Are there any more?"

Dern shrugged. "You'll find one in the SUV we arrived in."

"Eleven notebooks?" Calkins pressed.

"How should I know? I figured these were all there was."

Devlin willed himself not to blink or give away that a twelfth notebook was squirreled away in his apartment behind baking supplies.

"We're done here." Calkins gathered the notebooks. He seemed to note Devlin for the first time. "We'll have someone take you to a clinic to get that nose looked at, then home."

In the excitement, Devlin had nearly forgotten his injury, but at the agent's words, his nose began to throb. "Sure. What will happen to the men who kidnapped us?"

"You don't need to worry about them," Calkins said.

Kurimsky nodded toward the door. "This way, Dr. Mills."

Devlin exited the room, Kurimsky at his heels, assuming Calkins and Dern would follow, but the other pair stayed in the room. Kurimsky directed him to a navy-blue SUV. "Let's get you fixed up and back home."

Devlin leaned his head against the seat and closed his eyes. The strange events of the morning replayed through his mind. His stomach growled, reminding him lunch had come and gone. That three men from the German mafia had tried to get the Hoffman notebooks meant Lena had likely been right about her grandfather being involved in something so despicable, people were desperate to keep it from coming to light years later.

Tatiana's control slipped a notch as the door closed behind Mills and Kurimsky. He couldn't take the notebooks, not until she'd had a chance to decode their secrets. "Give me the notebooks."

Calkins laughed. "Come on, now, Dr. Dern. It's a matter of national security."

His words brought the picture into focus. She'd been such a fool. "His work."

"Whose work?" A wariness entered Calkins's eyes.

Tatiana clapped her hands together as memories surfaced from her time spent in Hoffman's lab as a student. "Of course. The trips, the lab work. It wasn't a continuation of what he did behind the Iron Curtain. It was a different project altogether." She laid a hand on the top notebook. "If the contents of these notebooks became public knowledge, more people might start digging into what Hoffman did in America."

"I would be very careful about what you say," Calkins warned. "You wouldn't want your career besmirched by scandal at this crucial stage."

Power surged through her at his words, which confirmed her suspicions. Finally, she had the upper hand. "You can talk about national security all you want, but you have no idea who you're dealing with. I'm not just some two-bit scientist toiling away on a cure for cancer."

"You're delusional." He picked up the notebooks. "Let's go."

Crossing her arms, she shook her head. "I think I'll stay and catch up on some paperwork." She cocked her head. "In fact, I think it's time you left. This is my lab, and you're trespassing."

Calkins shrugged. "Suit yourself."

She paced the office for ten minutes after his departure, then confirmed with the security office all agents had left the premises. Pulling out a burner cell from her stash in the safe's false bottom—which Calkins had neglected to search thoroughly once he had the notebooks—she dialed a familiar number.

"They took the notebooks."

The Butzemann cursed. "How did this happen?"

Tatiana relayed the events of the morning.

"Did you make a copy?"

The question irked her, as if she wouldn't have thought of that on her own. "I tried with one notebook, but the pages were too thin.

The copier picked up both the front and back sides of the paper, rendering the copy useless. Scanning and photographing were marginally better but still not readable."

"That is indeed unfortunate."

The understatement of the year. "However, I think Mills has one of the notebooks."

"What makes you think that?"

"He wasn't surprised to see I had one. I was watching him when Calkins asked if these were all the notebooks I had." She had caught a glimpse of indecision in the young doctor's eyes before he'd dropped his gaze to the floor. "So maybe we can—"

"I'm beginning to think you've oversold yourself as a scientist." His cold voice sliced over her words. "You assured me you were very, very close to making viral therapy a success, along with the development of a drug that would deliver the therapy to patients."

She bit her lip to avoid interrupting him with excuses as to why three years later, she had yet to deliver on her promises.

"I built you the state-of-the-art biosecure lab you requested. Allowed you free rein to staff it with loyal people. Provided security and a blank check."

All that and more he had done, but she had never forgotten the very strong string attached to his largess.

"Yet still this revolutionary therapy is a phantom, a wisp without solid form." His voice dropped softer.

Tatiana pressed the phone closer to her ear.

"I've now concluded the student will not outshine her teacher."

Her forehead and cheeks flushed with sweat, and her heart thumped quicker. If he pulled the plug on her lab, all her work would be for nothing.

"I will give you one last chance to redeem yourself. You have by the end of the week to bring Hoffman in." His voice conveyed she didn't want to find out what would happen if she failed.

He disconnected before she could respond. Absently, she removed the SIM card from the burner phone and dropped it into the shredder. She had three days. Plenty of time to put her escape plan into motion. He might think he had backed her into a corner, but he had severely underestimated her commitment to her work. She'd sacrificed her marriage and children to finding a cure for cancer. If it was all for naught, she was going to take him down with her.

THIRTY-EIGHT

Devlin pushed open his apartment door, weariness permeating every cell in his body. The clinic doctor had declared his nose broken, adjusted it into place, then slapped a piece of tape over it.

Something crinkled under his foot. He picked up the brown envelope, wincing as the downward movement brought blood rushing to his injured nose.

A sticky note clung to the outside. *Wanted to leave this on your car Sunday, but security walked me out that day. Stay safe. Nancy*

His stomach growled. Time for some Sustenance. Minutes later, sitting at the table with a plate of scrambled eggs and toast, he pulled out several sheets of paper from the envelope. The top one had the banner of a newspaper called the *Hooper Bay Advertiser*. Squinting, he made out the date of October 12, 1989.

Deaths Grieve Small Community

HOOPER BAY, Alaska – Malaya Tiktak has lived through many hardships in her nearly 90 years, but none have hit her as hard as the recent death of her grandson, Eli Nilgak. "He was such a good boy, always trying to provide for our family," she said. "Now he's dead, like so many others."

Nilgak died 10 days ago. "*The doctors, they said he had many, many tumors,*" *his grandmother said.* "*But not one can say how he got those tumors.*"

Tiktak listed seven other villagers—all of them in their twenties—who have died recently of similar tumors, sending this small town of less than 700 souls into profound grief. "*We all know each other, take care of each other,*" *said Mayor William Anghik.* "*It's such a shame these young men and women died before their time.*"

Devlin skimmed the middle of the article, which talked with other families of the dead. He started to set the paper aside when the last couple of paragraphs snagged his attention.

"I know what happened to them," Tiktak said, "but no one wants to listen to an old woman. It was that hush-hush study they participated in four years ago. That's what gave them the cancer."

Mayor Anghik laughed off Tiktak's assertion a secret study had sickened the young people. "Is it hard to explain why eight seemingly healthy young people died so close together? Not really, if you look at the cause of death for each one." He ticked off the list—tumors, lung cancer ("kid smoked like a chimney"), blood clot, childbirth, brain aneurysm, heart disease, stroke, and liver cancer. "For Ms. Tiktak to try to pin these deaths on BarosJanus Pharmaceutical is simply an old woman grasping at straws."

Devlin put the paper down and cleared his dishes, his mind whirring. Tiktak called the study "hush-hush," and the mayor had been quick to disavow any connection to BarosJanus Pharmaceutical. But so many deaths from so small a population with a connection to a medical study definitely bore more scrutiny.

He returned to the table to read the next paper, which listed company names, none of which were familiar until he got to the bottom. BarosJanus Pharmaceutical. Then he began to carefully read from the bottom up and realized it traced ownership of BarosJanus Pharmaceutical through a series of companies. The company at the top, Schaffung BJP, tickled his memory. Pulling out his phone, he Googled it.

Schaffung BJP was an international company with offices in New York City, Washington DC, London, Berlin, and Hong Kong. Drilling down into the About page, he managed to glean the company had its fingers in a lot of pies. Following additional links didn't bring clarity until he found an article in the *Washington Post* business section from two years ago that profiled the head of Schaffung BJP, Gideon Barclay, who mentioned the company had U.S. Department of Defense contracts.

Devlin grabbed his laptop and found a website listing all the Department of Defense contracts. Sure enough, Schaffung BJP had one to supply vaccinations to the U.S. military as well as to provide assistance countering biowarfare. To his limited knowledge, it appeared to be a fairly standard pharmaceutical defense contract. But, as they say, the devil was in the details. He'd be willing to bet his paycheck Dr. Dern's lab was connected to that contract, given the soldier guards. How Hoffman's research into liver cancer tied in, he hadn't figured out. But the puzzle pieces were beginning to form an ugly picture.

"You could have been killed, Devlin." Lena tucked empty takeout containers into a trash bag after dinner in his apartment again. She covered his hand with hers. "I'm so glad you weren't."

"Me too." He squeezed her hand.

"Does it hurt?" She pointed to his nose.

"A little. Ibuprofen is taking the edge off. The doctor said it would feel better tomorrow, but I'll look like I've been in a fight." He shrugged. "Good thing I'm on suspension, so I won't have to answer a lot of questions about what happened."

After putting the bag in his kitchen trashcan, she returned to the living room and slipped off her shoes. Tucking her feet underneath her, she settled into the couch beside him. "I'm so sorry you got dragged into this mess."

"I'm not."

The tender look in his eyes brought tears to her own. "But you've been shot at, punched in the face, and—"

He stopped the flow of words with a finger on her lips. "Shh." Leaning closer, he replaced his finger with his mouth.

With a sigh, she welcomed the kiss, glad to not think about what might have happened to Devlin for a few minutes. Instead, she reveled in the feel of his lips on hers, the strength of his shoulders under her hands, the heat of his body close to hers. Ending the kiss, he rested his forehead against hers.

"Lena, if those things hadn't happened, we might not have gotten the courage to speak to each other."

"I know." She pulled back, sliding her hands down his arms until she held his hands. "We've learned a lot of information, but we're no closer to figuring out who is behind the attacks."

"Agent Kurimsky said he would let us know if the Germans revealed anything, but they'll probably claim diplomatic immunity and get shipped back to their country without saying anything." He sighed. "I might have a different lead we can pursue. One of my colleagues slipped this under my door when I was out."

Lena released his hands as he reached for a brown envelope on the coffee table. Handing it to her, she removed two pieces of paper. "What's this?"

"One's a newspaper article. Read that first."

She placed the photocopied article on top and read the front-page story, "Deaths Grieve Small Community" from 1989. After finishing the piece, she contemplated how these pieces fit with the other info they'd gathered.

"What do you think?"

"I think it might explain what my grandfather was talking about in his journal." Her throat clogged as images of some of those words flashed across her mind, trapping the awful words inside her. How could her grandfather have been such a monster? Her eyes slid closed as she fought to retain her composure.

"Lena? Are you okay?"

Devlin's soft question brought her back to the present. She looked into his eyes, so warm and caring. He was a scientist with integrity, one who followed the rules even though it might mean taking a longer time to find the answers. She drew strength from him, knowing he wouldn't judge her because of the actions of a relative she never knew.

"It's hard to believe my grandfather experimented on human beings. He called it Operation Red Shoes."

"Last night, I read through most of the last one, where he began to have an attack of conscience." She exhaled. "He was being pressured to produce more results faster to bring glory to the regime for finding a cure for liver cancer. At first, the patients were criminals, those who had been convicted of violent crime like murder and rape, and sentenced to death. He convinced himself he gave them a chance to contribute something good to society before they died. But later, his patients were ordinary citizens targeted by the Stasi for crimes against the state."

"Which, as Henry told us, could have been as little as speaking out against a law or politician," Devlin added.

"I think he lost a couple of those patients, a very young husband and wife, who had been caught trying to escape East Berlin." She remembered the faint water marks on the page where he recorded their deaths. Had the great Dr. Hoffman shed tears over their loss? "Then he made contact with someone in the West who promised him a new life to continue his work."

"Did he name the source?"

She shook his head. "He only said, 'My Western friend.' But this person arranged for my grandfather to disappear."

"You think he has something to do with those cancer deaths in Alaska?"

Lena forced herself to answer honestly. "Yes, I do."

CHAPTER
THIRTY-NINE

Wolfgang ignored the argument by his next-door neighbors in the modest motel a few blocks from the Amtrak train station in Newton, Kansas. The slow journey via Greyhound bus and train had been long but safe. No one paid attention to an elderly man who kept to himself. The night clerk had given him a corner room on the ground floor of the two-story building, barely even glancing at his ID when Wolfgang paid for the room in cash.

Wolfgang slipped off his shoes, then set the room's digital alarm clock to wake him at six a.m. Awakening three hours later, he quickly showered and dressed in the same set of clothing. No matter. It would help to make him even more invisible to passersby.

Time to call an old friend. Picking up the burner phone he'd purchased along his journey, he dialed.

"Weißt du wie spät es ist?" Felicity Mayer sounded as annoyed by a middle-of-the-night phone call as she had of any request he'd made when she was his nurse. At least his friend had kept his promise to slip Felicity the prepaid phone.

"Es ist immer ein guter Zeitpunkt, um ein falsches zu korrigieren, ja?"

He was asking her to break her silence. But it was past time to right the wrong they'd both been complicit in, and he was banking she wouldn't want to die with their collective past sins on her conscience.

"*Ja.*" She paused, then added, "Your granddaughter called me."

"How—?" Then he bit off the rest of the question. How didn't matter.

"I told her nothing."

Relief turned his bones into gelatin, and he sagged against the headboard. "Good."

"But someone knew—or suspected—she'd called."

Felicity had always been the first to know when the Stasi were sniffing around the lab or one of the staff. Apparently age hadn't diminished that ability. "Why do you say that?"

"Someone added over-the-counter antihistamines to my medicines. Mixed with my current medications of tolterodine and spironolactone, those pills would trigger dementia symptoms these incompetent doctors would chalk up to old age." She chuckled. "Of course, I tricked them into thinking I took the new pills but instead checked them in the pharmacy to verify my suspicions."

Despite this fresh evidence of someone tying up loose ends, he smiled at the strength in her voice. Felicity Mayer had been the best nurse he'd ever worked with, better than some of the doctors even. Her passion for finding a cure for liver cancer had been instrumental in pushing him to cross into unethical territory.

"They should have remembered your nickname," he told her now. "*Die Stahlkrankenschwester.*"

"No one's called me the Steel Nurse in ages," she said. "I'd quite forgotten about that." She fell silent, perhaps as lost in the past as he was.

Clearing his throat, he brought the conversation back to the present. "I have been thinking a lot about the old days. There are some who want to remember in order to learn from our work."

"To save the suffering, like you and I did."

How noble they made it sound, when in reality, at least for him, it had been to bring glory to himself for his brilliance and his courage to do what so many refused. "Perhaps, but there are more who want to keep what I did in the dark forever."

She didn't reply immediately, then a soft sigh emanated over the phone. "Do you know why I helped you so faithfully and have kept quiet about it ever since?"

Shame heated his cheeks at the rebuke in her voice because he never asked. Not once during their years working together. "No."

"My son."

The words shocked him. He hadn't even realized she had been married, much less a mother. "I didn't know you have a son."

"I never told, and you never asked. The great man, only focused on his work, no time for chitchat—that's what the Americans say, *ja?*"

She described him perfectly, exactly the kind of arrogant monster he had been.

"But I would have told you nothing had you asked, because I couldn't share him with anyone. David died at fourteen from liver cancer, well before I worked with you."

"He's why you joined me?"

"*Ja.* I never wanted another boy, another mother, to suffer like we did. And those boys who were part of the program, they were *der grobianers*. David's life was worth ten of those delinquents."

A lifetime of pain gave her words poignancy, giving him belated insight into her almost fanatical approval of his plans. "David's father?"

"The Berlin Wall separated us when I was pregnant with David. He worked in the Western sector and got caught there when they closed the border."

So many families had been torn apart during that tumultuous time. "I'm sorry."

"What's done is done. All this reminiscing is not why you called me in the middle of the night."

"No." Gathering his thoughts, he squared his shoulders. *"Es ist an der Zeit, dies zu beenden."*

"Are you sure? Once we set this in motion, it cannot be undone."

The gentle warning in her voice only firmed his resolve. "Yes, the time has come to end this," he repeated. "You know what to do?"

"Ja. I will call the Bild reporter immediately. I do not think he will object to losing sleep."

"Probably not." He grimaced. "I never told you how much your support meant to me, nor how sorry I was to have left the way I did."

"It is all *wasser unter der Brücke.*"

How kind of her to say it was all water under the bridge when he knew his actions had caused Felicity to suffer.

"But you are right. It is time to tell the world what we did."

"And you'll be okay?"

"A little late to ask me that, yes?"

The amusement in her voice made him wince. He should have asked her permission, not told her his plans. Had he learned nothing in his years of exile from his homeland? "I'm sorry. I should have—"

"Nein! I am not ashamed of what we did. It was necessary, and it would have succeeded if you had had more time. Your work, our work, is a gift to humanity, and should be shared."

Many people, including the governments of both his former country and his adopted one, would disagree. *"Pass auf dich auf."*

Her chuckle brought another smile to his lips. "Dr. Hoffman, I always take care of myself."

IN THE QUIET OF HER OFFICE AFTER ALL THE OTHER LAB WORKERS HAD LEFT FOR the day, Tatiana reviewed her plan, testing it for missteps. She couldn't afford to make a single mistake. Hoffman's notebooks were out of her hands. Her career hung by a gossamer thread. Thank goodness those government agents had been distracted by the German nationals and the notebooks. No one had the sense to look into what exactly the lab assistants and scientists were doing. If they had, no amount of explaining could have glossed over the fact that her research wasn't on the right side of the dividing line between ethical and unethical.

Tossing a pen onto the desk blotter, she reached for another burner phone and dialed. "It's me," she said when the general answered. Quickly, she recapped the day's events.

"I thought you would have been more careful," General Pettigrew said. "You put your entire operation in jeopardy."

"How was I to know German agents would come after the notebooks?" She hated the whine in her voice, but she was tired of coming up short. She couldn't plan for every single contingency.

"You would have had you stopped to think beyond the end goal," he snapped. "Those notebooks hold more than the key to Dr. Hoffman's research into viral therapy. They also shed light on a time Germany would prefer to forget."

"But Hoffman worked in East Germany. I don't see the relevance—"

"Because your sole focus is on your research. If you paid even the slightest attention to the news, you'd know that Germany just announced the creation of a cutting-edge laboratory in Munich dedicated to finding a cure for various cancers with the goal of bringing together the top cancer researchers from all over the world. Funded by grants from pharmaceutical companies, hospitals, private businesses, and European Union governments, it will be the most collaborative project ever attempted."

Excitement and hope rushed through her body like twin jolts of electricity. What an audacious, wonderful idea. The snippet of an article in a recent medical journal surfaced in her mind, reminding her she had read about the possibility of such a facility, but she'd dismissed it as magical thinking. No way would anyone be able to actually pull off such a cooperative effort. Yet it appeared Germany had done it.

"If those notebooks surfaced, it would draw attention to a time Germany would like to forget," the general concluded.

"But surely it wouldn't be harmful, considering Hoffman worked for the East Germans at the time of his experiments." Then she frowned. "But why did the United States government swoop in and grab the notebooks from the Germans?"

"Dr. Dern, if you don't know the answer to that question, then you're not as brilliant as I thought you were." The general hung up.

Tatiana lowered the phone to the desk. How could she have missed such an obvious conclusion? Hoffman's work in East Germany. His defection not to Argentina as widely reported but to the United States. His secrecy about his work that she chalked up to being from a former Soviet Union country. The general was right. She had been stupid not to fit the pieces together before now. Or maybe she had been too laser focused on her own end goal of succeeding where Hoffman had failed.

She was so close to refining that cure, but there was something she was missing, which was why having Hoffman's notebooks had been imperative. Without them, the next best thing would be Hoffman himself. Good thing she knew the bait to draw him into her web.

LENA LOCKED UP HER OFFICE, WAVING GOODBYE TO A COLLEAGUE ON HER way out of the building. The temperature had dropped into the forties with the sunset. Drawing her scarf around her neck, she hurried to the Metro station, her thoughts on seeing Devlin. How he had come to mean so much to her in so short a time, she didn't question. All she knew was how her heart thumped faster in his presence, and how she couldn't wait to share the small details about her day with him.

Outside the Courthouse Metro stop, her steps quickened in anticipation of greeting Devlin with a kiss. Reaching their building, she stopped to get the day's mail, then on impulse, knocked on his door before going into her own apartment. He answered immediately, as if waiting by the door for her arrival.

"Hey, there." Devlin leaned against the doorframe, his tall frame filling the space. His eyes had dark bruises under them, and he still sported tape across the bridge of his nose.

"How are you feeling?"

He gestured toward his face. "The over-the-counter medicine is keeping the pain at bay. In other words, I look worse than I feel."

"I'm glad." She loosened the scarf as the heat of the building permeated her outerwear.

"How was work?"

"Okay." For a moment, she simply stared at him. "I found myself counting down the minutes until I could see you again."

"Me too." He leaned closer, and she followed suit. A smile drifted across his lips seconds before he closed the gap between them and kissed her.

The sense of belonging encased her heart as he deepened the kiss. This was where she belonged. This was her future. He broke the kiss, resting his forehead against hers. "A man could get used to a greeting like that."

"A girl could too." The scent of something spicy drifted out of the condo, and she stepped back, sniffing. "Something smells delicious."

"I'm trying a new recipe. Chicken mole." He shrugged. "Figured I might as well test some of these recipes I've been collecting now that I have more time."

"I, for one, am delighted you are expanding your culinary horizons."

He grinned. "I'm glad you're willing to be a test subject for my creations."

"Be back in a few?"

"I'll leave the door unlocked." He dropped a quick kiss on her forehead, then gave her a little push in the direction of her door. "Don't take too long."

"I won't," she promised. Hurrying across the hall, she inserted her key into the lock and entered her apartment. After shedding her coat, scarf, and gloves, she fed Goliath, then flipped through her mail. Nothing that couldn't wait.

She grabbed her phone and keys, then stepped into the hallway, turning back to check that the door handle was locked. Satisfied her condo was secure, she pivoted to cross to Devlin's when someone slapped a gloved hand over her mouth while simultaneously twisting her right arm up behind her back. The movement loosened her grip on the phone and keys, and the items dropped from her grasp. Her assailant leaned against her, the hard planes of his body telling her it was a man. His hand covered her mouth and one nostril, making breathing difficult. Her vision blurred.

"If you want your boyfriend to stay alive," the man hissed in her ear, "you'll come quietly."

CHAPTER
FORTY

Devlin surveyed the table with a critical eye. The glow from the trio of fat candles provided a romantic ambience. The chicken mole and accompanying side dish of rice steamed on either side of the candles. His favorite pinot noir wine had been uncorked to breathe. All he needed was the girl.

Checking his watch, Devlin frowned. It had been more than ten minutes since Lena had kissed him and darted to her own condo to feed Goliath and deposit her coat and mail. Maybe she was freshening up. He retreated to the kitchen and plucked two lids from the pot drawer to cover the mole and rice.

He read through some work email while he waited. Another ten minutes slipped by before he set down his phone and crossed to his front door. Better check on her. He stepped into the hall and froze as his eyes spotted keys and a phone lying on the floor near Lena's door. He scooped up the items, certain he recognized the phone case as belonging to Lena. A knock at the door went unanswered.

His gut told him this counted as an emergency, and he inserted her house key into the lock. Inside, her cat greeted him with a plaintive meow. Devlin checked the kitchen, spotting the Goliath's empty food dish and a can sitting upside down in the drainer. The coat closet held the winter coat and scarf she'd been wearing.

Panic flared, followed closely by visions of Lena hurt or worse. His own kidnapping ordeal with Dr. Dern flashed across his mind. Had someone taken Lena? She would never have left her keys and phone behind if she were helping a friend.

With her keys and phone in hand, he left her apartment, careful to ensure the door closed properly. Lena would never forgive him if her cat escaped. He re-entered his apartment and put Lena's items on the coffee table. He blew out the candles, then shrugged into his coat and left to search the condo grounds.

Forty minutes later, he had scoured every inch of the common area around the complex. No Lena. He'd asked everyone he met, showing them a photo of Lena on his phone he'd snapped during their first date. No one recalled seeing her. Frustration mounted as he trudged back to the condo. An older man who lived in the building next door approached with his Labrador retriever.

"Hi, Harold." Devlin greeted his dog, Molly, with a pat on her head. "Have you seen Lena?"

"I think you might have some competition there." Harold chuckled as he reined in Molly's leash before she could dart after a squirrel.

"What do you mean?" Devlin distracted the dog by scratching behind her ears.

"She left here with some other fellow when I was returning home from work."

Devlin stilled. Molly bumped him with her body. He absently rubbed the dog's head, his thoughts reeling with what it meant. "When exactly was this?"

Harold's brows knit together. "Oh, a little over an hour ago now, I think."

About the time Lena should have been making her way to his condo. "What did the man look like?"

His tone must have conveyed his anxiety because Harold peered at him, all joviality gone. "Is something wrong?"

Devlin blew out a breath in an attempt to calm his increasing sense of panic. "I don't know, but it's important I know what the man looked like."

"I didn't get a good look at him, but he was about your height with more muscle on his frame."

When the man didn't go on, Devlin prodded, "What color was his hair?"

Harold shrugged. "He was wearing a hoodie pulled low and sunglasses."

"At night?" The sense of foreboding increased.

"I thought that strange myself, but sometimes, if they're prescription sunglasses, people do forget to take them off or leave them on if they've left their regular glasses in the car." Harold took a few steps as Molly tugged at the leash. "That's about all I can tell you."

"Did you see which way they went?" Devlin wanted to grill the man for more information, but he could see Harold was anxious to get on with his evening.

"Yeah, they circled the building that way." Harold pointed to the right of Devlin and Lena's building. "I figured they were heading for the path."

"Thank you." Devlin took off at a jog toward the path, praying for Lena's safety and hoping he would find her before anything happened to her.

LENA'S ARMS ACHED FROM BEING SECURED BEHIND HER WITH A BINDING THAT bit into her wrists. Her assailant had placed a foul-smelling cloth over her mouth before shoving her into a vehicle. That was the last clear memory she had before regaining consciousness in this windowless room. Her feet, stripped of her boots, had been tied at the ankles to the straight-backed chair. A piece of fabric stuffed into her mouth made breathing difficult. Working her dry tongue, she spit out the fabric.

The single, dangling light bulb illuminated the small, rectangle room. As far as she could tell, she was the only thing in the room. Unpainted cinderblock walls surrounded her on three sides, while a corrugated metal door sealed her inside. Drag marks from the door to her seat indicated how she had arrived. Squinting, she spotted what might be mouse droppings in the corner and suppressed a shudder. So far, she'd seen no evidence she had company, and she prayed she wouldn't. Fear clawed at her throat, but she shoved it aside. She would not give into it. She would stay strong.

But then the room spun as a wave of dizziness swept over her like water over a dam. Closing her eyes, she gave into the darkness gobbling up the light.

When she awoke the second time, she had no idea how much time had passed. The temperature in the room had dropped. She shivered, and she wished she'd still had on her winter coat over her light sweater and dress pants. Wiggling her toes and fingers, she tried to warm them up, but she could barely feel them anymore. Nothing left to do but pray.

Dear God, please send someone to rescue me. Keep Devlin safe.

A warm peace filled her core, nurturing her soul. The door rattled, startling her awake. She must have dozed off again. Bracing herself, she watched the door slowly rise, bringing in a blast of cold air. Outside, darkness had fallen. Two figures slipped inside, backlit by a bright streetlight. Once inside, one of them lowered the door.

Both had heavy winter coats, hats, scarves, and gloves. Seeing them bundled up brought back her shivers. For a moment, her visitors didn't speak, then the shorter one pulled out a phone and aimed it at Lena. The flash hurt her eyes as the person took a series of photos.

"What do you want?" Lena hated the quiver in her voice, but with her whole body shaking, perhaps it wasn't noticeable.

The figure with the phone didn't respond, merely tapped on the screen with a gloved hand. Lena's eyes re-adjusted to the room light, allowing her to look over the two more carefully. Based on the height and build, the other might have been the man who'd brought Lena to this place. The other had the curves of a female.

"Please, I need water. A blanket." Her teeth chattered, but she clamped her lips together hard to stop them.

The woman pocketed the phone, then gazed straight at Lena. "Let's hope your grandfather isn't too slow to respond."

"My grandfather?" Lena didn't have to act confused at the woman's statement.

The woman cocked her head. "You should be happy Dr. Hoffman will be coming directly to you."

Her words made Lena even colder. "What are you talking about?"

The smile that sprang to the woman's lips had no warmth. "You'll see." To her companion, she motioned to the door. "Let's go."

"No! Please, it's cold in here and—"

The pair ignored her cries and raised the door, disappearing into the night.

As the door rattled closed, Lena sobbed, straining against her bonds. "Please, don't leave me!"

Tatiana hardened her heart against Lena's plaintive cries. She walked briskly beside the man recommended by General Pettigrew for his discretion and skills. Back at her SUV, she slid behind the wheel as the man climbed into the passenger seat. "How cold will it get tonight?"

The man shrugged. "Cold enough."

She bit her lip, picturing Lena's shivering body as she started the car and cranked the heat. "I have a blanket in the trunk. Take it to her."

"No."

"What did you say?" She couldn't believe he would defy her command.

The man's cold eyes frightened her, but she hid it behind her anger. "You do not give me orders."

"I most certainly do. Who do you think is running this operation?" She was doing what was necessary to bring Hoffman in.

"Drive."

She ignored the directive. "I want you to bring Lena the blanket."

The man moved so fast, she didn't even see his hand, only felt the gloved fingers clamping tight around her throat. "You will listen to me."

Tatiana didn't move, as she could barely breathe. The scientific part of her brain admired the skill in which he immobilized her but still allowed her enough air to stay alert. The other part of her brain screamed that if he exerted a little bit more pressure, he would kill her.

"You will drive home. You will wait for Hoffman to respond to your text. Are we clear?"

She managed a nod, then the man abruptly released her neck and sat back, fastening his seatbelt as if he hadn't threatened to end her life if she didn't cooperate. She clicked her own safety belt in place and put the car in gear. For the first time, fear took hold of her, digging its talons deep into her heart. But what frightened her more than the man beside her was the thought she had created the monster.

And now she would have to pay the price.

CHAPTER
FORTY-ONE

Wolfgang stared at the photo of Lena with her arms bound behind her and her shoeless feet tied to the legs of a wooden chair. The bewilderment and fear in her eyes tore at his heart. Of course he would obey the instructions to rescue his granddaughter. But what they didn't know is he had already set into motion plans of his own, a security measure for just such a possibility.

Using another prepaid phone, he called the general. "They've taken Lena Hoffman."

"I did tell you things could get messy," Pettigrew replied, caution in his voice.

"You have no idea who you're dealing with," Wolfgang snapped. "If Lena Hoffman is not returned to the safety of her apartment in three hours, I will destroy you."

"You destroy me?" The general laughed. "You know that's not possible without implicating yourself in far worse crimes."

"I'm ready to face my demons. Are you?" He hung up before the general could reply. The general might think Wolfgang was bluffing and do nothing. No, he needed to hedge his bets to ensure Lena's safety.

Dialing another number, he waited while the phone rang several times.

"Hello?" asked a male voice, sharp with worry.

"Dr. Devlin Mills?"

"Yes."

"This is Dr. Wolfgang Hoffman, Lena's grandfather." Hoffman waited a few seconds to give the other man time to digest that information. "I need your help in freeing Lena."

"Freeing Lena? You know where she is?"

The hope and concern in Devlin's voice told Wolfgang he had made the right call. This young man cared deeply for his granddaughter and would put her safety above everything else. "No, but I know who does. If you want to keep her safe, you'll do exactly what I tell you."

"I'm listening."

"Good. I believe you've met Dr. Tatiana Dern." Wolfgang had had a full report of his and Tatiana's kidnapping by German operatives but had known the danger hadn't passed. Someone still wanted him silenced.

"I have."

"She knows where Lena is."

"What? Where?"

"I don't have a location, but I know someone who can find out. Write this number down."

"Let me get a piece of paper and a pen." Rustling on the other end indicated Devlin's search for the items. "Okay, I'm ready."

Wolfgang gave him the number, then made Devlin repeat it. "When we hang up, call that number and tell the man who answers, 'Bei Mir Bist Du Schön.'"

"Like the old Andrew Sisters song?"

"How does one so young know that song?" Wolfgang couldn't keep the amazement from his voice.

"As a kid, I spent a lot of time with my grandparents in the summer. My grandmother loved the Andrew Sisters and was always playing one of their albums on her old record player."

"It was my late wife's favorite song." A memory washed over Wolfgang at the joy in Ida's face when he'd arranged to have the song played at the hotel during their honeymoon. "Then tell the man Dr. Dern knows where Lena is. He will take care of the rest."

"How can you be so sure?"

"You'll have to trust me. I want Lena safe as much as you do." Wolfgang disconnected. He had done what he could to ensure Lena's rescue. Now it was time to bring his misdeeds into the light of day.

DEVLIN STARED AT HIS CELL PHONE, BLINKING THE REMNANTS OF SLEEP FROM his eyes. He hadn't dreamed Dr. Hoffman called him about Lena at— he checked the time—4:58 a.m., had he? The piece of paper with a phone number was real. The Andrew Sisters' rendition of "Bei Mir Bist Du Schön (Means That Your Grand)" reverberated in his mind, as did the conviction in Hoffman's voice about wanting to keep Lena safe.

He thumbed in the number and waited while it rang once, twice, three times. The call rolled to voicemail, where a mechanical voice relayed the number, then informed Devlin the mailbox was full before disconnecting. Disappointment weighed heavy on his shoulders. He shoved the covers aside and padded to the kitchen. Coffee, hot and strong, was needed to power him through another long day.

As it brewed, he fished out Dr. Dern's business card from the junk drawer. Had her ambition led to kidnapping Lena? Hoffman hadn't had to spell out why Dern targeted Lena. The doctor's interest in Hoffman's notebooks had pointed to her knowing who Hoffman was. Snatching Lena must be Dern's attempt to flush Hoffman out of hiding.

He sipped the hot brew, the caffeine hitting his system with a welcome jolt. He'd drink this cup, shower, eat something, then figure out how to approach Dern without tipping his hand Hoffman had called. Having a plan—even a vague one—settled his nerves enough that he was able to eat a couple of scrambled eggs after dressing.

As he washed the pan, he concentrated on thinking about which of his NIH colleagues might know where Dern lived. Dr. Shan would have. His mentor's death struck him with fresh grief. The man hadn't deserved to die over decades old notebooks. The question of why the sudden interest in Hoffman's work behind the Iron Curtain continued to puzzle Devlin. The article detailing the doctor's breakthrough with viral therapy had given Devlin a new direction to pursue in the lab, but Hoffman hadn't found the cure everyone sought. Hoffman's research merely pushed them further along toward that cure.

Dern's interest in the notebooks, given her own cancer research, made sense. Why the Germans had been after the same thing didn't make sense to him. His phone pinged incoming email. He hadn't stopped reviewing his work email from those outside the NIH, which he could access on his phone. A quick scan revealed the usual assortment of newsletters, which he'd ignore for now. One headline caught his eye. A new state-of-the-art facility had opened in Munich.

Germany Announces Opening of Collaborative Cancer Research Facility

Scientists and medical researchers from all over the world will work together to find cures for cancer.

Skimming the article, he paused at the second-to-last paragraph.

German Chancellor Richard Heydrich said the facility will "show the world that Germany has the ability to produce cutting-edge medical research." The chancellor refused to answer questions regarding safeguards and protocols those working at the center will follow. "We have learned from the mistakes of our past and are looking to the future," he said.

Devlin lowered his phone, his mind spinning. Germany would not want any reminders of its past medical horrors like its Nazi-era experiments on unwilling patients. German officials especially would not want any more recent incidents of unethical medical experiments to come to light as they position themselves as a guiding light in world of cancer research. If Hoffman's notebooks had surfaced, it would have been extremely embarrassing to Germany, even though he worked for the East Germans. Ninety-plus years separated today's Germany from its Nazi past, but the distance between Hoffman's work and today could be measured in less than a lifetime.

His phone rang. Glancing down, he registered an unfamiliar number. Probably spam, although spammers usually waited until after nine a.m. to harass people. He picked up the call. "Hello?"

Silence.

A spammer after all. He was about to hang up, when it occurred to him it might be the man Hoffman told him to call ringing back. His number would have registered as a missed call on the man's phone. Might as well try the code phrase as Hoffman instructed.

"*Bei mir bist du schön,*" Devlin said.

A short pause, then a man said in a voice with a familiar ring to it, "Dr. Mills, what can I help you with?"

LENA COULD NOT RECALL A TIME WHEN SHE HAD FELT SO THIRSTY AND COLD. Her parched mouth generated little saliva, and the numbness in her feet and hands had ceased to alarm her. Part of her brain that still worked screamed she was slipping into hypothermia, but even that failed to strike fear in her heart. Devlin's face swam before her eyes. She would miss him. He had gone from being the hunky neighbor she hoped she'd exchange a smile with to someone near and dear to her heart. Who was she kidding? She'd fallen in love with the good doctor. But because of her dead-but-really-alive grandfather, she'd never get the chance to tell him.

Earlier, before the cold had sapped her brain of its ability to think clearly, she had connected the dots between Hoffman's research and

Germany's new medical research facility. If word got out about an East German's unethical use of human test subjects, it could tarnish Germany's reputation and potentially derail the work of the new facility. She also speculated that Hoffman must have had help escaping East Germany, help she was pretty sure had come from the United States, which, at the time, was locked in a Cold War one-upmanship with its Soviet rival. If Hoffman worked for the U.S. government, he might have been persuaded to carry on with his promising viral therapy experiments here.

Sleep dragged at her eyelids, but she lifted her head and stared straight at the corrugated metal door. The single light bulb cast the same shadows. Her throat ached from screaming for help off and on.

The door rattled. Fear drove its spikes into her flesh. *Please, God. Let it be a friend, not a foe.*

She let her head hang down, peering up through her eyelashes as a figure ducked under the door and approached her chair.

CHAPTER

FORTY-TWO

I n her home office, Tatiana stared at the subject line in her email, disbelief making the words incomprehensible.

East German Scientist Continued Experiments in US

Opening the message, she clicked on the link to a story in today's *New York Times*. The story detailed Dr. Wolfgang Hoffman's "unauthorized" use of human test subjects among the native Alaskan population in the 1980s, allegedly on behalf of the US government, which helped to smuggle him out of East Berlin in the early 1980s. The reporter, citing anonymous sources, provided details of Hoffman's East German experiments and alluded to a series of notebooks.

She reached for one of her burner phones while reviewing the rest of the article. Her hand stilled when her name jumped off the screen. Putting down the phone, she leaned closer to her laptop as she read:

Dr. Tatiana Dern, one of the foremost US cancer researchers, claimed in a recent interview that she was very close to finding a cure for liver cancer, the fourth deadliest form of cancer in the world. "We gain more knowledge every day on how this disease, which kills approximately

782,000 people worldwide annually, progresses, how it's acquired, and what works to stop it," she told CNN Medical in a taped interview that aired in December. She commented on why she studies liver cancer. "The rates of liver cancer incidence have increased three-fold since 1980, with the death rates more than doubling since then. I've been looking to the past, mining experiments related to liver cancer, for answers on how to move forward in the future."

Her landline office phone rang, sending her heart rate into overdrive. She fumbled the receiver, drew in a breath, and answered. "Dr. Dern."

"Dr. Tatiana Dern?" an unfamiliar male voice asked.

"Speaking." Her gaze strayed back to the story. She was only quoted because of her work with liver cancer research. No one could possibly know her connection with Hoffman.

"This is Lance James. I'm a medical reporter with the *New York Times*."

She bit back an expletive. Of all the times to answer her home office phone. "No comment." She pulled the receiver away from her ear, but the reporter's next words stalled her intention to hang up.

"I've received evidence that you're directly involved in the death of Dr. Walter Shan in order to gain access to Dr. Hoffman's notebooks."

"What did you say?" She should keep quiet, but she had to know what he knew.

"I have a recording of a conversation between you and a known assassin arranging for the recovery of the Hoffman papers."

Spots danced before her eyes, and she gulped air that didn't seem to make it to her lungs. The betrayal cut deep but even through the haze of disbelief and pain, admiration for the gutsy move on the Butzemann's part registered in her brain.

"Dr. Dern?" The reporter's voice had that edge of excitement, mirroring what she felt when reading lab results and knowing they would confirm what she had suspected.

Tatiana drew in a measured breath, counted to ten, then let it out slowly. The Butzemann had overplayed his hand if he thought a revelation like this would throw her out of the game for good. "You are only looking at half of the story. If you want the full picture, call me at this number in an hour." She gave him one of the burner cell phone numbers and disconnected without waiting for his confirmation. He'd call at the appointed time, and when he did, she would give him the story of his career.

DEVLIN PULLED INTO THE PARKING LOT OF STORAGE FOR YOU, TUCKED behind a Walmart off Route 1 in Alexandria, Virginia. Hope warred with concern that he was walking into a trap instead of rescuing Lena. Since realizing Lena had been kidnapped, he had wrestled with his reaction. On the one hand, he would have been concerned about the disappearance of a colleague or friend. But on the other hand, his visceral fear, his determination to find her no matter the cost to himself, had opened his eyes to his true feelings for Lena.

He loved her. Plain and simple. He suspected it had been building during their mailbox encounters, each too shy to do more than exchange smiles at the end of the workday. If he hadn't helped her after that SUV nearly ran her over, he wasn't sure he would have gotten the courage to ask her out. But something about the way she'd looked up at him from the pavement had made the words come easier.

Now he couldn't bear to think of his life without Lena by his side. Another vehicle pulled into the lot, and his phone dinged with an incoming text.

We'll take my car.

Sending a prayer for his safety and Lena's, he opened the door and crossed to the SUV, climbing into the passenger seat. Recognition dawned as he got a good look at the man Hoffman had told him to call. Agent Kurminsky nodded as he put the car in gear and approached the gate. Punching in a code to raise it, the other man drove through, navigating a series of turns toward the back of the matrix of storage units, each about the size of a single car garage.

Devlin didn't speak, following the other man's lead. He shouldn't be surprised but he was. Had Kurminsky known where Hoffman was all this time? Somehow, he didn't think so. From his conversation with Hoffman, it appeared Lena's grandfather had his own agenda.

Kurminsky halted before Unit 132, cutting the engine. "Get the blanket and water bottle from the back seat."

Devlin refrained from asking one of the dozens of questions crowding his mind and did as instructed, meeting the other man at the corrugated metal door of the unit. Kurminsky squatted by the padlock, which secured the chain looped through the door handle and a metal ring attached to the asphalt.

Hugging the silver warming blanket, he clutched the water bottle and prayed as he'd never prayed before. *Dear God, please let Lena be alive and okay. Please let this not be a wild goose chase. Please keep her grandfather safe. Please bring an end to this soon. Amen.* The chain rattled as the agent pulled it through the handle, tossing it to the side. He gripped the handle and yanked the door up, holding out a hand to stay Devlin's advance.

"Wait." As the door rose on its own, clattering along the track, Kurminsky drew his weapon.

Devlin bit back a gasp at the single bulb illuminated a figure tied to a straight-backed chair. Her head hung forward, her ankles lashed to the chair legs and her hands pulled behind her back. But even without seeing her beautiful face, he recognized Lena. Rushing forward, he knelt at her feet. "Lena?" He set down the blanket and water bottle, then cupped her face with his hands.

The chill of her skin alarmed him. He could hear Kurminsky requesting an ambulance and giving the address. Her eyes remained closed. "Lena, honey, can you hear me?"

"Hold her shoulders while I cut the ties on her wrists," the agent instructed.

Devlin moved his hands to her shoulders, supporting her as

Kurminsky released her hands. Her body shifted forward, its limpness driving spikes of fear into his heart. Devlin shifted to the right to give the other man access to the plastic ties securing her feet. Once free, Devlin scooped her up, then sat on the chair while Kurminsky draped the blanket over her. Devlin hugged her close, the coldness of her body seeping into his warmth.

"Sweetheart, it's going to be okay. I've got you now." Devlin rubbed her hands gently to restore circulation.

"An ambulance is on its way," Kurminsky said.

Continuing his ministrations, Devlin couldn't stop the questions from pouring out. "You've known Hoffman was alive all along?"

"I'm afraid there are things I can't disclose because of national security."

Frustration boiled over inside Devlin. Lena could have been killed because the agent standing in front of him kept silent. "Well, your precious national security nearly got the woman I love killed."

Amusement flickered in Kurminsky's eyes. "It was not our intention for any harm to come to Ms. Hoffman."

Devlin shifted Lena closer to him, tucking the blanket more secure around her still form. "You might not have intended for it to happen, but it did. And for what? Not for national security issues, but to cover up what Hoffman had done in the name of the US government."

The agent crossed his arms. "What is it you think Hoffman did?"

Devlin had fitted more pieces of the puzzle together in his mind while waiting for Kurminsky to come. "Continued the research he started in East Berlin on native Alaskans."

LENA SNUGGLED DOWN INTO THE WARMTH. HER TOES NO LONGER ACHED with cold. She didn't want to awaken, especially because of the dream. Devlin held her in his arms, saying he loved her. She never wanted to leave. Her lips struggled to form the words to tell him she felt the same, but a heaviness pressed down on her body, dragging her back to oblivion. She fought the weight, punching it with her fists as if it were something tangible. Under her head, the steady beat of Devlin's heart gave her strength to force herself out of the warm cocoon and back into the cold of the room. The memory of being tied to a chair jolted her out of the dream. For a moment, she lay still, taking inventory of her surroundings.

She no longer had her hands tied behind her back. She wasn't sitting in a chair but lying across someone's lap. Sniffing, she caught a whiff of Devlin's spicy cologne. Relief poured over her like hot fudge on cold ice cream. He was here. She was safe. *Thank you, Jesus.*

For a moment longer, she didn't open her eyes, trying to gauge to whom Devlin was talking. With her head against his chest, she couldn't hear everything, but caught a word or two. Dr. Hoffman. Devlin and another man were discussing her grandfather.

"Devlin?" Her voice came out softer than she'd expected.

"Lena?"

She blinked open her eyes, connecting with Devlin's worried gaze. "You came."

"I did." He brushed away a strand of hair off her cheek, the pads of his fingers gentle against her skin. "How are you feeling?"

"Warmer."

The other man stepped into view, handing Devlin an uncapped bottle of water without a word. Something about the man was familiar, but Lena's brain was too tired to figure out who he was. She sipped some water with Devlin's assistance, surprised her hands shook when she tried to hold the bottle.

"Thank you." She sank back into his embrace.

"The paramedics are here," the man said as the sound of other voices registered.

A female EMT approached, carrying a bag. "I'm Kate. What's your name?"

"Lena Hoffman," she whispered.

"Can you tell me what happened?" Kate strapped a blood pressure cuff on Lena's arm.

"Some man kidnapped me and brought me here, tied me to a chair, and left me." That much was clear in her mind.

"Do you remember when that was?" Kate inflated the cuff and checked the reading.

Lena frowned. "Around six p.m. last night?"

"That's right," Devlin put in. "It's now nearly six in the morning."

"Okay." Kate placed her fingers on Lena's wrist. "Let me check your heart rate."

Lena leaned against Devlin while Kate finished checking her out. Her eyelids didn't want to stay open, and she kept fighting to follow what Kate was saying to Devlin.

"Time for a ride in the ambulance." Devlin helped her onto the stretcher. "I'll be right behind you."

"Okay." She released his hand, not wanting to let go but knowing she had to. "Thanks for rescuing me."

He smiled, leaning down and kissing her forehead. "I couldn't lose my best girl, now could I?"

She hugged those words close to her heart as the EMTs loaded her into the ambulance.

CHAPTER
FORTY-THREE

Tatiana brewed a cup of espresso, allowing a smile to cross her lips. If she could whistle a jaunty tune, she would. Her second conversation with the reporter had gone according to plan. He had lapped up everything she'd fed him. By noon, her version of events would appear in the *New York Times*, then other news outlets would pick it up and broadcast it throughout the world. Both Hoffman and the Butzemann had underestimated her arsenal, and she hadn't even deployed her most destructive weapon. That one she was saving in case things went sideways despite her careful planning.

Her phone pinged an incoming text. Still smiling, she glanced at the message. Blood pounded in her head as she read the message.

You're not as smart as you think.

Below the words was a link to a *New York Times* article. Her finger slid off the link the first time she tried to press it, but she steadied her nerves and managed to connect to the article the second time.

Eminent Researcher Experimented on Humans
Dr. Tatiana Dern Bypassed Traditional Research Methods

ARLINGTON, Va.—Medical researcher Dr. Tatiana Dern deliberately infected human test subjects without their knowledge in an effort to find a cure for liver cancer, according to documents obtained by the *New York Times* and verified by several independent sources. Dr. Dern, who received the Oliver R. Grace Award for distinguished service in advancing cancer research from the Cancer Research Institute last year, had been running a secret lab funded by Wyn Pharmaceutical in collaboration with the US military. Dr. Dern, who was rumored to be on the short list for this year's Paul Marks Prize for Cancer Research, had been attempting to use viral therapy to halt the spread of liver cancer cells in the human body.

She scanned the rest of the article, her heart racing as fact after damning fact appeared in the story. The Butzemann's name wasn't mentioned, but that wouldn't appease him. Her work, her career as a doctor and researcher, was over. She had sacrificed her family and her entire life to finding a cure for liver cancer. And she had come so close. A few more months or years, and she would have succeeded where Hoffman had failed. Pressing her hands to her temples, she slid down to the floor. Her phone trilled the Looney Tunes theme music. Tom! She snatched the device from the counter.

"Tom." She couldn't choke out anything else.

"I saw the article," her husband replied. "How much of it is true?"

Tatiana bristled at his cool tone but told herself not to lash out. He had called her. That must mean he still cared. The lie sat on the tip of her tongue, but she swallowed it instead. What did appearances matter anymore? Her life lay in ruins, and she was tired of the double life she'd lead for so long. With one person, she wanted to tell the truth, even if it drove him away for good. "All of it."

Her quiet admission didn't elicit an immediate response. Then Tom sighed. "Oh, Tatiana."

The compassion in his voice broke the floodgates of her tears. As the tears rolled down her cheeks, she blurted, "I messed up. I thought I could find the cure. I was so close..."

Tom listened in silence as the entire story spilled out of her through heaving sobs. Finally, spent and cried out, Tatiana leaned her head against the wall. "What do I do now?"

He chuckled. "You're asking me for advice?"

She paused, reflecting how much she truly wanted to know his thoughts. "Yes."

"I think you need a good lawyer, then confess all to the proper authorities."

Her chest tightened. She couldn't do it. It was asking too much. "That would mean revocation of my medical license and possibly a prison sentence. I'd never be able to practice medicine again. My life would be over."

"You'd still have me and the kids."

Hope poked up like a tiny seedling sprouting through the ground. "I would?"

"Yes."

That one word filled her with strength. Maybe this wouldn't be the end but a new beginning. "I wouldn't even know who to call."

"It's a good thing I know an attorney who specializes in medical license defense."

"You do?" Love for her husband flooded Tatiana's senses. "Thank you, Tom." Maybe her life wouldn't be over after all but would be turning in a new direction.

~

WARMTH ENVELOPED LENA FROM HER FINGERTIPS TO HER TOES. SLEEP pulled her down into a cocoon of heat and softness, but something tapped in the back of her mind, telling her to resist the urge. She mentally batted away the insistent thought she should wake up. Then a male voice, softly calling her name, penetrated the haze. Devlin.

Lena forced her eyes open, blinking at the bright light. Devlin's face, fuzzy around the edges first, then sharpening as she became more fully awake, hovered in front of her.

"Lena?" Devlin leaned over her, his hand clasping hers.

"Devlin." Speaking made her throat ache, and the sudden need for water overwhelmed her.

"Here, drink this." Devlin supported her shoulders and guided a straw into her mouth, holding the plastic mug for her.

She drank deeply, the water cooling her throat and reviving her even more. Finished, she lay back against the pillows while he replaced the mug on a bedside table. A soft beep, then something tightened around her upper arm. Blood pressure cuff. Hospital. Being so cold and alone in that room...

"You found me." Her gaze flew to his face.

He retook her hand, lacing his fingers through hers. "Yes, thanks to your grandfather."

"My grandfather?" Memories of Dr. Dern and her companion flooded her senses. "Is he okay? Dr. Dern was using me as bait to draw him out."

Devlin settled into the chair beside the bed. "We still don't know where Dr. Hoffman is, but Dr. Dern turned herself into authorities a few hours ago."

"She did?" Lena hadn't thought the doctor capable of such a move.

"I think she had no other choice, not if she wanted any hope of leniency." Devlin released her hand to pull out his phone. "The *New York Times* posted an article early this morning detailing her rather unethical methods at her West Virginia lab."

He handed over the phone. She read the headline.

Eminent Researcher Experimented on Humans
Dr. Tatiana Dern Bypassed Traditional Research Methods

"Is this true?" She read the first few paragraphs, which provided details of Dr. Dern's experiments.

"One of my NIH colleagues says the medical research community is in shock but that the preponderance of evidence from the facility she ran leaves no doubt that the story is true." Devlin shook his head. "She worked with Hoffman during her residency."

"She did?" Lena handed the phone back, then relaxed back onto the pillows.

A nurse bustled in, her eyes brightening when she spotted Lena. "I see someone decided to wake up."

Lena summoned a smile. "Yes. How long have I been here?"

"About six hours," the nurse replied. "Let's get a vital check, and I'll send the doctor in."

Devlin stood. "I'm going to grab a cup of coffee."

Panic flared inside, and Lena reached out to him. "You don't have to go."

"Don't worry, I'll be back soon." He leaned over and kissed her forehead.

"Your fiancé has barely left your side since you were brought in," the nurse said. "He's been so worried about you, but we all told him that sleep was the best thing for you."

Fiancé? Lena started to correct the nurse, but then realized Devlin must have said that in order to be allowed in her room. The idea of marrying Devlin made her heart pound and her stomach flipflop. Thank goodness the nurse had already taken her pulse, or she might be concerned at Lena's rapid heart rate. Love for this man who had stuck by her through quite a crazy few weeks brought a smile to her lips.

WOLFGANG LAID THE BOUQUET OF FLOWERS ON THE HARD GROUND, HIS EYES tracing the words on the simple double headstone of his only son and daughter-in-law.

Here lies
Stefan Wolfgang Hoffman
and

Andrea Maike Mulherin Hoffman
Taken from this earth much too soon.
Besser zweimal erinnert als einmal vergessen.

The German proverb Lena had chosen touched his heart. "Better twice remembered than once forgotten." He would have been best forgotten, his work tossed out with the garbage. How arrogant he'd been at the age his son died, how sure he'd been that the remedy for liver cancer was within reach. What did the lives of a few degenerates mean when he found a cure for one of the deadliest cancers in the world?

But he hadn't done that. Instead, he'd left a wake of ruined lives, destroying not only those who came to him for help, but others whom the East German state deemed expendable. His own son and daughter-in-law suffered from his mistakes, and now his precious granddaughter's life had nearly been lost as well. All because of him.

"They died much too young, did they not?"

Wolfgang turned at the sound of the man's voice. It had been more than a quarter century since they'd met, but Wolfgang instantly recognized him. "Wyndermyer, it's been a long time."

Wyndermyer acknowledged the greeting with a crisp nod as he joined Wolfgang in front of the grave. "It has indeed."

"I'm surprised to see you alone." Wolfgang had no doubt the man had hidden minions throughout the cemetery but wasn't about to let Wyndermyer know his suspicions.

"Why would I bring others to greet an old friend?" The coldness of other man's eyes belied the joviality of his voice.

"Because we are not *freundes.*"

"Are we not? The enemy of my enemy is my friend. Is that not us?"

Maybe it had been at one time, but that was before Wolfgang's conscience had awakened to cry out that what he was doing in the name of science and humanity was nothing more than a man's vain attempt at glory. The desire to meet his granddaughter pushed all other thoughts away, and he tired of the sparring. "You're too late."

Wyndermyer chuckled. "Oh, I think I'm right on time."

Wolfgang faced him, turning away from Stefan and Andrea's grave. "Lena is safe."

An emotion crossed Wyndermyer's face too quickly for Wolfgang to identify, but the other man's slight stiffening told the doctor he hadn't known of Lena's rescue.

"And Dr. Dern has decided a caged bird is better than a dead one."

The other man's features hardened. "Have you decided to sing as well?"

Wolfgang sighed. "I have decided to stop hiding in the shadows."

"In that case..." Wyndermyer raised his gloved hand, and a man stepped out from behind a thick oak tree fifty feet away.

Wolfgang raised his eyebrows. "Rather risky, don't you think?"

"I've never been one to leave loose ends."

"It's what I used to admire about you. Now I see you for who you are—a greedy man only out for himself." Wolfgang waved toward the approaching man, who held a gun at his side. "But you've over-played your hand this time."

"It is you who have misjudged the situation." Wyndermyer nodded at the man, who raised the gun, aiming straight for Wolfgang's heart.

Wolfgang steadied himself. Surely Venedict Calkins wouldn't be late. He'd planned it so carefully, wanting to stay alive to meet his granddaughter and her young man.

"Freeze! FBI!" a male voice called as figures dressed in SWAT gear converged on the trio.

"Put down your weapon!" a man shouted.

The gunman slowly lowered his arm, bending to place the gun on the ground.

"Raise your hands over your heads." One of the men approached, his MP5 submachine gun at the ready.

Wyndermyer, Wolfgang, and the gunman obeyed. Relief made Wolfgang's hands shake slightly. He'd done it. He'd kept his granddaughter safe. Maybe his small act of valor, even at this late stage of his life, would atone for his earlier sins, along with what would surely be a prison sentence. Maybe then his heart would find peace.

FORTY-FOUR

Devlin rearranged the vase on his dining room table for the third time. Should the bouquet of lavender Peruvian lilies, white roses, and white carnations with baby's breath, assorted greenery, and seeded eucalyptus as accents go in the center or to the side? The stove timer buzzed, and he left the vase in the center to check on the spaghetti pie. The aromas of basil, oregano, tomato sauce, and mozzarella cheese filled the air. The lightly browned cheese and bubbly sauce indicated the pie was cooked to perfection. Using oven mitts, he set it to cool on a hot pad, then mentally reviewed the rest of the menu.

Salad chilled in the fridge with dressing on the side. Garlic bread toasted in the oven. Two servings of tiramisu wrapped in the fridge. Sparkling water ready to pour into goblets.

A knock at the door sent his heart into overdrive. Lena. He hurried to the door and yanked it open, his welcoming smile faltering at the sight of Venedict Calkins, Enno Kurimsky, and an older man.

Calkins sniffed the air. "Something smells delicious, Dr. Mills."

"Spaghetti pie," Devlin replied. "What are you doing here?"

Kurimsky raised his eyebrows. "Introducing you to Dr. Wolfgang Hoffman."

Devlin met the gaze of the older man. "Dr. Hoffman?" Now that he knew the man's identity, he could see a faint resemblance to Lena in the shape of his eyes and the paleness of his skin. "Lena's grandfather?"

Lena's front door opened, and she stepped into the hallway, halting when she caught sight of the men gathered around Devlin. "Devlin?"

"Hi, Lena. You look lovely." She looked beautiful, gorgeous, take-his-breath-away stunning, but he wasn't about to say that in front of an audience. She had been released from the hospital late yesterday, spending most of today resting. Devlin had arranged for her to come to his apartment for an early dinner but now that would be delayed.

"Are we interrupting something?" Calkins glanced from Devlin to Lena and back again, a sparkle in the Homeland Security agent's eyes.

Devlin set his jaw. "Nothing that can't wait. I think you'd better come in."

The men parted to allow Lena to enter first, then filed into his living room. He turned off the oven, then brought in the two dining room chairs for himself and Calkins. Lena and Hoffman sat on opposite ends of the sofa, the older man unable to take his eyes off his granddaughter. Kurminsky occupied the recliner.

Calkins accepted the chair Devlin brought for him, then cleared his throat. "As part of his plea agreement with the Justice Department, Dr. Hoffman requested this meeting."

Lena's eyes widened. "Dr. Hoffman?" Her voice sounded faint, and Devlin nearly rose to his feet to make sure she was okay.

"I prefer 'grandfather,'" Hoffman said. He reached out a hand toward her and she took it. "I have much to tell you, but first, let me simply look at you."

Tears streamed down Lena's cheeks. "I thought I was all alone."

"I know, *meine liebe Enkelin*." Hoffman squeezed her hand. "You are not alone anymore." The doctor switched to German, carrying on a short conversation with Lena in the language of his homeland.

Devlin watched the exchange, the tenderness in the old man's eyes, the light shining in Lena's, and thanked God for bringing these two lost souls together.

Then Hoffman turned to Calkins. "Thank you. I am ready for the explanations."

Calkins nodded. "Dr. Mills, Ms. Hoffman, since you both have top secret security clearances, we are able to share with you some of what Dr. Hoffman did for the US government when he came to America in the mid-1980s. I'm sure you will understand we will be unable to answer all of your questions. Dr. Hoffman has agreed to let me give the basic outline of his story."

Devlin settled back into his chair as Calkins began his narrative.

"You've pieced together much of what Hoffman worked on in East Germany from his notebooks and diary. After his wife died, Hoffman became increasingly disillusioned with the East Germans. When he learned his son's wife was pregnant, he determined to get Stefan and Andrea out of the country to America. He had been approached by an undercover West German agent about defecting and used that connection to get his son and daughter-in-law to the United States, following them soon after. The US government was very interested in his research into viral therapy and convinced him to run drug trial experiments in Alaska in collaboration with Wyndermyer Pharmaceutical. What Hoffman didn't realize at the time was that Wyndermyer Pharmaceutical had been paying East Germany to conduct Hoffman's experiments."

"What?" Devlin saw the same expression of shock on Lena's face.

"The German Democratic Republic desperately needed money to shore up its medical facilities and used the Stasi to set up drug and other medical trials for Western pharmaceutical companies for cash.

While the majority of those clinical trials were run strictly by the book, some, like Dr. Hoffman's, crossed ethical lines."

"Did you know about that?" Lena asked her grandfather.

"Yes, I recognized Wyndermyer himself from a visit he had made to my lab," Hoffman said. "We didn't actually meet then, but he's who I turned to for help in leaving East Germany after Ida's death, and Stefan and Andrea had gotten safely to America."

"Wyndermyer used his Stasi contacts to figure out how to get Hoffman out of the country, then set the doctor up in Alaska to continue his experiments," Calkins said. "Did you know from the beginning that Wyndermyer had deliberately infected the participating group prior to your arrival in order to speed up the clinical trial process?"

Hoffman protested he hadn't, while another piece of the puzzle fitted into place for Devlin. "That's why so many died of cancer after the trial ended," Devlin put in, recalling the articles his colleague had given him.

"Yes," Calkins agreed. "When Hoffman realized he hadn't left behind his previous work, he gathered all the evidence, then wrapped up the trial. The drug being tested hadn't worked, and Wyndermyer Pharmaceutical had eventually scrapped it. Hoffman worked on other trials, eventually setting up his own lab, where he mentored Dr. Tatiana Dern for a time."

"Then why did you disappear?" Lena asked her grandfather.

"Because Wyndermyer came back to me with another scheme to shortcut the clinical trial process. I refused. I was tired of working in the dark. But I knew he would not stop asking, so I disappeared, taking with me the evidence of the Alaskan trial," Hoffman explained.

"Dr. Dern's research brought you back," Devlin surmised. "She must have heard about the notebooks from Dr. Shan and wanted them for her own research."

"Yes, I had given the East Berlin notebooks to my son, who had foolishly given them to Dr. Shan."

"And my parents' car accident? Was it really an accident?" Lena said, her eyes filled with tears.

"I believe it was nothing more than a tragic accident," Hoffman assured her. "The driver of the other car had been drinking and drifted over the yellow line into Stefan and Andrea's lane, hitting their car head on."

Devlin leaned forward. "I've seen your notebooks—Dr. Shan showed me one and I found one left behind in his office after his death—but I still don't get why all the interest in decades-old medical research notes."

"Dr. Hoffman, I'll take this one, if you don't mind," Calkins said.

Hoffman agreed with a wave of his hand.

"When Hoffman first disappeared, the Germans chased down every rumor of sightings of the doctor all over world. When the Berlin Wall came down several years later and the Soviet Union started collapsing, their attention naturally turned to more immediate concerns surrounding re-unification," Calkins explained. "That allowed Hoffman to continue his work in relative safety here in America. As he mentioned, his son had passed along the notebooks to Dr. Shan. We believe Shan paid Stefan handsomely for them in the hopes their secrets would advance his own work in liver cancer research."

"But he couldn't decipher your shorthand," Devlin put in, "and so the notebooks were useless."

A slight smile crossed Hoffman's lips. "It wouldn't have done Dr. Shan any good had he been able to read them."

"Why is that?" Devlin asked.

"Because they were notes about all the ways my experiments failed." Hoffman shook his head. "I was a *sehr arrogant*, so sure that I would find a cure through viral therapy. I *übertrieben* my results in conversations and reports to my supervisors."

~

"You exaggerated your findings?" Lena couldn't believe she'd heard her grandfather correctly. "You weren't close to making viral therapy work against liver cancer?"

"No. There was some promising beginnings, one or two small successes, but I became more and more reckless, and that led to more patient deaths." Pain slashed the older man's features. "I will never forgive myself for the pain I've caused through my own sense of immortality. It is like the American saying about doctors playing God, yes? That was me. I was playing God with the lives of these young people I—and the German Democratic Republic—felt had no use. I had one major breakthrough early on using the virus JX-594 to attack cancer cells, but the virus couldn't sustain its momentum."

"I think we're close to solving that problem by adding a second virus to JX-594," Devlin said. "But we're still in the initial discovery stages."

Hoffman's eyes lit up, and he leaned forward. "Was it a derivative of the flu virus? I tried several but couldn't find the right combination."

"Not the flu virus but the coronavirus," Devlin said. "We're working our way through all the variants to see which would pair best with JX-594."

Lena recognized the look on both doctors' faces. They were settling into a long talk about scientific things. She wouldn't be able to keep her eyes open much longer, and she needed to hear the rest of the story. "As fascinating as this discussion is, I have another question. Why were the Germans after the notebooks now?"

"Someone in Germany must have gotten wind of Dr. Dern's search for the notebooks," Calkins said. "With a new trade agreement between the United States and Germany on the table, the Germans wanted to snuff out any hint of bad publicity about Hoffman's work and defection. We've confirmed the Germans were behind nearly running you down and the shooting incident—both of which, they claim, were aimed at frightening you into giving up the notebooks when their operative accosted you in your condo."

"What about the package bomb the dog found in the bushes?" Lena inquired, shuddering with the memory of the explosion.

Calkins grimaced. "That had nothing to do with the Germans, Wyndermyer, Hoffman, or Dern. It turned out a drug dealer had hidden the package there, rigged to explode if unwrapped, in order to flush out someone in his posse who the dealer suspected of stealing from him. Apparently, that particular gang has used the bushes around the complex to hide drug packages before. If the dog hadn't found it and ripped open the package, chances were the traitor would have slipped it into his pocket and opened it away from the complex."

"That couple and their dog ended up being collateral damage." Lena's heart ached for their families, but she couldn't help feeling relieved she hadn't caused their death by searching for her grandfather.

"What happens next?" Devlin linked his fingers through hers.

"Hoffman has more questions to answer, but I think the prosecutor is after bigger fish," Calkins said. "Namely Wyndermyer, who had his fingers in many pies but always managed to keep his hands clean until now."

"And Dr. Dern?" Lena asked.

"She's cooperating fully with the investigation, including passing along the information that Dr. Shan's suicide wasn't a suicide but murder and that she had paid people to harass Dr. Mills. She claims she didn't authorize physical force in the recovery of the notebooks that resulted in Dr. Shan's death."

"Do you believe her?" Devlin said.

"So far, her story checks out, but we're still in the early days of gathering evidence. Even if we can't make a murder-for-hire charge stick in the case of Dr. Shan, her kidnapping of Lena Hoffman in the hopes of drawing out Dr. Hoffman will put her away for a long time," Calkins said.

Lena ducked her head to stifle a yawn. Despite finally getting answers to the questions plaguing her for several weeks, she struggled to stay awake. As the others continued to discuss the events, she rested her head against the couch and closed her eyes. Her grandfather's accented voice rose and fell as he discussed something with Devlin. The voices of two men she loved soothed away the last remnants of her tattered nerves, and she gave up her fight against sleep.

CHAPTER

FORTY-FIVE

Devlin added a single rose in a bud vase to the tray, then surveyed his handiwork. Two travel mugs of coffee rested next to a covered dish of scrambled eggs and toast spread with strawberry jam. A cloth napkin wrapped around a knife and fork completed the breakfast. Perfection. His romantic dinner plans had withered after the arrival of Hoffman and the Homeland Security agents.

He switched to Plan B and decided to bring her the morning meal. One of the perks of living across the hall from one another made impromptu meals easy. If things progressed, they would soon reside at the same address. With a smile, he hefted the tray and managed to exit his apartment without dropping it. Stepping across to Lena's door, he balanced the tray in his arms to knock on the door.

"It's unlocked!" she hollered. "I'll be just a minute."

"Great," he muttered as he maneuvered the tray to allow one hand access to the knob. Somehow, he twisted it without dropping anything and entered her condo.

He peered around the entryway. No Lena in sight. He had put the tray on her small dining table when he heard footsteps behind him.

"Voila! Breakfast is served." He gestured to what he brought without taking his eyes off her lovely face. While her cheeks still held pallor from her ordeal, the smudges under her eyes had faded. Even dressed in casual jeans and a thick sweater to ward off the February cold, she looked like a million bucks to him.

Lena clapped her hands, delight bringing a sparkle to her eyes. "Devlin, this is marvelous."

He pulled out a chair for her, and she crossed to sit. He breathed in the light floral scent he'd come to associate with Lena, sending his heart rate into overdrive. Stepping away, he drew in air slowly, holding it to a count of three before exhaling in an attempt to calm his sudden attack of the nerves. "How are you feeling today?"

"Better." She squinted in the direction of the kitchen microwave. "I can't believe I slept for more than fourteen hours."

He took the chair opposite her. "Please, eat. I've already had my breakfast, but I did bring my own coffee." He snagged the mug with the NIH logo and took a sip.

She forked eggs into her mouth, then tasted her own coffee. "Delicious, and such a treat. I usually only have time to grab a toaster pastry on my way to work."

They made small talk while she finished breakfast, then moved to the couch to sip the remainder of their coffee. Devlin quickly drained his mug, setting it on the end table. "Lena, I've been thinking."

"About what?" She kept her gaze on her mug, turning it round and round in her hands.

He ran a hand through his hair, nerves zinging and pinging through his body and jumbling his thoughts. "You."

"Me?" Her voice came out in a squeak.

He gently removed the travel mug from her fingers, placing it next to his. Then he captured both of her hands in his own. "I suppose we have your grandfather to thank."

"We do?" Her voice had a breathless quality to it, sending his pulse racing even faster.

"If it wasn't for him, we might never have gotten the courage to speak to one another."

"We did exchange a lot of longing looks at the mailboxes," she said with a laugh.

He smiled. "We might have gone on that way for even longer hadn't I seen that car nearly run you down."

Her grin faded and her head dropped. "You were nearly killed because of me."

"Hey." Devlin let go of her hand and cupped her chin, bringing her gaze to his. "That wasn't your fault. Everything turned out okay."

Tears shimmered in her eyes. "But—"

He laid a finger on her lips. "But nothing. God kept us safe, brought your grandfather back from the dead and into your life. And brought you to me."

"And you to me," she added softly.

"Lena, I think I was a little in love with you from afar, and getting to know you these past few weeks has only made that feeling grow." As he poured out his heart, he stroked the soft skin of her cheek. "When you were taken, everything became crystal clear. I love you."

"You do?"

"Yes, I love you with my whole heart." He paused, wanting to give her time to respond before kissing her.

"Devlin?"

"Hmm?" was all he could manage without acting on his desire to cover her mouth with his.

"I love you too." Then she closed the gap between then, laying her lips on his in a kiss that sent tingles all the way down to his toes.

When she pulled back, her brow furrowed, he kissed her cheek, then proceeded to drop light kisses along her jawline.

"What do you think of June?"

Her question took a moment to penetrate his brain. He lifted his head. "The month of June?"

"Yes, I think that's the perfect time for a wedding, don't you?" Her eyes sparkled as her meaning sunk in.

"Are you asking me to marry you?" Devlin wrapped a strand of hair around his finger.

"Will you," Lena shifted closer, her breath brushing his cheek, "marry me?"

"I will." He gazed deep into her eyes. "And June seems like a fine month for a wedding, as long as it's this June, and not next year."

"Definitely this June," she agreed.

As he sealed the promise with another toe-tingling kiss, Devlin thanked God for bringing this woman into his life.

THE END

ABOUT THE AUTHOR

Sarah Hamaker loves writing books "where the hero and heroine fall in love while running for their lives." She's written romantic suspense novels and nonfiction books, as well as stories in *Chicken Soup for the Soul* volumes. As a AWSA certified writer coach, her heart is encouraging writers. She's a member of AWSA; Christian Authors Network; ACFW; ACFW Virginia Chapter; and Faith, Hope and Love, as well as the president of Capital Christian Writers Fellowship. Her podcast, "The Romantic Side of Suspense," can be found wherever you listen to podcasts. Sarah lives in Virginia with her husband, four teenagers, a preschool foster child and three cats.

Connect with Sarah!

Website: sarahhamakerfiction.com

BookBub: https://www.bookbub.com/profile/sarah-hamaker

Goodreads: https://www.goodreads.com/author/show/1804799.Sarah_Hamaker

YouTube: https://www.youtube.com/channel/UCzI8JVSzbms6-MoQbFc6SiLQ

LinkedIn: https://www.linkedin.com/in/sarah-hamaker-7295a01/

Amazon Author Page: https://www.amazon.com/-/e/B002TIARBS

OTHER BOOKS BY SARAH HAMAKER

Dangerous Christmas Memories (Love Inspired Suspense)

A witness in jeopardy...and a killer on the loose.

Hiding in witness protection is the only option for Priscilla Anderson after witnessing a murder. Then Lucas Langsdale shows up claiming to be her husband right when a hit man finds her. With partial amnesia, she has no memory of her marriage or the killer's identity. Yet she will have to put her faith in Luc if they both want to live to see another day.

THE COLD WAR LEGACY

The Cold War is long over, but The Wolf is still at the door.

THE
DARK GUEST

SARAH
HAMAKER

The Dark Guest (Seshva Press LLC) The Cold War Legacy Book 1

The Cold War is over, but The Wolf is still at the door.

When Violet Lundy isn't cleaning rooms at Happy Hills Assisted Living Facility, she loves spending her free time with resident Rainer Kopecek. Hearing his stories of the dangerous life he led behind the Iron Curtain in East Berlin makes her own life seem more tolerable. But when Rainer is found dead and his room in disarray, Violet suspects foul play.

Dr. Henry Silverton lives among his books, teaching and writing about the Cold War. A letter about an East German traitor known only as "The Wolf" propels Henry out of academia and into Violet's life. Together, they embark on a perilous quest to uncover the truth about Rainer's death and the traitor's identity.

Can Violet and Henry uncover the secrets of the past before one of them ends up as The Wolf's next victim?

Deadly Diamonds (Seshva Press LLC)

The race to find missing diamonds puts a widow in danger.

Three years ago, Dulce Honeycutt's life imploded when her husband died after a robbing a jewelry store and her 18-year-old son, Kieran, landed in prison as an accessory. The uncut diamonds were never recovered, and when rumors fly that she and Kieran know where the gems are hidden, their lives are in danger.

Veteran insurance investigator Miles Sharp believes Dulce knows more about the diamonds than she's revealing. But as the attacks on the beautiful widow's life multiply, he struggles to maintain his professional objectivity. Is Dulce a victim or is her story a sweet web of lies?

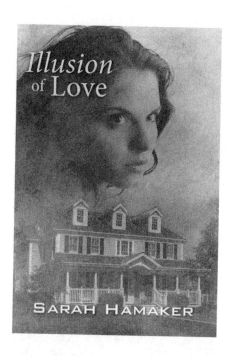

Illusion of Love (Seshva Press LLC)

A suspicious online romance reconnects an agoraphobe and an old friend.

Psychiatrist Jared Quinby's investigation for the FBI leads him to his childhood friend, Mary Divers. Agoraphobic Mary has found love with online beau David. When David reveals his intention of becoming a missionary, Mary takes a leap of faith and accepts David's marriage proposal.

When Jared's case intersects with Mary's online relationship, she refuses to believe anything's amiss with David. When tragedy strikes, Mary pushes Jared away.

Will Jared convince Mary of the truth—and of his love for her—before it's too late?

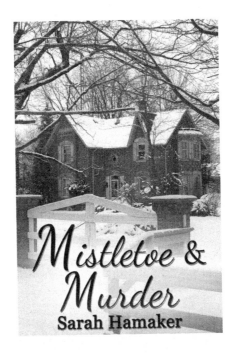

Mistletoe & Murder (Seshva Press LLC)

Alec Stratman comes home to Twin Oaks, Virginia, after his Army retirement to contemplate his reentry into civilian life. Instead he's greeted with the murder of his beloved Great-Aunt Heloise.

For Isabella Montoya, the loss of Heloise Stratman Thatcher goes beyond the end of a job. Heloise had encouraged Isabella to follow her dreams and helped fund her studies. Now, accused of her mentor's murder, Isabella is scrambling to prove her innocence.

Since his great-aunt had written glowing letters about Isabella, Alec is unwilling to believe the police's suspicion of the former housekeeper. Instead, he works to help clear her name.

Will Isabella and Alec be able to navigate the secrets that threaten to derail their budding romance and uncover the truth about Heloise's death before the killer strikes again?

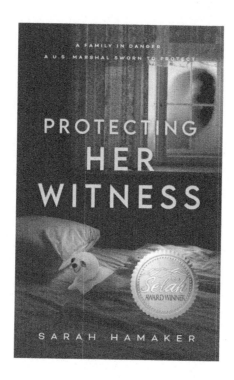

Protecting Her Witness (Seshva Press LLC)

Winner of the 2022 Selah Award for romantic suspense.

A family in danger...a U.S. Marshal sworn to protect.

U.S. Marshal Chalissa Manning has been running from her past and God for most of her life. When she meets widower Titus Davis and his son, Sam, her well-built defenses begin to crumble. But someone is targeting Titus and Sam, and it's up to Chalissa to both protect them and to find out who is behind the attacks.

As the threats pile up, will Chalissa be able to keep the family she's grown to love safe?

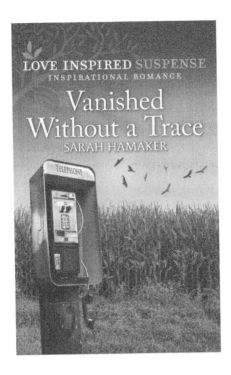

Vanished Without a Trace (Love Inspired Suspense)

A missing person case. A new clue. And a fight for survival.

After nine years searching for his missing sister, attorney Henderson Parker uncovers a clue that leads him to Twin Oaks, Virginia—and podcaster Elle Updike investigating the case. Partnering with the journalist is the last thing Henderson wants, until mysterious thugs make multiple attacks on both their lives. Now they'll have to trust each other...before the suspected kidnappers make them disappear for good.

Coming early 2023....

The Dark Reckoning (Seshva Press LLC) The Cold War Legacy Book 3

A mysterious list of names links a dangerous past to the present.

When Isana Thomas finds a smartphone among the cherry trees, her life is put in jeopardy. Isana discovers the phone belongs to Lillian Hillam, whose son, Cyrus "Cy" Hillam, works at The Heritage Museum with Isana. But Lillian is missing, and someone doesn't want the pair to find her.

Cy can't believe his mother would disappear without telling him, not after his father's suicide when he was a child. Then kidnappers claiming to have Lillian contact him, asking to exchange her life for a list of names. Cy and Isana must delve deep into his parents' past to find the list and save his mother's life.

But someone doesn't want them to succeed and will do anything to stop their search. Will Cy and Isana uncover the truth about the list before their lives are snuffed out?

Made in the USA
Middletown, DE
19 September 2022

73417125R00205